S0-ACT-733

WITHDRAWN

THE PROFESSIONALS

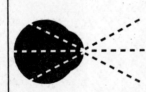 This Large Print Book carries the Seal of Approval of N.A.V.H.

THE PROFESSIONALS

OWEN LAUKKANEN

THORNDIKE PRESS
A part of Gale, Cengage Learning

Mount Laurel Library
100 Walt Whitman Avenue
Mount Laurel, NJ 08054-9539
856-234-7319
www.mtlaurel.lib.nj.us

GALE
CENGAGE Learning·

Detroit • New York • San Francisco • New Haven, Conn • Waterville, Maine • London

Copyright © 2012 by Owen Laukkanen.
Thorndike Press, a part of Gale, Cengage Learning.

ALL RIGHTS RESERVED
This is a work of fiction. Names, characters, places, and incidents either are the product of the author's imagination or are used fictitiously, and any resemblance to actual persons, living or dead, business, companies, events, or locales is entirely coincidental.

While the author has made every effort to provide accurate telephone numbers and Internet addresses at the time of publication, neither the publisher nor the author assumes any responsibility for errors, or for changes that occur after publication. Further, the publisher does not have any control over and does not assume any responsibility for author or third-party websites or their content.

Thorndike Press® Large Print Core.
The text of this Large Print edition is unabridged.
Other aspects of the book may vary from the original edition.
Set in 16 pt. Plantin.

LIBRARY OF CONGRESS CATALOGING-IN-PUBLICATION DATA

Laukkanen, Owen.
    The professionals / by Owen Laukkanen. — Large print ed.
        p. cm. — (Thorndike Press large print core)
    ISBN-13: 978-1-4104-4692-3 (hardcover)
    ISBN-10: 1-4104-4692-1 (hardcover)
    1. United States. Federal Bureau of Investigation—Fiction.
  2. Kidnapping—Fiction. 3. Organized crime—Fiction. 4. Suspense fiction.
  gsafd 5. Large type books. I. Title.
  PS3612.A93255P76 2012
  813'.6—dc23   2011049474

Published in 2012 by arrangement with G. P. Putnam's Sons, a member of Penguin Group (USA) Inc.

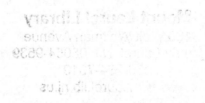

Printed in the United States of America
1 2 3 4 5 6 7 16 15 14 13 12

For my parents

ONE

Martin Warner checked his watch as the train slowed for Highland Park. Quarter to seven. Not early, but not terribly late, either; time enough for a relaxed dinner and a couple hours babysitting the Bulls before putting Sarah and Tim to bed.

The train jostled and the brakes squealed and Warner stood, thinking about a hot lasagna and a cold beer and maybe, if Leanne wasn't too tired, a little bit of fun in the master bedroom before they turned in for the night.

It was dusk by the time he stepped onto the platform, the crisp October air and the chill wind off Lake Michigan already hinting at the long winter ahead, and Warner shivered involuntarily and pulled his coat close around him as he joined the rest of the Highland Park commuters, a uniform crush of tailored suits and tasteful ties and thousand-dollar briefcases, a collective desire to get home, get warm, get fed.

The arrivals streamed out of the station, and Warner moved with the current toward the far end of the parking lot, the herd thinning around him until only a few stragglers remained. When he was alone on the pavement, he stopped and surveyed the archipelago of cars, searching in vain for his own. The light was dim in the back corners of the lot, and he couldn't see his car. He squinted into the shadows, turned around, and realized after a moment that someone had parked a van in front of it, a white Ford cargo van.

I must be tired, he thought, fingering his keys in his pocket and skirting the van to where his Lexus sat waiting. He pressed a button on his key fob and the car chirped in response as he reached for the door handle. Before he could open the door, however, a woman's voice called out behind him.

"Marty?" she said. "Martin Warner? Is that you?"

It was a younger woman's voice, a happy, what-a-coincidence voice, and Warner set his briefcase down and turned around with a smile to match. But when he turned to greet the mystery woman, hoping a little guiltily that her face was as attractive as her voice, he found no smiling beauty but instead two men, their faces hidden behind black ski masks. Behind them stood the van, its sliding side door wide open, and Warner stared inside, not comprehending, before someone wrapped something over his eyes and he could no longer see.

He felt hands grip his shoulders and shove him into the back of the van, and Warner heard the men talking around him, low voices tinged with urgency.

"Got him?"

"We're clear."

The door slammed shut, and Warner lay stunned in the rear compartment as the van rumbled to life and reversed. He was blindfolded, his hands tied behind him, and he had sudden nightmarish thoughts, visceral, involuntary images of his broken body, bloody and anonymous in death. "You're making a mistake," he said, his voice pitiful and weak. "Whoever you're looking for, I'm not the guy."

The woman spoke again. "You're Martin Warner of 15 Linden Park Place? Married to Leanne Warner, father of Sarah and Tim Warner?"

Warner felt like he was going to be sick. "Don't hurt them," he said.

"Your kids are fine, Martin. Sit back and relax."

"Why are you doing this?" He twisted in his bindings, craning his neck toward the sound of her voice. "Where are you taking me?"

"Don't worry about it now," she said. "We'll explain it all when we get there."

The van drove fifteen, maybe twenty, minutes, before pulling in somewhere and stopping. Someone cut the ignition. "Have a look." A door opened and slammed shut.

A minute later, the rear door slid open. "We're clear."

Someone lifted Warner to his feet and pushed him out of the van. *"Hurry."* He let them guide him up a flight of stairs and down a long hallway before they turned him left, walked him a few paces, and deposited him on what felt like a bed.

"Sit," said the man. "Listen."

Warner sat up. Listened to the sounds around him: the rustle of feet on carpet, chairs being moved. A door shut and was locked.

"Okay, Marty." A third voice, a man's, youngish but assertive. "I apologize for the blindfold. Just a precaution. If you promise not to take it off, I'll untie your hands. Deal?"

Warner nodded. "Okay."

"If you take off the blindfold and see our faces, Marty, we'll have to kill you."

Warner swallowed. "I promise I won't look."

Someone untied his hands, and he rubbed his wrists gingerly. A glass was pressed into his hands, and he brought it to his lips. Water. He realized he was thirsty and drank, emptying the glass.

"You're wondering why we've brought you here," the third voice continued. Warner was already thinking of him as the boss. "Yeah?"

Warner nodded. "I . . . am."

"It's really simple. You've been kidnapped, Marty. We're holding you for ransom. We don't want to hurt you. We don't even want to inconvenience you that much. If all goes according to plan, we'll have you back home tomorrow."

"The police," said Warner. "They'll find you."

"They won't," said the man. "Because they're not going to know about it. We're watching your house, Marty. We have eyes on your family right now. If anyone calls the police, we'll know about it. And then we'll have to react."

Warner swallowed again. "No police."

Someone pressed a phone into his hand.

"This is not a big deal," the man said. "You're going to call Leanne and tell her you're all right. You're going to tell her not to call the police. You're going to tell her if she does call the police, she'll never see you again."

"How much do you want?"

"Then you're going to tell her she can have you back tomorrow. Good as new. All we want is a small finder's fee."

"How much, damn it?" said Warner.

"Sixty grand, Marty," said the man. "Unmarked twenties. We need it within twenty-four hours. Tell your wife she'll get the drop details once she's secured the money."

"Sixty thousand dollars?" said Warner. "That's absurd. I expensed more than sixty grand last year alone."

"We know that," said the man. "And we know you made a million dollars last year speculating on oil futures, yeah? Sixty grand should be a cinch."

Warner paused. "How do you know this stuff?"

"We did our research, Marty." He could feel someone beside him, punching numbers into the phone. "Now, go ahead and make that call."

TWO

Arthur Pender stared out the window of the restaurant, watching cars pull in and out of the parking lot as the night settled in beyond. Another perfect score, he thought. This is easier than flipping burgers.

Sawyer had purchased the van in Kansas City on Monday, the day after LaSalle's wife paid his ransom. The four of them had driven up to Chicagoland that night, arriving in Highland Park around four in the morning. They found a cheap motel by the highway and turned in at dawn. For Pender, it was the first time he'd slept, really slept, in a week.

Tuesday was decompression day. Mouse and Sawyer rented a little Toyota, headed into Chicago, caught a Blackhawks game. Pender and Marie hit Lake Michigan. Took a long walk. Ate a nice dinner. Got a bit drunk and made the best of their alone time.

They spent Wednesday doing preliminary

intel, scoping out Warner, getting a feel for his routine. Confirming travel times. Double-checking Mouse's computer work with practice and old-fashioned observation.

Thursday: dress rehearsal. Everyone a bit antsy. Fraying tempers. Everything nailed down and nothing to do. Sawyer and Mouse fighting over the remote. Marie withdrawn, worried.

Friday was D-day. Pender didn't sleep much, as usual. Game day always gave him a rush. Like waiting for Santa Claus on Christmas Eve.

He kept Marie awake with his tossing and turning and finally left her around three in the morning, headed to Sawyer and Mouse's room. Found them watching action movies on cable. Watched for a while and fell asleep in an easy chair.

They spent the morning doing final recon work. Parked the van beside Warner's Lexus in the Metra lot, babysat Leanne Warner all day in the Toyota, and then headed back to the motel. The hostage room all set up. Marie locked in the bathroom, rehearsing her lines in the mirror. Sawyer taking a nap and Mouse watching TV. Loose.

They drove back to the parking lot in the late afternoon. Pender and Sawyer in the van. Mouse in the Toyota. Marie on the platform. Everybody focused. Everybody calm.

Ten to seven. The train arrived. Marie found Warner on the platform. Followed him out into the parking lot. Pender phoned Mouse and gave him the all clear. Mouse flashed the high beams at Marie. Point of no return. No quitting now. Go go go.

It played exactly as they drew it up. They snagged Warner no problem, got him back to the motel, made the pitch.

Warner called his wife. Calmed down a little. What's sixty grand to this guy? Probably kept that kind of change in a jam jar in his basement. Walking-around money.

Leanne Warner had no trouble producing the ransom. Had the money by Saturday afternoon with plenty of time to spare. No police. Mouse tailed her in the Toyota to be sure.

She drove a black Lincoln Navigator, and came alone, as instructed. Left the money in a duffel bag at the drop site and parked nearby to wait.

Mouse scoped the scene in the Toyota and phoned in the all clear. Sawyer and Pender drove up in the van, sunglasses on and hats pulled low. Pender grabbed the cash bag. Checked it, counted it, found it clean. All glorious, well-used twenties. Kicked Warner from the van blindfolded. Slid the door shut behind him and drove off into traffic.

Perfect execution.

Leanne Warner was good with instructions. She didn't try to follow. According to Mouse, she played the usual tune: ran to her husband, hugged him, took off the blindfold, tearful reunion. Then they drove home.

"No cops," Pender warned them both. "Even after it's over. We'll be watching the house. You call the cops, and we come for the kids."

They divvied up the money in Racine, just across the state line. Pender set aside twenty thousand for expenses: van, rental car, cell phones, motel, food, and gas. That left forty thousand for the team. Ten thousand apiece. Even split. Ten thousand for the Warner job and ten thousand from Kansas City made twenty for the month. Add it to the twenty-five or so from the September jobs and you had the makings of a decent autumn.

They stripped the van clean and abandoned it behind a warehouse in Waukegan. Pender and Sawyer paid cash for a GMC Savana on lease return at a used-car dealership in Lake Forest, and they threw the burner phones and the old plates into Lake

16

Michigan when they dropped off the rental car.

Now they sat in a Denny's in Racine, trying to figure the next move. "We could do Milwaukee next week," Mouse was saying. "Won't take much looking to find something suitable."

"Milwaukee's too close," said Pender. "We pull a job in Wisconsin, there's a chance someone catches on. I was thinking Minneapolis. Quick, before it gets too cold. Then down to Detroit and then south to the sunny stuff."

"I like that," said Marie. "Can we do Florida?"

"Disney World," said Mouse.

"Disney World," said Pender. "You want to kidnap Mickey Mouse?"

"You know he's filthy rich," said Mouse. "Minnie pays the ransom and we're set for life."

Pender laughed. "How about it, Sawyer? Florida?"

Sawyer looked up from his Grand Slam breakfast. He nodded. "Would be nice to try some surfing."

"Cheers to that," said Mouse, lifting his glass. They drank to the plan and then ate in silence, reflecting on the success of the job, and when the plates had been cleared and the bill was on the table, Pender cleared his throat. "All right," he said. "Sawyer and Mouse, you guys drive up to Minnesota tonight. Grab a motel and try and find someone for us to key on."

Pender smiled at Marie. "We'll take the train, you and me. These guys can pick us up at the station tomorrow." He pulled out his wallet and put cash on the bill. "Great work, everyone," he said. "See you in Minnesota."

THREE

Kirk Stevens stared down at the body on the pavement and shivered. He blew on his hands and rubbed them together and looked back longingly at his Cherokee, parked some thirty yards back in the shadows. He shivered again and looked down at the body, and then into the yawning cab of the Peterbilt parked behind.

The sheriff's deputy glanced into the cab and then looked back at Stevens. He was a young guy, buzz-cut and brash. "Don't know why they had to call you all the way out here," he said, frowning. "Not like we can't solve a murder or nothing."

Stevens crouched down to get a closer look at the body. "I don't know anything about that," he said.

The dead man was barely more than a kid himself. He wore a Twins hat cocked sideways and a big camouflage parka, and his 9 mm pistol lay on the pavement where it

19

had scattered off behind him. His chest was a mess of blood and goose down and buckshot.

The deputy leaned against the cab of the Peterbilt. He looked down at Stevens. "So what do you think happened?" he said.

Stevens glanced up at him, and then at the truck, lit up in the blue-and-red glow of the deputy's patrol car lights. Besides the truck and the patrol car and Stevens's old Cherokee, the rest stop was deserted, though through the trees Stevens could trace the lights of the cars headed north to St. Paul on Interstate 35.

The cab door was open. The dead kid had eaten a hot buckshot dinner. The truck driver was nowhere to be found.

"I'll tell you what happened," the deputy said. "This yo tried to hijack the truck. Driver let him have it. Then he panicked and ran. Stole the yo's car and he vanished. Sound good?"

Stevens looked up at him. "Maybe," he said.

The deputy snorted. "Sounds better than good. This is open-and-shut, is what it is. No reason to get the BCA out here."

No argument there, Stevens thought, feeling his muscles groan as he pulled himself to his feet. He'd been watching a movie —

a good movie for once — with Nancy and the kids when the call came down the line. Stevens was next up on the rotation, and for his luck he'd earned a sixty-mile drive and a smart-ass rookie companion out in the bitter air of the Minnesota hinterlands, any hope of rest or relaxation now gone.

Life with the Bureau of Criminal Apprehension. Stevens had been a city cop, once, fifteen years ago now. Five years in Duluth. Five years was enough. He'd gotten sick of the murders and the drug grabs and the cheap dollar-store robberies, the boring sawed-off crimes of desperation. A job came up at the BCA and he took it, and the requisite move to St. Paul, and had never regretted the decision. These days, however, life with the state's police force seemed to consist mainly of paperwork and whodunit homicides, another small town with another new body, a rate of about a couple per month.

Robberies gone bad, drug deals gone bad, marital squabbles gone bad. It wasn't exactly world-changing stuff.

Stevens looked around at the crime scene. The cab of the big truck was riddled with holes, and the mirror hung half shot off its stanchion. Stevens walked around the back of the truck to where the rear door had been wrenched open. The cargo inside — a mountain of DVD players in slim cardboard boxes — was strewn haphazardly across the floor of the trailer. He peered in and kept walking.

He walked alongside the rig to the passenger-side door. The truck was parked close to the trees, and the light from the trooper's blue-and-reds didn't quite permeate. Stevens squinted in the darkness at the door. He reached out and touched it and felt the door give. He let it go and it swung back, a half inch or so open.

Stevens called out to the deputy, who came around with a flashlight. He held the light up to Stevens and then at the door. "Shit," he said. "What does this mean?"

Stevens looked down at the pavement leading up to the brush. "Shine a light down there," he said, and the deputy obliged him.

"Shit," said the deputy.

"Sure looks like blood," said Stevens. He glanced into the brush. In the dim light, he could just make out an impromptu path. "Follow me with that light."

They found the truck driver about fifteen feet in, the shotgun by his side and a bullet hole in his head. Stevens looked back at the deputy. "There's a third player," he said. "Probably headed north to St. Paul."

The deputy nodded and disappeared down the path. Stevens looked down at the dead truck driver in the shadows for a moment. Then he turned back toward the truck. The wind howled through the trees and he shivered again, thinking about Nancy and the kids and the movie he'd missed. He walked back to the pavement and around the truck and back to where the deputy sat in his patrol car, hollering excited instructions into his radio.

Stevens stood alongside the patrol car, waiting for the deputy to finish. In Duluth, he thought, I was just like this kid. I thought every case made me a hero.

He caught his dim reflection in the patrol car's rear window as he waited, and he stared at it a moment, a forty-three-year-old career cop with thinning hair and a paunch, his tired eyes betraying a mounting fatigue. Sooner or later they would catch the third player, some woebegone kid with a gun and a trunk full of hot electronics. They'd lock him up and he'd cop to the robbery and do time and be ruined, and someone else would jump in and hijack tractor trailers, and sooner or later they'd wind up a body themselves.

Another botched robbery, Stevens thought

to himself. Another day in the glamorous
life.

FOUR

They arrived in Minnesota on Sunday afternoon, and by noon Tuesday they'd picked out a target.

"His name's Terrence Harper," said Mouse, reading off the screen of his laptop. "Junior vice president at North Star Investors Group. Age forty-seven. Wife Sandra Harper, daughter Alice. Lives close to downtown and two major highways."

Pender stared at the computer over Mouse's shoulder. "His finances?"

"A-1," said Mouse. He turned in his chair, caught Pender's eye. "Says this guy made a million-six betting against the housing meltdown. That's on top of his half-million-dollar salary and bonuses."

Mouse turned back to the computer, brought up Harper's bank statements. The target was certainly liquid. His wife would have no problem scraping together the finder's fee.

25

Moreover, Terrence Harper looked like just the kind of target Pender had had in mind when he'd started making scores. A fat-cat day trader, grown rich short-selling the American Dream while the rest of the country struggled to pay the mortgage.

Guys like Harper, thought Pender, were the reason they were kidnapping bankers in the first place.

In the beginning, the whole thing had been Marie's idea. It had started as a joke, some throwaway line spouted off one rainy night in Seattle, the gang holed up at Sawyer's place bitching about the job market over cheap beer and pizza, scholarships almost gone and graduation upon them, nobody but Mouse with a future to speak of.

"Listen," Marie said. "Maybe Mouse can hack his way to a million dollars, but for me it's either robbing banks or making lattes."

They laughed at her, half drunk and rueful, some shitty action movie on in the background, buildings blowing up and machine guns blasting full bore. Pender reached for the remote, changed the channel. Got the news, the grim forecast: unemployment, foreclosures.

"This is what I'm talking about," Marie said. "My parents lost half their savings in the last six months alone."

Mouse nodded. "My dad nearly gave up his house."

"You think anyone's got time for three kids with three useless degrees?" Marie said. "Nobody's making money but investment bankers. And they're getting paid with our taxes."

"Construction," said Sawyer.

"Maybe *you* could build houses," Marie told him. "I don't have the muscle. Anyway, the housing boom's over. Construction workers aren't getting paid, either."

"So what," Pender asked her. "You want to work on Wall Street?"

"No," said Marie. "I want to rob those bastards." She smiled as she said it, and she caught Pender's eye. "Think about it. A couple big scores and then we could retire."

Pender laughed again. His eyes met Sawyer's. "One more time, Marie," Pender said. "You want to rob banks for a living?"

"I have a history degree, Pender." Marie twisted around to look up at him from the floor. "I don't want to make coffee my whole life."

Pender glanced around the room. They all had reason to be desperate, each one of his friends. Marie's history degree was worth just enough to overqualify her for most entry-level jobs. If she wanted a career, she'd have to go back to school, and her parents, both doctors, still smarted from their daughter's choosing arts over science. They weren't writing any more checks for tuition.

After six years of flunking and fighting, meanwhile, Sawyer's GPA was a punch line. He'd flirted with dropping out more than once, spent a couple nights in jail, and it was only with Pender's help that he'd qualified — barely — for his degree.

Mouse had it best of them all, having landed himself a programming internship with Microsoft with the potential for lucrative full-time employment. But Mouse was a hacker at heart, and his anarchist tendencies didn't mesh with the Microsoft ethic. At the end of the semester, he found himself unemployed, and with his father out of work and his own finances dwindling, Mouse needed money and fast.

They all needed money. They all had degrees, and degrees were supposed to pave the way to careers. They hadn't, and it was time for another solution. But crime? Crime seemed a little extreme. Pender shook his head. "Robbing banks is tough work. Dangerous."

"What about kidnapping?" That was Sawyer, slow and thoughtful.

"Kidnapping, yeah." Marie nodded. "Mouse could get us close to Bill Gates."

"Screw off."

"We could make a million dollars in one shot."

"No," said Pender. "That's how people get caught. Greed. If you were going to kidnap someone and get away with it, you'd need to stay out of the spotlight."

"What do you mean?" said Mouse. Nobody was smiling now.

"I mean, you could grab one movie star and ask for a million dollars or you could get ten normal people and ask for a hundred grand," said Pender, making it up as he went. "You get a junior VP at a Fortune 500 company, tell his wife to hand over a hundred grand in the next twenty-four hours, and she'll do it without thinking. It's an inconvenience at those stakes, not a crime."

"You want to kidnap ten people? Won't the police catch on?"

"Not if you keep moving," said Sawyer.

"Yeah," said Pender. "Yeah. You make a score and then you hit the next city down the road. Rinse and repeat."

Nobody spoke for a minute or two. Nobody made eye contact. Sawyer stared at the floor, Mouse into his beer, Marie out onto the avenue, watching drunk students stream past. Pender changed channels again, back to the action movie. This time he watched closer, his stomach turning to jelly and his mind moving nonstop.

Then Marie straightened. "Well," she said. "We don't have to make a career out of it."

Pender nodded. "Of course not."

Mouse sat up. "If we pulled one job, like you said, we walk away with a hundred grand. That's twenty-five for each person. Not a bad summer project."

"Nobody gets hurt."

"I could go back to Microsoft. Beg for my job."

"And we could buy time to figure out options," said Marie. She sat up on the couch and looked at Pender, hard. "Let's just do it," she said. "Just once. Just to see if we can."

Pender looked at Sawyer. Sawyer looked back, said nothing, waited. "I say we do it," said Mouse. "We're smart enough. We can pull this thing off."

Pender hesitated a moment. Then he nodded. "Let's try it," he said. "Just to see if we can."

Now, sitting in the work van outside a Minneapolis bank tower two years down the road, Pender waited for Terrence Harper to show and he wondered whether his friends had ever really imagined they would wind up career criminals. Maybe we were all just daring each other, he thought. Maybe none of us wanted to be the one who pulled the cord.

Mouse pointed across the sidewalk, jolting Pender back to the present. A squat middle-aged man had just exited the North Star offices and was walking quickly down the sidewalk. "That's our guy."

Pender glanced down at the laptop. Compared the picture on the screen with the real thing outside. Same jowls, same receding hairline. A paunch and a wrinkled tie and the look of a man who didn't want his time wasted. Pender looked at the laptop again. Then he opened the van door. "That's him," he said. "Let's go for a walk."

FIVE

They took Terry Harper on another Friday evening, nabbing him on the sidewalk as he turned to walk the last block to his home. He was a struggler; he bit at Sawyer and screamed as the big guy, cursing and bloody, dragged him into the van.

They drove Harper to the Super 8 and got Sawyer bandaged up. Marie took off in the rental car to stake out the Harper residence, and Pender made his speech to Harper, laid it out and promised to remove the gag and untie his wrists if he'd promise to behave.

Harper promised. He seemed broken by the situation and incredulous, as they always were, about the low sum being demanded for his ransom. Pender made the call and pressed the phone to Harper's cheek, and the mark played his tune perfectly until the end.

"It's just sixty thousand, honey," he told

32

his wife. "Just take it from savings first thing tomorrow." Then he paused. Glanced around despite his blindfold. "There are three, maybe four, of them. One woman. I'm in an apartment, I think —"

Sawyer backhanded him, hard, and down he went. Pender hung up the phone before Sandra Harper could connect the dots, and Sawyer kept going, his fists hammering down on the hostage, his face contorted with rage.

"Don't you *ever* try to get cute like that again," he said. Harper curled up on the floor beneath him, ducking the punches and sobbing.

Pender put his arm on his shoulder. "All right."

Sawyer straightened. He glanced at Pender. "Had to," he said, breathing heavily.

Pender knew Sawyer was right, even if he didn't like it. Harper needed to be taught that he was dealing with professionals, and Sawyer had established that, brutally and effectively.

It was a part of his friend's personality that sometimes scared Pender. Matt Sawyer could be smart, articulate, and deadly funny, his infectious smile and slow, steady baritone a favorite with the women on campus. But Sawyer's parents had divorced

33

when he was a teenager, leaving him moody and violent and itching to fight, and even ten years later the big guy had a temper, could still get pissed off and black out, swinging his fists until his problems were solved. Pender could remember the first time he'd met Sawyer, a big scrappy freshman talking trash in the wrong kind of bar. Pender had talked the kid down and out of the place before a dozen drunk longshoremen did them both in.

Even in their new lives as kidnappers, though, Pender had hoped to get more use out of Sawyer's brain than his brawn. He held out hope that cuties like Terry Harper would continue to prove few and far between.

Marie phoned in on her new burner phone every couple hours. She'd parked the rental car a couple houses down and was taking periodic walks around the block to make sure Sandra Harper didn't take after her husband in the cuteness department.

Marie reported lights on at the Harper residence until one in the morning, when the final second-floor light was extinguished. She hung around outside, sitting low in the driver's seat of the Hyundai, listening to rock music at low volume and calling in until dawn.

Pender stayed up all night to take the calls. He never slept, anyway, when Marie was playing the point. Hell, he could barely sit down. Kept pacing the room. Turning on the TV, flipping through channels. On the second bed, Terry Harper shifted in his sleep, groaning every time Pender made a move.

"You gonna stay up all night?" he said finally. "Thought I'd at least get a good night's sleep out of this deal."

Pender stopped pacing. Stared at Harper a minute. "Yeah, fine," he said. "Sorry. I'll keep it down."

"I just got one question for you, though." Harper pointed his face in Pender's vague direction. "Why me? I'm nobody special."

The same old question. "You're special to me," said Pender.

"Seriously. Why me? And why so little money?"

"Don't worry about it. Go back to sleep."

Harper sat back on the bed. "I guess you're thinking it's easier to get sixty thousand than six hundred thousand. Quicker." He sighed. "Well, pal, I gotta tell you. You could have had six hundred grand for me. Easy."

"Sleep," said Pender. "Now."

I'm glad nobody else heard him say that,

35

he thought, as Harper turned back onto his side and began snoring a tractor-trailer snore. We're risking enough just by pulling these jobs. We don't need to get greedy besides.

Of all of his worries, it was greed that kept Arthur Pender awake at night. It wasn't his own greed that bothered him; Pender was happy with sixty-thousand-dollar scores. He worried, though, that the long grind would wear on his team.

Most would-be kidnappers treated the job like a Hail Mary. Tried to knock down some CEO, some pop star, tried to take ten million and disappear after one big haul. One shot for all the glory. To Pender, that kind of thinking was stupidity, plain and simple. Those heroes who aimed for the big scores always attracted the big crowds. Police. Feds. TV cameras. Publicity like that made it impossible to remain anonymous. Publicity like that meant investigations, manhunts, Wanted posters. Ultimately, publicity like that meant jail or death. Nobody got away from the Big American Machine.

Far better, then, to pull quick scores. Lower numbers, but higher volume. The Pender method. Snatch guys like Terry Harper, Martin Warner. Midlevel executives, hedge-fund managers, guys with enough cash to make the job worthwhile, with families to pay the ransoms, but with no glamour to their names. No romance. Anonymous upper-class fellas who just wanted to see things return to normal.

The first of their marks had been a Silicon Valley systems engineer, a tech-boom millionaire whose girlfriend delivered the ransom in a bright red Ferrari. Marcus Sinclair, an arrogant braggart in thousand-dollar sneakers and a solid-gold Rolex, a prick with a fake tan and a potty mouth. To a gang of impoverished students used to part-time jobs and ramen noodles, Sinclair's hundred grand seemed like a fortune.

Afterward, walking on a long, empty stretch of California coastline, Marie had wrapped her arms around Pender, staring out at the Pacific Ocean, eyes wide and bright, and asked if he really thought they should retire right now or if they could maybe manage one more score.

The question had surprised him. He'd been asking himself the same thing. He had believed from the start they could make a career as kidnappers, but it had been a daydream to Pender, a theory. He figured they'd cash out and go home and try and find normal jobs. He had never imagined

Marie would get off on the rush as much as he did. He'd turned to her. "You're serious."

She smiled at him, drunk off success, beautiful in the dying light of the day. She kissed him. "Just one more time," she said.

"You know we'll go to jail for this," he said. "This is a major crime."

"We won't go to jail," said Marie. "We won't get caught. Anyway, we're not hurting anyone. Not really."

"That guy was an asshole."

"He was an asshole," she said. "We didn't hurt him. What's a hundred thousand dollars to a guy like that?"

"Nothing," said Pender. "Less than nothing."

"To us, though." She kissed him again. Smiled. She was beautiful that night, even more than normal, the way her eyes caught the light, the way that thick mane of deep chestnut hair fell over her shoulders — and, above all, her perfect, carefree smile. She was *happy* tonight, Pender realized. He hadn't seen her this happy in weeks.

"I don't want to go back to Seattle," she said. "Wondering what I'm going to do with my life. Not yet, Arthur. Think what we could do with another hundred grand."

She had visions of a long vacation, a

chance to see the world — Machu Picchu and South Africa and Rome — and then a master's degree in something useful and a chance at some kind of career. Just one more score to get a head start on real life. One more perfect crime.

But Pender was dreaming bigger. And when he told her that in four years they could afford to retire in the Maldives or New Zealand, she'd laughed him off, disbelieving. But he'd mapped it out for her, for the team, showed them his projections, and now they held tight to that image, a little grass-roofed hut at the edge of a sparkling sea a million miles from anywhere.

The goal. The Dream. Pender's five-year plan. Criminals in the short term. The only way to get ahead. No job market, no unemployment lines, no Social Security or foreclosures. No 401(k) and no taxpayer bailouts. Just five years making low-risk, no-violence scores and then a worry-free existence forever.

Sawyer and Mouse, he knew, had similar aspirations. Maybe not the Maldives and maybe not a grass-roofed hut, but dreams nonetheless. Sawyer, Pender remembered, had been taken with that Silicon Valley man's Ferrari. Mouse was more into the guy's girlfriend, a pneumatic blonde with enhanced breasts and legs up to her ears. Both men saw their current occupations as a means toward those ends, toward fast cars and girls with fake breasts, a long life of leisure and luxury.

As they'd migrated eastward after those first big scores, however, away from the slacker-rich Silicon Valley geeks and gaudy Hollywood players and inland toward Middle America, even a hundred grand began to sound like an exorbitant ransom. Now, two years into the project, working sixty-thousand-dollar deals in frigid Minnesota, Pender knew it would be easy to forget the grind. It would be tempting to get greedy, to go for one big haul to end the show and set each of them up for life. And though nobody on the team had said anything yet, Pender still lay awake nights, fearing his teammates' greed and praying they'd stay on the program — *his* program — for as long as it would take to make the Dream something real.

Six

Sandra Harper paid the ransom by sunset.

Pender chose a suburban McDonald's for the drop spot and gave the woman fifteen minutes to be there. Told her put the money in a trash bag, leave it by the dumpster out back. Come alone. Park in the northwest corner of the lot. Way out in back. Do not follow us after the drop. Any deviation and your husband gets it.

They got there first. Pender watched from the van as Sandra drove in a few minutes later, a slight, graying woman in a navy blue Infiniti. She dropped the money bag beside the dumpster and parked as instructed.

Sawyer drove up, and Pender counted the money. All of it there. Pender nodded and Mouse kicked Harper to the curb and the men drove off in the van.

Marie hung around the parking lot in the rented Hyundai, watching Terry Harper pick himself up off the pavement and walk,

41

indignant, to his car, where his wife had vacated the driver's seat and waited on the passenger side, darting nervous glances at her husband and then back into the lot.

Marie followed them home and waited outside for a few hours, watching the lights go on and off, watching the shadows and silhouettes playing in the windows. Then Pender called and, with no police in sight, told Marie to bring it home.

They drove the Savana out to a nature reserve northwest of town. Marie met them in the barrens in the Hyundai, and they wiped the van clean, parked it deep in the woods at the end of a long dirt road, and said prayers for early snow. Then they drove the Hyundai back into Minneapolis and checked out of the Super 8 and checked into a Best Western across town and divvied up the money in the room.

The next day Pender and Marie took the rental car out and went van shopping, putting cash down on a red Ford E-Series passenger van and using another of Mouse's fake IDs for the registration. They took the rental car back to the airport and swung back to the Best Western to pick up Mouse and Sawyer.

Then Pender drove them out onto the highway, pointing the van northeast on a bearing for Green Bay and Michigan's Upper Peninsula, the late afternoon sunset a fire show over the Twin Cities in the rearview mirror.

"They said no police," said Sandra Harper, peering through the living room blinds and out into the shadows beyond. "They said they'd hurt Alice if we did."

"Bullshit." Terry Harper paced the room behind his wife. "They're not out there anymore. They're not watching us."

"But how do you know?"

"They have their money. Makes no sense them sticking around. They throw a threat at us and get the hell outta Dodge."

"But how do you *know?*"

"Goddamn it, Sandra, I just know."

In a corner of the living room, Alice Harper lingered, watching her father pace the room as her mother stared out into the street. Sandra replaced the curtain, looked back, and noticed her daughter, her eyes wide. "We're safe, Terry."

Her husband stopped pacing. "What?"

"We're safe. All of us. Safe." She gestured around the room. "You're safe. Alice is safe. I'm safe. So we lost some money. Big deal. Do you really want to risk our lives to get it back?"

For the first time that evening, Terry Harper looked his wife in the eye. "Yes," he said. "We have to send a message. You don't fuck with Terry Harper and expect to get away with it. Whether it's two dollars or two million."

Sandra sank into a couch. "I just want this to be over."

Her husband followed her, stood staring down at her. "If we don't make a stand, it will never be over," he said. "It could be you next, or Alice, God forbid. We have to make a stand."

His wife looked up at him, her eyes tired and swollen. His daughter crept out from the corner. "Daddy," she said. "What if someone else gets kidnapped like you were?"

Harper looked at his daughter, then at his wife. Sandra stared at Alice. "You're right," she said finally. "Let's call the police."

Seven

Kirk Stevens's third player was not at all hard to find.

A Burger King employee found a pistol in the trash outside a restaurant in Burnsville and a ballistics test confirmed it for the semitruck shooting. Stevens checked out the gun and followed it back to a retired schoolteacher in Dayton's Bluff. The teacher was clean; he'd bought the gun for protection and reported it stolen a week or so prior, but Stevens called in a favor with the St. Paul city cops and they came back with the news that the teacher had hired an old student of his to do the occasional odd job — rake leaves or buy groceries or whatever else. Wayne Harris was the kid's name.

Stevens and the St. Paul police did some looking around. Found Wayne Harris holed up in his grandmother's home in Burns Park. The kid played innocent for a minute, told the St. Paul city cop he was at a party that night. Stevens came around later and followed the kid to a pawnshop downtown, where Stevens made him unloading four or five hot DVD players from the back of his granny's Corolla.

Stevens hauled the kid in and it didn't take long. A couple hours in an interrogation room, a line or two about a long sentence and a brokenhearted grandmother and Harris burst into tears and confessed the whole thing. It wasn't supposed to go bad, he said. Nobody was supposed to die.

Stevens bought the kid a sandwich and a Coke and then brought him down to be charged. He spent the rest of his afternoon doing paperwork at his desk, and by about eight his stomach was growling and he was ready to call the case closed. He shut down his computer and was halfway out of his chair when his phone started ringing, loud and obnoxious in the near-empty confines of the BCA headquarters. Stevens stared at it a moment, his stomach rumbling its impatience. Then he sighed and sank back in his seat and picked up the handset. "Stevens."

"This is Special Investigations?"

"You got it," said Stevens. "Who am I talking to?"

"Powell, Minneapolis PD. Agent, we've

got a case you're probably going to want to hear about."

Minneapolis PD, thought Stevens. This ought to be good. In general, the police on the Twin Cities forces worked separate beats from their BCA counterparts. When Minneapolis PD came calling, it could only mean something major.

"Shoot," said Stevens, reaching for his notepad. "I'm all ears."

"Well, Agent," said the detective. "We got a kidnapping."

Stevens straightened, any thought of food now forgotten. "You're serious." Kidnappings were about as rare in Minnesota as swimsuits in January. "If it's a kid gone missing, you gotta take it to the FBI."

"Not a kid," said Powell. "A grown man. Name's Harper, Terrence. Late forties. Taken two days ago from the sidewalk outside his home in Lowry Hill. Walking home from work."

Stevens leaned forward on his desk and started copying Powell's dictation, his heart rate quickening. A kidnapping in Minneapolis, he thought. Bona fide. "Who is this guy Harper?" he said. "He a rich guy? Poor guy?"

"He's rich," said Powell. "Some kind of stockbroker or something."

"All right. Family get any kind of note? Phone call? Any ransom demanded?"

"Phone call, night of. Harper himself, asking for sixty grand in unmarked twenties."

"Small-time crooks."

"You said it. Wife paid in full the next day. Harper released safe and sound."

Stevens felt his stomach start to growl again. "The husband's safe."

"Yes, sir."

"Not missing any fingers, toes, ears, eyes."

"Everything present and accounted for."

Stevens sighed. He rubbed his eyes. Probably just some kids going out on a dare. Not likely to be any fun at all.

"Sorry to disappoint," said Powell. "If you don't want it, I can tell my sergeant you're passing."

Stevens sat back in his chair. He glanced around the room, catching his own face reflected momentarily in a darkened window. He saw the career cop again, the bags under the eyes and the latest spiderweb wrinkles, the face of an agent who'd once dreamed of making a difference but who'd seen those dreams replaced by an admirable service record and a decent outlook and a comfortable chair in a comfortable office.

Cheer up, he told himself. A middle-aged man gets himself stolen and brought back within twenty-four hours. A sixty-thousand-dollar ransom. Maybe it wasn't going to change the world, this case, but it sure beat the hell out of paperwork.

"I'll take it," he told Powell. "What else am I gonna do tonight?"

EIGHT

Terry Harper was a bulldog of a man, a round ball of indignation who would not be calmed despite the presence of the state police and the best efforts of his wife and daughter, both of whom had given up by this point and slunk, defeated, to the margins of the room.

Stevens stood in the living room doorway, watching him pace and feeling his own stomach churn. He'd stopped for Taco Bell on the way over and the molten cheese and low-grade beef weren't playing nice with his digestive tract. He swallowed a burp and fixed his eyes on Harper. "Give it to me from the beginning," he said.

Harper didn't break stride as he launched into his story. He had been walking home from work, he said, just before dusk. He was turning onto his block when a young woman called to him by name. No, he did not see the woman; she was behind him.

Though he may have caught a glimpse of brown curls. She was, he believed, white.

Before he could notice anything else, he was wrapped up and tossed in the back of a van, his arms tied, his eyes blindfolded, and his mouth gagged. He was driven to some sort of compound — an apartment, it seemed like — where he was instructed to phone his wife and then beaten by an assailant.

There were probably three kidnappers, he thought, including the girl, and he had talked to one of them during the night. "The guy didn't sleep," said Harper. "Kept pacing the room. Changing channels on the TV."

Ultimately, Harper slept, and spent the morning listening to the television before being tossed in the back of the van again and driven to a McDonald's parking lot. No, he didn't get a good look at the van. It was blue. Navy. The make? No idea.

"They said they were watching the house," he said. "And we shouldn't talk to the police."

Sandra Harper eyed Stevens and stepped forward. "They said they'd come for Alice," she said.

"They're not coming for your daughter," said Stevens. "Your family is safe."

"I know we're safe," said Harper. He stopped pacing and fixed Stevens with a glare. "I'm not afraid. I'm *mad.* I want you to do your damn job. Find them."

Stevens sighed to himself. You'd almost wish a guy like this would stay kidnapped, he thought. "These people," he said. "Two men. One woman. All white?"

"Far as I could tell."

"Weapons?"

Harper shrugged. "I was blindfolded. Maybe a handgun."

"How old were they?"

"Young." He started pacing again. "Late twenties, early thirties."

"Catch any names?"

"No. Everything was tight. No wasted words. Everything quick."

"Tell him the other thing," said Sandra Harper. "The money thing."

"Sixty grand," said Harper. "Kind of small, don't you think?"

"Sure."

"You'd think, you're kidnapping someone, you ask for more money. Big money. I've got it. I told the guy straight up. He could have asked for a million, and he would have got it."

Stevens scratched his head. "What did he say?"

"Didn't say anything. Told me go to sleep. But I figured they wanted me in and out, quick, before anyone else caught on. Twenty-four hours."

"You figured, hey?"

"Why else would they aim so low?"

Maybe they were junkies, thought Stevens. Addicts looking to make a quick score. But junkies would be sloppy and desperate. They would make mistakes. If these kids had made a mistake, it wasn't showing through yet.

A woman with curly brown hair. A blue panel van. A low ransom demand and a quick turnaround. A hit-and-run job.

Agent Stevens could count the number of kidnappings he'd worked on one hand. And they'd all been easy compared to this: a couple jealous parents playing musical kids, a drug dealer snatching his rival off a street corner. The kids came back overdosed on ice cream, and the rival came back in a block of concrete. Not exactly whodunits. Nothing like this job.

But he had to start somewhere. Kids in an apartment. A bunch of students, maybe, having a laugh. An elaborate senior prank. Minneapolis had a number of universities. Get a detail of Metro uniforms to canvass the campuses, ask around.

The McDonald's may have had a security camera. And there was the blue van. Had to be hundreds in the Twin Cities, but it wouldn't hurt to put out a notice, get people looking around. The phone records might work, too. Figure out where the calls were coming from and you get your kidnappers' geography. The more Stevens figured, the better he liked it. Maybe it wasn't such a dead end after all.

Stevens turned to Harper. "You have any enemies? Anyone who'd want to hurt you?"

Harper gave him a withering look. "I'm no asshole, buddy. I play the goddamn stock market."

"These days," said Stevens, "that might just make you an asshole."

NINE

They drove over the top of northern Michigan, stopping for the night at a deserted roadside motel just north of the Straits of Mackinac. In the morning it snowed, a few flakes of dandruff and a bitter wind off the lake. It took Sawyer ten minutes to scrape the frost from the van's windows.

It was a nice little spot, Pender thought, the cold notwithstanding. Would be amazing in the summer. Fishing, boating, maybe some swimming. A little chunk of heaven.

They slept in that morning, Sawyer and Mouse in one room and Pender and Marie in the other.

Marie woke first and when Pender opened his eyes he saw her, curled up in a baggy university sweatshirt and her nose in a paperback novel. She smiled at him when he sat up, her frizzy hair an explosion and her eyes still bleary. He leaned over and kissed her. "Getting ideas?" he said.

She shook her head. "It's a romance novel."

"What do you need with a romance novel?" He kissed her again. "You have me."

She smiled again and kissed him back, and then she sank back into the sheets and stared up at the ceiling. "It's nice here," she said.

"Would be better in the summer."

"I was thinking," she said. "It would be nice if we could stay."

He watched her. "Yeah?"

"If we weren't always in such a hurry." She sighed. "I just wish we could be normal sometimes."

"In a couple more years, we'll be done with this stuff. We can be normal the rest of our lives."

She sat up again. "I'm just kind of tired," she said. "Motel rooms and minivans and stuff. I feel dirty, Pender. Unhealthy. This isn't really what I had in mind when I thought about seeing the world."

He reached out to her and ran his hands over her hip and her side. Slid his hand underneath her sweatshirt and along the contours of her body. "You look pretty healthy to me," he told her.

She sighed again. "We need exercise, Pender," she said. "Maybe we should start doing yoga or something."

"I have a better idea." He pulled her closer and kissed her long and hard, loving the way her body curved to fit his. He tugged at her sweatshirt and she sat up to pull it over her head, casting a sideways look down at him.

"This is your idea of exercise?" she said.

He grinned at her. "It's better than yoga. No offense."

She swatted playfully at him and then he pulled her back to him. He admired her for another long minute, and then he closed his eyes and kissed her some more.

They stayed in bed until noon. Then the phone rang and it was Mouse and Sawyer, ready to go. They showered and dressed and ate breakfast with the guys in an empty diner down the road, and then they piled back in the van and drove on.

They made Detroit by the middle of the afternoon, swooping down on the I-75 into the city's grimy suburbs under a sky as bleak as the surroundings. They found a Super 8 off the highway and paid cash for two double rooms. When they got in and got settled, Mouse booted up his computer and started looking for prospects.

"This is good," he said, staring at a map on his screen. "Looks like we're pretty close to a lot of rich neighborhoods."

"Rich?" said Sawyer. "Who the hell are we going to nab in this broke-ass town?"

"No kidding," said Marie. "If we take the president of GM, they'll make us pay to give him back."

They had a point, Pender thought. He worried a little about the target possibilities in this part of the country. The whole southern half of the state looked like a fallout zone, and Detroit itself wasn't exactly millionaires' row these days. It almost felt wrong taking money from the people around here.

But Mouse was confident, and he was good. By next morning he had pulled up three worthy candidates, none of whom seemed to have suffered at all in the recession. By noon, Pender had made his decision.

The target was Sam Porter, a forty-two-year-old executive with an agricultural engineering firm headquartered outside the Detroit city limits. Porter lived with his young family in Royal Oak, an affluent bedroom community and an easy highway drive from the Super 8.

"House is worth about a million, and he's got stock," said Mouse. "Must have got in early with his company and rode it north.

He's perfect."

The target acquired, they settled in to the work. There was plenty of it. Burner phones to buy and a car to rent. Routines to establish and intelligence to gather. The team was at its best with a job to do, Pender believed, himself included. With tasks at hand, he could forget about the bigger worries and throw himself into the grind. And he did. They all did, enjoying the anticipation of a job coming together, another D-day just two days away.

TEN

For all of Agent Stevens's initial enthusiasm, the Harper job didn't exactly hightail it out of the gate. There were few leads to start with, and none of them seemed to be leading to much.

The drop site McDonald's did indeed have a security camera, but whoever had taken Harper had gone to great lengths to stay out of the shot. Stevens had watched Harper stomp over to his Infiniti eight or nine times, peering at the edges of the frame for any hint of the kidnappers' ride, but to no avail. Shit outta luck in that regard.

SOL university-wise, too. The Minneapolis PD had canvassed the U of M campus as well as the North-Central, Capella, Walden, and St. Thomas schools. Nobody was saying anything about any kidnapping, and as for girls with curly brown hair, well, there were only about eight thousand of them.

Stevens left word with the Minneapolis

PD and the various campus police forces to watch out for kids who were throwing money around and had even hauled one sophomore in a Hummer down to the BCA for questioning. But the kid was a basketball player and the Hummer was a loaner from a booster — a clear violation of NCAA rules, but not something the BCA was looking to prosecute.

He still doubted his perps were addicts, but just to be on the safe side, Stevens asked the knockos at the Minneapolis PD to keep an eye out for blue vans and rich junkies in the poorer neighborhoods.

Blue vans. Every time Stevens saw a blue van, he had to resist the urge to pull it over. It happened probably five or six times a day. Still, he looked close at every van he saw, hoping for that perfect combination, praying for a brown-haired girl in the driver's seat.

The phone records weren't much help, either. The kidnappers had made two calls to the Harper residence, one each from a pair of T-Mobile pay-as-you-go cellular phones. Simple. Only the phone company wouldn't give up the locations of the calls without a warrant.

Lawyers, Stevens thought. It's a kidnapping case. These are the kidnappers calling with ransom demands. There's obvious probable cause. The company has to know we'll come back with a warrant. They're just slowing down the process with this bullshit insistence on protocol. Meanwhile, the case is getting colder by the minute.

The phone company did, however, allow that the phones had been purchased from the T-Mobile kiosk at Mall of America on the Monday before the kidnapping. A clerk named Aziz had made the sale.

Earlier in the day, Stevens had driven over to the Mall and searched out Aziz and the T-Mobile kiosk. The guy looked barely out of high school and half stoned besides, but Stevens tried it on anyway, asking Aziz if he remembered anyone coming in and buying two burners last Monday afternoon.

The results were predictable. Aziz shrugged. "Lots of people buy phones."

"These people bought two phones. At once."

"Lots of people buy two phones."

Stevens shot the guy a look. "Come on," he said. "Help me out. Young people. A white girl with curly brown hair."

Aziz shrugged and gestured to the ceiling. "You check the security cameras?"

Stevens hit up the security console, explained the situation. Ran straight into a stonewalling rent-a-cop with an attitude problem.

Management was a bit more obliging, but the tapes, they said, were on a three-day cycle. Every three days they were erased and reused. Monday was five days ago. Therefore, no tapes.

Police work. Sometimes it made Stevens want to be a long-haul trucker.

Night after night, he found himself shackled to his desk in the BCA long after sundown, his wife and kids having given up on dinner with Daddy yet again, his eyes bleary and his head aching. Tim Lesley, Special Agent in Charge of Special Investigations, was riding him for answers — and Lesley, a tall, mean bastard whose wire-rimmed glasses belied a long history as a shit-kicking homicide cop in the old vein, wasn't trying to hear about Stevens's lack of progress. A case was a case, and a kidnapping, goddamn it, didn't happen in Minnesota without someone getting their ass locked up.

Now Stevens sat in the BCA offices, watching the clock make its idle circuit, waiting for his break. Another weary night.

Then the phone rang. Loud. Scared the shit out of him. Stevens sat up at his desk. Fingers crossed, he thought. "Stevens."

"Hi, honey." Nancy.

"Oh, hey," said Stevens. "I was just thinking about you."

"Really?"

"Sure. You're wanted for armed robbery. The kids turned state's witness."

"Those brats. Never should have brought them along."

"Hard to find a good babysitter."

"I never figured they would squeal." He could hear the smile in her voice. Nancy Monroe's wicked sense of humor was one of the first things that had attracted Stevens to his wife. That and she was the prettiest girl he'd ever seen.

Tonight, he couldn't see her, but he could picture her smile and it was almost enough. She was just calling to say hi, she said, and to remind Stevens how lucky he was to have a wife who understood a state policeman's long hours — though he hardly needed reminding. The sound of her voice perked him up, brightened his mood, and he hoped she'd be awake when he finally got home.

As his wife gave him the daily report, Stevens fiddled around with the security footage from the drop site, playing it on a loop and staring, mindless, into the grainy black-and-white footage, watching the pixels move back and forth on his screen.

"So the teacher says that J.J. is going to have to take the remedial math program," Nancy was saying. "At least until he figures out long division."

"Long division," said Stevens. "A dead language. Who needs it?"

"Means he spends lunch hour inside with Mr. Davidson and some other kids. I guess it's not a big deal, right?"

"Should be fine." Stevens blinked. He stared at the screen, rewound the loop. Terrence Harper storming over to his car. Sandra Harper ditching, getting in on the passenger side. The Harpers sitting in the car for a couple minutes, Terrence yelling something at his wife. Then the headlights turning on and Terrence adjusting the rearview mirror before slowly pulling out of the lot.

All fine. Stevens had watched the footage a hundred times already.

But now, as he kept watching, a small Korean sedan moved into the frame. The car stopped for a moment, directly in front of the camera, and Stevens caught a half-second glimpse of the driver before the car pulled out of the lot, headed in the same direction as the Harpers.

"Honey?"

"What?"

"I was just saying that Andrea needs to be picked up from volleyball practice tomorrow."

"Oh." Stevens paused the tape, his heart pounding. "Sure. I can do that."

"Great."

"Listen," he said. "Can I call you back? I think I just found something."

Nancy paused. "Fine," she said, sighing. "Come home soon."

After Nancy hung up the phone, Stevens turned back to the screen. He rewound the tape, playing it forward to that brief moment when the driver of the sedan was visible to the camera.

She was a white woman, young by the looks of it. The camera footage was grainy, and Stevens couldn't make out much of her facial features. What he *could* see, however, was her hair: a mass of dark curls that spilled over her face and her shoulders, partially obscuring her eyes.

ELEVEN

Sam Porter was a major disappointment.

The guy should have been the perfect score. He had a big house and a couple of nice foreign cars and a blond wife who was obviously a decade or so his junior. He was the kind of guy who enjoyed being rich, who would throw money at a problem and expect it to disappear. The kind of guy who would pay off sixty thousand dollars with a smirk and then go home and make it all back plus interest playing the stock market the next day.

He was the kind of guy who would spend his Novembers on a beach in the Turks and Caicos.

They lost him Thursday morning. One day before D-day. Mouse was on shadow detail, hanging out down the street from Porter's place and babysitting him on the drive in to work. Thursday, though, Porter was running late. Mouse cruised the block a couple times, thinking he'd missed him, but both cars stayed put in the driveway, and after a while, Mouse realized he hadn't seen the guy's kid leave for school yet, either.

At quarter to ten, the whole family — Porter, the wife, the fourteen-year-old son — piled into Grace Porter's Mercedes SUV and backed out onto the street. Mouse followed in the rental Impala, tailing the Benz southwest to the airport, where the Porters parked in the long-term lot and disappeared into the terminal.

Mouse called Pender, panicked. Pender called Porter's office and got the goods from a secretary. The family was gone for three weeks. The West Indies — isn't that nice? Howard Bartley would be handling Porter's accounts.

Pender half debated switching the job over to Bartley, just to maintain the theme, but then Mouse punched a couple keys on his laptop and revealed that Bartley was a bachelor with serious credit problems. No chance they'd get a penny in ransom.

Pender gathered the gang at the Super 8 that afternoon. "What now?" he asked them. "What do you guys want to do?"

"No worries," said Mouse. He started typing again. "We can find another mark in a minute and a half. Easy."

Pender stared at Mouse's computer screen. "We could just ditch and go on vacation."

Sawyer frowned. "No sense coming to Detroit if we're not getting paid for it."

"Besides, who's going to pay for the hotel if it's not the mark?" said Mouse. "And the rental car? It ain't coming out of my share."

Pender turned to his girlfriend. "What do you think, Marie?"

She was quiet a moment, but then she sighed and looked up. "Let's just do it."

"You're sure?"

"Yeah," she said. "Let's get paid and get out of here. Go somewhere warm."

Pender stared at her a second, almost wishing she'd wanted to jet. I really don't like these slapdash encounters, he thought. We work best when we're prepared. But he mulled it over a little longer, and then he thought, man up. You'll pull this job and spend a week on the beach. Nothing to it. He looked around the room, the gang waiting for him, and he squared his shoulders and looked down at Mouse's laptop. "All right," he told Mouse. "Bring up those targets again. Let's find us a good one."

They picked Donald Beneteau. But Donald

Beneteau did not go easy.

They collared him in Birmingham, a couple blocks from his house, as he walked back from the grocery store with a half gallon of milk and the day's *Free Press*. He turned around nice and easy when Marie called out his name, but once Sawyer and Pender put their hands on him he broke free and bolted.

Beneteau made it half a block before they got him in the van, punching and kicking and swearing his lungs out. Sawyer fed him a right cross and he calmed down enough that Pender could rope him up, but the man got his kicks in, nailing Pender square in the jaw as he tried to fit the gag.

"Do you know who I am?" he kept saying. "Do you *know* who the fuck I am?"

Pender and Sawyer swapped looks. They knew what Mouse knew. Beneteau owned his own tool-and-die operation. Four factories. Thirty million dollars in annual revenue. Commuted to work daily in a Mercedes-Benz sedan. Married fifteen years to Patricia Beneteau, forty, VP of Marketing for the Motown Casino. Three sons. Million and a half dollars in real estate, another couple million in the bank. Perfect target.

Perfect targets, though, didn't tend to put up such a fight. Perfect targets didn't act like their kidnappers should know who the fuck they were.

They got Beneteau back to the Super 8 and let him cool down a little while Pender took Mouse into the other bedroom. "Why's this guy acting like a superstar?" he asked. "Is there something we should know about him?"

Mouse shrugged. "Guy thinks he's a big shot. No big deal."

"You sure?"

"Yeah." Mouse gave him a smile. "It's fine, boss. Do your thing."

Pender gave it a minute. He shrugged. Of course it was fine. The guy was just pissed off, was all. "Fine," he said. He went back to Beneteau's room.

There, Pender lay out the story, closing with a hundred-thousand-dollar payoff. Beneteau looked like he could stand to pay a premium, and the extra forty grand would make a nice vacation bonus when they hit Florida next week. When Pender finished his spiel, however, Beneteau laughed in his face.

"Nice speech, pal," he said. "But you won't get a dime from me."

Sawyer smacked him. Beneteau came up bloody, but he kept laughing.

"We're going to put you on the phone to your wife," said Pender, trying to sound calmer than he felt. "You can lay out the situation. Talk it over."

"Think about your wife," said Sawyer. "Think about your kids."

"Think about fuck you," said Beneteau. "Let me go now and maybe you live."

Pender picked up the phone. "Call your wife."

"Last chance. I make this call and you fuckers are roadkill."

Sawyer smacked him again. "Dial the number."

Pender dialed. Beneteau put the phone to his ear. After a few seconds, he spoke. "Honey," he said. "I've been kidnapped. Some chumps. I'm all right. They want a ransom. No, listen. Hundred grand. That's the price. Twenty-four hours. You know what to do . . . All right. All right."

Beneteau hung up the phone. He turned his face in Sawyer's direction and flashed a bloody grin. "You motherfuckers just made the biggest mistake of your lives."

TWELVE

"Yeah, I remember her. How could I forget?"

Agent Stevens found himself at the Avis counter at the Minneapolis–St. Paul International Airport, listening to the clerk nearly blow his wad as he tried to describe the girl who'd rented the brown Hyundai last Tuesday.

It hadn't taken much for Stevens to follow the McDonald's security footage to the rental car agency. Just a couple frames forward on the tape to where the car waited to pull into traffic and Stevens could almost read the full license plate straight off the screen. A few keystrokes later and he'd traced the car back to Avis. If only all police work was that easy.

"She was *hot,* man," said the guy, Brian, a fat twentysomething. He leered at Stevens as he spoke. "Big brown eyes, pretty smile. *Nice* rack. She was something."

"Curly hair?"

"Curly hair." Brian nodded. "A lot of it, too."

"She came alone?"

"Nah, she had this big guy with her. Kind of lurking in the background."

Stevens took out his notepad. "Could you describe him?"

"Probably six-two, six-three, I guess? Mid- to late twenties. Short brown hair. Chin-strap beard. Maybe two hundred pounds." He shrugged. "I was looking at the girl, you know?"

"They come off a plane?"

Brian shrugged. "Hard to say. Didn't think they had any bags, though." He glanced up at Stevens. "What'd they do with the car, anyway?"

"Took it to McDonald's," said Stevens. "You got the paperwork?"

Brian nodded and knelt below the counter. He stood up with a sheaf of documents and passed them across. Stevens took a look.

According to the file, the renter was an Ashley McAdams. Gave an address in Atlanta, Georgia, a 404 area code. Twenty-six years old. Paid with a Visa card.

Stevens put down the folder. "You were here when she brought back the car?"

"Nah. Wish I was, though."

"Yeah," said Stevens. "Can you come down to the BCA tomorrow, talk to a composite artist about these two?"

"Guess so." Brian shrugged. "We could do it tonight if you want. I'm off in a half hour."

"No, thanks," said Stevens, already walking away. "I gotta pick up my daughter from volleyball practice."

A couple hours later, with Andrea home from practice, dinner consumed, and the dishes done, the kids having vanished to their rooms, Stevens left his wife snoring into her files and crept to the front door. His hand was on the doorknob when she spoke up behind him. "You know, a lesser wife might accuse you of sneaking around," she said, a clutch of papers in her hand and her face set to a frown everywhere but her eyes.

"I am sneaking around," Stevens told her.

"You got a new girlfriend?"

Stevens took his hand off the doorknob and placed it, instead, on his wife's hip. "I do," he said. "Name's Lesley."

Nancy moved closer, moving his hand up to her sweater. "Sounds sexy."

"Very," said Stevens. "His first name's Tim."

"Tim Lesley. You dog."

"I think I have a problem." He was cupping her breast now, watching her eyes half close as he touched her.

"You have more than one problem," she said. "You passing me up for Tim Lesley is your biggest." She slid her hand slow down the front of his pants.

He forced himself to pull away. "I'll be back soon."

"I'll be asleep."

"That never stopped me before."

She smacked his arm. "Get out of here. But come back quick, understand?"

He left her at the doorway and stepped out into the cold, wondering what kind of fool passed up good sex and a warm home on a night like tonight. A fool cop with a dead-end case, apparently, but at least the case was getting better. T-Mobile's snarky lawyer had run off with his tail between his legs when Stevens came back with a warrant, and the company had promised to fax over the call locations that afternoon. And this Ashley McAdams lead was the most promising development yet.

Stevens pulled into the bureau lot, nearly empty so late at night. Still a couple lights on upstairs: the keeners. The guys with no wives and no lives.

Upstairs, he found the T-Mobile information waiting on his desk. Three sheets of paper: one cover letter and two lists, one for each phone. Each list contained a breakdown of calls made and received with a corresponding cell phone tower for each call. The first phone hung mainly around a cell tower in Brooklyn Center, northwest of Minneapolis along the 694.

The second phone moved around a bit more, calling in on a cell tower out near the airport a couple times and then, six or seven times, from a tower near Harper's place the night he was nabbed and then again for a couple hours after he'd been given back. Ballsy.

The last phone call on each list was a head-scratcher. Both phones used a tower way to the northwest of the city off I-94. Out near the Crow-Hassan Reserve. Interesting.

Stevens looked over the T-Mobile sheets once more, searching in vain for something else he could use. Then he turned to his computer and brought up the FBI's National Crime Information Center database. He typed in "Ashley McAdams" and pressed the search key, sending the FBI's digital bloodhounds on a search for Ms. McAdams's criminal record.

A minute or so later, the Fed computers called off the search. Ashley McAdams was clean.

Fifteen minutes later, Stevens was driving west on the 694 across the Mississippi River. His little extracurricular field trip would mean taking a rain check on Nancy's quality time, but Stevens was onto something and he knew if he went home he would spend most of the night awake in his bed, wishing he'd followed up on his instinct.

As he drove, he made a list of tasks. He would need to look deeper into the McAdams situation, find out all he could about the curly-haired girl from Georgia. And he would need to look into the phone calls out by the Crow-Hassan Reserve.

But for now, he was going to check out the locale around the kidnappers' first cell tower. It was a little ambitious, searching for an apartment in a sea of apartment buildings, but Stevens had never lost a case because of too much legwork. He drove north, humming along to an old Springsteen song on the radio, and when the 694 merged with I-94 and he drove into Brooklyn Center, Stevens saw exactly what he was looking for.

On the side of the highway stood a collection of cheap motels, some privately owned and some national brands, some plain and some plain sleazy. Harper thought he'd been held in an apartment. Could he have been wrong?

Stevens pulled off the highway and aimed for the motels. He pulled into the first lot, a sleepy little two-story shoe box called the Stay Inn. He got out of the Crown Vic and started up toward the office, staring down the strip at a sky full of neon signs and identical fishbowl lobbies.

THIRTEEN

It took three motels and some serious bullshit before Stevens came up with the catch.

The Stay Inn produced nothing, and the Motel 6 was no better. Neither desk clerk gave up anything more than a baleful stare and a half-assed search of the records. Nobody remembered; nobody wanted to talk.

Things went better at the Super 8, though the clerk took some convincing at first. She was a young girl, early twenties. Her name tag said "Sheena," and she looked up from her romance novel long enough to give Stevens's badge a cursory glance before returning to the book. "Nah," she said, snapping her gum. "I didn't see anyone."

"You were working here Friday?"

"Yeah," she said. "Haven't had a day off in about a month."

"Always the night shift?"

The girl sighed and dog-eared her novel. "Yeah," she said. "Me and Jimmy handle nights. He's the maintenance guy. They make him stick around so nobody tries to rape me."

"Where's Jimmy now?"

"Having a nap in back," she said. "He's usually sleeping."

"Some guard dog," said Stevens. "You sure you don't remember anybody? Pretty girl in her mid-twenties, long curly hair? Big guy with brown hair and a chinstrap beard? Probably driving a blue van, probably rolling with a third person?"

The girl blinked. "Wait a sec," she said. "We had a big guy like you said roll in here Saturday before last, real late. Wasn't with no curly-haired girl, though. He had with him a little runty fella. Young, maybe my age. They got two rooms."

"What did they drive?"

"Didn't see," she said. "I can check the registry."

"Please."

She put her novel aside and punched a few keys on her desktop computer. "Good stuff," she said. "Here we go."

She spun the monitor around to face Stevens, pointed out the entry in question. Adam Tarver and Eugene Moy. An address in Maryland. "Paid cash?"

"Yup," said Sheena. "Far as I can remember."

Stevens examined the entry. Under the vehicle heading, they'd listed a blue GMC Savana. No plates. "You didn't get the plates on this van?"

"It's not in there?"

Stevens shook his head.

"Guess not, then. We're not real sticklers for that. Long as you put the make and model."

"You don't remember anything else about these two? No curly-haired girl come along for the ride?"

"One sec," she said. She leaned back behind the counter. "Jimmy!" Then she turned back to Stevens. Shrugged. "I don't really remember."

A middle-aged man came shambling out of the back room, rubbing his eyes and blinking in the light. "Jimmy," said Sheena. "This is Officer Stevens. He's got a few questions."

Jimmy raised his hands. "Not guilty."

"Sure you are. You remember those kids came through in the blue van last week? One tall, one small. Came in real late, stayed a few days?"

Jimmy scratched his head. "Met up with

those other two, right?"

Two, thought Stevens. Interesting. "Which two, Jimmy?"

"A woman and a man. Pretty girl. Curly hair. They came later. Stayed in the one room, and the other two took the first one. Drove a little brown Japanese car."

"Maybe a Hyundai?"

Jimmy shrugged. "You tell me."

"What did the third man look like?"

"Well, tall. Maybe six feet. Thinner. Light-colored hair. It was dark when I seen them."

"Sure. You remember anything else about them? Maybe about the van?"

"Nah." He shook his head. "Except the van had Illinois plates. Figured they were passing through, but they stuck around a few days." He scratched his head, yawning. "That's about all I got, Officer."

"All right," said Stevens. "Go back to sleep."

Jimmy disappeared, and Stevens turned back to Sheena. "You guys had anyone stay in those rooms since our gang disappeared?"

"Yeah," said Sheena. "Couple nights ago in the one, and yesterday and today in the other. They been cleaned and put back to normal already."

"I figured," said Stevens. He straightened up. "Probably going to need you and Jimmy to come downtown and talk to a sketch artist at some point."

Sheena nodded absently, reaching for her novel. Stevens watched her a moment. Then he turned and left the lobby.

Once outside, he took out his phone and punched in a number. The phone rang a couple times, and then the sleepy voice of Tim Lesley, Special Agent in Charge, came on the line. "Yes?"

"Sir, it's Agent Stevens."

"Stevens. What time is it?"

"It's late, sir. Sorry to wake you."

"You didn't wake me, Stevens. What's the matter?"

"Sir, I've made some progress on this kidnapping case," said Stevens. "I'm going to need some help chasing down leads."

"What do you need?"

"Well, sir, we might want to give the FBI a heads-up. These guys are from out of state. Could be a professional job."

Lesley was quiet for a moment. "What happened to the university angle?"

"Gone," said Stevens. "These guys have Maryland and Georgia addresses and Illinois plates on their car. They stayed in a Super 8 to work the job."

"You can have Singer and Rotundi," said Lesley. "Leave the Feds out of it for now.

We can work our own case. And I'm not convinced the student angle's so wrong. Those kids could be out-of-state students who knew what they were doing."

"That's true, sir."

"Don't discount the university possibility yet, Stevens. Keep me posted."

"Will do, sir," said Stevens. "Good night."

Maybe Lesley was right, Stevens thought, climbing back into the Crown Vic. Maybe the motel didn't mean anything but that the kidnappers wanted to do business somewhere transient and anonymous.

Maybe they're students, he thought. Maybe these guys have been right in front of us all along.

Somehow, though, he knew otherwise. Some basic cop instinct told him Lesley was wrong.

FOURTEEN

Patricia Beneteau hung up the phone, her eyes diamond-hard and just as sharp. She inhaled slowly, looking around the study, trying to keep her heart rate steady. She heard footsteps outside the door, and Matthew, the eldest, came running into the room.

"Mom," he said, panting. "Ian found a bird on the deck. I think its wing's broken."

Beneteau turned to her son. Forced a smile. "I'm a little busy now, honey," she said. "I'll come see your bird later, okay?"

The fourteen-year-old stared at her a moment, then shrugged and disappeared down the hall. Beneteau listened to his footsteps. Heard the back door slam and then she was alone again.

Kidnapping, she thought. Those maniacs. Stealing my husband for a hundred thousand dollars. *My* husband. Must have been crackheads. Crackheads or maniacs. Either way, they're in for a surprise.

She walked back to the phone and dialed Rialto. "This is Mrs. B," she said. "We have a situation."

Pender could feel the bile welling up in his stomach as he stared at Mouse's computer screen. My God, he thought. We've kidnapped John Gotti.

A few minutes earlier, Mouse had pulled him out of the hostage room where Beneteau lay bound and blindfolded. He dragged Pender down the hall to the next room, his face ashen.

"We might have a little problem," Mouse told him. "This guy Beneteau? We were right. He owns those tool-and-die shops or whatever. He's just your everyday rube, yeah?"

"Yeah," said Pender. "So? The hell's going on?"

"It's his wife, boss." Mouse's eyes were oh-shit wide. "His wife's not quite so everyday."

Now Pender peered over Mouse's shoulder and wanted to throw up. In less than twenty minutes, Mouse had come up with an encyclopedia of news reports, all concerning Patricia Beneteau and her alleged organized crime connections at the city's

Motown Casino. The reports suggested the casino was run by a low-profile offshoot of a prominent New York crime family and that the majority of the company's executives possessed strong ties back to the Manhattan home office. Beneteau — née Liakos — was mentioned repeatedly by name.

"Holy shit," said Pender. "This is straight out of a mob movie."

Mouse looked up at him. "What do we do, boss?"

"I'm not sure yet," he said. "We don't get killed, that's the main thing."

His phone rang. Marie, standing guard at the Beneteau house. Pender felt his heart start to pump even faster. She might as well be wearing a target, he thought. "Arthur?"

"Yeah," he said, trying to keep his voice calm. "How's it going out there?"

"I'm not sure," said Marie. She sounded shaky. "No cops yet, anyway."

"No cops," said Pender. Probably the last thing we have to worry about now. "Okay. What else?"

"Arthur — these cars just started showing up. Fifteen minutes ago, maybe. People just started rolling into the house."

"What cars? What people?"

"Big black cars," she said. "Cadillacs. And

a big truck. People everywhere, Arthur. Scary-looking people."

"All right," said Pender. "Get the hell out of there. Come on back to the motel."

"What if they call the police?"

"They're not calling the police, Marie," he said. "These aren't the calling-the-police kind of people. Get out of there. Now."

Twenty minutes later, Marie was at the Super 8, and Pender called a team meeting. They left Beneteau bound in the first room, and the four of them crowded into the second, everyone jumpy and confused and scared.

"So here's the deal," Pender said. He cleared his throat. Tried to sound confident. "Beneteau's wife is connected."

"Connected?" said Marie. "What does that even mean?"

"Means she's in the mob," said Mouse. "She knows people who know people. *Sopranos* shit."

"Those people you saw at her place were thugs," said Pender. "Goons? Henchmen? I don't even know what they call them." He surveyed the room. "The point is, what are we going to do?"

"We let him go," said Marie. "Right, Pender? We cut our losses and leave him by the side of the road. Get the hell out of

Detroit and forget all of this."

"Yeah," said Mouse. "We don't need this headache. Those guys will kill us."

"Bullshit." Suddenly Sawyer had a gun in his hands, a big black pistol that freeze-framed the room. "Nobody's going to kill us."

Marie gasped. The room went silent. Pender stared at the gun like it was a lit stick of dynamite, the whole room moving faster and faster around him. He glanced at Mouse. The kid stared back, one eyebrow raised. "Jesus, Sawyer," Marie said at last. "Where the hell did you get that?"

Sawyer kept his eyes on Pender. "Thought we might need it."

"Need it for what, exactly?"

"We never needed guns before," said Pender.

"My God, Sawyer. What are you thinking? We're not *killers.*"

Marie was this close to hysterical. Pender put his arm around her. "It's okay," he said. "We'll figure this out."

"He has a goddamn *gun,* Pender."

"I know. I don't know where the hell it came from." He glared at Sawyer. "But it's not our biggest problem right now. We gotta figure out this Beneteau thing first. Put the gun away, Matt."

Sawyer shrugged. The gun disappeared.

Pender looked around the room, the dim light, the claustrophobic walls. Fought the rising tide of panic. "Let's work through this. We ditch Beneteau tonight and skip town."

"You guys watch too many mob movies," said Sawyer. "These guys are businessmen. They'll pay up."

"You don't watch enough mob movies," said Mouse. "They'll come looking for us."

"Big deal. We ditch the van and catch a plane somewhere they won't find us."

"It doesn't matter where we go, Sawyer. They'll find us."

"How?"

"Look," said Pender. "Maybe they pay. Maybe they don't find us. But why risk it? We don't need the money that bad. We ditch this guy and we run another score next week. We do better research and we get back on the grind. It doesn't make sense to start pissing off mobsters. Not if we want to stay clean."

Sawyer stared at him. Said nothing. "Please, Matt," said Marie. "Let's just let this one go."

Sawyer sighed. "Whatever," he said. "I guess I'm outvoted."

■ ■ ■ ■

Patricia Beneteau stared out into the street as the last of the day's light slipped away. Behind her, Rialto's three goons sat waiting, looking oversized and uncomfortable on her sofas and easy chairs. She turned and examined them: two Italian, one Greek. Muscle from top to bottom. Shaved heads, dead eyes, long scars. Might as well have been clones.

A car door slammed outside. Beneteau turned back to the window to see another mammoth of a man step out of his Escalade and start up toward the house. A minute later he was inside, rubbing his hands together, his cheeks rosy and his eyes bright. He looks like an overgrown child, she thought. A teddy bear. He peeled off his coat and fixed his eyes on hers. "You're Mrs. B?"

"That's right," she said. She watched him walk into the room. He surveyed the muscle, nodded slightly, and then examined her in the same way.

"You would be Mr. D'Antonio," she said. He didn't look like a teddy bear now. Not when his eyes got so hard, anyway. "Would you like some coffee?"

"Just D'Antonio. And no coffee." He waved at an empty chair. "May I?"

"Please."

"You had a girl parked down the street in a Chevy Impala watching the house, talking into a cell phone."

Patricia spun. "She's not ours. Go back out there and get her."

D'Antonio shook his head. "She bolted. Either something spooked her or she got called back to home base."

She stared at him. "So you lost her."

He shrugged. "I took down her plates. We'll find her again."

Patricia walked away from the window and sat down opposite. The muscle watched her with uniform disinterest. She ignored them and kept her eyes on D'Antonio. "So what do we do?" she said. "How do we punish these people?"

FIFTEEN

Ashley McAdams was no student. Neither was Adam Tarver or Eugene Moy. Stevens had Singer double-check with every university in the state. No luck. Not students.

Neither were they criminals, though. The NCIC database spit out no results for either Tarver or Moy. No criminal records, no warrants, no nothing.

Either they were rookies or they just never got caught. Or they had aliases. Could be they were keeping their real names to themselves.

Rotundi brought in Sheena and Jimmy, and after a couple hours with a composite artist they had a couple pretty good sketches making Tarver and Moy. Then Brian came in from Avis and gave them the girl, McAdams, leaving only the fourth suspect, the nameless man who'd come in with McAdams. Jimmy begged off working the last sketch. It was dark, he said. He could barely trust his eyes in the daytime.

Stevens examined the sketches, searching the faces of his suspects. Who are you, he wondered. *Where* are you?

He had Rotundi put the sketches on the wire. Every cop shop in the region would get a copy. Lesley was still pushing the university angle, so every post-secondary institution in the state would get a nice poster to tack up in campus security. As for Georgia and Maryland and Illinois, don't ask. "I don't want those Fed bastards thinking we can't compete," Lesley told him. "We solve this in-house, understand?"

Stevens spent a couple hours paging through the FBI's Most Wanted lists, comparing the pictures and looking for matches, but the closest he came was making Tarver as James Walter Lawson, a fugitive from Alaska in his late thirties who was suspected to have died somewhere in the wilderness, fleeing from an armed robbery gone wrong. No dice.

Stevens clicked off the FBI database and turned to where Nick Singer sat at his computer, going hard at a roast beef sandwich. "Hey, Nick," he said. "Maybe call Avis, some of the other rental companies. See if McAdams, Tarver, or Moy ever rented cars from them elsewhere."

Singer chewed slowly. "Probably need a warrant for that stuff."

"Fine," said Stevens, silently cursing Tim Lesley. Singer and Rotundi weren't exactly the BCA's ringers. "Maybe get a warrant, then."

Singer nodded and kept chewing. Stevens was about to say something else when his phone rang. He answered.

"Is this Agent Stevens?"

"Speaking."

"This is Stu Courtney with the highway patrol. Understand you're looking for blue vans."

"Sure," said Stevens. "GMCs in particular. Savanas."

"Perfect," said Courtney. "I've got just the car for you."

Ten minutes later, Stevens was on I-94 in his Crown Vic headed northwest and out of the city. He glanced at Courtney's directions. Town called Rogers, the trooper had said. Out by the Crow-Hassan Reserve.

The suspects had made one phone call to each other at the Crow-Hassan Reserve the day after the kidnapping. This had to be connected. Someone's looking out for us, he thought.

He turned off the I-94 at Rogers and took the back roads west toward the park border.

Fifteen minutes and a couple of three-point turns later, he found himself squinting down an unmarked dirt road, trying to make out if there was a black-and-white at the end.

As he drove closer he could make out the trooper's sedan and Courtney inside it, the windows starting to fog up and the exhaust a white cloud billowing around the rear of the car. Stevens parked behind and got out, shivering in the bracing air as Courtney turned off his ignition. Stevens looked around at his surroundings: forest in all directions, dark and tangled and dense.

"Couple of hunters found it," said Courtney. "Thought it was a little weird, this van sitting out there in the middle of nowhere. Mentioned it to a state trooper friend who remembered you guys were looking for vans. Figured we'd let you take a look."

Stevens pulled his coat tighter. "Where is it?"

Courtney gestured ahead of his patrol car, and Stevens could see the van now, parked off the road and half hidden in the underbrush. The General Motors logo was just barely visible through the camouflage.

"Guess they did a decent job of hiding it," said the trooper. "Didn't figure anyone was coming down this road anytime soon."

"Didn't plan on hunting season. That car

97

got plates?"

Courtney shook his head. "No plates. No personal effects inside, either, far as I can tell. You gonna wipe it for prints?"

"Sure," said Stevens. "Doubt they left any, but maybe we'll get lucky."

"Well, all right." Courtney shivered. "You need me to stick around?"

Stevens shook his head. "I'll call in my team. Thanks."

The trooper tipped his hat and climbed back into his patrol car. Stevens watched him drive off, momentarily jealous of the man's warm vehicle. Then he turned back to the van and all jealousy was forgotten. He was too damn excited to be cold.

SIXTEEN

Stevens watched the tow truck yank the van out of the trees, lurching and jostling as it pulled out onto the dirt road. Things are finally picking up, he thought. Good things to those who wait.

An hour earlier, Nick Singer had called with a tidbit of good news. According to the girl at Hertz, Eugene Moy had rented a Ford Taurus from the airport in Memphis about a month and a half ago. Used it for a couple days, Friday through Monday, then ditched. Paid with a Visa. "That's all I got," he said. "Nobody else'd even heard of these guys."

"That's good enough," Stevens told him, thinking, Memphis. How the hell did they get all the way up here?

Then Rotundi came in with his own bit of news.

After Courtney left Stevens alone with his little bit of buried treasure, the agent had called in a team of forensic technicians to analyze the scene. As expected, the van had been mostly clean. No latent fingerprints, no blood. No long strands of curly brown hair.

What they did come up with, though, was the van's Vehicle Identification Number. Rotundi ran the VIN through the Driver and Vehicle Services database and called back with the good stuff: the van had been sold a couple weeks back from a dealership in Lake Forest, Illinois. Bought by one Ryan Carew.

Ryan Carew, thought Stevens. Hot damn. The fourth man.

The tow truck driver gave the van one last tug and then rolled to a stop beside him. The driver leaned out the window. "We all set here?"

"Sure," said Stevens. "Go ahead and bring her back to town."

Forty-five minutes later, he was back in the bureau building, staring at his phone and wondering if he had time for a couple more calls before dinner. I'm on a roll, he decided. Gotta keep up the momentum. He picked up the phone.

First thing he did was call up the used-car dealer in Lake Forest. Millennium Auto, it was called. He dialed the number and was greeted by a gravel-patch voice. "Millennium."

Stevens introduced himself. "Got a couple questions about a van you sold a couple weeks ago. Was used to commit a crime up here in Minneapolis."

"You got a warrant?"

"Not yet," said Stevens. Can't get a warrant without jurisdiction, he thought.

"So what makes you think I'll answer your questions?" the guy said. "I don't have to tell you a thing."

"Guess I'm thinking you're just a caring citizen, right?"

"Caring citizen." The guy laughed. "You got the wrong number, fella."

"Sure," said Stevens. "Maybe I'm thinking something else, then. Maybe I'm thinking you don't want the Lake Forest boys to come through with a warrant and a fine-toothed comb."

"I didn't do nothing."

"I just have a couple questions," said Stevens. "It was a blue GMC Savana, came off lease return. Guy paid cash."

The dealer sighed. "All right."

"Guy named Ryan Carew bought it. You remember?"

"Yeah, maybe. Medium height. Maybe six foot? Blond hair. Sunglasses. What do you want me to say?"

"That's fine. How'd he get to the dealership?"

"Brought a friend with him. Drove a Camry, I think. Real big guy. Brown hair. Kind of a beard. I would have said he was there to intimidate, except your boy didn't want to negotiate."

"Paid sticker?"

"Like that. In and out. We insured on the spot."

"He give an address?"

"Let me check." The line went silent for a minute or two. "Yeah, we got an address. Joliet. Got a pen?"

Stevens copied down the address and thanked the man.

"I didn't do anything wrong, right?"

"You're clean enough for me, anyway."

"All right," the man said, and hung up.

Stevens replaced the phone and leaned back in his chair. The kid's home base is Joliet, he thought. But he buys his van in Lake Forest. That's on the other side of Chicago. Doesn't make much sense unless he's got a thing for blue GMC Savanas.

He picked up the phone again. Called the Illinois State Police in Des Plaines. Got himself routed to Crimes Against Persons, where a hard-ass named Taylor picked up the phone. "Who'd you say you were again?"

"Stevens, Minnesota BCA," he said. "I'm looking for any unsolved kidnappings you guys may have had in the last month or so. Specifically north of Chicago, but maybe around Joliet as well."

"Kidnappings?" said Taylor. "You want to be more specific."

Stevens laid out the Harper case. "I trace these guys to Lake Forest about two weeks ago. They may have tried the same play down there as well."

"Don't think so," said Taylor. "Most of our kidnappings are drug-related. Anyway, we haven't seen any reported in over a month."

"What was the last case you got?"

"Drug-related. Unpaid debt in the southeast. Victim wound up dead a week or so later."

"Sure," said Stevens. "That doesn't sound like my guys."

"Nah, it wasn't your guys. Good luck, though."

Stevens thanked him and hung up. He stared at his computer screen, trying to figure out his next move. We've got to check out Carew's residence in Joliet, he thought. And McAdams's in Georgia and Tarver's in Maryland. That's not something I can handle on my own.

Stevens stood up and walked down the row of cubicles to the row of private offices at the edge of the room. He knocked on Tim Lesley's door and stuck his head inside the room. His boss looked up from his desk. "Stevens," he said. "Come on in. What can I do for you?"

Stevens walked in and sat down. "We've made progress on the Harper case," he said. He laid out the van development and Carew's home address in Joliet, Illinois.

Lesley tented his fingers. "So much for the university angle."

Stevens shook his head. "They're too organized to be students, sir. This is big-time. You don't come all the way to Minneapolis and run a kidnapping job like this just to walk with sixty grand and be done with it."

"You think these guys are some kind of crew."

"I do."

Lesley leaned back in his chair. He fixed Stevens with a stare. "And you want me to hand this over to the FBI, do you? Make the BCA look like we can't solve a goddamn case on our own."

Stevens held Lesley's stare. "I don't think we have a choice, sir. We've got this kid in

Illinois, the girl in Georgia, and his friends in Maryland. If we want to move forward, someone's got to start breaking down doors."

Lesley stared at Stevens for a long moment. Then he nodded. "Fine," he said. "We'll hand it off. But Stevens?"

"Yes, sir?"

The Special Agent in Charge stood. "You'd damn well better be right."

Seventeen

Birmingham, Michigan, after dark. The streets were lifeless and black, the only lights visible a few dim reading lamps in upstairs windows. Quiet, too: nothing moving on the sidewalks, the lawns, inside the long shadowy rows of cars on either side of the street.

Pender brought the van to a stop at the head of the block. He looked over at Marie in the passenger seat. Her eyes met his, expressionless. He glanced back into the rearview mirror, where Mouse and Sawyer sat silent, their mouths drawn tight, one hand each gripping Donald Beneteau's arms.

Only Beneteau seemed satisfied. He had been talkative when they left the motel, outlining in painstaking detail the ways his family would take their revenge. Then Sawyer fed him a backhand slap and told him shut up. Now Beneteau sat smirking into his blindfold, humming softly to himself.

Pender released the brake and the van crept forward, the engine sounding like a nuclear explosion in the silence of the night. He let the van roll down the block, fully expecting Patricia Beneteau and her henchmen to jump out from a parked car, packing heavy artillery and hell-bent on revenge.

But the street stayed quiet, even as Pender brought the van to an easy stop a few houses down from the Beneteau place. "All right," he said. "We drop him here."

Mouse slid open the rear door, and it sounded like an Amtrak train. Pender flinched, staring out into the darkness, searching out the ambush. Sawyer kicked Beneteau to his feet. "End of the line."

Beneteau stood and let Sawyer untie his hands. "You pukes fucked up," he said. "You fucked up real good." Then he turned toward the front of the van. "Which one of you is Pender, anyway?"

All of the air seemed to rush out of the van. Pender felt like he'd swallowed a brick. Marie was staring at him, shocked. Mouse stood frozen in the back.

"Which one of you little fucks is Pender?"

Sawyer was already reaching for his gun. "I gotta shoot him, right?"

Beneteau smiled wide. He cackled, triumphant and incessant. Sawyer rammed the gun into the back of his head. Beneteau kept laughing.

Pender's brain went to overdrive. He knows my name, he thought. *How?* Who cares? What now? If we kill him, we set the whole goddamn mob against us. *Jesus — shut that guy up.* If we let him go, he knows who I am. Somehow. *How?* Calm down. He knows Pender. How many Penders in the world? In Detroit alone? We're good. We're fine. They'll never find me.

He looked up, relieved. "It's all right," he told Sawyer. "He doesn't —"

BAM. The gun roared, and Beneteau's head exploded. Blood everywhere. His body pitched forward, out of the van and onto the pavement below. Car alarms sounded outside. Marie screamed. Sawyer yelled at him. "Go, go, go!"

Mouse slammed the door shut, and now he started yelling, too. Lights started blinking on outside. Pender's head rang from the shot, the sound. Marie screamed. "We gotta go, Pender. We gotta go!"

Sawyer smacked him, hard, and he stomped on the gas. A reflex. The van jumped forward, and the tires squealed. The noise came in loud. Lights on at the Beneteau residence. People at the window. Go, go, *go.*

Pender stood on the gas pedal, and the van fishtailed down the block. He got traction, got the van back under control, and made it to the end of the street. Hard right and more speed. He drove fast, not daring to look in the mirrors, not wanting to know who was behind him.

They made the main roads and he was still standing on the gas pedal and Sawyer and Marie were grabbing onto his sweater, shouting, and finally he heard them. "We gotta slow down, man. We gotta slow down," Sawyer was saying. "We can't be driving so fast right now."

Pender realized he was right. He slowed down and tried to blend into traffic. Tried to breathe.

"How the hell did he know your name, Pender?" said Marie.

"He must have heard us arguing in the other room," said Mouse. "Walls are so goddamn thin." Pender glanced at him in the rearview mirror. He was pale, shaking. Pender was shaking, too. The adrenaline rush.

"We were too loud," said Sawyer. "We should have shut the fuck up."

Pender watched a blue-and-white patrol

car cruise past them in the opposite direction. "We didn't have to kill him," he said.

Mouse stared. "He knew your name."

"My last name. So what?"

"We had to do it, man," said Sawyer. "We had to get rid of him."

Pender shook his head. "There's gotta be a million Penders in the United States. There's probably a couple hundred in Detroit alone. They were never going to find us based on one fucking last name, Sawyer."

"We couldn't take the chance."

"Bullshit," said Pender. "That's bullshit, and you know it. You just wanted an excuse to use that gun."

"Hey." Sawyer leaned forward between the two seats. "I was trying to protect us. I shot him so we'd get away clean."

"Yeah, well, now we've got a body on our hands." Pender couldn't keep the anger from his voice. "Not just any body, a mobster's body. That means not only do we have the police looking for us, we've got Carmela fucking Soprano as well. If you'd let the guy go, he would have gone back to his family and started searching Penders in the phone book. The *Detroit* phone book. We would have been hundreds of miles away before he figured out his Pender wasn't from around here. *If* he figured it out."

Pender turned to look Sawyer in the eye. "You fucked us up, Matt. You fucked us up, bad."

Pender drove. He pointed the van away from Birmingham, and he drove the speed limit as he tried to keep his heart from pounding out of his chest. Tried to keep his hands from wrenching off the steering wheel. We're screwed, he thought. What a stupid goddamn play. What the hell are we supposed to do now?

EIGHTEEN

They got rid of the van in River Rouge, parking it on a deserted industrial back lot, wiping it down, stripping the plates, and setting it aflame. Pender watched it burn for a minute or two before he turned back and joined the others in the Impala.

They threw the license plates and the gun into the Detroit River a few miles downstream, and then they pointed the car west and drove out to the airport. They rode in silence, each of them staring out a different window, cringing with every police car and trying to forget.

Only Pender couldn't forget. He could still hear Beneteau cackling, could hear the smirk in the man's voice as he played Pender's name like a trump card, could see the back of the man's head explode as Sawyer pulled the trigger. It had been a brutal act, an unnecessary act. An unprofessional act.

We could have done this forever, he

thought. We could have worked these scores for as long as we wanted. Now, because of one lapse in judgment, we're on the run. We've killed a man, and we're on the run.

He sank back in his seat and watched Detroit through the window, rainy and miserable.

They stopped at a motel a mile from the terminal. Pender paid cash for a double room, and they all piled in, dragging ass, exhausted. Marie collapsed on one bed and Sawyer on the other. Mouse sank into a chair, and for a couple minutes they said nothing. Pender leaned against the wall and closed his eyes and tried again to wipe Beneteau's death from his mind.

He should have known that they would find themselves in a situation like this, he thought. He should have foreseen it. One day they were bound to meet a person who didn't want to be kidnapped. A person whose family didn't really want to pay the ransom. He should have foreseen that one day they were going to have to make good on their threats.

But he'd never imagined they would kill anyone. They'd bluffed in the past, and Pender supposed he had figured they would bluff every time. And if the bluffs didn't work now and again, they could call off the deal and get back on the road and nobody would be the wiser. He'd never intended to kill anyone. He'd never really thought of his team as the bad guys.

They'd never talked about it, not ever, not in two full years pulling jobs. As a team, they had never acknowledged the reality of what they were doing. The implications, morally and legally. In the beginning it was easy to get caught up in the rush, the madcap spitballing in that motel in Salinas after the Sinclair job, everyone yelling over top of one another, the ideas coming fast and exciting as each of them realized that, yes, they could do this, go pro and pull more scores and never get caught.

The first few jobs had been a balls-out adrenaline high. No time to think of the consequences. The tech geek in Silicon Valley, that first awkward terrifying job, and then the accountant in Long Beach, Robert Thompson. It was all about the challenge. It was about cheating the system and not getting caught. It was about some crazy Robin Hood thing, this gang of broke kids outsmarting the rich, redistributing the wealth, and proving that yeah, crime *could* pay, and a hell of a lot more than some useless college degree besides.

But there was never any acknowledgment

that what they were doing was wrong. That what they were doing, besides causing a bit of stress to a bunch of upper-class families, was hard-core, no safe word, *wrong*. If we get caught, he thought, we'll go to jail for life.

Of course, he had thought about the consequences of failure before. He was Arthur Pender; he worried about everything. It was his fear of failing that had led them to their MO: the quick scores, the low ransoms, the constant moves around the country. But he had always worried about failure in the abstract. It was always a question of how to avoid getting caught. He didn't let himself think about what would happen if the police did catch up, just as he tried not to think about the families they left in their wake.

Jail, though, was a terrifying prospect.

Pender lay awake in bed deep into the night, thinking about jail, about murder, about Donald Beneteau and Marie and Sawyer and Mouse. Sawyer had acted rashly and unprofessionally, and Pender could not — *could not* — believe his friend could be so stupid. Even now as he lay awake in the motel room bed, listening to airplanes take off and land in the distance, Pender felt sick with anger as he replayed the moment, his

115

mind running loops as he imagined what fates must await them, and considered what they'd become.

He lay awake, looking for a way out. He listened to his friends asleep around him and he pictured them in prison cells. He pictured them shot dead by mobsters. What the hell are we going to do, he thought. How do we come back from this mess?

Pender thought back to his life in Seattle, his precriminal days. He thought about his family in Port Angeles. His parents. His dad on his fish boat and his brothers alongside. Proud men, hardworking and honest. Men who struggled with boat payments and money for rent, who starved in the winters when the salmon didn't run. Men who'd never lain awake nights in some shitty hotel room, thinking about murder and jail.

He remembered learning to drive on the Olympic Peninsula, ten or twelve years ago. Driving his dad's battered pickup down the 101 from Port Angeles to Dungeness Bay and back, his mind running through every worst-case scenario a driver could encounter. All it takes is one slipup and we're all dead, he would think to himself, his stomach winding itself into knots and his foot lifting unconsciously off the accelerator. One blink at the wrong time and we're toast.

"You gotta banish those thoughts," his dad told him. "You gotta focus on the road. Stay alert. You're not helping anybody by worrying so much."

He'd found, once he could stomach it, that his dad was right. If he stayed focused and kept aware — and yeah, got a little lucky — he'd get down the road all right. If he panicked and gave into the fear, all he'd do is wind up at the side of the road, a terrified little boy in his daddy's truck, too scared to become a man.

Time to become a man, Pender decided. There's no bringing Beneteau back. You can only move forward. Stay focused on the job. Stop worrying about jail. If you take care of your business, you'll never see the inside of one. We're a good team. We can get out of this.

We were fugitives before, he thought. We're fugitives still. Nothing has changed. It's time to put your foot on the gas.

NINETEEN

Patricia Beneteau stood on her front porch, watching the parade of police officers and forensic technicians on the sidewalk before her. The night sky was cloudy and sullen, and a miserable drizzle was pissing down on the cops, washing away the chalk that outlined her husband's body.

She watched as a detective walked up the lawn toward her, gripping a flimsy umbrella in one hand and a fresh cigarette in the other. He was a tired-looking man — even his mustache looked worn out.

"Mrs. Beneteau," he said when he'd reached the porch. "I'm Detective Landry." He didn't offer to shake hands. "Awfully sorry about your loss."

She sighed. "I can only imagine."

He examined her face. "Any idea who did this?"

"Not a clue."

"Some of your neighbors saw a van speed

away after they heard the gunshot. Don't suppose you'd have any idea who that might have been."

"No idea."

The detective sighed and took a drag from his cigarette. "Did your husband have any enemies, Mrs. Beneteau?"

The front door swung open, and D'Antonio emerged from the house. "Mrs. Beneteau didn't see anything," he said. "She has nothing to tell you."

Landry turned to him. "And who are you?"

"I'm her lawyer," D'Antonio told him. "She's not answering questions."

"We could bring her downtown."

"You'd have to arrest her."

Landry stared at them for a moment. Then he shrugged. "Suit yourselves." He took a last drag from his cigarette and snuffed the butt beneath his feet. Then he started down the steps. When he reached the lawn, he turned back. "I just hope this whole mess doesn't point back at you, Mrs. Beneteau. I'd hate to see your kids have to suffer any further."

He turned and walked back to the crime scene, and Patricia watched him disappear among the rest of the rumpled suits and soaking uniforms milling about on the street. Then she turned to D'Antonio. "Where do we stand?"

D'Antonio stared out into the street beside her. "The girl's Chevy was a rental," he said. "We've got a couple guys posted at the Budget desk at the airport."

"That's assuming they bring the car back."

D'Antonio nodded.

"What if they don't?"

"I've got a guy at Detroit PD," he said. "We're keeping track of the investigation through him. Anything they know, we'll know."

Beneteau turned her eyes to his. "I want you to find those bastards," she said. "Find them before the police do."

"We'll find them," he told her. "Don't you worry about that."

Down the street, Detective Paul Landry stood silent on the sidewalk, watching the forensic techs as they scurried around Donald Beneteau's body. His coat was thin and his umbrella leaked, making Landry perhaps the unhappiest person at the crime scene besides Beneteau himself.

He stared down at the body. Donald Beneteau lay splayed out on the sidewalk at an impossible angle, his arms outstretched and a smirk on his face. A hole in the back of his head, probably a 9 mm round, close range. The climax to the poor bastard's life.

Landry glanced back up to the house, where Patricia Beneteau and her quote-unquote lawyer stood silhouetted on the front porch. Of course she didn't want to talk, he thought. Who the hell would want to talk to the police anymore? We're only trying to find the goddamn killer.

He'd heard the stories about Patricia Beneteau, of course. To Landry's way of thinking, this case just about closed the proverbial book. Husband shot dead, execution-style. Large, ominous men lurking around the house. No cooperation with the police. This was a goddamn mob hit.

"What'd the old woman say?" Bill Garvey, with a thicker coat and a working umbrella, was relishing the investigation. The kid was still new enough to homicide that even getting called out to the suburbs for a stone whodunit on a bleak November night wasn't enough to dampen his enthusiasm. Landry watched his partner navigate the crime scene, grinning like a puppy with a tennis ball.

"The old woman said nothing, Garv," Landry told him. "She hadn't got a clue."

"You believe her?"

"Course not. Anything from the rest of

the block?"

"Guy down the road says it was a red Ford dropped off the body." Garvey gestured in the vague direction of his witness. "Said he was walking the dog, watched the van come creeping up the block, lights off. Stopped about here for a minute or so, then the gunshot, then the body. Then the van sped off thataway."

"He get the license plate?"

Garvey shook his head. "Too dark."

"A red Ford van. Full-sized?"

"Yeah. Passenger van, not cargo. Some other guy said he saw a cute brunette hanging around in her car in the evening," said Garvey. "Said he didn't know whether it was relevant or not, but she seemed to be casing the Beneteau place."

"A brunette, huh?"

"Yeah. Curly hair." Garvey shrugged. "I dunno. Could just be a coincidence."

"What kind of car?"

"Some kind of late-model Chevy, he said. Big car. Maybe an Impala?"

"An Impala. Okay."

Garvey watched him, smile a mile wide, eyes bright. He's feeling the rush, thought Landry. Loving this stuff.

"So what do we do, Paul?" Garvey asked. "What's the story?"

Landry shrugged. "We let them handle it, I guess. Unless the family opens up, there's not a hell of a lot we can do. Keep an eye out for red Ford vans, but that's a long shot and a half."

"We're going to let them get away?"

"No," said Landry. "We're going to go back to the station, type up a report, come back tomorrow, and canvass the block again. We'll put in the time. But without a statement from the old lady or any kind of solid lead on the Ford, we're stuck."

He turned back toward the house, where Patricia Beneteau and her so-called lawyer were no longer visible in the light from the front room. They'd gone inside to the warmth, pretty much the only sensible thing to do on a night like this one. Even the techs were finishing up. In ten minutes, Beneteau's body would be loaded into the medical examiner's van and driven down to the morgue, and the street, chalk and bloodstains notwithstanding, would return to normal. Landry shivered under his umbrella. "All right, Bill," he said. "Let's go home."

TWENTY

Agent Stevens parked his Cherokee downtown and walked into the FBI's Minneapolis field office. A fifteen-story skyscraper in the heart of the city, the Feds' Minnesota headquarters looked like nothing more than the head office of some financial firm — North Star Investors, perhaps. It certainly didn't look like a police station, and that, Stevens thought, was probably how the Feds wanted it.

He walked inside the building and introduced himself at the front desk, surrendered his sidearm, and made a couple passes through the metal detector before he got it right. Then he climbed into an elevator and rode it up to the Criminal Investigative Division.

When the elevator doors slid open Stevens stepped out onto a vast, open floor not unlike his own at the BCA, an expansive room of low cubicles and glass partitions ringed by private offices on the outside. It was the kind of office you'd expect to find at an investment bank or a software company, its long banks of monitors and server farms speaking to the reality of police investigation in the computer age.

"Agent Stevens?"

Stevens found himself staring into the eyes of the woman who had called his name. She was beautiful — she must have been about thirty, tall and slender, her brown skin rich and her hair coal black and ruler-straight — but it was her eyes that got him. Deep shimmering pools with startling hazel centers, they seemed to bore deep inside him as he stood rooted in the lobby, watching her approach.

She came closer and proffered her hand, a polite smile on her lips. "I'm Carla Windermere," she said. She spoke with the hint of an accent, somewhere southern. "We spoke on the phone."

Stevens took her hand and they shook. "Kirk Stevens," he said. She had a firm, cool grip. "It's good to meet you in person."

Windermere led him out of the reception area and down the first line of cubicles, stopping at a desk close to the end of the row. "I don't have much of an office, I'm afraid."

She stole a chair from the cubicle beside hers and offered it to Stevens, then sat down in her own. Stevens glanced around the workstation. It was impeccably neat, almost obsessively so. One picture decorated the low walls, a snapshot of a man about her age in a Hawaiian shirt, posing on a dock with an enormous swordfish. "They told me when I came to Minneapolis I'd get my own office." Windermere smiled. "Little did I know."

"You've been here long?"

"Almost a year now," she said. "Transferred from Miami in December."

"Wow. I'm very sorry."

She laughed. "It's not so bad. I figured it would be worse. Like that old comedy bit about Prince being the only black person in Minnesota. I figured me and my boyfriend would triple the score."

She smiled at Stevens. He found himself smiling back at her. "Your accent doesn't quite sound like South Beach."

"Mississippi," she said. Then she paused. "Well, more like Tennessee. I grew up across the state line from Memphis."

"So you're a warm-weather person all the way."

Windermere shrugged. "I don't mind the cold so much. I can't drive in the snow, but

I'm learning. My boyfriend, though. He hates it."

"He'll get used to it," Stevens told her. "Wait till he tries ice fishing."

"We'll see." She straightened. "Anyway, enough of me wasting your time. You said you had a case, Agent Stevens."

"Sure," he said. "A kidnapping."

"A kidnapping. In Minnesota."

Stevens nodded. "Just like the movies. Ransom demand and all." He gave her the full story, from Terry Harper through Ashley McAdams to Ryan Carew and his Joliet address. Windermere listened intently, staring at him with those piercing eyes.

She sat forward when he was finished. "What makes you so sure they've done this in other jurisdictions?"

"It's just a hunch," he said. "These guys aren't buying a van and driving it to Minneapolis for a sixty-thousand-dollar score unless they're stringing multiples together."

She nodded. "All right," she said. "I can see that. So you think we should check out the Carew kid's address in Joliet."

"And I want to check out the Georgia and Maryland addresses. And take a look in Memphis and anywhere else for other unsolved hit-and-run kidnappings. I don't have jurisdiction, obviously, so I thought you guys could take over."

"Okay," she said. "I have to run this by my Special Agent in Charge. You got a card?"

He gave her a card. "We'll be in touch, Agent Stevens," she said, standing. "I'll get back to you when the boss gives me his thoughts."

Stevens stood. Looked around. "I almost wish I could be here to see this case through," he said.

"Why's that?" Windermere smiled. "Don't trust the Feds?"

"I trust you guys," he said. "But this case — if I'm right — it could be a blockbuster."

"*If* you're right," she said. "Are you?"

He caught her eyes on him and paused. "I think so."

She winked. "Relax, Stevens. I'm messing with you. I'll give you a call."

Windermere walked him back to the elevator. He shook her hand again and got on board, watching her walk away as the doors slid shut, her eyes still burning holes inside him.

Later that night, Stevens did the dishes, watching his wife from the corner of his eye, admiring the curve of her neck as she pored over a mess of files at the kitchen table. She caught him looking, stuck out her tongue, and then leaned back in her chair. "Oh, Jesus," she said. "It's going to be a hell of a week."

"Tough cases?"

"Too many of them. Brennan's on vacation, so I'm covering his people as well as my own. The bastard, running off to the tropics when the whole goddamn state can't afford an attorney."

"They did the crime." Stevens put down his dish towel. "Let them do the time."

"They didn't all do the crime," Nancy said. "That's why I have a job."

Stevens walked over to his wife and stood behind her, his hands on her shoulders. He bent down to nuzzle her hair. "You have this job because you're too nice to be a tax lawyer," he said.

Nancy sighed. "Nice isn't the word. Disinclined to make money, more like."

"You and me both," said Stevens. "We could have been rock stars. Or doctors. On the plus side, I think my case finally flipped."

"You solved it?"

"Almost as good. The kids were operating out of state. Means it's FBI territory. I talked to a field agent today, and she's going to take over."

Nancy leaned back in her chair. She stared

up at him. "Really?"

He nodded. "Just waiting for official confirmation."

"Oh, thank God," she said. "Andrea has volleyball all week, and I think J.J. is coming down with something. It would be great if you were around."

He bent down and kissed her on the forehead. "I'll be around," he said.

Fifteen minutes later, he was sitting in the living room, just settling into the Timberwolves game when the phone rang. "I'll get it," he called, reaching for the handset, but it was too late. Nancy was already on the line.

"Agent Stevens?" she said. "I'll just get him." He heard her put the phone down, and she poked her head into the living room a couple seconds later, wearing a mischievous smile. *Agent Stevens,* she said. "Your other girlfriend is calling."

"What, Lesley? Great." He made a show of rushing for the telephone. "Hello?"

"Agent Stevens, it's Carla Windermere." Her voice was warm and buttery. "Good news. The SAC okayed the case."

"Excellent," said Stevens. "I'll forward you the paperwork tomorrow, then."

"Actually, you might as well just bring it by yourself."

"Why's that?"

"We're shorthanded here, Stevens. Homeland Security and all. My boss called your boss and asked if he wouldn't mind detailing you to the FBI for the duration. Looks like we're going to be working together."

Lesley. That bastard. "You really think that's necessary?"

"Couldn't hurt," said Windermere. "This is your baby. Anyway, I thought you wanted to solve this thing with me."

"I want to." Stevens sighed. "It's just a hell of a week."

"Get your game face on, Stevens. This is the big time. We're going to take down these kids, you and me."

"Sure," he said. "Sure. I'll see you tomorrow." He hung up the phone and sat back in his chair as Nancy came into the room.

"So?" she said, smiling. "You gonna be my knight in shining armor this week?"

TWENTY-ONE

Pender woke up early and turned on the television. He watched the news with the volume turned down, and when the Beneteau case came up, he sat close to the screen, straining for information and watching the reporter deliver her monologue a few feet from where they'd dumped Beneteau's body. According to the reporter, the police had no suspects and were appealing to witnesses to come forward. From Pender's point of view, that sounded like success.

After lying awake for most of the night, Pender had nearly convinced himself to forget about the murder. To feel nothing. Beneteau was dead. That was a fact. They had to deal with it, and they had to get as far away from the crime scene as possible, lest they end up paying with their own lives for their first major mistake.

By dawn, Sawyer was awake on the opposite bed. He'd said nothing since they left the crime scene, and he looked shrunken in the dim light, his eyes swollen and his face pale. Pender caught his eye. "You all right?"

Sawyer didn't move. Didn't look up. "Fine," he said.

"Forget about it," Pender told him. "It could have happened to any of us."

The big guy laughed, rueful and cold. "That's a lie."

"You gotta get over it. We gotta get over it. Professionals deal with stuff like this. They don't let it bring them down."

Sawyer stared up at the ceiling. "I keep seeing his face."

Pender watched him a long moment. "What do you want to do?" he said finally. "You want to quit? We could hop a flight to Seattle this morning."

Sawyer said nothing. He looked across at Pender, searching his eyes.

"You want to quit, we can walk away right now."

Mouse sat up, rubbing his eyes. "Walk away from what?"

"From the job," said Pender. "We have to decide. How do we deal with what happened last night?"

He looked at Sawyer, then Mouse. Foot on the gas, he thought. "Last night was a

133

speed bump. It doesn't change anything. If we can get out of Detroit, we can keep making money."

"We killed a mobster," said Sawyer. "The police *and* the mafia are going to be looking for us."

"What do the police know?" said Pender. "What does anyone know about us?"

"Maybe they saw the van," said Mouse. "Worst-case scenario, they can trace the burners. Who cares?"

"I say we go to Florida," said Pender. "We take a week or two off. Then we start hitting jobs again. We do it quiet, no guns, and we do it professional. We forget about what happened and we watch our backs. All right?"

"I'm in," said Mouse. "Let's do it."

"Sawyer?"

Sawyer stared at him for a minute. Pender watched his friend try to work his head around it. "All right," he said at last. "We keep going."

Mouse caught Pender's eye. "What about Marie?"

They all three shifted around to where Marie lay sleeping, her back to them, her body rigid as a piece of steel rebar. Pender turned back to his friends. "I'll talk to Marie," he said.

Later that morning, Pender and Marie took the Impala back into Detroit. Neither of them spoke until Pender merged onto I-75 and pointed the car north toward the suburbs and the Super 8 motel. Then Pender glanced across at Marie. "How are you doing?" he said.

Marie looked at him. Her eyes were tired and swollen. "I can't get that noise out of my head," she said. "The gunshot. And then the — I don't know. The body."

Pender nodded. "I've been thinking about it, too."

Marie stared out the window. "I didn't ever think we'd end up like this. We killed a man, Pender. We ended his life."

Pender said nothing for a mile or two, tried to pick out his words. Finally he sighed. "You didn't think that was at all a possibility, Marie?"

Marie turned to face him. "What?"

"We're kidnappers," he said. "Criminals. You didn't think there was a chance it would escalate?"

"I never would have done this if I thought it would escalate." Her voice was deadly calm. "I never wanted to be a murderer."

"None of us wanted it. But it happened. It's over."

"Did you know it would happen, Pender?

Did you plan for this?"

"Of course not," he said. "But I don't think I had any illusions that what we were doing was right."

"We weren't killing people."

"The guy was a mobster."

"His wife was a mobster. Maybe. Allegedly. He had three kids. That's a fact."

Pender pulled over to the side of the highway and stopped the car on the shoulder. He stared across at her. "What do you want to do, Marie? He's dead. Nothing I can say is going to make it better. He's dead. We're not. So what do you want to do?"

Marie said nothing.

"We can go to the police right now if that's what you really want."

Outside, cars sped past, horns blaring. "I don't want to go to the police," she said. "I don't want to go to jail, Arthur."

"Then what?" he said. "What do you want?"

She didn't answer for a long moment. Then she sighed. "I want my life back," she said. "I want to be normal again. I want a good job and a house and a dog and everything normal people are supposed to have. I want *normal*, Pender."

"We'll have normal," he told her. "Another

couple years, tops. Then we'll be free. We'll find a beach and —"

"That's not normal, Pender. That's a dream and it's great, but it's nowhere near normal."

Pender stared out the front windshield. Cars blurred by around them. "How long have you felt this way?"

She paused. "A while. I don't know."

"That life doesn't exist anymore." He kept his eyes hidden. "That's why we got into this business, Marie. That's why *you* suggested it. Because normal wasn't an option for us."

"So what, we're just stuck here?"

Pender glanced in the rearview. "I thought that was the point." He waited a moment, and then he stomped on the gas and the car howled forward, picking up speed as they merged into traffic.

Marie stared out the window. "I just never thought I'd kill anyone."

"I know. Me, neither."

"Do you think we'll be okay?"

"I think if we get out of Detroit, we'll be fine," he said.

She sat back in her seat. "That's not what I meant."

They drove the Impala into Troy and to the Super 8, where Marie packed up the

137

gear as Pender waited outside, watching the parking lot for police or Beneteau's goons. They left the room keys on the counter at the front desk and were gone within fifteen minutes.

Sawyer and Mouse were eating Hardee's when they returned. The TV was turned to an action movie, volume extra-loud, and some Italian motherfuckers were shooting at some black motherfuckers as bystanders ducked for cover. Sawyer was eating a cheeseburger, wrapped up in the flick. Guess he's over it, Pender thought. Marie made a face and went to wait in the car.

They let the boys finish their meal and checked out. Then they drove across the interstate and into the airport. Pender glanced at the gang in the rearview. "If anyone's looking for us, they're looking for four," he said. "We should split up here and meet in Miami."

Sawyer and Mouse nodded. Marie paused. "I think I might go back to Seattle," she said. "I need to think some things over."

Pender looked at her. "Marie."

"I'll meet you guys in Florida. I just need some time."

Pender watched Sawyer and Mouse swap looks in the rearview mirror, but he said nothing. They drove in silence. When they arrived at the terminal, Pender pulled the Impala into the drop-off lane.

"You guys grab tickets to Miami," he said. "We'll take back the car. I'll catch the next flight down, and we'll meet up on the beach. You guys have burners?"

"We got 'em." Mouse opened the door. "See you in Florida, boss. See you whenever, Marie." He got out of the car, and Sawyer followed and closed the door firm behind.

Marie watched them shoulder their luggage and disappear into the terminal. "They're mad at me," she said. "They think I'm ditching."

Pender glanced at her. "Aren't you?"

"No, I'm not ditching," she said. "I told you I'd see you in Florida."

Pender drove the car to the rental lot and parked. They got out and walked toward the terminal. "This is a mistake," Pender told her. "This isn't the time to be alone."

Marie shook her head. "It's just a couple of days. I'll be fine."

They walked into the terminal. Pender scoped out the crowd, feeling like he'd swallowed a time bomb. Be professional, he told himself. Get out of Detroit.

He didn't make anyone in the concourse for cops or goons, so they walked to the ticket counter and he bought a ticket to Miami for the Kyle Miller alias and a ticket to Seattle for Ashley McAdams. Then they walked to the security checkpoint and into the terminal proper and down to her gate, where they stood as the aircraft boarded and he took her hands in his. "I don't think you should go," he said.

"I know." She gave him a forced smile. "I love you. I'll see you again soon."

He tried to kiss her, but she turned away. "I can't," she said. "I'm sorry." She squeezed his hands and walked. She didn't look back.

Twenty-Two

Twenty miles away from Detroit Metro Airport, where Marie McAllister's Delta 757 was already taxiing for takeoff and Arthur Pender's Continental 737 was in preboarding, D'Antonio was sitting in a Cadillac truck outside the Beneteau residence, waiting for a phone call as a plainclothes cop knocked on every door on the other side of the street.

A half hour earlier, Dmitri had called from the terminal with the news: The kidnappers were fleeing the city. Well, let them run. The stupid kids would have to flee the hemisphere before they'd be safe, and even then D'Antonio was certain he could dig up a Korean hit squad to put the problem to bed.

Miami wouldn't be a problem. The organization had family down there, did plenty of business in Florida. Somebody in South Beach would know somebody who could take on the job. One punk-ass white boy wouldn't be an issue at all.

Seattle was another story. D'Antonio didn't know anyone in that part of the world. Meant he'd have to send goons to take care of it. Or kill the girl himself. Either way, it could get complicated. They'd pull the Miami kid's card first, then deal with the girl in Seattle.

He'd left the house then, dialing a number with one hand as he opened his umbrella with the other. "It's D," he said when his contact picked up. "I need a job done in Miami."

Paul Landry sat at his desk, shuffling through printouts with one hand and eating a Subway sandwich with the other. He'd had Garvey requisition any and all recent unsolved crimes featuring a red Ford van, and the kid had brought back an encyclopedia, effectively chaining the detective to his desk while his rookie partner went back out to Beneteau's block and kept looking for witnesses.

It was like he told the kid, though. If the family didn't want to talk, then they didn't really have a case, unless the phantom Chevy came back loaded with good prints or the neighbor from across the way suddenly woke up and realized she'd had a good look at every one of the killers' faces.

Or if I manage to make some gold out of all this straw here, Landry thought, as he stared down at the reports. Maybe someone used a red Ford van in some other contract killing and I can make a connection.

From the looks of things, multiple people had used multiple Ford vans for all sorts of criminal endeavors. Most of them were drug-related, though, and Landry had a hard time figuring how a yo from the Cass Corridor was going to wind up in Birmingham laying waste to a mob boss's husband.

Still, there were a handful of cases that seemed like they might lead somewhere, and Landry set them aside. Something to work on until the kid comes back from the neighborhood, he thought. At least I'll stay warm and dry.

The phone rang. A uniform with the Detroit PD, somewhere in the southwest. River Rouge. "Heard you guys were looking for vans."

"Is it a Ford?"

"Used to be, anyway."

Beautiful, Landry thought. "All right," he sighed. "I'll add it to the pile."

TWENTY-THREE

Windermere was at her desk when Stevens showed up at the FBI building the next day. She shook his hand when he arrived, then gestured to an empty cubicle across from her own. "Welcome to the big show," she said. "There's our command station."

Stevens sat down, testing the chair. "It feels so glamorous."

"It gets better."

"Do I get my own trench coat?"

"If you behave yourself," Windermere said, "you might even get a badge. Bring the stuff?"

Stevens opened his briefcase and produced a file folder. Inside was every scrap of evidence he'd managed to obtain thus far. He handed it to the Fed, and she paged through.

"Work many kidnappings in Miami?" he asked her.

She shook her head. "One or two. Drug-related. You?"

"Same. Minnesota ain't exactly crime central."

"I helped out on an abduction here a couple months back," she said. "Daddy didn't think mommy was doing a good enough job. Never saw a scheme like you're talking, though." Windermere put down the folder and picked up some paperwork of her own. "Search warrant and plane tickets."

Stevens shuddered. "Plane tickets."

"The Windy City, Stevens. You don't look thrilled."

He forced a smile. "I'm fine," he said. "Just not much of a flier."

Windermere smiled back. "Stick with me and that'll change, and fast. We've got Georgia and Maryland down the road if Chicago doesn't work out." She stood. "Ready to go find Carew?"

They were in Chicago within three torturous hours. Stevens spent the flight sipping ginger ale and staring at the back of the seat in front of him, while Windermere paged through the in-flight magazine, pausing now and then to chuckle at his predicament. "How can you be so calm?" Stevens asked her. "We're thirty thousand feet above the earth right now. Doesn't that freak you out?"

Windermere shook her head. "I grew up

around planes, Stevens. My dad worked for Delta growing up."

"He was a pilot?"

"Chief mechanic," she said. "In Memphis. He worked on everything from DC-9s to those big 767s. Taught me all about how they fly. There's nothing to be scared of. It's just physics."

She looked closer at him. "Look, you're not going to yack, are you? You throw up on me and I might regret bringing you along."

Stevens gripped his armrest tighter. "I regret it already."

A local Fed, an Agent Davis, was waiting at O'Hare. To Stevens he looked everything like the stereotypical G-man: He had the trench coat, the suit, the shades, and the ride, an all-black GMC Yukon he'd double-parked in the loading lane. He flashed Windermere a shark-toothed grin when he saw her. "Hot damn," he said. "And who might you be?"

Windermere held out her hand. "Carla Windermere. You're Davis?"

"That's right." He held on to her hand a beat too long. Then he glanced over at Stevens. "This the local?"

"Kirk Stevens," said Stevens. "Minnesota BCA."

Davis looked him over a second. Then he

gestured to the Yukon. "Truck's right here," he said. He turned back to Windermere. "You been down to Chicago before?"

Windermere shook her head. "Never really saw the point."

She climbed into the Yukon and Stevens followed. Davis walked around to the driver's side of the truck. "You might think about paying a visit," he said as he slid behind the wheel. He glanced back at Stevens and then gave Windermere another toothy grin. "I imagine Minnesota can get kind of boring."

Davis started the truck and navigated out of the airport's labyrinthine service roads, gabbing like a second-rate tour guide. Stevens stared out the window at the outskirts of Chicagoland, tuning out the G-man and wondering what he was getting himself into.

He'd had just enough time to leave a message for Nancy at her office before they'd boarded the flight, and though Windermere had assured him they'd be back in the evening, Stevens couldn't see his wife being thrilled by his absence. It was a tough enough week as it was.

They'd weathered busy streaks before, though. And the kids loved Natalie, the teenager they hired at times like these, when the courthouse and the state police got wild simultaneously. But Stevens knew his wife, and he knew she hadn't been happy when he'd told her about the FBI detail the night previous. She'd sighed a long, expressive sigh and muttered something about the babysitter and then returned to the kitchen table, where she put herself to sleep reviewing case files and briefs. She wasn't mad, she said, just tired and busy, and her husband had found her facedown on a stack of *American Criminal Law Review*s when he woke up the next morning.

Davis was eyeing him in the rearview mirror. "State policeman, huh? You must be pumped to get to run with the big dogs."

"Dream come true," said Stevens. "Always wanted to be an FBI. All that flying around."

Windermere stifled a smile. "You get me a tactical unit, Davis?"

Davis nodded. "Could have saved you the trip, though. This Carew address is in the middle of nowhere. Industrial Joliet. No way the guy lives there."

"He's got ID says he does."

"Yeah. Maybe the state patrolman didn't copy the address right. Forgot to carry the one or something."

Davis wasn't lying. They arrived on Carew's alleged block about forty minutes later, and Stevens stared through the truck windows at pallet factories and stamping plants and a long line of low warehouses that hardly looked like the home base for a merry band of kidnappers.

Davis pulled onto a side street and stopped behind a big black bread van that Stevens knew must be the tactical unit. He turned back in his seat toward Windermere. "See what I mean?"

Windermere glanced at Stevens. "Anything's possible," she said. "They could use this place as a hangout. Somewhere to store hostages."

"Or it's a fake address," said Stevens. "Carew's banking that nobody checks up on his story."

Windermere nodded. "That's assuming his name's even Carew."

"My thoughts exactly. Probably an alias."

Davis cleared his throat. "The address you gave me is down the block that way," he said, pointing. "The Avenue Tool Company."

Windermere opened her door. "Let's have a look."

They left the truck and walked up the block to the Avenue building, a two-story gray box built of corrugated steel and a dearth of imagination. The parking lot was half full, and a succession of hammering noises was coming from inside.

"Looks like business as usual," said Windermere. "Tell the Tac squad to hang back for now."

They found an entrance and walked inside, where a middle-aged woman waited behind a service desk with a scowl and a *People* magazine. "Help you?" she said.

Windermere brandished the warrant. "FBI. We need to have a look around."

The woman blinked. "I'll get the manager."

The manager was a droopy-looking man with a face as bleak as his surroundings. He introduced himself as Bob McNulty and gave the warrant a thorough read.

"We're looking for Ryan Carew," said Windermere. "You know where we could find him?"

McNulty looked up at the mention of the name. "No," he said slowly. "But maybe you could answer a couple questions for me."

TWENTY-FOUR

The man stood in the arrivals concourse at Miami International, watching another crowd of passengers emerge from the terminal. He ran his fingers through his slicked-back hair and checked his watch, then the flight information monitors. Then he turned his gaze back to the steady stream of travelers, most of them dressed for the northern winter and already sweating in the city's seventy-five-degree heat.

He wore a loose Hawaiian shirt, cutoff shorts, and Ray-Bans, and he kept his pistol in his waistband, hidden by the folds of his shirt. He stood leaned up against a pillar, a newspaper in his hands, looking for all the world like another local waiting to pick up his brother-in-law for a winter vacation in the sun.

Three hours ago he'd been asleep, his girl lying beside him in the cool dark of his bedroom. Then the phone rang.

151

"Got a job for you." It was Zeke. "Some friends up north have a problem flying in this afternoon. They need someone to play welcome wagon. The Continental flight from Detroit. Maybe bring a friend."

Zeke described the guy and hung up, and the man had lain in bed for a few more minutes, listening to his girl sound asleep, admiring the long curve of her back and the swell of her hips through the thin sheet. Then he'd picked up the phone and called Carlos.

Now Carlos sat waiting in the loading zone in his Trans Am, an Uzi under the passenger seat and an extra clip in the glove box. The man didn't necessarily like teaming up for jobs, but Zeke had ordered the hit and Zeke wanted a doubles act and whatever Zeke wanted, Zeke got.

So now the man waited in the airport, searching out a tall white boy with sandy hair and a blue coat as a mob of tall people, white people, blond people walked past. Tall black people in blue coats, short white blond people, tall white blond people in red coats. He checked the monitors again. The Detroit flight was at the gate. The target should have shown by now.

Then he saw him. In his mid-twenties, about six feet even, maybe six one. Short

152

blond hair and a navy blue coat. It was the kid's expression that sold him out. Came strolling down the tunnel like your everyday rich kid headed for the beach, but he hit the baggage carousels, and just for a second as he scanned the room, his nonchalance melted away. He frowned and sped up through the crowd, shouldering his carry-on bag and slipping out toward the taxi stand.

The man followed the kid outside and watched him stand, blinking, in the sunlight. He took off his coat and hailed a cab, smiling now, a little bit, like he knew he was going to get away with it. The man watched him from a distance, saw him climb into the taxi, and then he gestured to Carlos, who pulled up in the Trans Am.

"That's the guy," he told Carlos as the Trans Am slipped into traffic. "Let's go make some money."

Pender sat in the back of the taxicab and rolled the window down. It feels so good to be warm and dry, he thought, after all those rainy days. He told the driver to take him to South Beach, and he pulled out his phone and sent a text to Mouse's burner.

The flight down had been nerve-racking. Pender spent the majority of his time paging through the in-flight magazine or staring out the window, worrying about Marie and trying to convince himself they'd made it out of Detroit undetected. Then they touched down in Miami, and when he walked into the arrivals lounge he felt panicked, sure there was somebody waiting for him in the crowd. But nobody came for him, and he walked outside and felt the sun on his face and the warmth and he realized, you're being ridiculous, Pender. Nobody within a thousand miles knows anything about you.

Mouse texted him back. The Dauphin on Ocean Drive. Pender passed the instructions on to his driver and then sat back to enjoy the wind in his hair as the taxi took him over the MacArthur Causeway and into South Beach.

I hope Marie's okay, he thought. For a moment, he felt the tightness in his chest again and he missed her almost palpably. We're not meant to be apart like this, he thought. She's supposed to be here.

He wondered if she would even come to Florida. Maybe she'd go home and decide she was done. Maybe she'd already decided. The idea made him feel sick, and he forced himself to look out at the ocean and the palm trees and pretend she hadn't walked away like she did. She'll come back, he told himself. She said she'd come back in a couple of days.

The Dauphin was a classic South Beach hotel, a squat, art deco complex with a big neon sign and a faded paint job. It looked like it had lived out its glory days before *Scarface* started shooting and had endured a long, slow decline ever since. Now it sat almost forgotten amidst the gleaming condo high-rises and refurbished boutique hotels, and Pender examined the place as the cab pulled up alongside. It was largely anonymous, and it faced the beach. A good base for a little vacation.

Pender paid the driver and got out of the car. He stood on the pavement for a moment, staring up at the hotel, and then he picked up his carry-on bag and walked inside, pausing once to look back at the ocean and thinking, I wish Marie could be here to see this.

Carlos pulled the Trans Am to the curb a half a block down from the Dauphin, and they watched the kid stand on the sidewalk, staring up at the hotel. He looked like an accountant, a student, or something else preppy. Nothing like the usual targets at all. "How do you want to do it?" Carlos asked.

"We'll hang out a little bit," said the man.

"Then when it gets dark, we'll park in the alley. Use the rear door to get out."

"How will we find him?"

"The kid's a tourist. He's headed for the beach, man. We let him work on his tan and then follow him when he comes back."

Carlos nodded. The man stared out the window, watching the girls walk by and wondering if his own girl would be around when he got home. He settled in to wait, wishing the darkness would come faster, anticipating the kill.

TWENTY-FIVE

Marie McAllister sat onboard her plane, watching the lights of Seattle come ghosting through the clouds, trying not to throw up as the 757 made its final approach to Sea-Tac International.

The plane bumped and careened to a landing on the rain-slick runway tarmac, but her churning stomach had nothing to do with the turbulence. She was afraid, for herself and for Pender and the gang, and as the plane taxied toward the terminal, she felt sick with the sense that the whole sordid scheme had spiraled out of control.

She knew Pender was right about needing to move on, and she knew she was a hypocrite for taking Beneteau's death so personally, but Marie couldn't help it. Every time she blinked, she saw the bastard's blood spatter against the roof of the van. Every time she heard a noise, she swore it was the gunshot.

The plane arrived at the gate, and Marie stood, stretching, anxious to be free. She stood in line waiting for the doors to be opened, and then she realized that the man across the aisle was staring at her.

She watched him from the corner of her eye, panic welling up inside her. He was an older man, probably sixty, with a thick head of hair and a bushy white beard. He was smiling at her like he was trying to get her attention.

He recognizes me, Marie realized. He's probably one of those mobster guys, sent here to kill me. She was starting to hyperventilate. The line shuffled ahead slowly, and the crowd murmured, impatient. The man kept staring at her. Marie felt like she was suffocating. She wanted to scream.

Finally, the aisle cleared. Marie grabbed her bag and hurried ahead, walking quickly through the rows of seats, her head down. She ignored the stewardess at the front of the plane and burst out onto the loading gate, breathing the cool damp kiss of fresh air and then hurrying up the ramp into the terminal.

She was halfway to the baggage claim when he caught her. "Excuse me," he said, and she pretended she hadn't heard him. He touched her arm. "Aren't you Marie

McAllister?"

She stopped. The game was up. She turned to find the old man smiling wider now, panting slightly from the chase.

Marie looked around for police. Sooner or later they'd be here, she thought, and she'd be led away in handcuffs. It was no use running anymore. "You got me," she said. "I'm her."

The man laughed. "I knew it. I bet you don't remember me."

Marie stared at his face. The man smiled back, waiting. He wasn't a cop, she realized, recalling roast turkey and stuffing and pumpkin pie. He wasn't an assassin, either. "Dr. Tavares," she said finally.

He laughed again, delighted, and Marie remembered him now, though she'd been much younger the last time she'd seen him. Dr. Vincent Tavares. A friend of her father's and a guest at Thanksgiving dinner a long time ago. She must have been all of ten.

"My goodness," said Tavares now. "How you've grown, Marie."

"It's been so long," she said, willing herself to act normal. "How have you been?"

"Fine, dear. Just fine. I'm coming back from a surgical conference in Ann Arbor. What about you? What brought you to Detroit?"

"Oh," said Marie. "You know. Work."

They had talked about this, she and Pender. They had to tell people *something*. They decided they would be marketing personnel, the kind of people who flew all over the country to open up franchises and network at trade shows. It sounded boring and normal and reasonable, and as she gave Tavares the spiel, she could tell it was working. His eyes glazed over. He didn't suspect a thing.

"Oh," he said. "Won't your parents be excited to see you."

"Yeah," she said smiling, ad-libbing. "I'm going to surprise them. It's Mom's birthday in a couple days, and I thought I'd just show up at the party."

"That sounds wonderful." Tavares winked. "I won't tell a soul I saw you."

They chatted on the way to the bag claim, and the doctor offered her a ride home. But she begged off, making up a story about a friend waiting outside, and then she fled the terminal and jumped into a taxi before Tavares's suitcase could emerge on the carousel.

The taxi wound its way toward the city and through the downtown core, and Marie watched the skyline pass as she'd watched Detroit the night before and Minneapolis

160

before that. Seattle had been home, once, but tonight through rain-streaked windows the city looked as bleak as any other. Though Pender and Marie still kept an apartment in Queen Anne for appearance's sake, she'd been back only three or four times since they started the kidnappings.

At first, her parents had been hurt and confused by their daughter's sudden absence. She'd created her marketing job, invented little stories about long hours at the office and no free time for anything but sleep, but that only made her parents worry more. Her dad warned her not to burn herself out and her mother worried that she wasn't eating right, and in the end it was easier to just shut them out entirely. Even now, she'd lied to Dr. Tavares because she couldn't bear the thought of facing her father's earnest curiosity and her mother's concern and her med-school sister's smug satisfaction.

Pender tried to encourage her to see her family. He hated to think he was taking her away from the people she loved. He just thought they should remember to be cautious. To be *professional* — God, he loved that word. Anyway, Pender had it easy. His parents barely sent Christmas cards anymore.

And Mouse was like Pender, familywise. He'd told his dad he'd taken a tech support job with Microsoft and that's why he was gone so much and his dad had grunted his approval over the top of his beer and that had been that. Sawyer's parents were too busy with their own lives to pay much attention, though the big guy had a younger sister he adored and to whom he sent vague, cheerful — for Sawyer — e-mails every week or so. He told his sister he was an online poker player and he could work whenever and wherever he wanted.

The boys had it easier. They still had each other. She had dropped what few friends she had as soon as they'd decided to hit scores full time. She knew the guys had done the same, sort of, but it was different; they were each other's best friends. Marie's best friends were getting master's degrees or working at Starbucks, struggling to make lives for themselves in the real world. Marie hadn't seen most of them in years.

She had given up everything, her friends and her family, and for what? Well, for the promise of a decent life, somewhere down the road. For a life outside retail sales, a low hourly wage, the constant threat of unemployment. And for Pender. She did love him, and she did love his coconut-oil dreams. But Marie often felt that she'd given up her own life, a decent life with decent, caring people, in exchange for an endless succession of motel rooms and fast-food joints and a whole lot of lies.

And now they were murderers, too.

The cab dropped her off outside her apartment, the old building looking black and empty in the naked trees and the rain. She dug out her key and hurried upstairs to her door. The place was cold and damp and musty, but Marie hardly noticed. She left her shoes by the door and threw her coat on a chair and crawled into bed fully dressed, listening to the rain beat against the windows as she drifted into an unhappy, uneasy sleep.

TWENTY-SIX

Agent Stevens leaned forward and stared through the window of the Yukon, looking down the highway at a calamitous knot of angry, slow-moving traffic. "So this is what I'm missing," he said, sighing. "The glamorous life of an FBI agent."

Windermere laughed. Davis didn't. Windermere turned to face Stevens from the front seat. "What do we do now?"

The Avenue Tool Company was a dead end. Bob McNulty had led them into his office, where he dug into a filing cabinet and returned with a manila folder bulging with junk mail, credit card solicitations, grocery store flyers, and the like, all addressed to Ryan Carew.

"These things started coming maybe a year and a half ago," said McNulty. "We couldn't figure it out. Nobody named Carew works in this place. Nobody named Carew *ever* worked in this place."

"Maybe he moved," said Windermere. "Forgot to change his address."

McNulty shook his head. "Avenue Tool Company's been on this spot since 1946. He's been gone a long time if that's the case."

Davis chuckled to himself. Windermere and Stevens traded glances.

"Who is this Carew, anyway?" said McNulty. "What does the FBI want with him?"

"He's a suspect in an ongoing investigation. He listed this place as his home address."

"Yeah, well, he's not here." McNulty paged idly through the stack of mail. "If you happen to find him, tell him go ahead and change his address."

So Ryan Carew was a dud. The name was never anything but an alias. And if these kids were going to the trouble to make up phony names and addresses, they weren't wasting their talents on one puny sixty-grand score. These were serial kidnappers. A professional crew.

"I'll get in touch with someone from the Georgia and Maryland offices," said Windermere. "Save us the trip. Save you a couple of barf bags."

"We're not finding anything in those places, either," said Stevens. "They're all of them fake."

Windermere nodded. "You think?"

"These kids are serious," Stevens told her. "We're not getting them easy."

Davis pounded on the steering wheel and leaned on the horn, cursing. "What time is your flight?"

Windermere checked her watch. "An hour or so."

"You ain't making it."

"Come on, Larry."

"What, come on?" He gestured through the windshield. "It's like trying to fit a hundred-gauge rail inside a Japanese condom out there."

Stevens glanced up at Windermere. "Guess we're catching the late flight."

"Bad news," said Windermere. "This is the late flight."

Goddamn it, thought Stevens. Nancy's going to kill me. "Maybe there's something at Midway?"

Davis shrugged. "In this mess? You ain't getting to Midway, pal." He grinned at Windermere. "Now's your chance to see some of the sights."

Windermere shook her head. "I've seen all I need to see," she said. "Scenic Joliet was enough for one day."

"Then, how about dinner?" Davis said.

"You and me. I know a place —"

"Davis." Windermere looked across the truck at him. "I get it, okay? And I'm flattered. But it's been a long day and I'm tired, you know?"

Davis looked at her a moment. Then he shrugged and turned back to the road. "Best I can do is drop you at a hotel by the airport," he said. "You guys can stay the night."

It was nearly nine in the evening by the time Davis picked his way through the traffic to O'Hare. The Fed dropped them off in front of the airport Sheraton and looked ready to bolt before Windermere closed her door. "So long," Stevens told him. "Thanks for the company."

Davis grunted something and stared straight ahead. Windermere climbed out of the truck and peered back in at him. "You'll book us on a morning flight, Larry?"

Davis grunted again. "Sure thing," he said, rolling his eyes. "Have a good night." Then he stepped on the gas and peeled out of the lot, the big Yukon howling as he made for the highway.

Stevens and Windermere watched him go. "I think I pissed him off," Windermere said.

Stevens nodded. "I'd say so. He really wanted to show you Chicago."

"I know what he wanted to show me, Stevens. It wasn't anywhere as big as Chicago." She turned and started toward the lobby doors. "I'm starving. You hungry? How about a steak dinner on the Federal dime?"

Stevens begged off dinner for ten minutes to call home. "Just to check in," he said.

"Good idea," said Windermere. "I'll probably need about twenty. Sometimes Mark needs a little sweet talk."

They checked in together, and then parted at the elevators. Stevens called Nancy from his room. She was angry, though Stevens could tell she was trying not to show it. "I thought you were going to be around this week," she said.

"I know," he replied. "I'm really sorry, honey. This just came up."

"How the hell did you end up in Chicago, anyway?"

"We had to check out a place in Joliet. They told me I'd be back this evening, and then traffic just screwed us over."

"You're with that FBI agent? Windsor?"

"Windermere, yeah. We're holed up by the airport. The Sheraton."

"Oh, how nice for you both," said Nancy. "Use protection."

"Ha-ha. We got separate rooms."

168

"I know. Come back soon."

Stevens promised he would and hung up the phone. He surveyed the room, a bland business traveler's vacuum, and his stomach growled. The phone rang and he picked it up. Windermere. "You watching the news?"

"Not yet," said Stevens. "Everything all right back home?"

"Mark was in a mood," said Windermere. "Sweet talk wasn't cutting it. Turn on Channel 5."

Stevens turned on the television. Switched over to Windermere's channel. The reporter was in some grimy corner of Detroit, of all places, standing out in the rain. She was explaining how the van used in the murder of Birmingham's Donald Beneteau had been found, gutted by fire, in an industrial neighborhood in River Rouge.

Beneteau, the reporter said, was the husband of the infamous and controversial Patricia Beneteau, a Motown Casino exec with alleged ties to the Bartholdi crime family in New York City. He'd been shot once and then dumped from a red Ford van outside his tony Birmingham mansion late Wednesday evening. The family refused to comment, and the suspects remained at large.

Stevens spoke into the phone. "What are

you saying, Windermere?"

"You watching? Some mob guy got clipped out of a red Ford van. Van was found burned up a few days later, no plates. Could have been our kids, no?"

Stevens ran the math in his head. They dumped the body on Saturday, he thought. They could easily have been in Minneapolis the week before.

"Could just be a coincidence," said Windermere. "But it sounds like their MO, you know what I mean?"

"Sure," said Stevens. "Anyway, what else have we got right now?"

"We can at least call up Detroit and see if they know anything."

"Let's get the Michigan office involved."

"Already done," Windermere told him. "Now, are you ready for dinner or what?"

TWENTY-SEVEN

He found them on the beach.

They'd commandeered board shorts and a couple beach towels, and they were stretched out on the sand about thirty feet from the surf, their pale bodies incongruous amid acres of tanned flesh. Sawyer was laid out flat on his back, staring up through a brand-new pair of Oakleys at some girl in a yellow bikini. Mouse was pretending to read a mystery novel while sneaking glances at Sawyer's new friend.

Pender thought about sneaking up on them and maybe pretending to be the cops, but quickly thought better of it. Too soon, he decided. Besides, Sawyer had probably found himself another gun already. So he played it straight: walked up, cast a shadow over Mouse, and kicked sand on Sawyer's chest.

The big guy sprang up. "Yo, what the fuck?" He was ready to brawl, showing off for the girl. She had long blond hair and a tight, toned body, a gorgeous face that probably put plenty of miles on her fake ID. Beautiful, definitely, and knowing Sawyer, probably dangerous. He wondered how much they'd told her.

Mouse looked up from his novel, laughed. "Penderrrr."

"Oh, shit." Sawyer relaxed. "I almost decked you, bro."

Pender stuck out his hand, and they shook. "See you guys are settling in nicely."

"Yeah." Sawyer grinned. He gestured to the girl. "This is Tiffany. She's from Pennsylvania."

Tiffany gave a little wave and a world-melting smile. "Bryn Mawr," she said. "Taking a little impromptu winter break from school. So you're the famous Pender."

Pender glanced at Sawyer. "I don't know if I'm famous."

"The way these guys talk about you, you might as well be," she said. "I kept telling them we should go for food, and they kept insisting we had to wait for Pender. And now here you are. So can we eat or what?"

"All right." Sawyer grabbed the girl and lifted her up off the ground, spinning and bouncing her in his arms as she screamed, laughing, for mercy. "You're gonna give him a big head."

Pender watched Sawyer and Tiffany flirt, shuffling his feet in the sand and feeling more than a little overdressed in his Michigan street clothes. "Where'd she come from?" he asked Mouse.

Mouse looked up, shrugged, gestured around the beach.

"Sawyer gonna fall in love with her?"

"For tonight, probably."

"Yeah," said Pender. "What did you guys tell her?"

"The truth." Mouse sat up, grinning. "Told her we're energy drink representatives from Manhattan come down to pitch the new product line."

"The truth." Pender smiled, relieved. "So where's your girl?"

Mouse frowned. His eyes swept the horizon, paused hungrily at Tiffany, and then continued, surveying the bronzed skin and bikini-clad bodies that littered the beach. "Somewhere out there," he said, shaking his head.

"You're a funny guy, Mouse. And you're rich. What are you waiting for?"

"I'm not rich enough for South Beach," he said. "And I'm just funny *looking*."

Sawyer and Tiffany returned, laughing and jostling each other. "We're starving," said

Tiffany. "Let's eat, please?"

"I gotta pick up some clothes first. I'll meet you?"

"Back at the hotel," said Sawyer. "We gotta get changed, anyway."

They walked back up the road, Sawyer mugging for Tiffany, goofing off, the girl giggling, sticking close. Mouse walked a couple steps behind, his eyes on permanent roll. When they got off the sand, they split up, Pender bearing right, heading for the shops, and the others bearing left toward the Dauphin.

"Catch you later, bro," said Sawyer, lifting Tiffany into a piggyback. Mouse shot Pender a look.

"Just once, I want to be that lucky," he said. Then he shook Pender's hand. "See you in a bit. Don't get caught."

The man sat in the passenger seat of the Trans Am, watching the crowds ebb and flow along Ocean Drive. Beside him, Carlos sat snoring in the driver's seat, a small puddle of drool forming on the comics section of *The Miami Herald.* The blond kid had left the hotel an hour or so beforehand and headed for the beach, his jeans and collared shirt giving him away amid the throngs of passersby in shorts and tees and halter tops.

Now the man waited in the waning light, antsy now, ready. He watched as a trio of gringos passed them on the sidewalk, walking up to the front door of the Dauphin, the men pale as albinos and the girl tanned a buttery brown. The bigger guy eyed the Trans Am as he passed, and his eyes briefly met the man's before he turned toward the hotel. They were hard eyes, even as the kid was smiling, and the man looked away, unsettled.

He watched the kids disappear into the hotel, and then he nudged Carlos awake, told him bring the car around the back of the building and wait by the rear door for his signal. Then he got out of the car and stood on the sidewalk, enjoying the breeze off the ocean and the sound of the surf in the background. He pulled the sports section from his back pocket, unrolled it, and leaned up against a palm tree, pretending to read as he surveyed the landscape, the Glock in his waistband pressing up against his back, begging to be used.

TWENTY-EIGHT

The kid returned with shopping bags at a quarter past six. The man was reading the sports pages for the third time when he strolled past, walking quick and swinging the shopping bags from his arms, in a hurry, but not urgently. He passed the man at the palm tree, didn't even slow down, and turned up the walk toward the front door of the Dauphin. The man forced himself to read a sentence or two more and then came up the walk just as the kid was disappearing inside.

The man entered the hotel and walked through the lobby, ignoring the front desk clerk who sat reading his own newspaper, oblivious. The kid was on the elevator, and the man watched the lights above the door until the elevator stopped on the fourth floor. Then he walked quickly through the first-floor hallway to the back of the building, where Carlos sat on the rear steps, the

Trans Am parked in the alley behind.

"Fourth floor," he told Carlos, holding the door open and letting him inside. Carlos cradled his Uzi beneath a Miami Heat warm-up jacket, the extra clip bulging in his pants pocket. They made for the rear stairwell and climbed up into the building, listening close for any noises from above as each footstep echoed around them.

They reached the fourth floor, Carlos panting from the climb, and the man let him catch his breath as he peered out the stairwell window into the hall. Deserted. He looked back and gestured to Carlos, who nodded, and he pushed open the door and crept out into the hallway, listening at each door for the sounds of habitation. The man lifted the Glock from his waistband, enjoying the feel of it in his hands as he crept along the wall, pressing his ear close to the doors as he passed them.

Sawyer was in the shower when Pender arrived at the room, and Mouse and Tiffany shared an uneasy silence in the bedroom. The place was dark; nobody had bothered to turn on the lamp, and the dusty windowpane filtered out what little sunlight remained.

Mouse lay sprawled on the bed like a kid

on Saturday morning, staring blank-faced at the television as a couple of overweight moms battled over one bucktoothed groom. Tiffany sat in an easy chair by the window, barely watching the TV. She'd found herself a denim miniskirt and a white tank top. Mouse was still in his bathing suit.

"Knock-knock," said Pender, entering the room. He set down the bags and stood blinking in the darkness, letting his eyes shift from Mouse to the television to the girl. "What are you guys watching?"

"Springer," said Mouse, not bothering to look up from the screen.

Pender glanced at Tiffany. "How's that working out for you?"

"It's fine," she said, shrugging. "I don't really watch talk shows."

"Mouse," said Pender. "Get some manners, will you? Find something the lady wants to watch."

Mouse sighed, letting every last breath escape his body, and rolled over to face Pender. He was opening his mouth to argue when a knock at the door shut him up.

It was a firm knock, insistent. Pender felt his stomach tighten. "You guys order room service?"

Mouse shook his head, frowning.

"It's probably just housekeeping," said Tiffany.

"It's not fucking housekeeping," said Mouse.

Pender put a finger to his lips and crept to the door. He peered through the peephole. It was dark. What the hell? Then he got it. *"Motherfucker."*

He was on the floor when the first shot came, crouching, crawling back toward the bedroom. The shot came through the door and then the door swung open with a sick crack, the deadbolt swinging useless as two angels of death stood silhouetted in the light from the hallway.

"Get down!" Pender shouted, and Tiffany screamed, diving for cover behind the bed. The shots kept coming, flying past Pender as he turned the corner, bracing for the end as he hid against the wall and waited for the gunmen to come farther into the room.

The first guy came quickly, a scar-faced kid in a Hawaiian shirt brandishing a big pistol and shouting in Spanish as he let shots go, tearing up the place. He fired at the bed and Pender heard Mouse cry out, and then Pender leapt at the gunman and tackled him from the side. The man cursed in Spanish and swung, firing wildly, shooting out the window as Pender held on for dear life. He wrestled with the guy, climbing on his back and clawing at him, grabbing for the pistol and feeling the guy's strength draining, feeling like he might be winning. Then he glanced at the door and saw the big guy with the Uzi.

The blond kid was climbing all over him and the man fired wildly, screaming in Spanish for Carlos to ice the motherfucker and now. He hadn't expected so many people in the room, but he'd hit the girl, he thought, and definitely the scrawny guy on the bed. Then the blond kid ambushed him from the side, jumping all over him, fucking up his aim. But that's why you brought backup, and why the hell wasn't Carlos using that big goddamn Uzi already?

The man swung around, the kid hanging on his back like a Superman cape. Carlos was still standing there, the Uzi raised, looking for a clean shot and yelling something about move, boss, move. The man moved, tried to swing the kid off his back, but the kid held on and wouldn't let go, and the man swung around to face Carlos just in time to see the big guy get his face punched in by the hard kid from the street.

He'd come out of the bathroom wrapped in a towel, eyes murderous, and he'd surprised the shit out of Carlos, who was still fucking around trying to get a clean shot. The hard kid hit him square in the face, a knockout punch, and Carlos reeled into the wall, his finger on the trigger and the Uzi spraying bullets now, clean shot or no.

The man felt the first couple catch him in the chest, then a couple more in the stomach, and then he stopped counting. The hard kid jumped all over Carlos, socking him, knocking him to the floor as the Uzi fired nonstop, catching the ceiling, the floor, the walls — and the man. He kept fighting the kid, barely felt the bullets, kept trying to swing the kid off so Carlos would have a decent shot, but the kid held on and the man felt his strength start to go, felt light-headed a little and sick, and he looked down and saw blood blossoming like crimson flowers on his Hawaiian shirt.

The hard kid had Carlos lying on the floor, all bloodied with the Uzi spent and smoking beside him. The hard kid picked it up and turned to the man, looking him in the eye once more as the man crumpled to the carpet, feeling the pain now, feeling the blood pouring out of him.

The blond kid stepped back and let him fall, and he did, heavy, onto the carpet, staring at Carlos's beaten body and the hard kid beside, hearing the screams and the vague sirens in the distance and watching as the blond kid stepped over his body and walked to Carlos, pistol in hand. He stood over Carlos's body, his eyes as hard as his friend's now, and with his jaw set firm he held the pistol steady and put one shot between Carlos's eyes.

Then the man closed his eyes and let go.

TWENTY-NINE

Tiffany was screaming. Tiffany was screaming and Mouse was moaning, and sirens were already starting to blare in the distance. Sawyer stood beside him, handling the empty Uzi, staring at the big guy and the kid in the Hawaiian shirt who lay bleeding to death on the hallway floor. Tiffany kept screaming. Mouse kept groaning. Pender dropped the pistol, the empty reminder of the gunshots still echoing in his head. He stepped over the Spanish kid and returned to the bedroom, a tableau of destruction: windows shattered, the TV, too, the prints on the wall all shot up and crooked. Stuffing lingering in the air from where the bedding had been torn to pieces.

Mouse lay on the other side of the bed, Tiffany on top of him, her hand pressing down on his chest, bloody. She stopped screaming when she saw Pender. Mouse stared up at him. "Motherfucker," he said.

He'd been shot high in the chest, right side. Plenty of blood. Pender felt his knees go weak.

"We gotta go," said Sawyer. He'd pulled on a pair of pants and a T-shirt, and he stood now in the doorway. "We gotta go, now."

Pender stared down at Mouse. The girl was sobbing now. Mouse was calmer. "You guys go," he said. "I'll sit this one out."

Pender blinked. The world seemed to coalesce around him, and he was thinking straight again. "Forget it," he said. "You're not hurt that bad."

He lifted Tiffany to her feet. "Let's go," he told her. She let him point her to the door. Sawyer beckoned her along, and she came, slowly, eyes clenched shut as she stepped over the body of the Spanish kid, eyes clenched even tighter as she ignored what remained of the big guy. Sawyer took her in his arms.

"Look for car keys," Pender told him. "We have to move."

He turned back to Mouse, who lay on his back on the floor with his hand over his wound. He grabbed one of his shopping bags from the floor and took out a T-shirt. Tore it into a strip and knelt down over Mouse. He wrapped the T-shirt over

Mouse's shoulder and under his armpit, bandaging the wound as best he could. "All right, Mouse," he said, inspecting his work. "Let's get you out of here."

Sawyer was kneeling down, rummaging through the big guy's pocket. He came up with a key ring as Pender lifted Mouse to his feet. "Trans Am," he said. "I saw these bastards earlier."

He pocketed the keys and then knelt again, picking up the Spanish kid's pistol and the big guy's extra ammunition. He shoved both in his pocket and turned back to Pender. "You ready?"

Pender knelt at his carry-on and pulled out a manila envelope. "Money," he said, standing. "Let's go."

They staggered out into the hallway. Sawyer led, holding the Uzi in one hand and Tiffany in the other. Pender hung behind playing human crutch for Mouse. The hallway was empty. "Back stairs," he told Sawyer.

They made it to the stairwell and labored down, Mouse breathing heavily, struggling. "Leave me behind," he said. "I'm slowing you down."

"Shut up, drama queen," Sawyer called from a flight or two below. "Takes a lot more than a flesh wound before you get to be hero."

They went slow down the stairwell. Pender felt like he was dreaming, running in place and never getting anywhere. Mouse leaned heavy on his shoulders and every step took an hour and Pender felt the panic rising. Stay calm, he told himself. Be professional. Get through this.

They reached the first floor, and Sawyer poked his head out into the hallway, then quickly back in. "Cops," he said. "Down the other end."

"We take the back way," said Pender. "Then we find the ride."

They burst out the back of the hotel, and Pender heard Sawyer give a little whoop as he emerged into the alley. A bright orange Trans Am was parked in back, angled out for a quick getaway. Sawyer slid behind the wheel and fired up the engine, and Pender and the girl helped Mouse in back. Pender climbed in and slammed the passenger door, and Sawyer peeled out, headed west, away from Ocean Drive and the Dauphin and the bodies of the two assassins.

Sawyer drove them to the MacArthur Causeway, and they crossed back into Miami proper, Pender half expecting a roadblock on the other side of the bay and telling Sawyer slow down, blend in, act normal. There was no roadblock, but Sawyer slowed down regardless as Pender tried to calm down his heart.

He turned around to where Mouse slumped in the backseat. "How you doing, buddy?" Mouse was breathing heavily, and he was pale. But he gave Pender a weak grin and a thumbs-up.

"Still alive," he said.

Sawyer glanced at Pender. "Hospital?"

"No way." Pender shook his head. "They'd arrest us as soon as we walked through the door."

"Just leave me outside the emergency room," said Mouse. "I'm slowing you down."

"You watch too many movies," said Pender. "We're not leaving you, Mouse."

"What the hell are you guys talking about?" Tiffany's voice was rising. "Why aren't we going to the hospital — or the police? Who the hell were those guys?"

"Calm down," said Sawyer. "We'll explain later. We're not going to the hospital."

"But your friend is *dying.*"

"I'm not dying," said Mouse. "I'm a drama queen. Don't listen to me."

"He's shot in the shoulder," said Pender. "He's in a lot of pain, and he's probably going to go into shock. We're getting the hell out of the area, and then we're going to stabilize him. That all right with you, Mouse?"

"Whatever you say, boss."

"All right," said Pender. "Let's get as far away from South Beach as possible. Find a place to lie low for a bit and ditch this car. We'll keep an eye on Mouse, and if everything goes all right we'll fix him up and keep moving. If it doesn't, we'll find a hospital in the county or something, bribe a doctor to keep him quiet. Cool?"

Sawyer nodded. "Very cool, boss."

In the backseat, Tiffany leaned forward. She stared at Sawyer, and then she stared at Pender. "Jesus," she said. "Who *are* you guys?"

THIRTY

Detective Landry led the two agents through the police impound lot in downtown Detroit, shivering in the constant rain. He turned back to his companions, one male, one female, one white, one black, one FBI with a southern accent and the other some kind of Minnesota state police, which didn't make sense to Landry but he'd learned in this job there were questions you asked and questions you forgot to ask. "Van's over here," he said, leading them past a couple street-racer Hondas. "What's left of it, anyways."

Agent Stevens followed the detective, wishing he'd remembered an umbrella. He hadn't figured on spending much time outdoors on this trip, and besides, Windermere hadn't given him much time to pack. In this miserable weather, though, Stevens would have traded in his toothbrush for an umbrella in a heartbeat.

As it was, he was living out of a Walmart shopping bag since they'd left Chicago. After the McAdams and Tarver addresses came back as false as Ryan Carew's, Windermere had checked on the Beneteau angle with her SAC and returned with instructions to proceed to Detroit. Now here they were in the Motor City, checking on this burned-out van, while back in Minnesota Nancy simmered quietly amid a mountain of casework and two needy children. "Fine," she'd sighed, when he told her the new development. "You have any idea when you're going to be home?"

"After Detroit," he'd told her. "I'll be home after Detroit, I promise."

Now, marooned in the gray rain in some police lot in southern Michigan, Stevens could think of nowhere else he'd rather be but back in Minnesota with his sick kid and his busy, angry wife. He ran his fingers through his thinning hair and found it utterly soaked.

Windermere moved closer to him, holding her own umbrella high. "Here," she said. "Grab some shelter."

"I'm fine," said Stevens. "Thanks."

"I insist, Agent Stevens. You're representing the FBI, and you look like shit. Come on."

He shrugged and took the umbrella, feeling her press against him as they huddled underneath. Stevens could just make out the scent of her perfume as they followed the detective through the lot and toward the charnel-house remains of what had apparently been a Ford E-Series passenger van. The detective paused before it, gesturing like Vanna White at its burned-out hulk.

The bodywork was almost entirely burned away, and what remained had been charred black in the blaze. The thing was destroyed, but the Detroit police swore it was a Ford and they figured it had probably been red once, too.

Stevens circled the vehicle. "Plates?"

Landry shook his head. "Stripped."

"We're looking for a van that was sold in Minnesota. You guys run the VIN?"

"VIN's melted off. No way to identify the car."

"So how do you know this is your van?"

"Night watchman at the Ford plant in River Rouge said he saw a red Ford van drive past on the night in question, followed by a gray Chevy Impala. Half hour or so later, the Impala drove back but the van stayed put. One of the victim's neighbors puts a girl in a gray Chevy outside Donald Beneteau's house the day he was killed."

"She have curls?"

"That's the one," said Landry.

"Watchman called in the fire?"

Landry shook his head again. "Wasn't on Ford property, so he didn't think much of it until he got off shift the next day. Drove down the block on his way home and found the van burned out on a side street. He thought it was a drug hit and didn't want to talk, but we got him."

"All right," said Stevens. "So we make the van for the Beneteau hit. And we've got an Impala with our pretty girl inside."

Windermere spoke up. "You said you had a witness who saw the van drive off, correct?"

"That's right," said Landry.

"He didn't see the plates, though."

"Nah," said Landry. "Too dark."

"Huh," said Windermere. "You mind if we take him for a spin?"

The Birmingham witness took all of ten minutes to remember that the van he'd seen wasn't wearing the standard Michigan plates but rather a white plate with a light-blue bar across the top — spot-on for a Minnesota tag.

Then Stevens started calling rental car agencies. Struck gold with the Budget office at the airport. Sure, they told him, we rented a gray Impala to a woman named Darcy Wellman out of Louisville, Kentucky. Yeah, she paid with her own MasterCard. No, we can't remember what she looked like. No, we don't remember if she had anyone with her. Sure, we'll call if we remember anything else.

Circumstantial evidence, maybe. But way too big to be a coincidence. "Can you freeze that credit card?" Stevens asked Windermere.

"I can do one better," she replied. "I'll have MasterCard alert us when the card is used. We can trail her from a distance."

"Let's do the same with Ashley McAdams's Visa."

"Already done." She winked at him. "You're dealing with a pro right here. Get in the car."

Now they drove back southwest on I-94, the wipers working double time and the traffic starting to thin as they passed through the outskirts of town. Stevens glanced at Windermere. "You going to tell me where you're taking me?" he asked her. "You know something I don't know?"

"Maybe," she replied, the hint of a smile playing on her face.

"Jesus, Carla," he said. "Don't play coy. What do you have?"

"Just wait and see, Stevens," she said. "Just wait and see."

Stevens sighed and sat back in his seat, watching Detroit pass by out the window. Whatever she's got, he thought, it's been a hell of a good day already.

Her phone rang a few minutes later. Windermere winked at Stevens again and picked up. "Windermere." She paused. "My man. That's perfect. Can you text me the details?" Paused. "Already, great. I owe you."

She ended the call and turned back to Stevens, unable to hide her smile. "You ready for the surprise?"

"Spill."

"We're headed for the airport, Stevens. That was a friend of mine on the phone just now. Works at the FAA. I had him run some names for me."

Her smile was contagious. "And?"

"Turns out a woman by the name of Ashley McAdams took a flight from Detroit to Seattle-Tacoma International Airport just a couple days ago," she said. Her smile got wider. "You don't think that could be a coincidence, do you?"

THIRTY-ONE

D'Antonio swore and hung up the phone. He lit a cigarette and stared out the window of the Escalade and swore again. Teach anyone to trust that motherfucker Zeke again.

The news out of Miami was not good. The news out of Miami was fucking awful. Zeke had delegated to this kid, Manny, supposed to be a real hard-ass. Supposed to be good at what he was good at. Apparently, he wasn't.

"Told him bring backup," said Zeke. "They must have run into a goddamn war."

As best as D'Antonio could tell, the two men had got themselves outsmarted by one skinny little geek kid who didn't even have a gun. Word out of Miami PD was ballistics had found only two types of ammunition: the 200-grain bullets from a .45 caliber pistol and the 9 mm Parabellum rounds that according to the officers on scene probably came from a submachine gun. The 9 mm rounds were in Manny. The other guy had taken a shell from a .45 to the brain. Meaning either they'd shot each other or the skinny kid had managed to overpower them both. Without a weapon of his own. Impossible.

Fingerprints were too plentiful to matter and witnesses were nonexistent, and frankly, D'Antonio's contact told him, the homicide police would have been all too willing to run with the idea that the men had shot each other but for one minor problem: a shitload of extra blood on the floor of the hotel room. The conventional wisdom in Miami put a third person in the room while the killings went down.

The kid. All that blood meant the bastard was hurting.

D'Antonio stepped out of the Escalade and into the rain. He stared up at the Beneteau residence, wondering if the old lady was watching him. Lately he seemed to be living in her driveway or in her living room, taking phone calls and directing traffic while she brooded in the background, the kids wandering like ghosts through the home. Poor bastards lost their dad to this asshole, he thought. Who knows when they lost their mom.

He walked up to the front door and let himself in. One of the kids, the youngest, met him in the foyer as he took off his shoes. "Your mom around?"

The kid stared at him a second, then pointed to the study. Said nothing. D'Antonio nodded. "Thanks."

The kid followed him to the doorway, watching from a distance. D'Antonio opened the door and then noticed the kid staring at him. "What's up, little man?"

The kid's eyes were cartoonish wide. "You're going to get the men who killed my dad."

"That's right," said D'Antonio.

"You're going to make them pay."

"Yeah."

The kid said nothing more. D'Antonio hung there a moment and then let himself into the study, where Patricia Beneteau waited like a winter coat waits for a blizzard. "Close the door," she said.

D'Antonio closed the door. "We had a problem," he said. "The Miami job didn't play."

She fixed her cold eyes on him. "What does that mean, exactly?"

"The kid got away. Fired the help and stole their car."

"They don't sound like good help," she

said. "What about the girl?"

"I'm working on a Seattle connection. We'll find her."

"Jesus," she said. She walked to a bookshelf. Examined a row of books. Then she turned back to him, her eyes sharp and her voice like ice. "My husband is dead because of a couple of kids, and all the manpower in this organization can't seem to catch up to them. So tell me, can you find these people? Or should I have Rialto send over someone better?"

"There's no one better," he told her. "There's me, and that's it."

She stared at D'Antonio, her eyebrow raised. D'Antonio stared back. Waited her out. Mercifully, his phone rang. "Excuse me," he told her, and he ducked out into the hall.

It was his man at Detroit PD. "I have news."

"Go."

"FBI's taking over your case."

D'Antonio felt his heart sink even further. "Bullshit."

"True story. Not racketeering, though. Different Feds. That homicide cop, Landry, brought them downtown from Birmingham, had 'em looking at vans in the impound lot. Two agents out of Minnesota working a

198

kidnapping angle. They make your killers as a group, probably four people, working jobs state to state."

Those clowns? thought D'Antonio. No way. Those kids were barely out of high school. "Feds," he said. "What does that mean for us?"

"Means I can't get you much more information unless Birmingham homicide stays involved somehow. Otherwise the Feds shut us out."

"So what do you want to do?"

"We can feed them information," said the man. "Small stuff. Just enough to keep the Feds around. We can admit Beneteau was kidnapped, for starters."

"Let me think on it," said D'Antonio. "Anything else?"

"Yeah. Got a name for your Seattle bird."

"No shit."

"Ticket was booked under the name Ashley McAdams. Flew out the day after. Might be a fake, but it's probably worth chasing."

"We'll chase it," said D'Antonio.

He hung up the phone and stood in the hall for a minute. Kidnappers. They thought kidnappers took Beneteau. Well, the theory made sense as far as Miami went. Those guys figured they were taking out one unarmed kid. Turned out they were walking into a viper's nest. Interesting.

D'Antonio let himself back into the study. Patricia Beneteau looked up at him from her desk. "Well?" she said. "Have you figured out how you're going to catch these people?"

"Yeah," D'Antonio told her. "I'm going to Seattle."

THIRTY-TWO

I killed a man, Pender thought. I killed a man in cold blood. Killed him while he was lying barely conscious and defenseless on the floor. I stood over him and shot him dead, and I would do it again if I had to.

They holed up in a shitty motel in Hollywood, just up the interstate from Miami. Parked the Trans Am in the back of the lot and piled into a dirty little room with no air conditioner and no cable. They carried Mouse into the room and laid him on the bed and made sure he was stable, and then they left Tiffany to babysit while they hiked up the road to a 7-Eleven for supplies.

"How bad do you think he's hurt?" Pender asked Sawyer as they walked. "Do you think he's all right?"

"How the hell should I know?" said Sawyer. "He's conscious, isn't he?"

"He's maybe in shock."

"Nothing vital up there where he was

shot, I don't think. Probably hurts like a bitch, but he should be all right, right?"

"I hope so," said Pender. "You can't just walk off a gunshot wound."

"You can in the movies," said Sawyer.

"Yeah, for whatever that's worth."

They walked a ways farther. "We can try to bribe a doctor," said Pender. "But we gotta make it quick, and we gotta keep moving. Those guys are going to come after us again."

"What about the girl?" said Sawyer. "Tiffany. How much do we tell her?"

"How much do you like her?"

Sawyer glanced at Pender. "I only just met her, dude. She's some rich Princeton kid. Who knows what she's thinking right now?"

"Can we let her go?"

They let the question hang there and kept walking. If we can think of a reasonable story, Pender thought, we can let her go. If we can be sure she's not going to talk. But what happens if we can't?

"Maybe we tell her my dad's someone famous," he said finally. "Like a politician."

"Yeah," said Sawyer. "Those guys were trying to kidnap you."

"That works, right?"

They bought the 7-Eleven out of bandages and aspirin and grabbed some cheap snack food and alcohol, and then they walked back down along the dark road, honing the cover story until it was sharp as a prison toothbrush. They walked across the back of the motel, ready to feed the girl the lie and cut her loose.

They opened the door to the room and found Mouse lying on the bed, still in his bloody bathing suit and bloodier homemade bandages, head propped up by pillows, and an action movie on the television. Tiffany sat beside him, her hand over his.

Mouse looked up when Pender and Sawyer came into the room. "Hey, fellas." He gestured to the TV. "These things are a whole lot cooler when you know what they're going through."

Tiffany rolled her eyes at Pender. "What did you guys get?"

"Bandages, drugs, Ho Hos, and vodka," said Sawyer. "Everything our shot-up little bastard could ever want."

"How's he doing?"

"I'm fine," said Mouse. "I really just want to take a nap."

"No naps," said Pender. "How's your arm feel? You need a doctor?"

"Shit, no," said Mouse. "Just give me a shot of something and tell me if there's an exit wound."

They gave Mouse a bottle of vodka and a plastic motel cup and told him to get ready while Tiffany spread bath towels over the bedspread. Mouse poured a shot and forced it down and came up coughing and grimacing.

"Lightweight," said Sawyer.

Mouse glared at him. "Screw off."

Pender poured him another double, just in case, and then they lifted up Mouse and deposited him gently on the bath towel lining. They rolled him onto his left side. Pender and Sawyer held him in place while Tiffany examined his back. She made a face. "Yeah," she said. "There's an exit wound."

"How's it look?" said Mouse.

"Fucking gross," she said. "How should I know?"

"I think that guy had a forty-five. That's a big fucking gun."

"It's a big fucking hole," said Tiffany.

Mouse reached for his cup and drained it again. "Yeah," he said. "I'll be fine. We just gotta stop the bleeding and keep it bandaged up."

Pender and Sawyer glanced at each other. "You're sure?"

"I think so." He gestured to the plastic shopping bags. "Let's see what kind of stuff

204

you bought."

They plugged up the exit wound with the bandages from 7-Eleven and then wrapped up his arm and shoulder in the rest of the clean towels. Then they lowered him to the bed and told him to take a rest.

"No more booze," said Tiffany. "It thins the blood."

Mouse groaned, a stage groan. "At least let me have some Ho Hos."

"Eat up." Pender tossed Tiffany a package of snack cakes. Then he turned to Sawyer. "You want to run her through the story?"

Sawyer nodded. "Yeah, all right."

Pender turned back to where Tiffany was feeding Mouse the Ho Hos, laughing as he nibbled them in her hand. "Tiffany, why don't you let me take over? You and Sawyer can take a break. Take a walk."

Tiffany looked up, her eyes wide. "You want me to take a walk with Sawyer."

"Nah, boss, let her stay," said Mouse. "We're having fun."

"Just for a couple minutes," said Pender.

Tiffany was pale. "You guys are going to kill me, aren't you?"

Mouse sat up. "What?" He grimaced and sunk back. "Who's killing who?"

She stood. "You think I know too much."

"Nobody's killing anyone," Pender told

her. "I thought you and Sawyer could have a talk about the situation here. He could answer any questions. That sort of thing."

"No need," said Tiffany. "Mouse explained it all already."

Pender stared at her. Then at Mouse, who shrugged and smiled weakly. "She forced it out of me, guys. Advanced interrogation techniques."

Tiffany blushed, but Pender kept his eyes on Mouse. "What exactly did you tell her?"

"He told me the truth," said Tiffany.

"Uh-huh," said Pender. "What truth?"

"He told me you guys travel around kidnapping people for money," she said. "He told me those guys who came into the hotel room were pissed because you tried to kidnap a mobster in Detroit, and now you're on the run. That's what he told me."

Pender stared hard at Mouse, but the kid was focused on Tiffany, still wearing that same stupid grin. Pender could have killed him himself.

"So, what?" Tiffany's eyes were on Pender. "You guys have a better story?"

THIRTY-THREE

Nancy was still awake when Stevens got home. He found her sitting at the kitchen table, an array of file folders and photocopies spread out before her. "Agent Stevens," she said, looking up as he came in from the garage. "Back from saving the world?"

He was back, that was true, but it was only a brief respite from the road. Windermere wanted to be on a plane to Seattle by noon the next day.

"Kiss your wife, hug your kids, and pack a bag," she'd told Stevens as they parted ways at the airport, and Stevens had spent the cab ride home wondering just what he was going to tell Nancy.

Now he stood over her, bending down to kiss her forehead, and he still hadn't come up with any kind of a plan. She looked up at him, smiled through sleepy eyes. "How's your day?" he asked her.

"Busy," she said, closing her eyes as he rubbed her back. "I missed you."

"Yeah," said Stevens. "I sure missed you."

He massaged her back for a few minutes, working out the knots and feeling the tension in her shoulders. She leaned back into his touch, a contented smile playing on her face.

"The kids asleep?"

She nodded. "Been about an hour."

"Rats. How's J.J. feeling?"

"Better. Fever's down. You could wake them."

"Nah. Let them sleep."

She opened her eyes and stared up into his. "I guess you're flying out again."

He blinked. "How did you know?"

"I know you, Agent Stevens," she said. "You look like you're into something deep and you don't think I'm going to like it."

Stevens stared down at his wife. "Some poker face I've got."

Nancy smiled. Reached back to rub his arm. "We can't all be born liars."

"Seattle." He sighed. "Couple days, maybe more." He felt like nothing he could say would fix it. "I'm sorry, honey."

Nancy reached back to pull him closer. "You don't have to apologize."

"I do."

"I knew what I was getting into when I married a policeman. It's just crummy that it all has to come together this week of all weeks."

"It plain sucks," said Stevens. "I figured when I joined the BCA I'd get to sleep in my own bed every night."

"We'll get through it. Brennan will come back and you'll figure out this case and we'll all go back to normal. All right?"

She tilted her head back, and he kissed her. "All right," he said.

She smiled up at him. "So tell me about this case of yours."

"This case of mine," he said, walking around the table and taking a seat opposite hers. "We got these kids pulling kidnapping jobs all over the place. Minnesota. Detroit. Seattle, maybe. They've got aliases, fake addresses, credit cards. It's insane."

"It better be, you leaving like this," she said. "What time's your flight?"

"Eleven-thirty."

She stood, stretching, and walked over to where he sat. "Well, then, Agent Stevens, I guess you'd better fulfill your marital responsibilities while you have the chance."

She sat down in his lap and he tilted his head up toward hers and they kissed again, long and slow and deep.

"Was your wife upset?" Windermere glanced across the aisle of the Delta A320 as Stevens settled into his seat.

Stevens fastened his seat belt and stared up the aisle, willing his stomach to stay settled. "We worked our way through it," he said. "What about Mark?"

Windermere frowned. "Mark. Yeah, he had some issues with it." She smiled at Stevens. "He's jealous of you."

"You tell him I'm married?"

"I could have told him you were gay and he wouldn't have cared." She sighed. "We agreed to disagree."

"Yikes."

She sighed again. "He's just moody," she said. "Ever since we moved up here. He can't find any work, so he just sits at home and mopes around all day. Can't even go out because he hates the cold."

"You tell him about ice-fishing?"

"I told him," she said. "He told me I was insane and went to turn up the heat." She dug around in her briefcase and handed him a sheaf of paper. "Anyway, we've got homework to do."

"Credit cards?"

"Partly. That's Ashley McAdams's Visa statements for the last twelve months. Take a look."

Stevens flipped through the first few pages. He started from the front, working backward from the October statement. There was the deposit on the Avis rental car in Minneapolis, but apart from that single transaction, no activity whatsoever. Stevens looked back at Windermere. "They're all blank."

Windermere nodded. "Same with the Wellman card. One charge in Detroit and nothing else."

"Maybe they're new cards?"

"Nope." She shook her head. "Those cards were issued and activated about a year ago. The girl just never used them."

"Then why use them now?"

"She has other aliases we don't know about," said Windermere. "She could have twelve, for all we know. Uses one card, then ditches the alias."

"Except Ashley McAdams got on a flight to Seattle a couple weeks after using her credit card."

"Yeah, but she paid cash. Maybe she didn't think anyone would make the connection."

"Hot damn," said Stevens. "Let's hope she

slips up again. Unless we want to start interrogating all the curly-haired girls in Seattle."

"In other news," said Windermere, "Landry at Birmingham homicide called with an update. Someone in Beneteau's household caved. They're admitting he was kidnapped."

Stevens looked up. "And the kids asked for sixty grand, right?"

"A hundred this time, but still. Just when we'd figured it out for ourselves. I thanked the detective, told him we were past that already. Told him we were headed to Seattle to check on the curly-haired girl, but keep us in the loop if they heard anything else."

The flight attendants closed the cabin doors, and Stevens filed the folio away while the plane taxied from the terminal. When the plane was pointed down the runway, Stevens gripped the armrests, his knuckles straining the skin. Windermere looked over at him. "You're really hating this, aren't you?"

He glanced out the window and felt his stomach flip over. "I've been like this since I was a kid."

She reached over and touched his hand. "Look at me, Stevens. Forget about the airplane a second and just try and breathe."

He held on to her hand and stared straight ahead.

"Let's just talk," said Windermere. "Forget about flying and talk to me for a minute. Your hobbies, Stevens. What do you do for fun?"

Stevens looked at her. She was staring back at him, her eyes calm. He felt the plane start its surge forward and made himself exhale slowly. "Basketball," he said. "I played varsity, back in the day."

"Basketball." She examined him. "You were a guard?"

He shook his head. "A center in high school, believe it or not. I was tall for my age." He found himself smiling. "All I ever wanted was to do play-by-play for the Milwaukee Bucks home games. Somehow I got sidetracked."

Windermere kept her hand on top of his. "Basketball, huh? I was more into football. Of course, girls couldn't *play* football, so I was shit out of luck."

Stevens exhaled again. Felt a little bit calmer. "What did you do?"

"Back then? I ran track. Now I do kick-boxing three nights a week. Take out my aggression without worrying about lawsuits or criminal charges."

The plane sped up off the runway and the

ground fell away. Windermere squeezed his hand. "Takeoff's over, Stevens. We made it. You gonna live through this or what?"

"Yeah," he said. "Thanks." He gripped her hand in his. "I'm just going to borrow your hand for another few hours."

Later on, when the plane was well up in the air and Stevens had a cocktail in front of him and could relax a little, he turned back to Windermere. "So what do we do?"

Windermere looked over at him. She gestured to the folio. "We read, Stevens. I brought more than credit card statements. In that folder is a list of every unsolved kidnapping in the continental United States for the last five years. If we can find anything that fits, we can put together a time line for these guys."

Stevens leafed through the folder. It was thick. "Jesus," he said. "These kids are too good to leave much of their history lying around. We'll lose them if we can't get ahead somehow."

"We'll get ahead." Windermere shuffled her papers. "Maybe history will repeat itself."

Stevens started reading. Kidnappings in Delaware, in Houston, in Atlanta. None of them fit the profile. This is like searching for a marble in a room full of ball bearings, he thought.

He drained his cocktail and gestured to the flight attendant for another. Then he started reading again. The plane shuddered and dove on its way over the Rocky Mountains, and Stevens stared glumly at the long list of kidnappings, unable to shake the desperate feeling they were losing the case.

THIRTY-FOUR

D'Antonio sat in the business-class seat of another Delta airliner, staring out at the clouds as the plane sped toward the coast.

Earlier in the day, the Detroit PD contact had called with good news. "They bit on the Beneteau scoop," he told D'Antonio. "The Fed told me they're headed to Seattle to check on the McAdams girl."

He was on his way to the airport and on board the next flight to Seattle within the hour, booked under an alias he used sometimes, Pistone. Name of the FBI cop from *Donnie Brasco;* kind of a joke. Now he sat watching the plains pass beneath him, hoping the Feds had a better lead on Ashley McAdams than he did.

He pictured the cops in his head. The tall black woman and her partner, the older guy. Windermere and Stevens. He'd watched the two agents when they came back with Landry to talk to the neighbor again. They weren't local, and they sure as hell weren't in racketeering. From Minnesota, his contact said. Sniffing out a kidnapping ring dumb enough to snatch a made guy. What the fuck was this world coming to?

The plane touched down in Seattle, and D'Antonio checked his BlackBerry as they taxied to the gate. More news waited: He had missed calls all over the map, but one in particular from Miami. He called back from inside the terminal. "It's D'Antonio," he said when his contact picked up. "What do you have?"

"You're not going to believe this," said the contact. "It wasn't just the blond kid working alone."

"No shit," said D'Antonio. "He had at least two other people."

"Three, but how'd you know?"

"Doesn't matter how I know. What I want to know is how you know."

"Few things," said the man. "First, the room was rented out to some guy named Howard. According to the clerk, he was tall and muscular. Brown hair. Paid cash. Came with another kid, shorter. They brought a girl back to the room before it all went down."

"Let me guess," said D'Antonio. "She had curly brown hair."

"No, sir. Blond hair. Hot body. Real gorgeous, apparently."

"What else?"

"Police found clothes in the room, enough for three guys. Duffel bags with winter gear and a couple shopping bags from down the road."

"What else?"

"You're going to love this part. They also recovered like five grand in cash. Twenty-dollar bills, the lot of it. Four thousand in one bag and a grand in another. And a laptop computer, all shot up. They're trying to save the hard drive as we speak."

"Make sure they save it," said D'Antonio. "I need to know what's on that computer."

"Might be tough. I can't just walk into the lab and ask to see what everyone's working on, you know?"

"You're not listening to me."

The man sighed. "I'll get you the computer."

D'Antonio ended the call. That computer could have everything anyone ever needed to know about those kids. It would be a goddamn shame if the goons had fucked up the computer at the same time they *weren't* fucking up the kids. Speaking of which —

He called Zeke from the cab on the way downtown. "How we doing on our project?"

"It's not good," said Zeke. "The kid disappeared."

"You mean kids," said D'Antonio. "You have multiple projects now. Kid named Howard, big guy with brown hair. Shorter guy, that's all I know about him. The blond kid who you already know about and a girl, supposed to be beautiful. Blond as well."

"Okay," said Zeke. "But how are we supposed to find them?"

"I don't know," said D'Antonio. "Look for them."

He put down his phone and watched the Seattle skyline come closer. Somewhere in this city, he thought, is a pretty little curly-haired girl who knows everything I need to know about the bullet in the back of Donald Beneteau's brain. Somewhere in this city are the answers. I just need to find them.

THIRTY-FIVE

Marie McAllister finally left her apartment after a day and a half indoors. She'd slept for twelve hours the first night and woken up disoriented, reaching for Pender and calling his name, dreaming that he was in some kind of trouble. She opened her eyes to the dusty bedroom in Seattle, the plain white walls and the too-perfect double bed, and she stood alone at the windows looking out into the alleyway where homeless men would root through the dumpsters at dawn, waking up Pender and pissing him off.

She'd lain in bed until the room became unbearable, and then she stood and forced herself to get undressed and shower. She turned the water as hot as she could stand, filling the bathroom with clouds of steam and taking her breath away as she stood beneath the flow, scrubbing at her body with a washcloth and imagining she would never be clean.

She showered for what seemed like hours, but when she'd dried off and dressed she couldn't find the strength to show her face outdoors. She sat inside on the shitty little couch, watching the shadows move across the cold hardwood floor and trying not to think about Detroit. She ordered in Chinese food and tried to hide her face behind the door, certain her picture must be on Wanted posters throughout the country, but the delivery boy just looked at her like she was crazy and handed her her change and that was that.

She tried to sleep but couldn't, tried to read but her eyes wouldn't focus. So she sat in front of the television instead, watching infomercials until they ran out of things to sell, and then she slumped down on the couch and tipped halfway over and fell asleep like that.

When she woke up, it was morning again, and she felt claustrophobic, suffocated by the dingy apartment. She showered again, quickly, and then she dressed and went down to the street.

She walked, enjoying the cool fresh air and the hint of salt on the breeze. She had lunch at the market at Pike Place, mingling with the tourists and the fishmongers and feeling utterly anonymous, and then she started home, stopping at the Safeway a few blocks from her house and filling a basket with fresh fruit and vegetables, whole grain breads, and yogurt, wanting to purge her system of the deep-fried diet she'd grown sick of after two years of diners and drive-thru.

Then she reached the checkout counter, and she realized she'd run out of cash.

It was a strange feeling, not having any money; she'd gotten used to having hundreds, if not thousands, of dollars on her person most of the time. But she'd forgotten to refill her wallet before she left the apartment and had spent her last ten dollars on lunch, and as she reached for the plastic she handed over the Darcy Wellman card without even realizing she was doing it. Shit, she thought, and snatched the card back from the cashier's hand, swapping it for her Visa. The teenaged princess behind the counter gave her a look and then glanced down at the card. She looked back at Marie and narrowed her eyes. "So who are you?" she said. "Ashley McAdams or Delores Wellman?"

"What?"

The girl gestured with the Visa. "This card says Ashley McAdams. That last one said Delores something. Which one's you?"

Christ, thought Marie. Neither of them's me. "I'm Ashley," she said.

"Then who's Delores?"

Marie sighed. "Darcy Wellman. She's a friend of mine, all right? She left her credit card at my house, and I accidentally gave you her card instead of mine. All right? Come on, it's not like I tried to pass it off as my own."

The girl glared at her. "I'm going to need to see some ID."

Marie dug around in her purse and came up with the Ashley McAdams driver's license. She handed it over. "There, all right?"

"Long way from home."

"I'm a student," she said. "You want to call the cops? My ice cream's melting."

"You didn't buy ice cream."

"Look," said Marie, "just run the god-damn card before I find the manager."

The girl gave her a long sigh and rolled her eyes. But she ran the card through, and Marie signed. The cashier didn't even bother to check the signature.

Shit, Marie thought as she walked out the store. I have to be more careful.

Later on, she made a stir-fry and grabbed her old laptop for something to do as she ate. She surfed the Internet and checked her e-mail and decided she should write her parents.

She didn't feel like writing e-mails, though, couldn't think up any good lies to tell, so instead she went to travel websites and looked at pictures of the Maldives. She stared at the pictures and she thought about a little cottage on an empty beach, thought about Pender relaxing, reading novels, taking walks again. Thought about cooking elaborate dinners and tanning on the white sand and making love in a hammock while the surf crashed in the distance.

Yeah, she thought to herself. You keep dreaming that. Maybe it will make the whole killing people thing go down a little easier.

She wondered what Pender and the boys were up to, and she Googled Miami, picturing the boys on South Beach. Sawyer and Mouse would be roughhousing in the water, hitting on girls, and Pender would be relaxing, reading some nonfiction book he'd bought at the airport because he figured it would help them do their jobs better. She wondered if Pender missed her. She wished she'd kissed him good-bye.

Then the search results came up and at the top of the page was a news alert that made her sit up and her heart start to pound. "Two men dead in South Beach drug slaying," went the headline, and even though none of the boys were really into drugs Marie had to click through to be sure.

She paled as she read the article. Miami police, it said, had recovered a laptop computer and a substantial amount of cash from what appeared to be a drug deal gone wrong. The police believed a pair of local dealers had been overpowered by as many as four armed assassins, and now authorities were looking for three white men in their mid- to late twenties as well as a younger white woman. One of the suspects was believed to be injured in the gunfight.

She stared at the computer screen, her body ice-cold with fear and tense with frustration. The article was sparse on details, but it described the suspects and Marie knew it was them. Three men, one named Howard. Two tall guys, one blond and one brown-haired, one skinny and one bigger. A shorter man with brown hair and the mystery blonde.

Howard was one of Sawyer's aliases. He'd used it on the Memphis job.

She'd have to go to Miami. She'd have to find Pender and the boys and help them escape. It made no sense for her to be sitting in Seattle when the rest of the gang was neck deep in trouble. She imagined the boys hiding out somewhere, terrified. Imagined the hit men bursting through the door.

She spent the rest of the night staring at the walls in her apartment, picturing all of the awful things that were about to happen.

Thirty-Six

"Absolutely not," Pender said. "I can't believe we're even having this discussion." He leaned back against the wall and stared up at the mottled ceiling. We don't have time for this crap, he thought. We have to keep moving.

They were sitting alone in the motel room, the three of them, Mouse propped up on the bed and Sawyer in an easy chair. They'd slept off the shock of Mouse's big revelation, and now it was morning and time was wasting. No time for anger, thought Pender. It's time to react.

He'd called a team meeting and they'd asked Tiffany to wait outside and now Pender stood, staring down at his friends and wondering again what in hell they were going to do. Mouse, at least, looked better, though his bandages were still bloody and he'd taken a lot of drugs. They were running out of clean towels to dress the wounds.

Sawyer stood and walked to the window overlooking the parking lot. They'd opened the curtains partway, and he was staring out at Tiffany as she sat on the curb, staring down at her feet. "Why not?" he asked.

"We're not just going to add her to the team," said Pender. "We don't even know her."

"What do you want to know?" said Mouse. "She's rich. She goes to Princeton. Her dad's worth like a hundred million dollars."

"Okay," said Pender. "So why does she need us?"

"You know these rich girls. They get bored. She just up and ditched school last week. Came down here on vacation. Said she was looking for some kind of adventure."

"So she's a tourist," said Pender. "Absolutely not."

Sawyer sighed. "So we can bring your girlfriend along and that's it."

"Girlfriend?" said Pender. "And whose girlfriend is she, exactly?"

Sawyer glanced at Mouse. Mouse kept his eyes on Pender. Nobody wanted to answer. Then Mouse shook his head. "Look, just forget about the girl for a second," he said. "We've got other things to figure out."

"If you forget about her, I'll take her back," said Sawyer.

"Shut up, Sawyer," said Pender. "Be serious a second. We have to ditch that car. Today."

"Then we gotta get some clothes," said Sawyer. "For Mouse especially. I'm sick of staring at his skinny little body."

"You love it," Mouse said. He turned back to Pender. "Here's the big thing, boss. We left the laptop at the hotel in Miami."

Pender felt his heart stop. That laptop was the key to the whole operation. If someone managed to hack it they'd find everything they needed to put the whole damn team away for life — full names and addresses, banking information and aliases, and a shit ton more incriminating evidence. He groaned. "We're screwed."

"We're not screwed," said Mouse. "I put beaucoup security on that thing. Anyone even looks at it wrong it will self-destruct. Erase everything. Anyways, I have everything we need memorized or backed up somewhere safe. But I need a new machine so we can keep operating, and also," he shrugged, "we kind of need money."

"Yeah, we do," said Sawyer. "I left four grand in that hotel room."

Pender glanced at Sawyer. "You're broke?"

Sawyer nodded.

"I left a grand," said Mouse, "but I still have about fifteen hundred dollars in cash."

"Okay," said Pender. "I still have plenty left over from the Minnesota expenses. Ten grand or thereabouts. We're fine for a little while."

"Good," said Mouse. "But we're going to want to get our hands on more money sooner or later, right? So you guys have to get me a new machine."

"Fine," said Pender. "Any requests?"

Mouse read off some specs, and Pender dutifully copied them down. The whole damn thing might as well be in Russian, he thought. Thank God, Mouse knows what he's doing. "Where would we get one of these?"

"Best Buy. Any decent computer store. Just go in and give that to a salesman, and he'll sort you out."

"Right," said Pender. He straightened. "Now, listen. About Tiffany. We're not just going to let some new girl waltz in and hang with us just because she happens to be hot."

"That's not why —"

"Can it, Mouse," said Pender. "You gave the whole goddamn game away because you wanted to get in her pants. That doesn't mean you get to keep her." He glanced at

Sawyer. "You guys can't even figure out which one of you is going to be the one to —"

There was a knock on the door, cutting him off. Sawyer opened it partway, and Tiffany peered in at him. "Hey, guys," she said. "Can I come in?"

Sawyer glanced back at Pender. "We're not done yet," he said.

"Look, I had an idea," she said. "I'll just hang around with you guys a little while. A few days. We'll get to know each other. You can figure out if you like me or not."

Pender cleared his throat. "Tiffany," he said. "Come on. You're what, nineteen?"

"Twenty."

"You're a beautiful girl. The boys say you're rich. You've got so much going for you. Why would you want to just give all that up?"

She shrugged. "I'm sick of real life," she said. "It's all parties and douche bags, anyway."

"We're fugitives, Tiffany. This *is* our real life."

"I *know*," she said. "That's what's so great about it. Look, there's nobody waiting for me. I'm supposed to be in class right now. The only person who knows I'm here is my friend Haley, and she's too busy meeting boys to care about me. Nobody's going to miss me if I just hang with you guys for a while."

She stared at Pender, watching his face. Giving him that world-beater smile. She was certainly beautiful, he thought. And she was certainly dangerous.

A car horn honked outside, and Pender's heart rate quickened. "We don't have time for this." He turned to Sawyer. "We gotta ditch that car and get out of here. Sawyer, come ride with me. We'll ditch the Trans Am and find something bigger."

"Don't forget the computer."

Pender was halfway out the door. "Yeah, we'll get your computer."

"And clothes."

"And clothes."

"Wait," said Tiffany. "What about me?"

Pender stopped. Stared back at her. "Hang out with Mouse," he sighed. "Keep him alive until we get back. We'll figure out what to do with you later."

THIRTY-SEVEN

"You're never going to believe this," said Windermere. Stevens opened the door a little wider, stared out into the hallway where she stood, excited, clutching her laptop. He pulled his hotel bathrobe tighter.

"It's three in the morning," he said.

"I know," she said. "Sorry. Can I come in?"

He stared at her a second, then turned around and padded back into the room. He switched on the overhead light, blinked, and turned it off, then turned on a couple of lamps instead. Soft light spread into the room, leaving darkness in the corners and shadows on the walls. His pile of unsolved kidnappings sat scattered on the desk; he'd put himself to sleep trying to work out a pattern.

Stevens sat down on the bed. He'd been dreaming about Nancy and the kids. Summer on Lake Superior. He rubbed his eyes and turned back to Windermere. "What have you got?"

She sat down beside him and angled her laptop so he could see. She was dressed down, in jeans and a Stetson Law sweatshirt, and she'd washed off her makeup. Her face looked fresh-scrubbed now, bare, and Stevens felt almost guilty, seeing her this way. He felt flushed and looked away from her face, forcing his eyes down to the computer screen.

Windermere brought up the Ashley McAdams Visa statement. "We caught a break," she said. "I didn't think she'd ever use that credit card again."

Stevens sat up. "But she did."

Windermere nodded. "She bought groceries. Yesterday, at a Safeway in Seattle. You believe it?"

"No," said Stevens. Groceries and a used credit card. Something was different. Something had changed. "What's the neighborhood like?"

"Residential. But it's close enough to downtown and the highways. Route 99 passes just east of there."

"Why's she paying with a credit card?"

"I don't know," said Windermere, turning to face him on the bed. "But I don't much care, either, so long as it gets us closer to her."

Stevens stared back at her, the fog in his head slowly starting to lift. Whatever the reason, he thought, I'm not complaining, either. Those case files are getting us nowhere. This could be the break we need.

They hit the Safeway the next morning. Windermere took charge, searching out the store manager and explaining the situation. We need the tapes, she told him, and we'd like to talk to the cashier, too. The manager, a middle-aged guy with rings under his eyes, told them no problem.

"Got the tapes upstairs," he said. "Might have to wait for the cashier. She's not due in until four or so, after school gets out."

The manager led them up a flight of stairs at the front of the store. He punched a code into a door and then led them into a tiny cluttered office. A window with one-way glass looked out over the store, and a chair and a desk took up most of the room. In the corner of the office was a bank of four televisions, each cycling through a series of security camera views in grainy black and white.

"You wanted yesterday afternoon, right?" said the manager. "Just the cash registers?"

"Yeah," said Windermere.

"No," said Stevens. "You have any footage from the parking lots?"

The manager dug out a couple of tapes and keyed up the first in the VCR. Then he turned to the window. He stiffened.

"Key-rist," he said, heading for the door. "That kid never learns. Excuse me, would you?"

When he was gone, Stevens hit Play on the VCR, and he and Windermere settled in to watch as a parade of shoppers made their way through the checkout counter. It took about ten minutes before Stevens saw her. He reached forward and stopped the tape. "There," he said, pointing. "That's gotta be her." The girl had just entered the line, her hair tied up in a bun but still undeniably curly. She was carrying her groceries in a green plastic basket, and she was alone.

Stevens pressed Play and they watched the girl unload her basket. The cashier scanned her purchases and then turned to the girl to wait for her payment. The girl fumbled in her purse for a second or two before coming out with a credit card. Before the cashier could run it, though, the girl reached out and took the credit card back and handed over another one. The cashier put up a fuss, and the girl seemed to get a little riled up. Then she reached back into her purse and showed the cashier something. "ID," said Stevens. "You see that?"

"What's she doing?"

"She pulled two cards. Took back the first and gave her the second. Cashier didn't like it and asked for ID. Now she's showing her the Ashley McAdams ID."

"What does that mean?"

"I don't know. Maybe she gave over her real credit card first and thought better of it."

"But the cashier had already seen the name." Windermere nodded. "Interesting. She nearly screwed up."

Stevens pressed Play again and watched the girl finish her purchase, stuffing the groceries into a couple of canvas bags and then walking away from the counter, disappearing offscreen. "She was alone," said Windermere.

"Maybe the boys are in the car. Let's check the parking lot."

He put the second tape in the VCR and pressed Play again. They watched as grainy cars shunted back and forth throughout the lot, searching for the car that would bring them Ashley McAdams.

Stevens glanced at Windermere. The office was small, and they were sitting close, her thigh against his. She was made up again, dressed for the workday, and Stevens felt his cheeks burn as he remembered how he'd felt when he saw her the night before.

"What's the matter?" said Windermere, catching his eye. "You see something?"

"No," said Stevens. "Not yet."

She gave him a lopsided smile. "Just enjoying the view?"

Stevens forced a laugh. "No way." He leaned forward, focusing on the TV, feeling her eyes on him. Christ, he thought, remembering how coolly she'd shut down Davis in Chicago. She must think I'm the same kind of asshole, staring at her like that. He turned back to her. "Look, I'm sorry."

"You mean you *weren't* enjoying the view?" She was still smiling. Her eyes were hypnotic. "Spit it out, Stevens. You falling in love here or something?"

Stevens felt his collar tighten. What was she trying to do? "No," he said. He fumbled for an answer. "I'm just tired. Late nights, right?"

Her smile widened. "Relax, Stevens. I'm just messing with you. I know you're an honest man."

"Yeah," he said. "I am."

"We're just two cops doing our jobs." She kept her eyes on him, and he turned away, back to the screens. Felt his face getting redder as the silence grew.

Then he sat up and grabbed her arm. "There," he said, pointing to a smudge in the bottom corner. "You see her? She came walking into the lot from the right-hand side. That's our girl, right there."

Windermere peered at the screen. "You think?"

There was a noise from behind them as the manager let himself back into the office. "You get what you were looking for?" he said.

He stared over their shoulders at the TVs. Scratched his head. "Marie, right?" He glanced at Stevens. "That's who you're after?"

Stevens looked at Windermere. "I don't know," he said. "Who's Marie?"

The manager shrugged. "This girl used to come into the store all the time. Her and her boyfriend. Real good-looking couple, lived up on Sixth. They stopped coming in a while back. I figured they moved away." He squinted at the screen. "That's her, right?"

Stevens pressed Fast Forward as the girl disappeared into the store. About a minute later she emerged, a grocery bag in each hand. She made her way through the parking lot and then, just at the very top of the frame, disappeared onto the sidewalk and started walking away. "That's her," said the manager. "I'd put money on it. She's back in town. Isn't that something?"

Windermere glanced at Stevens. "Yeah," she said, flashing another smile. "Isn't that something?"

THIRTY-EIGHT

D'Antonio watched from the rental car as the FBI agents emerged from the grocery store. They had another person with them, a little man in a rumpled shirt and tie — the manager, D'Antonio guessed. The man walked with the agents to their own car and pointed up the street. They said a few words to one another, and then the agents got into the car and drove away. D'Antonio shifted into drive and followed them.

The cops hadn't been any sort of tough to find. D'Antonio had dealt with enough Federal agents to have a decent idea of their habits, and after he'd gotten himself settled in at the Hyatt and fixed himself a gin and tonic from the minibar, he'd pulled out the phone book and started dialing around for the businessmen's hotels in the center of town, pretending to be Windermere's husband or Stevens's older brother. He found them, after two or three tries, at the Crowne

Plaza a few blocks away.

In the morning he'd had a rental car brought around, a decent Lincoln that maybe looked a little too much like a Ford for his liking, but what were you going to do? Then he camped out in front of the Crowne and pretended to be a limo driver until the Feds came out in their own rental, a little cookie-cutter Nissan.

He'd followed them to the Safeway and waited while they screwed around inside, and now he followed them out of the lot and west into an older residential neighborhood.

The Feds must have found something in that Safeway, he thought. The manager had showed them a lead. He followed in the Lincoln, hanging back a ways and letting the Feds clear the block before he followed, letting them show him what they'd learned.

The Feds were just turning onto 6th Avenue when he saw her. Had to be her. Curly brown hair. Pretty face. He'd only caught a glimpse of her outside the Beneteau house but the image had stayed with him, and now, watching her walk up toward an old brick apartment on the corner, he knew he'd found her.

D'Antonio steered the Lincoln to the curb and stepped out of the car. He jogged across the street, oblivious to the shouts and horns from the motorists behind him. "Ashley," he called as he caught up to her. "Ashley, over here."

Windermere glanced in the rearview mirror again. "That Lincoln," she said. "You think it looks familiar?"

Stevens twisted in his seat. "Looks like every other Lincoln I've ever seen."

"I think he's following us," she said. "I've seen him a couple times now."

"Probably a lost limo driver. Who would want to follow us?"

Windermere turned up onto 6th Avenue and watched in the mirror as the Lincoln pulled over at the corner. The driver got out, a big burly guy in a long, expensive-looking coat. She watched as he ran out into traffic, nearly causing chaos as he hurried across the street. He seemed to be calling to someone.

"The manager said a big brick apartment building," said Windermere. She slid down in her seat, straining to see through the rearview mirror. There was a big brick apartment building back there, no doubt. But it wasn't on 6th, exactly.

"Watch out!" said Stevens, and she slammed on the brakes, narrowly avoiding the rear bumper of the BMW in front of her.

"All right," said Windermere. She looked back in the mirror but the Lincoln — and the man — was too far behind her. Windermere stared up the street. Nothing but houses. No apartments in sight. She made a quick right at the first cross street. "We're going back," she said. "I don't like the looks of that car."

THIRTY-NINE

Marie was on her way to the front door of her apartment building when the big black Lincoln pulled over behind her. She'd been walking in Kinnear Park, staring out at the bay and trying to decide whether she should fly to Miami first or try to contact Pender before she left. For all she knew, they were out of the city by now. They might have even fled the country.

She was about to put her key in the front door when she heard the car pull up behind her. The driver turned on his four-ways and stepped out of the vehicle, and for a moment Marie thought he was looking right at her. But she'd never seen him before in her life, and she told herself she was just being paranoid. She turned back to the door. Then the man started yelling.

"Ashley," he called. "Ashley, over here."

Marie watched him jog across the street toward her. No freaking way, she thought.

Nobody knows I'm Ashley McAdams. Not here, not anywhere. But he was beckoning her to come closer.

He was a big guy in expensive clothes and a haircut to match. His face was friendly; he looked like somebody's father, someone who would drive his son to basketball practice and look the other way if the kid happened to steal a couple of his beers. But he was coming her way, and he was calling her Ashley. And that was bad news.

He was about ten feet away from her and coming in fast. "Ashley McAdams?" he said, smiling down at her. Marie felt the bottom fall out of her stomach.

"No." She forced a smile. "Sorry. You must have me confused with somebody."

He narrowed his eyes. "I'm not confused, Ashley. You need to come with me."

"Who are you?" she said. "Are you the police or something?"

"I'm a kind of police, yes."

He can't do anything here, she thought. You're in a public place, and there are people around. Whatever he wants to do, he can't do it here. "Could I see your ID?" she said.

"No." He grabbed her arm. "You need to come with me."

She tried to shake free. She couldn't. "I'll

scream."

He reached inside his coat. "You won't." He looked anything but friendly now. "I'll shoot you dead right here."

Marie looked around, searching for help, trying to gauge her chances. The man said he had a gun, and if he had a gun her chances weren't good. He'd shoot her before she got ten feet away. But if she let him take her, he'd kill her anyway. Someone call the police, she thought. Someone get in on this, *please.*

The man wrenched her arm. "Get in the goddamn car."

Windermere circled the block and turned the car back down toward the apartment building. The Lincoln was still parked curbside, midway down the street, its four-ways flashing. The big guy was across the road, standing in the awning of an old brick walkup, talking to a girl. Talking to *the* girl. "Holy shit," said Stevens. "Is that —"

"Yeah," said Windermere. "Let's go."

She pulled over to the curb and threw on her emergency lights. Then she got out and ran. Stevens followed, dodging cars and a pissed-off cyclist, watching the scene unfold as he came closer. The big guy had his hand on the girl's arm and was gesturing back to the Lincoln. Then he put his hand inside his coat.

"Freeze," Windermere shouted. Heads turned. "FBI!"

The man looked up for a moment, and the girl saw her chance, wrenching free and bolting around back of the apartment. The man took his hand from his coat, and Windermere reached for her sidearm. But the man came up clean, his hands empty. "You take this guy," said Windermere. "I'll get the girl."

She took off around the apartment, and Stevens started for the big guy, who saw him coming and ran, cutting back across the street toward his Lincoln. Stevens was just about on him when the guy reached his car and dove in, punching the gas and lurching forward with tires squealing, shooting off down the street. Stevens watched as the guy kept his foot down, squeezing down the centerline to avoid the traffic, bouncing off cars going both directions and disappearing down the street.

"Goddamn it." Stevens pulled out his cell phone and punched in Seattle PD. Relayed the situation to the dispatcher, who promised radio cars on scene within minutes.

D'Antonio drove, shoving the car hard

down the middle of the road, the engine howling and the car squealing metal on metal. He cleared the block and made a hard right and then doubled back on the next street over, hoping to cut off the girl and the cop in back of the apartment. I had her, he thought. I had the little bitch.

He searched through the trees as he drove, looking for signs of his target. Midway down the block was an alley, and he steered the Lincoln down it, fishtailing, careening off somebody's wall and sliding all over the place.

Halfway down the alley and the girl appeared, just burst out from one of the apartment complexes, and nearly ran right into D'Antonio and the Lincoln. He gunned it, swerving to try and hit her, but she dodged at the last second and ran behind the car.

D'Antonio shifted into reverse and kept his foot on the gas, the wheels shrieking in protest as he steered one-handed back toward the girl, who was fleeing now along the side of the alley, hugging the garages, looking for a way out.

He had the Lincoln lined up, closing fast, and was ready to run the bitch down when someone took a shot through the front windshield and he let his foot off the accelerator, lost focus, and twisted back to face forward, where the girl Fed stood in your classic Weaver stance, aiming the barrel of her Glock right through the windshield and directly at his head. She was yelling something, but he couldn't hear it for the distance and the scraping of the car against the brick of some fucker's garage, but she got what she wanted. He'd let the car slow just for a second, and when he looked back in the rearview mirror the bitch was out of sight, had ducked into somebody's backyard and disappeared, leaving D'Antonio alone with the Fed.

FORTY

Windermere stood in the alley, both hands on her pistol, staring down the driver of the black Lincoln. Whoever this clown thinks he is, she thought, there's no way in hell he's killing my suspect.

She advanced toward the car, hearing the first few sirens in the distance and hoping Stevens was still around front to catch up with the girl. Goddamn this guy, she thought. I had her. "Turn off the car," she called out. "Throw the keys out the window."

The driver stared at her for a few moments, watching her advance. Then he glanced down, and Windermere let out her breath. He's giving up, she thought. At least we can get this guy into custody, try and figure out his beef.

But the driver wasn't giving up. Windermere heard the roar of the engine and the chirp of the tires scrabbling for traction as the car leapt forward toward her. She had time for one shot, but missed, and then she was diving for cover as the Lincoln sped past.

Windermere slammed against a garage door, feeling the rush of the wind in the car's slipstream and the gravel spat back from the tires. She hauled herself to her feet and watched the car speed away down the alley. The car reached the end of the block and made a right-hand turn and disappeared.

Windermere stood in the alley a moment, catching her breath. Then she swore, loud, and walked around to the front of the apartment building to find Stevens.

Marie heard the gunshot and nearly froze up, thinking the big guy was somehow shooting at her from behind the wheel. But she looked back and saw the female agent take aim while she yelled at the driver, and he slowed down just as Marie reached another open gate and ducked through it, cutting across a back lawn, nearly tripping over a sandbox, and then hurrying around the side of the house and back out onto the sidewalk.

She could hear the sirens now, and her heart was pounding. Somewhere behind her was the male police officer, and soon the whole street would be filled with police cars. So she kept her head down, ran as fast as she could out of the neighborhood and down toward Kinnear Park again, where the sound of sirens dissipated and she could slow down to a walk, blending in with the crowds walking the paths and enjoying the sunshine.

This was bad, she knew. Really bad. That guy had found her right at her door. Somehow he knew where she lived. Somehow the police knew, too. They were compromised. They were found out. She had to tell Pender, and she had to get out of Seattle.

She wanted to sit down on a park bench and cry. She was tired and scared, and she had no idea how anyone had figured out where they lived or how the cops had been on her so fast. She wanted to slow things down and think things over, but she knew if she stopped she wouldn't get started again. She'd lie there until the police or the bad guys caught up.

She forced herself to keep moving. Let's figure this out. The apartment's blown. Can't go back. You're stuck with what you've got, right now, on your person. She looked through her purse. No cash. ID and credit cards for Ashley McAdams, Darcy

Wellman, and Rebecca Decoursey. And Marie McAllister. The McAdams alias was done. So was Marie McAllister. The thought made her want to cry again. Marie McAllister was as good as dead. So was Arthur Pender.

Still two good aliases left. Darcy Wellman was used in Detroit, though. One good alias left. Rebecca Decoursey was never used. Marie dug around in her purse some more. What else? The backup burner. Thank God for that. Anything else? A pack of spearmint Trident. What the hell, she thought, trying to think like Arthur. One alias, one cell phone, and some chewing gum. Let's hope that's enough to get out of here safe.

FORTY-ONE

The clerk at the Hollywood Motor Lodge yawned as he watched the Trans Am pull out of the parking lot and onto the highway. Damn, but that car looked familiar. Those kids had been hanging around for a day now, and they hadn't done a thing. Hadn't gone sightseeing, hadn't even gone out to eat. Three or four of them, Florida plates, car parked at the very back of the lot. The clerk wasn't stupid; he'd seen plenty of people come stay at the Hollywood who didn't want to be seen. Question wasn't were they on the run, it's what they were running from. And was it worth getting involved?

The clerk sat down at the front desk and shuffled his newspaper. Had to be the kids from that South Beach shooting, he figured. He dug up the local news and paged through it. Sure enough. Trans Am, kids in their twenties. Three men, one woman, one presumed injured. Probably bleeding on the furniture, the bastard.

Paper said the Dauphin — that was the South Beach hotel — got torn up, said it looked like drugs. Well, damn it. Drug shootings and bullet holes were something the Hollywood didn't quite need. Hard enough keeping customers around without wireless Internet, these days.

He didn't like to get involved in these things, not usually. People had a right to privacy, and who was he to judge? But when their presence started to interfere with another man's commerce, well. It was time to put a stop to things.

The clerk put down the newspaper. He glanced around the lobby. All right, he thought. If you're gonna do it, you're gonna do it. He reached for the phone with one hand and dug around in the desk drawer with the other, reaching for the old .38 while he dialed for the police.

Pender and Sawyer drove the Trans Am into Hollywood on the Federal Highway, Pender at the wheel and Sawyer on the lookout for cops. It gave Pender a funny feeling, driving around in broad daylight, but how else were they going to get out of here? We've gotta swap this rig somehow, he thought.

They found a used-car dealership on a slummy main drag, a little corner lot with a shitty corrugated-iron shack in the back and a razor-wire fence around the perimeter. "These guys will do fine," he told Sawyer. "Probably criminals themselves."

Pender parked the car on a side street, and they wiped it, threw the plates in a dumpster a few blocks down, and hiked onto the lot, where a man in a bad suit and a wrinkled tie shook their hands and squinted through the sun and tried to sell them on a repossessed Porsche Boxster.

Pender talked him away from the sports car long enough to set his eyes on a big Dodge truck, a Durango, and then pulled out his wallet and got the salesman to sign off for seven thousand in cash, no undercoating necessary.

He purchased the car in Ryan Carew's name, and they were off the lot within forty-five minutes and feeling a hell of a lot better about the situation.

"Clothes and a computer," said Sawyer. "And then let's get the hell out of Florida."

They drove until they came to a shopping mall, and Pender found them a computer store inside. He handed Mouse's note to the first salesman he saw and came out ten minutes later with a brand-new computer.

Then they hit JCPenney and set about buying clothes.

Pender hooked himself up with a decent wardrobe and started working on getting Mouse some clothing of his own. Then he caught sight of Sawyer a couple aisles down, working his way through women's wear. Pender wandered over to him. "Don't think they have your size, guy."

Sawyer held up a purple sweater. "You think she'll like this?"

"Who?"

"Tiffany, who else? She can't wear that tank top forever."

Pender shook his head. "Christ, Sawyer."

"What?" Sawyer stared back. "She needs clothes as much as we do."

"She has clothes. At her hotel room."

Sawyer glanced at the sweater once more, then draped it over his arm and kept walking. "I think she'll like it."

Pender sighed. "We get her one change of clothes," he said. "Then we cut her loose."

Pender paid for the clothing, and they made for the exits, stopping once at a drugstore for more bandages and painkillers before retreating to the Durango. They piled all the bags in the back, and Pender was about to climb behind the wheel when his burner started ringing.

"Arthur?" It was Marie. Sounding shaky. "It's me. Where are you?"

"We're in Florida," he told her. "North of Miami. We had a little problem."

"I know," she said. "So did I."

"How so?"

"Arthur, we screwed up," she said. "I don't know how, but there are people after us. There were cops at the apartment. And someone else, too. Someone bad. They were waiting for me. Somehow they figured out where we live."

Pender leaned back against the truck. Felt dizzy all of a sudden. "But you got out all right. You're okay."

"I'm fine," she said. "I'm — yeah, I'm fine. But I gotta get out of Seattle."

"Where are you now?"

"I'm at a motel by the airport. Tell me where you're headed, and I'll fly out there to meet you. I'll fly tonight."

"You have cash? ID?"

"One credit card. One ID. Rebecca Decoursey. McAdams and Wellman are shot. Arthur, so is Marie McAllister. So is Arthur Pender."

Jesus Christ. "That's fine," he said. "You're doing great. Just let me think for a second, and I'll tell you where to meet us."

He closed his eyes, trying to visualize a

map of Florida in his head. Sawyer knocked on the window from inside the Durango. Leaned over and opened the door. "Everything all right?"

"Give me an airport north of here," said Pender.

"Fort Lauderdale?"

"Too close."

"Orlando?"

"Maybe. Can we make Jacksonville?"

"Time frame?"

"Tonight. Tomorrow morning at the latest."

"Yeah," said Sawyer. "It's like three hundred miles."

"Okay." Pender picked up the phone. "Marie? Fly to Jacksonville. Orlando if you can't make it by tomorrow morning. Text me your flight info, and we'll meet you at the airport."

"Jacksonville," said Marie. "Okay."

"Marie," said Pender. "You did great. Everything's going to be fine." He hung up the phone and stood in the parking lot for a minute, staring up at the sky. Cops and somebody else, too. Somebody bad. Beneteau's people. How the hell had they found the apartment? Nobody in the world could connect Marie McAllister and Arthur Pender to the kidnappings. Nobody. But they'd found the apartment, and they'd almost caught Marie. The thought made him sick.

Sawyer knocked on the window again. Pender swung open the door and climbed into the truck. He glanced at Sawyer. "They made us. Marie and me. I don't know how."

"She's all right?"

"She's fine. Terrified, but she got away."

"So Jacksonville."

"Jacksonville," said Pender. "Tonight or tomorrow."

He turned the key in the ignition. He was about to drive away when the phone rang again. He picked it up. "Yeah."

"Pender?" A whisper. "It's Tiffany."

"Tiffany. What's up?"

"Pender, we're at the motel, and I'm afraid," she said, and Pender felt his stomach flip all over again.

"What's going on? Is Mouse okay?"

"Mouse is fine, Pender. But the cops just pulled into the parking lot," she said. "They're out there in a police cruiser, and I think they're coming to get us."

FORTY-TWO

The superintendent jangled his keys as he climbed the steps to the second floor, and the sound echoed through the stairwell. He was an older guy, white hair and thick glasses, and he'd sounded like he was asleep when Stevens knocked on the door.

"That curly-haired girl," he said as he reached the landing. "Unit 204. Lives with her boyfriend."

Stevens glanced back at Windermere. "Which one's her boyfriend?"

"Tall kid," said the super. "Blond hair. Good-looking guy. Nice and quiet."

Carew, thought Stevens. We're getting the two-fer.

The super started down the hall. "They weren't around much. Either of them. Traveled for work, they said."

"You have names for these two?"

"Pender," said the super. "That's the boyfriend. Arthur Pender. His name's on the lease. The girl's Marie something. I can't remember."

They'd lost the girl in the alley when the big guy in the Lincoln had showed up. Stevens hadn't seen her come out on his end, and Windermere hadn't found her when she squeezed back onto the street. The patrol cars were searching the neighborhood but the girl was gone.

Ditto the driver. They'd had Seattle police put a notice to all units to keep an eye out for busted-ass Town Cars, and the FBI's Seattle office had detailed an agent to start looking at livery companies and car rentals as well. But Stevens knew the driver would likely be long gone even if they did manage to find the car.

Windermere hadn't taken either loss very well. Stevens had caught up to her outside of the apartment building, found her staring into her hands, swearing under her breath. He walked up and sat down beside her. "You all right?"

She didn't look up. "I had a shot at them both, Stevens. I didn't get either."

"We'll get them," he told her. "The whole city's looking by now."

"I played that like a rookie. A goddamn city cop. We had a wide-open shot and we missed it." She looked at him and her eyes were dark. "We missed our big chance here, Kirk."

She was right, Stevens knew. Still, it was impossible to stay disappointed when the consolation prize was so good. The Seattle office had come through with a search and seizure warrant almost immediately, and Stevens felt his insides prickling as he and Windermere waited outside the kidnappers' door. Here it is, he thought. The inner sanctum. Even Windermere looked excited again.

The super fumbled with his keys outside unit 204 and then unlocked the door. He pushed it open. "Go ahead, Officers."

As far as interstate crime ring headquarters went, the place was a bit spartan. It was a little one-bedroom apartment: scuffed hardwood floors, plain off-white walls with cheap posters and prints hung up for color. There was a kitchenette off to one side and a bathroom to the other, a bedroom dead ahead and a living room with a modest little couch and a beat-up old coffee table facing a medium-sized TV.

"I thought these kids were supposed to be rich," said Windermere.

"Maybe they spend it all on candy bars."

"They sure don't spend it here."

Stevens looked around. "They're professionals," he said. "They know they can't explain a mansion and a yacht if the IRS figures them out. They've got the money stashed off somewhere."

They searched the place. Windermere took the bed and bathroom, and Stevens took a tour of the rest of the place. The kitchenette was empty — a few dishes drying in the rack and a few more in the cupboards, but that was it. The girl's groceries were in the fridge, and there was a romance novel on the coffee table and a handful of DVDs underneath the TV. Otherwise, the place was bare.

"Stevens," said Windermere. "Come on in here."

Stevens walked into the bedroom — the same modest aesthetic as the rest of the apartment — and found Windermere waiting by the bed, grinning like she'd just won the jackpot. She held a laptop computer in one hand and was gesturing down to her feet, where the girl's duffel bag lay half open on the bedroom floor.

"This is the good stuff," she said. "Let's have a look in that bag."

Stevens looked. Clothes, for starters. Plenty of warm winter clothes. He picked up a pair of jeans and felt something rustling in the pocket. Took it out and examined it

— a receipt. A receipt from a White Castle restaurant in Troy, Michigan. "Bingo," he said.

"Keep looking."

He pushed clothing aside until he came to the bottom of the bag, where he felt out a flat paper envelope and brought it to the surface. He opened it and peered inside. Money. Well-used twenties, and lots of them. "Must be like four grand in here," he told Windermere. "Told you they stashed it somewhere."

"That's nothing," said Windermere. "Four grand must be walking-around money to these kids."

Windermere sat down on the bed and opened the laptop. "Let's call the Seattle office," she said. "Get them to start looking into Pender and his girlfriend. Assuming those aren't aliases, too."

"They're not aliases," said Stevens. "They never expected to be found here. This was home."

"Some home."

"Probably temporary. They wouldn't have wanted to stick around here too long." Stevens took out his phone and called the Seattle office. Asked for a background check on Arthur Pender and Marie —

"McAllister." Windermere looked up from

266

the computer. "Marie McAllister."

"Gotcha," said the Seattle agent, a young guy named Vance. "I'm on it."

"Thanks. Any word on the Lincoln?"

"As a matter of fact," said Vance, "we got a lead on that. None of the big companies reported renting out a Town Car like you described. But we talked to a smaller outfit, Emerald City Cars, said they'd dropped off a black Lincoln at the Hyatt this morning. Rented to an Antonio Pistone of Royal Oak, Michigan."

There it is, Stevens thought. "They get the car back?"

"Not yet."

"All right," he said. "We're heading to the Hyatt right now. Do me a favor and run this Pistone through the computer, see what comes up."

"Already done," Vance told him. "Pistone's a known alias for Alessandro D'Antonio, a made guy in the Bartholdi family. Pretty high up in their Detroit operations, I guess. Kind of a badass."

Stevens thanked him and hung up the phone. D'Antonio, he thought. Out of Michigan. Isn't that cute.

FORTY-THREE

D'Antonio left the car in a parking garage a couple blocks from the Hyatt and walked back to the hotel. Those goddamn cops would be looking for him by now, he knew, and he scanned for plainclothesmen as he walked through the lobby. Nobody seemed to notice his arrival. They haven't come this far, he thought. I still have time.

He took the elevator to his room and packed quickly. Then he made a phone call to book a ticket to Detroit and fast. I would have had her, he thought as he ended the call. If those cops hadn't fucked everything up.

So the kill was blown. Unusual for him, but it happened sometimes. It didn't mean anything. Maybe he was gripping too hard, like a baseball hitter in a slump. Maybe he wanted it too much. Time to step back, regroup, rethink.

The girl wouldn't dare go back to the

apartment. If she was smart, she'd flee the country immediately, try to stay off the grid until the Feds forgot about her. But very few people were that smart. Very few people could walk away when the time came, especially if they still had attachments waiting for them.

The girl would go to Florida. She'd run back to her friends, he was sure of it. That would make it easy to kill the lot of them. He could use her to lead him to the rest of the gang, and there would sure as shit be no more screwups when D'Antonio caught the ringleader.

He got back on the phone and cancelled the ticket. Paid two hundred dollars in fees, but if he was right it would be worth it. He ended the call without booking a new ticket, grabbed his overnight bag and took the elevator back down to the lobby, where he checked out of the hotel and climbed into a yellow cab.

"The airport," he told the driver, hoping the girl wasn't too far gone already.

Stevens kept the Nissan close to the taxi, not wanting to risk losing D'Antonio on the drive out of town. They'd picked him up outside the Hyatt within an hour of Vance's call, and now, Stevens hoped, they could

269

use the bad guy to lead them to the girl. Windermere was on the phone as he drove, rapping away to Vance at headquarters with a shopping list of things she wanted done.

"You got that computer I sent you, right?" she was saying. "There's a picture of the girl on there. We need that picture in the hands of every airport security guard like yesterday. Then you can look for pictures of the other three goofballs and get them on the Wanted list. Anything come back for McAllister and Pender?"

She listened for a moment. "No kidding. Talk to their families and see if you can get anything there. Anywhere they might run to, that sort of thing. Try and ID the other two kidnappers. What?" she said. "No. Hadn't heard that."

She listened. "Could be related. Hard to say. Let me know if you hear anything."

She hung up the phone and turned to Stevens. "Vance says McAllister and Pender were students at the U of Washington a few years back. She got a history degree. He got a master's in English lit."

"Christ," said Stevens. "How do a couple of nerds suddenly become kidnappers?"

"Couldn't get real jobs, I guess. Vance also said there was a big ruckus down in Miami yesterday. Wondered if we'd heard about it."

Stevens shrugged. "Nope."

"Couple of kids got into a shooting match down on South Beach. Police found two bodies shot up in a room at the Dauphin. Big-time hard-asses. Known killers. But they got shot by their own guns."

"Argument?"

"Police say no way. There were guests in that hotel room. Three or four kids. Three guys and a girl."

"No kidding," said Stevens. "You're thinking it's them."

Windermere glanced at him. "I guess we'll find out."

D'Antonio's cab signaled right and took the Sea-Tac exit. Stevens followed, and the two cars skirted the runways for a few miles before reaching the terminal, where D'Antonio's car pulled over under the Delta departures sign. "Hang back," said Windermere. "Let me out here and go grab a parking spot."

Stevens slowed to a stop just long enough for Windermere to climb out of the car. Then he drove on as Windermere followed D'Antonio, keeping her distance. She watched the big man walk up to the Delta sales desk and loitered nearby as he booked a ticket. He paid by credit card, flirting with the Delta agent, who smiled and said something funny and they both laughed. Then he took his ticket and picked up his bag and walked away from the counter, joining the crush of travelers headed for the security gates.

Windermere gave him a minute or two and then walked over to the same Delta agent just as Stevens came into the terminal. He spotted her quickly and came over. "Where'd he go?"

Windermere pointed to the gates. "That way." She turned to the Delta agent and flashed her badge. "FBI, ma'am. Quick question."

The woman looked up, startled. "Yeah?"

"That big teddy bear who just bought a ticket. Where's he going?"

"He's going to Miami on the red-eye," she said. "Is there a problem? I can call security and have him stopped."

Windermere shook her head. "Don't worry about it. But maybe you could hook us up. You have any other flights to Miami tonight?"

The agent punched a few keys and booked them through Detroit, touching down in Miami an hour and a half after D'Antonio. Windermere got on the phone with Vance. "Vance," she said. "Listen up. You were right about the Miami job. I need you to get a picture of Alessandro D'Antonio to the FBI office in Miami and tell them to meet our guy when he gets off his plane."

She read him the flight information. "No arrests. Just tail him. Also, ship a picture of McAllister to the Miami airport people. Tell them to keep an eye out for the girl as well. All right?"

She hung up the phone. Stevens examined the tickets. "You know what," he said. "If those kids got into so much trouble in Miami, they probably didn't stick around."

Windermere frowned. "What are you saying?"

He shrugged. "If I'd just shot up a hotel room in South Beach, I think I'd get the hell out of the neighborhood. I'm just thinking we should cover our bases if she's headed somewhere other than Miami."

"You think they're on the move," said Windermere. "Fine. We'll notify airport security at Fort Lauderdale, Tampa, Orlando, Jacksonville, and Tallahassee. Cool? If they made it out of Florida, we've still got D'Antonio to lead us to them. But we'll put the word out and maybe we'll get lucky."

She picked up the phone and dialed. "Agent Vance," she said, when he came on the line. "Do you hate me yet?"

FORTY-FOUR

Tiffany Prentice stood at the window, clutching the phone. The police cruiser was outside in the parking lot, and the officer, a tall, scary-looking guy in boots and sunglasses, was talking to the motel manager. The manager was pointing down the line of units to their own, and Tiffany shrank back, afraid he'd seen her.

"Tiffany," Pender said from the other end of the line. "You've gotta handle this. Take a deep breath and let's figure this out."

"Okay." Tiffany glanced around the room. Mouse was laid out on the bed, pale as the sheets. The bloody towels were draped all around him.

"First thing you need to do is hide Mouse. Put him in the bathroom or something and make sure he stays quiet. Get rid of the towels, too. Anything bloody, hide it. Act like you're there alone."

"Okay."

"Charm him. Stall him. We'll be there in a half hour, but you gotta hold him off until then. Get him out of there if you can. Do you think you can do that?"

"Yeah," said Tiffany. You can do this, she thought. You've charmed cops before. They're human beings. They're men.

"Just don't get caught. You gotta be strong, all right?"

"All right." Tiffany ended the call. She turned back from the window. "Okay, Mr. Mouse," she said. "You gotta get moving."

She drew the curtains and moved Mouse to the bathroom. Set him up in the bathtub on a bed of bloody towels and told him to keep quiet. Fortunately, she thought, the bathroom was at the back of the unit. If they were lucky, the cop wouldn't even see it. Working quickly, she threw the rest of the towels into the bathroom and tossed the bloody bedspread in behind. Then she looked in at Mouse one more time and shut the door.

She looked around the motel room. The place looked okay. She moved some of the garbage out of sight, and then she heard the knock on the door.

Deep breath. Tiffany glanced at herself in the mirror. She ran her fingers through her hair. Pouted. Surveyed her outfit and tied the back of her tank top to show off her tanned stomach. The knocks came again, louder.

Tiffany walked to the door and opened it partway. Stood in the entryway and stared out at the cop. He loomed over her, massive and muscular, all coiled tension and the promise of violence. Tiffany looked him up and down. Forced a smile onto her face. "Good morning, Officer," she said. "What can I do for you?"

The officer examined her behind his mirrored sunglasses. He peered over her, trying to get a look inside the room. Tiffany kept the door closed as tight as possible, trying to act casual. The officer cleared his throat. "Ma'am, my name's Officer Cope, with the Hollywood Police Department. Do you mind if I have a look around the room?"

"I'm sorry," said Tiffany. "My friend's sleeping inside."

"That's fine," said Cope. "She can put a robe on. This will only take a minute."

Tiffany kept the smile on her face. "Did you say you had a warrant, Officer?"

Cope stared down at her. "I beg your pardon?"

"A search warrant."

The officer sighed. "You're asking me if I have a warrant."

"Uh-huh."

"You have something you want to hide in there?"

Tiffany shook her head. "Nothing more than a naked roommate," she said. "But my daddy always told me never let a policeman search your stuff unless he has a warrant."

"Oh yeah?" said Cope. "Who's your daddy?"

"Andrew Prentice. Maybe you've heard of him?"

Cope shook his head. "Afraid not."

"Oh well," said Tiffany. "Maybe you want to phone that one in. He was on the Forbes 400 last year. So was his lawyer."

She held her ground and held her smile, feeling her insides turn to Jell-O as the officer examined her. "What's your name, ma'am?"

"Tiffany Prentice, sir," she said. "You want to see my ID?"

"What are you doing here in Hollywood?"

"Vacation. My best friend and I decided to take a little winter break. You know how those midterms get."

"Why aren't you out at the beach if you're here on vacation?"

Tiffany winked at him. "We were out late last night. Didn't get much sleep. We'll be out again later, don't you worry."

The policeman looked around the parking lot. He was getting frustrated, Tiffany could tell. "You got something you want to hide in there, don't you?"

"No, sir."

"I could step past you and walk through that door right now," he said. "Tell the judge I saw drugs on the table. Call it probable cause."

"Go ahead," said Tiffany. "Do what you have to do. But make sure your department has a good lawyer first. I'd hate to see a good police officer like you lose his job because he was afraid of a little bit of paper-work."

Cope swore. Then he spat down onto the pavement. "I'll be back," he said. "Count on it."

Tiffany watched him walk back to his car. "I look forward to it, Officer," she said. "Just don't forget that warrant next time."

Cope stood at his patrol car for a minute, shielding his eyes, staring back at her. She gave him a little wave, and he climbed into his car and pulled it around the front of the building and out of sight. Tiffany watched him go. Then she closed the door and leaned back against it and sunk down to the ground, her whole body shaking. She sat

there for a long time, trying to catch her
breath.

FORTY-FIVE

The police were nowhere in sight when they pulled back into the motel lot. Pender drove slowly to the back of the building and parked far away from the unit, anticipating a trap and knowing there was someone in the motel who must have sold them out. "What do you think?" he asked Sawyer as they sat in the Durango. "Coast is clear?"

Sawyer gazed out at the parking lot. Nobody moving. A couple beat-up old road warriors and an RV from Ohio that had been sitting there since they'd arrived. "Looks good to me," he said.

They got out of the Durango and walked cautiously along the back of the building until they got to the room. Pender knocked on the door, and after a moment, it opened a crack. Tiffany peered out.

"Open up," Pender said. "It's us."

She swung the door open. "Holy crap," she said. She ambushed Pender with a monster hug. "We actually made it."

Pender hugged her back despite himself. She did good, he thought. Saved our asses.

"Where's Mouse?" said Sawyer.

"Bathroom." Tiffany backed away from Pender. "Holy crap, that was cool."

"How did you do it?" Pender asked.

Tiffany laughed. "I played the poor little rich girl. Told him he'd better have a warrant, and if he didn't, my dad would sue him and his whole department. I did good, right?"

"You were perfect."

"So I can stay?"

Pender paused. "I don't know yet."

"Come on, Pender," she said. "I just lied to the cops. I'm a criminal, too."

Pender stared at her a long moment. Then he sighed. "You can stay. For now."

Sawyer poked his head in the bathroom. Then he glanced back at Pender and Tiffany. "When's the last time you checked on Mouse?"

Tiffany frowned. "I was with him the whole time."

Sawyer gave her a long stare. "Boss, you better have a look in there."

Pender walked over and peered into the bathroom. Mouse was lying in the bathtub on a pile of bloody towels. He was dead pale, his head leaned back against the tile, his eyes closed. Pender turned to Tiffany. "Was he conscious when you left him?"

"He was tired," she said. "He said he was tired."

Sawyer knelt by the bathtub and felt around on Mouse's neck. After a few seconds, he looked up, relieved. "He's got a pulse."

"Of course I have a pulse," said Mouse, opening his eyes a crack. "I'm just taking a nap in here. Can't a brother get some sleep?"

Sawyer stood up, forced a laugh. "Fucking guy."

"How are you feeling, Mouse?" asked Pender.

"I feel like shit," said Mouse. "Somebody shot me, I'm tired as hell, and I'm sleeping in a bathtub. How would you feel?"

Tiffany helped Mouse to his feet. He leaned on her, half grinning at the other guys. "You keep Tiffany around and I'm sure I'll be fine," he said.

"We'll keep that in mind," said Pender. "Now get your ass in gear. We're moving out in ten."

They drove out of Hollywood and headed north on Interstate 95, and Pender watched Mouse in the rearview mirror as he drove.

His friend was lying with his head in Tiffany's lap as she played with his hair, the two of them curled up like a couple of middle-school kids after the dance. Sawyer, Pender noticed, was ignoring the lovebirds. Fine. The absolute last thing they needed right now was a fight over a woman.

He watched Mouse cuddle with Tiffany. The kid could play tough all he wanted, but sooner or later he was going to need fixing and all the drugstore doctoring in the world wasn't going to make him better. As they'd packed up the Durango, Pender had noticed his friend couldn't even lift his right arm. He's probably got nerve damage, he thought. If we don't get him to a hospital, he might never use that arm again. "Mouse," he said, catching his friend's eye in the mirror. "How are you feeling?"

Mouse looked up from Tiffany's lap. He winked at Pender. "A lot better now."

"For real, though. We gotta get you to a hospital."

Mouse struggled to sit up. "What? Pender, no way. I'm cool."

"I saw you back there. You couldn't lift your arm at all."

"It's just superficial," said Mouse. "I'll be fine in a few days."

Pender stared at him. "Come on, Mouse."

Mouse sighed. He sank back into Tiffany's lap. "All right," he said finally. "I just gotta get us some money if we're going to bribe a doctor."

"No problem," said Pender. "You can do it tomorrow after we pick up Marie."

Mouse stretched out and closed his eyes and Pender turned his attention back to the highway. Sawyer glanced over at him. "Jacksonville?"

Pender nodded. "Delta 1720. She gets in at eight-thirty tomorrow morning. We'll crash at the airport tonight and meet her tomorrow."

"You need me to drive?"

"I'm fine."

Sawyer nodded. He leaned against the window and closed his eyes, and within a few minutes Pender could hear him snoring softly. By the time they hit Boca Raton, Mouse and Tiffany were out, too. Pender drove in silence, watching the sun set over the lowlands and the brake lights flashing on the highway.

FORTY-SIX

D'Antonio touched down in Miami at dawn and immediately knew that something was wrong. The terminal building was filled with cops of all kinds, security guards and plain-clothesmen, everyone pretending they weren't looking his way when he walked through the terminal past them.

So the Feds had made him. Moreover, they'd figured out he was headed for Miami. D'Antonio wasn't worried. Cops — even Feds — weren't much of a threat. They stuck out in crowds and got bogged down with rules. And the Bartholdis kept excellent lawyers. If the FBI wanted to book him on some bullshit charge, they could slap on the cuffs and then get slapped with a lawsuit.

To his surprise, though, the cops let him walk right out of the terminal and into Zeke's waiting Coupe de Ville without so much as a word. D'Antonio glanced back at the exit once and saw the security guard looking straight at him. They locked eyes for a second, and then D'Antonio climbed into the car. "Drive fast," he told Zeke. "We're going to have tails."

Zeke swore and stepped on the gas. "You bring a fucking tail on me?"

"Relax," said D'Antonio. "What are you, a rookie?"

Zeke swore again and glanced in the rearview mirror as they swung out into traffic. Behind them an unmarked Crown Victoria pulled out a few cars back. "Got him," he said.

"Good. Give him some time and then lose him."

They cruised for a couple miles, putting space between them and the airport. Traffic was light, and Zeke kept the Caddy rolling at a clip. D'Antonio lowered the window and enjoyed the sunshine on his face. Today's going to be a good day, he thought. Just as soon as we lose these cops.

He dug out his BlackBerry and called his contact at Miami PD. The guy answered late, his voice far off and alien. "Time is it?"

"Time to get up," said D'Antonio. "What do you have for me?"

"Aw, fuck. Where are you?"

"I'm here."

"All right, I got bad news and worse news. You wanna hear it?"

D'Antonio frowned. "What's up?"

"First thing is that damn computer nearly blew up when we tried to hack it. It's toast. Totally erased itself right in front of us."

"Jesus Christ."

"I'm sorry, D," said the cop. He paused. "The other thing is they found the kids holed up in a motel in Hollywood."

"And that's bad why?"

"Motel owner called the police. First car on the scene was a patrolman from Hollywood PD. Cope, his name was. Real straight man. Always by the rules, this guy. He gets stood up at the door by some chick demands to see a warrant."

"Motherfuck. The guy never heard of probable cause?"

"She was some rich girl, said Daddy would sue the force if he played it wrong. He took her serious and bailed out, spent the rest of the day trying to wrangle a warrant from a judge on a golf course."

"And the kids?"

"Got away clean. Motel owner called back in the evening, said the room was empty. Nothing but a pile of bloody towels and some empty bottles of aspirin. He didn't see them leave."

"Great," said D'Antonio. "You just let a bunch of kids make a fool out of your whole department. Do you clowns have any leads whatsoever?"

"Not so much." The guy paused. "Maybe your Feds will come up with something."

D'Antonio ended the call. He felt like chucking his phone out the window, but took a deep breath, drawing it in slow and then letting the air out.

Zeke looked over at him. "You all right, boss?"

"Those kids were in Hollywood," said D'Antonio. "Cops found them, let them go. Couldn't get a warrant in time, and they vanished."

"No shit," said Zeke. "They still got Carlos's Trans Am?"

Good point, thought D'Antonio. He picked up his cell phone and called back his contact. The guy picked up quick this time. "Johnston."

"It's D. Make damn sure Hollywood PD is looking for an orange Trans Am. Those kids probably dumped the car somewhere before they blew. Tell the state patrol, too."

D'Antonio pocketed the phone again. He swiveled in his seat and made the unmarked Crown Vic a couple cars behind, hanging back. Those Feds wanted to use him as a tour guide, fuck them. He turned to Zeke. "All right, enough," he said. "Lose the goddamn tail."

Zeke nodded, signaled left, and pulled into the left-hand turn lane. Then at the last possible moment, he swerved right, cutting across three lanes of traffic and standing on the accelerator as horns blared and tires squealed behind him. The Caddy rocketed down the side street, and Zeke made another quick right and then a left before he finally let off the gas. He glanced in the rearview mirror. "Tail's gone," he said.

"Good," said D'Antonio. "Now take me to the beach."

FORTY-SEVEN

Marie sat up, gasping, as the plane banked and turned into its final approach above Jacksonville. She'd spent the night dozing, drifting between her seat in the plane and a nightmare of Pender and the boys and the bad things they'd stirred up. Now she blinked, rubbing her eyes, and stared out the window and down toward the Jacksonville airport. Arthur was right, she thought. We should have stayed together after Detroit. At least if something happens now, it will happen to both of us.

The plane touched down on the runway, bounced and shuddered and finally found solid ground. Within five minutes they had taxied to the gate, and Marie shouldered her bag and made her way up into the terminal, following the flow of passengers toward the baggage claim area, her senses deadened by the sleepless night.

She walked through the baggage claim,

searching the room for Arthur's sandy hair and not finding it. She kept walking, found an exit, and walked out into the sunlight and the diesel-exhaust air of the loading area.

Marie looked up and down the sidewalk. Parked cars, buses, a line of taxis, and a crowd of passengers. And twenty feet away, leaning up against a big blue SUV, Arthur Pender stood waiting for her, watching the steady stream of arrivals. He seemed to see her at the same time she saw him, and they smiled at each other as she tried to push her way through the riptide crowd.

But as she came closer, she could see his smile disappear. He was staring at her now, shaking his head almost imperceptibly, and she stopped, confused, in midstream. Arthur was pale now. Marie shrugged at him, feeling panic start to well.

Then she felt a hand on her shoulder, sudden and firm. Someone spoke her name in her ear. "Marie McAllister? Could you come with me, please?"

Pender watched as the plainclothes cop double-checked the photocopy in his hand and then started toward Marie. The man caught up with her, and Pender saw the look of panic on his girlfriend's face as he touched her shoulder and turned her toward him. The cop was flanked by two uniformed security guards, and they stood by, warily, as the crowds started to thin out around them.

Pender watched Marie answer the cop, feeling his stomach churn as she stared across the sidewalk at him, plaintive. He shook his head at her, tried to blend in to the background while his brain screamed at him to act. *Save her. Do something.*

The cop kept his arm on Marie's shoulder and turned her back toward the terminal building. One security guard was scanning the sidewalk, and Pender turned away, watching the scene from the corner of his eye. The other security guard produced a pair of handcuffs. If there was a time to move, it was now.

Pender pushed off from the Durango and started toward Marie, trying to figure out a plan. Easiest way might be to get physical, try to jar Marie away from the cops and then run with her. Marie was struggling now, fighting off the police, and a crowd was gathering around her. Pender shoved bystanders aside, trying to get to his girl-friend before the cops put the handcuffs on her, dimly aware that more security guards were appearing from the exits now. A siren whooped, and an airport police car pulled up to the curb. The whole goddamn place was a trap.

Pender kept pushing, getting closer now, people starting to complain as he jostled past them. He felt a hand on his own shoulder, and he swung around, fists balled, ready to fight, but when he turned it was Sawyer holding him back. "We gotta go," Sawyer told him. "We stay here they catch us all."

"They got Marie," said Pender. "We have to get her back."

"Impossible. There's cops everywhere." Sawyer leaned close, hissed in Pender's ear. "We got about a minute and a half before we're in cuffs, too, bro. We gotta move."

He grabbed Pender's other shoulder and spun him around. Pender struggled but Sawyer held tight, pushing him back to the Durango while he twisted to watch the cop turn Marie back to the terminal. Sawyer threw him into the passenger seat and dashed around to the driver's side as Pender stared back at Marie. She was fighting, but she was losing, and just before the police pushed her into the airport, she swung her head around and caught Pender's eye, her face a mask of desperation.

Then she was gone, disappeared inside

the building, and Sawyer was speeding out into traffic. Pender doubled over in the passenger seat, gasping for breath and replaying the last moments in his head, seeing over and over the look of resignation in Marie's eyes when she realized he wasn't coming to save her.

FORTY-EIGHT

Stevens and Windermere touched down in Miami just after nine in the morning, and they were on a plane to Jacksonville by a quarter to ten. Agent Vance had paged them as soon as they touched down in Dade County, passing along the good news about Marie McAllister and hooking them up with two new tickets north. It was six in the morning in Seattle. If the kid had slept at all, it was a miracle.

"Pender's people live out in Port Angeles," he told Windermere, "but I made a little midnight visit to the McAllister family home. Couple of sleepy doctors. Surprised as anyone to hear their daughter was a fugitive."

"Not the kind of thing you tell your parents," said Windermere.

"True enough. I showed them a couple pictures from Marie's laptop. The parents didn't have a clue, but the girl's sister recognized the other two suspects. The big guy's Matt Sawyer. Seattle kid, father's in advertising. He went to school here as well. The little one's Ben Stirzaker — she kept calling him Mouse, whatever that means. Kid's supposed to be some kind of computer genius."

"Can you e-mail this stuff?" said Windermere. "We'll review it when we touch down in Jacksonville."

"On it," said Vance. He paused. "One more thing. This guy D'Antonio slipped our tail. Miami guys lost him about a half hour after he left airport property."

D'Antonio's driver, a Hispanic cat in a boat of a Cadillac, had managed to duck the Feds without much of a problem, Vance explained. The agents made the driver as one Eddy "Zeke" Sevillano, a middleman in the Miami drug and prostitution racket, but so far, nobody could pin down where the man slept at night — or how he tied in with Alessandro D'Antonio. "Either way," said Vance, "this guy D'Antonio's clearly a pro."

"The bastard nearly killed me," said Windermere. "We catch up with him again, and I'll show him who's pro. Keep looking for him. In the meantime, we still have the girl."

"She'll have to do," said Vance.

"She'll more than do, Vance. She'll get us the rest of her gang. You running out of things to do yet?"

Vance laughed. "Pile it on, lady."

"First things first, let's freeze their bank accounts," said Windermere. "We know they've got money somewhere, so let's find it and take it from them. And get McAllister transferred to the Jacksonville regional office. We'll interview her when we're on the ground."

Then they were on another plane, Windermere bouncing in her seat as the tiny commuter jet roared down the runway. She looks pumped, thought Stevens, watching his partner humming to herself, her eyes darting to look out the window and then back around to the cabin. She couldn't wait for the plane to land.

Stevens couldn't wait, either. He had a splitting headache, and the little commuter plane scared him worse than any big jetliner. But he was pumped up as well. The hunch had paid off. Somehow, somebody in the Jacksonville airport had recognized Marie McAllister and had managed to corral her before she disappeared again. It was a goddamn Hail Mary and it had worked, and now Stevens was eager to get into an interrogation room with McAllister and see what she had to say.

The flight touched down in Jacksonville at a quarter past eleven, and Windermere and Stevens were first in the terminal. They were met by a big plainclothes cop named French and an FBI agent in a pantsuit with a briefcase in one hand and a tray of Starbucks in the other. Windermere smiled wide when she saw her. "Wendy Gallant," she said. "What the hell are you doing here?"

Gallant smiled identically. "Jacksonville, baby. Moving up in the world. You still drinking lattes?"

"As long as you're buying." Windermere reached for a cup. She turned to Stevens. "Agent Gallant was my mentor in Miami. Taught me everything I know about police work."

"Bullshit," said Gallant. "You taught yourself." She smiled at Stevens. "I swear Windermere here didn't sleep the first year and a half out of Quantico. Spent her life in the field, on the street. Any assignment you had, she was there."

Windermere shrugged. "The street's a hell of a lot more exciting than classrooms and theory. I wanted to get out and do something."

"Do something." Gallant winked at Stevens. "This girl took down four Miami

PD undercover drug runners before the AD could finally corral her."

"Goddamn city cops," said Windermere. "A bunch of pylons."

"Anyway, it sounds like the teacher's become the student. Got a phone call from an Agent Vance this morning telling me to get my ass to the airport to help out with your little kidnapping situation. So I brought you coffee, boss."

"Don't call me boss," said Windermere. "Stevens runs the show around here."

"If you can stand taking orders from a state policeman," said Stevens. He shook Gallant's hand.

"You're FBI now, big guy," Windermere said, punching his arm. She turned back to Gallant. "Where's the prisoner?"

French cleared his throat. "We got a holding cell in the security zone. I'll take you to her."

The plainclothesman led them through the airport, and Stevens walked beside him. "You spotted the girl getting off the plane?" he said.

French nodded without breaking stride. "She was on the fifth or sixth flight in this morning. You guys sent a pretty good picture."

"She go quietly?"

"Hell, no," said French. "Had to cuff her on the sidewalk. Took three guys to get her inside. Kept screaming about there'd been a mistake. Called herself Rebecca something."

"You get a look at any of the other suspects?"

The plainclothesman shook his head. "Had our hands full with the girl. Whole damn sidewalk was a zoo." He glanced at Stevens. "Guess we should have let her lead us to the rest of them, but we didn't want to lose her. Your man Vance said you've had a bit of trouble keeping her contained."

Stevens nodded. "She's been slippery. Glad you guys were on the ball."

French led them along a back hallway, keyed a code into a heavy door, and swung it open, gesturing Stevens inside. He held it until Windermere and Gallant were inside as well and then closed it firm behind.

The airport's security office was all linoleum and fluorescent light, generic plastic office furniture, and a sound track of electronic chirps and whirls. Beside the door was a bulletin board hung with security notices and Wanted posters. Marie McAllister's face was tacked dead center.

"This way," said French. He took out a key ring and fit it into a locked door at the

300

rear of the room, swinging the door out and open. He gestured inside and Stevens peered in, finding himself on the threshold of a miserable green box, empty save a bench and a stainless-steel toilet and one solitary occupant: in the corner of the room, curled up on the unforgiving bench, the girl who called herself Rebecca Decoursey sat swollen-eyed and hunched, her knees to her chest, her curly hair flat and lifeless.

FORTY-NINE

"God*damn*." Pender punched the wall. *"Motherfucker."*

He punched the wall again and pulled back, his hand already starting to throb. He looked around for something to throw and then he stopped and closed his eyes and forced himself to steady his breathing.

They were holed up in the Jacksonville Fly-Inn, about a mile and a half from the airport. Sawyer, Mouse, and Tiffany sat arrayed around the room, watching him, Sawyer in a chair in the corner and Tiffany and Mouse curled up on the bed. Pender paced the room. He'd been pacing for over an hour, and he couldn't make himself stop. Every time he closed his eyes, he saw Marie's face and he felt sick all over again.

Sawyer caught his eye. "We had to let her go."

"We could have done something," said Pender. "We could have snatched her and thrown her in the truck and ran. We didn't need to leave her."

Sawyer stood. "Pender, man. Did you see that place? Cops everywhere. If we hung around, we would have gone down with her. We had to get out."

"Bullshit."

"We can't do her any good if we're on the inside with her, bro." Sawyer put his arm around him. "If you and I get picked up, then we're all screwed. Mouse needs us, and Tiffany doesn't know the score yet. We gotta be cool, all right?"

Pender looked at Sawyer. Finally, he nodded. "You're right," he said. He ran his fingers through his hair. "I just cannot believe this is happening."

Mouse cleared his throat. "Um, guys."

Sawyer turned around. "What?"

"You said you were like twenty feet away from her when it happened, right?" Mouse glanced at Pender. "Are you sure you didn't get made?"

Sawyer looked at Pender. Neither man replied.

"There could be cops on our asses right now," said Mouse. "If they got our plates, we're screwed. We need to ditch the ride fast and get out of the city."

Pender shook his head. "No way. We're

not leaving until we spring Marie."

"Pender —"

Tiffany spoke up from the bed. "You've known this girl a long time, right? You've been with her for a while?"

"Four years," said Pender.

Tiffany nodded. "Okay."

"Why?"

She stayed quiet for a second. Then she sighed. "Don't get mad, Pender. I'm not saying she'll flip. If you trust her, that's great. But look, they probably make it damn tough in those interrogation rooms."

Mouse struggled to sit up. "She's not going to flip. She knows we have a plan."

They had talked about this — after Tucson, when a stray city cop in an unmarked Impala nearly busted up the whole enterprise. Snuck up on Mouse outside the target's home, flashed his cherry lights, and informed Mouse his taillight was busted. Nearly gave the kid a heart attack.

Mouse stayed polite and somehow stayed calm and the cop let him off with a warning. The target paid the ransom and the cop never made the connection. But for weeks afterward, Pender felt sick when he considered what might have gone wrong.

If we're going to be professional criminals, he'd decided, we have to figure out what we do if someone gets picked up.

"Let 'em rot," Sawyer had announced. "It'll probably be Mouse, anyway."

"Mouse is indispensable," Marie told him. "You're not."

"Fine," said Sawyer. "Then I'll rot. Big deal. I've done jail time before. If I'm dumb enough to get caught, I deserve to go back."

"You did an overnight stay for a bar brawl," said Marie. "Don't talk like you're some kind of federal hard-time badass."

Pender put his hands up. "Sawyer's got a point," he said. "A professional crew would take the charge and keep quiet."

"No snitching," said Mouse.

"We don't talk to the police," said Pender. "That's the first thing. Whatever they say, they're lying. Don't take the bait. We'll get you a lawyer, and he'll get you out."

Marie looked at him. "And what if he can't?"

Pender smiled at her. "With our money, he can."

Now, stuck in a Jacksonville hotel room two years down the road, Pender thought back to that conversation and wanted to implode. I should have kept her safer, he thought. I shouldn't have let her go home on her own.

He stopped pacing and breathed again,

slow. He took out his wallet and pulled out a business card. I planned for this, he thought. I just thought the scenario would remain hypothetical. But if we keep cool and stay rational, we can get Marie out in no time. Pender walked to the phone and punched in a Seattle number. Then he waited. He looked at Sawyer, forced a smile. "Friends in high places," he said.

Someone picked up. "Torrance and Steinberg," said the man. "Victor Carter speaking."

"Victor," said Pender. "It's Arthur Pender. Long time."

There was a long pause. "Arthur Pender," the man said finally. "Long time is right. Must be two years at least."

"I have a situation, Victor," said Pender. "One of my friends is in trouble. Kidnapping. And murder. She's innocent, but the FBI is involved. We need a lawyer, and quick."

Carter let out a low whistle. "You're talking big bucks here."

"Big bucks is fine."

"I mean, a hundred thousand just to retain anyone in this office. Can you do that kind of money?"

"A hundred thousand," said Pender, "is not a problem. How soon can you be in

Jacksonville?"

"Florida? Tomorrow evening, I guess." Carter exhaled. "I just need to see the money first. It's a big commitment we're talking."

"I understand," Pender told him. "I'll get you the money. No problem."

Pender hung up the phone. He turned back to the room. "Got us a lawyer," he said. "How soon can we get a hundred grand for a retainer?"

Mouse winked at him. "An hour or so, tops," he said. "Tiff, can you hand me that computer?"

Sawyer caught Pender's eye as Tiffany handed over the computer. "We still don't know if we got away clean from the airport, boss."

Pender stayed quiet a moment. "Christ," he said finally. "All right. We keep moving. We get a new ride and some new IDs. We get the money to Carter, and he springs Marie."

Pender turned to Mouse. "Can you handle new aliases?"

Mouse stared down at his screen. "You know it."

"Time frame?"

"Twenty-four hours to get us into the system. A few days for the paperwork."

"We need some cash, too," said Pender. "I'm down to scratch. And we gotta find you a doctor, probably out of state. I don't think we can risk it in Florida."

"Georgia's up the road," said Sawyer. "We could do Atlanta or Savannah."

"Let's think on it," said Pender. "The lawyer will be here tomorrow evening. With any luck we can spring Marie and get Mouse fixed within days."

Mouse pounded into his keyboard, frowned. Punched a few more keys and came up frowning harder. "Except, Pender," he said, "we might have a problem."

"What now?"

Mouse looked up at him, his eyes wide. "They got our bank accounts," he said. "All our money's frozen solid."

FIFTY

Marie rested her elbows on the desk and leaned forward, her shoulders hunched and her eyes low. She stared down at the table, counting its pockmarks, imagining she was on a beach in the Maldives with Pender, a million miles away.

The FBI agents had taken her from the airport to an interrogation room in the Jacksonville field office. They'd ignored her on the drive, riding in silence except for the radio, and then they'd dumped her in her shitty little room and locked the door and let her sit and think about her situation for what seemed like days.

She sat in the little room and waited, and she closed her eyes and tried not to be sick. The inevitable had happened, as she guessed she'd always known it would. For all of Pender's careful planning, someone was bound to catch up to them sooner or later.

Marie closed her eyes again, and she saw

Beneteau's body and the scared, sallow faces of the targets before him — Martin Warner and Robert Thompson and the rest. She saw their terrified wives and their families. This was bound to happen, she thought. We made our choice, and we knew they'd come after us.

She knew Pender was out there, somewhere, finding her a lawyer and figuring a way to get her out of jail. As the hours passed in that miserable little room, though, Marie pictured Beneteau's children and wondered why she deserved to be free.

Then the FBI agents came back, the younger woman and the man, and they stood watching her from different corners of the room, letting her feel their eyes on her as she stared down at the table, determined to ignore them.

Finally the man cleared his throat. "Marie, I'm Agent Stevens and this is Agent Windermere. Are you ready to answer some questions?"

Marie ignored him. Even if she deserved it, she wasn't giving up. They'd talked about what to do if someone got caught. Pender said keep your head down. Don't volunteer information. Don't listen. Don't talk.

The lawyer's coming, she thought. You'll have plenty of time to feel guilty when you're in the Maldives.

She stared down at the table. Windermere stepped forward. "Wake up, Marie," she said. "We got you. You killed Donald Beneteau in Detroit, and you kidnapped Terry Harper in Minneapolis. You're in deep shit, girl. It's time to start cooperating."

Marie kept her head down. "My name is Rebecca Decoursey," she said. "I'd like to speak to my lawyer."

"We've got witnesses who put you at the murder, Marie," said Stevens. "Said they saw you dump the body."

"That right there would put you away for life," said Windermere. "Hate to see a pretty girl like you take a murder rap just because she was too stupid to reach out for the lifeline."

"My name is Rebecca Decoursey," Marie said. "I'd like to talk to my lawyer."

"You want to talk to a lawyer, fine," said Stevens. "We can't stop you. But you gotta know that once you go down that path, anything we could have done to help you gets erased."

Pender said they'd say that. He said that they were lying, that detectives were like used-car salesmen, willing to say whatever it took to get you to close the deal. If they're talking, they don't have you, he'd said.

They're trying to bluff you into giving yourself away.

"We talked to your parents," said Stevens. He let out a long stream of air. "Man oh man, are they disappointed."

"My parents are dead," said Marie. Then she wished like hell she hadn't. Quit volunteering information. "You're supposed to let me talk to my lawyer."

Stevens winked at Windermere. "No," he said. "Your parents aren't dead. Your parents are Michael and Allison McAllister of 56 Hawthorne Way in Bothell, Washington. They're still alive, Marie. And you broke their hearts."

"Told them you were in marketing, huh?" said Windermere. "Pretty little lie. Should have seen their faces when they found out the truth."

"You talk to us, we can work something out," said Stevens. "We know this wasn't your idea. You're practically a victim here. You give up Pender, give up Stirzaker and Sawyer, and we'll throw you a bone. Probation, maybe some community service. You like?"

Windermere leaned forward. "It's a good deal, Marie."

Marie looked up into the cop's eyes. "Go to hell," she said.

"Sure," said Stevens. "Admirable. You love your boyfriend. These are your best friends, right?"

He waited, but Marie didn't answer. "Listen up, though," he continued. "Your friends are supposed to be there for you, right? Your boyfriend's supposed to love you. So where the hell are they?"

"Think about what you're looking at here," said Windermere. "What we've got on you, you'll do twenty-five years if you do a day."

"You guys have pulled a shitload of jobs," said Stevens. "You have the money. So where's Pender, Marie? Where's his fat-cat lawyer in the Armani suit who's going to get you off on a technicality?"

Marie avoided their eyes. He's coming, she thought. Pender's calling his lawyer right now, and he's coming to get me. He'll bail me out of this mess and we'll fly to the Maldives and I swear to God I'll never so much as steal an MP3 for the rest of my life. I'll be perfect, she thought. Just get me out of here.

"Don't tell me you're thinking about a public defender," said Stevens.

Windermere laughed, hollow and cold. "We get you a lawyer, it's gonna be some twenty-five-year-old rookie racking up hours on the taxpayer's dime. He's gonna push you for a plea bargain 'cause he's got no idea how to argue a conspiracy kidnapping charge, and you'll wind up doing ten years if you're lucky," she said. "You've got to face the facts. You've been abandoned. It's time to start playing for self."

Marie bit her lip. She stared down at the table and said nothing. The lawyer should have been here by now. Where was he? Where the hell was Pender?

Maybe the guys figured their cover was blown and they'd better lie low for a while. Maybe they freaked out and ran. They could be on an airplane right now, headed for retirement and freedom. Marie knew if the situation were reversed, Pender would beg her to cut loose and run. But he wouldn't just abandon her, would he?

Then Marie felt her stomach lurch. *Somebody got shot.* She'd seen it on the news. "We had a little problem," Pender had said. She hadn't let him finish. Somebody got shot. *Who?*

Her stomach lurched again and she realized she was going to be sick and she threw up a split-second later, spattering the floor with bile.

Windermere jumped back. "Christ."

Pender had been waiting to meet her. He

seemed fine. He wasn't shot. She thought she remembered seeing Sawyer drag Pender back to the truck. He seemed okay as well.

Mouse, then. Mouse had been shot. Mouse had been shot and was probably dead or dying and here she was worried about jail. You selfish bitch, she thought. Wake up. Your friend's dead.

She threw up again. The detectives swore, but Marie didn't care. She looked up at them, wiped her mouth, the room a blur. "I'm not saying another word," she said, trying to keep her voice strong. "Not one more word until my lawyer gets here."

Windermere glanced at Stevens. Stevens shrugged. Windermere stepped forward again, eyeing the splatter of vomit on the ground. "Have it your way," she said. "We'll get you your lawyer. Gonna be a slight delay, though."

"We're taking you north," said Stevens. "Extradition."

"You want to do this, we're going to do it right." Windermere winked at her. "It's road trip time. You want to see your lawyer, you're going to see him in Detroit."

FIFTY-ONE

Pender stared at the white checks on the highway as he drove the Durango north toward the Georgia border. The gang was quiet in the back, all of them sleeping, and Pender was alone with his thoughts. Right now, his thoughts were cold comfort. The whole situation was spiraling out of control, and every time Pender thought about Mouse or Marie, he felt fresh panic start to rise in his throat.

Pender had called Victor Carter as soon as Mouse reported the bank accounts frozen. He told the lawyer he could only muster a two-thousand-dollar retainer, short term. Carter shut him down cold.

"No offense," he said, "but there's no way I can fly down to Florida until you come up with the full hundred thousand. Maybe try somebody closer?"

Someone closer. As soon as the sun rose, Pender started visiting law offices. Mouse looked up Jacksonville criminal lawyers on his laptop, and Pender picked out a couple of candidates. They snuck out in the Durango, expecting every cop they passed to be the green flag to a high-speed chase. But nobody seemed even to glance in their direction, and by the time they reached the first lawyer's office, Pender was starting to think the cops maybe hadn't made the car after all.

They would have to ditch it anyway, he knew, but it was a relief to think they could wait until Mouse scrounged them up some money before they had to act. Money. The Jacksonville lawyer, a middle-aged fat cat named Wise, had nearly laughed in Pender's face when he explained the situation. "I don't put on pants for less than ten thousand," he said. "And for kidnapping and conspiracy, I'm going to need a big payment up front."

Their problems ran deeper than money, though. As Wise was guiding Pender out of his office, he'd dropped one tidbit of wisdom.

"Money or no," he told Pender, "if it's a case like you're talking, there's a good chance your friend doesn't get bail regardless. You could have the best lawyer in the world, but if the judge rules she's a flight risk, she's staying behind bars."

A flight risk. Well, that was the point, wasn't it? Bail her out and be gone.

So now they were driving north, headed to Macon, Georgia, where with any luck they would find an unscrupulous doctor who could get Mouse fixed up overnight — assuming, of course, he would work for cheap.

"Money ain't a thing," Mouse had told them once the initial shock had worn off. "We've got money hidden so far overseas it needs its own passport. It's just going to take time to get it back ashore."

"How long?" said Pender.

"A week," said Mouse. "Maybe more. We figured we would never need to access that money while we were still in the United States. It's the retirement fund, right? So I set it up thinking we could avoid dealing with American banks."

"How so?"

Mouse sat up. "Look, any international wire transfer coming into the United States goes through the government. The Office of Foreign Assets Control. The amount of money we're going to need, we're raising red flags all over the place if we go through the States."

"But you can bypass that."

He shook his head. "Can't bypass it. But if you give me a week, I can set it up so the transfers look clean. I'll work out a way that we get the money without anyone getting wise."

A week, Pender thought as he drove north toward Georgia. He glanced back at Mouse, laid out and pale in the backseat of the Durango. How do we know the kid's even going to last that long? We need money now.

He drove on, trying not to think about Marie and failing at it. She must think we've abandoned her, he thought. She must be terrified, the things those cops must be telling her. How the hell are we going to get her out?

Not for the first time, Pender wondered what exactly the cops had on her. On any of them. Where did we go wrong, he thought. Where did we screw up? We were pretty damn careful. Until the Beneteau job, anyway.

The cops were on Marie in Seattle, which meant they must have followed her from Detroit. And if they followed her from Detroit, it meant they got her scent from what? Why didn't they follow the gang down to Miami?

Ashley McAdams. Marie said they'd made her as Ashley McAdams. She'd flown home on a plane ticket he'd bought for that alias. So they spotted her in the airport? She'd rented the car as Darcy Wellman. The only other time they'd used McAdams was in Minnesota, and they'd gotten out of Minneapolis clean, right?

Pender felt his thoughts swim in and out of focus. Maybe they hadn't screwed up, he thought. Maybe someone spotted Marie outside Beneteau's place and that's all they've got, a little bit of circumstantial evidence putting her at the scene of the crime. Pender felt better for a minute, but he couldn't let the notion survive. They're onto us, he thought. We've got to get Marie out of the mix and then get out of the country.

And what if we can't get Marie out, the pessimist in him wanted to know. What if we never see her again? Can you walk away before it's too late? Can you let her take the weight for the team and retire without her?

A professional would walk, he knew. A professional would be on a plane right now, headed for a sandy beach and a hefty international wire transfer and a life of relaxation and privacy. A professional would have cut loose days ago.

So what's stopping us from running, he thought. What's keeping us from switching off to a private airfield, chartering a plane, and flying to South America?

Money, for starters. Money in the short term and money in the long term. Short term, they were sitting on a little more than three grand, and that had to last a week. Pender wondered how much their hypothetical Macon doctor would want, and three grand, he figured, was the absolute minimum.

Even if they got Mouse fixed and got out of the country, Pender didn't figure on his having enough cash socked away just yet. He didn't know the exact number, but he estimated he probably had around half a million saved up in Mouse's offshore accounts. With Marie's share, that meant about a million. He'd figured two would do them for retirement, so that left them a million short, and their work prospects, Pender knew, were diminishing rapidly.

Sawyer looked over from the passenger seat. "Everything all right, boss?"

"Yeah." Pender shook his head, let the numbers vanish. "Everything's fine."

"What are you thinking?"

"Money," he said. "We're going to need some real quick. We gotta get Mouse fixed up and Marie sprung, and even with everything in the offshore accounts, I don't know if we have enough to disappear on."

"You're thinking we should pull more jobs?"

Pender frowned. "I don't know. This net is closing fast."

"Yeah."

"We're going to want to get the hell out of here once we get Marie back onboard. But where does that leave us financially?"

Sawyer stared out at the road. "We'll figure out something," he said. "We'll live frugally. Maybe we find jobs at a tropical McDonald's. We'll be all right. We get out of here, we'll be all right."

Pender opened his mouth to reply, but couldn't figure a decent answer. He let it sit for a couple minutes, letting the road hypnotize him. Frugally, he thought. What happened to the Dream?

Then Tiffany leaned forward and tapped him on the shoulder. "Hey," she said. "You said you guys need money? Maybe I can help."

FIFTY-TWO

"So," said Windermere. "When's the last time you talked to your wife?"

Stevens put down his fork and stared across the table at her, trying to think. "I guess it was back in Minnesota," he said. "Just before we went to Seattle."

They were in a steak house near the hotel in Jacksonville, dining once again on the Federal government's dime. I could get used to this, Stevens thought. It almost makes up for all the flying around.

Windermere chewed her steak. "Your wife doesn't know you're in Florida?"

Stevens shrugged, smiled sheepishly. "I guess I should call her, huh?" He took a long pull from his beer, looked across the table at Windermere, watched her cut another piece of steak. He suddenly felt guilty about Nancy. He hadn't given her much thought since the case started to turn.

"If it makes you feel better," said Windermere, "I haven't talked to Mark in a couple days, either."

"There's so much going on," Stevens said. "It's just tough to find time."

He'd meant to call Nancy today, before the McAllister girl started puking her guts out in the interrogation room. They'd gotten nothing from the interview except a good look at the girl's lunch, and from the looks of things it was going to take the hard sell to convince her to stop puking and cooperate.

Wendy Gallant, however, had been a little more productive.

She was waiting outside the room when Windermere and Stevens exited, the rank smell of vomit behind them. "My God," she said, gagging. "What the hell did you do?"

"It was Stevens," said Windermere. "He has that effect on women."

"Rejected, huh?" Gallant winked at Stevens. "I've got something might cheer you up."

They followed Gallant into her office, a private room with a window overlooking the parking lot and a highway beyond. "I see you got one of these office offices," said Windermere. "They told me I'd get something like this in Minnesota."

"And?"

"Got me a nice little cubicle instead. Shit."

"Ha," said Gallant. "You come back to Florida, we'll hook you up."

"Uh-huh." Windermere shook her head. "I fell for that before. What's up?"

Gallant flashed another smile. "Miami's up. We found that orange Trans Am on a side road in Hollywood. Anonymous tip."

"Prints?"

"No prints. Whole car was wiped. But it was parked five or six blocks from a street full of used-car dealerships. Figure someone in the neighborhood must have sold them a new car."

"Try running the aliases through the DMV," said Stevens. "See if anybody registered a car under any of those names in the last few days."

"Will do," said Gallant. "We'll canvass the dealers, too. Put the fear of God in them. That's not all, though."

"No?"

"You heard about those kids getting looked up in some Hollywood fleabag motel, right?"

"Yeah," said Stevens. Vance had filled them in. "Trooper let them go because he didn't have a warrant, right?"

"That's right. The girl he talked to was on a power trip. Some hot little blonde with a

325

rich daddy. Anyway, Miami Police got a call earlier today from a girl on South Beach, girl named, let me see, Haley Whittaker. Rich girl, pretty girl — but she's a brunette."

"Hair dye?" said Windermere.

"Not quite. She was calling in because her hot little blond friend had gone missing. Disappeared a few days ago. Haley figured her friend was just off with some guy somewhere, but they were supposed to head back up to Princeton today and the girl hadn't turned up."

"No shit," said Windermere. "So what do we know?"

"The blonde is Tiffany Prentice. Daughter of Andrew Prentice, who is apparently some big-shot investment banker. Anyway, the girl is rich and she's blond and she's missing."

"Parents know?" Stevens asked.

"Not yet," said Gallant. "Family's divorced, Mom's AWOL somewhere in California. We're trying to get in touch with the father now, but he's a busy son of a bitch. I don't think this girl had much in the way of parental guidance."

"Let's find Daddy," said Stevens. "If we can get him involved, we get monster publicity. Those kids won't breathe without a witness phoning it in."

"Hot damn," said Windermere. "I love it

when you talk like that."

"Those kids want to stay under the radar so bad," said Stevens, "let's shine a spotlight up their asses."

They'd spent the rest of the day chasing leads on Andrew Prentice and the Hollywood car dealerships, and now, after an afternoon of futility, Stevens stared across the table at Windermere and felt guilty about Nancy some more. Tried to imagine a career like this, making a relationship work through the phone lines.

He cut a piece of his steak. "You haven't talked to Mark, either, huh?"

Windermere frowned, looked down at her meal. "I called him in Seattle, I guess. We kind of left it on a bad note."

"Yeah?"

"He's stressed," she said. "He's looking for work. And he hates that I'm on the road so much."

"He shouldn't have shacked up with an FBI agent," said Stevens.

"He liked it at first. The whole FBI thing. He found it exciting. He liked telling people he was dating some cute federal agent. Like it made him a big shot or something." She looked up and caught his eye. "I know I should feel guilty about being away for so long. I should be hoping this case will end so I can go home and be with my boyfriend. But honestly, Stevens? I don't feel guilty at all."

Stevens took another bite. She was right, he realized. He felt the same way.

"I'm *enjoying* this case," said Windermere. "I mean, most of the time I'm working little bullshit files. If I'm lucky, I see a bank robbery. This is a career case, Stevens. You know that. Mark has to know that."

"This is a blockbuster," said Stevens. "Didn't I tell you?"

"I mean, this is kind of why you join the FBI, right? Or the BCA? This is professional stuff. You hear guys talk about how they didn't want a case to end and you think, that's stupid, why wouldn't you want to solve a case?"

"But it doesn't work like that."

"When we crack this thing open, we're back to drug deals and anonymous terrorist tips." Windermere sighed. "Back to the cubicle. It's fun, I guess, but this is *fun*. I just wish Mark could see that. I wish he could be happy for me."

"Maybe it doesn't matter," said Stevens. "You'd still feel guilty even if he was your biggest cheerleader."

"You think?"

"Sure," he said, taking another sip of beer.

"I've been enjoying myself, too. I guess now that you mention it, I *am* dreading this case coming to an end. And I bet if I told my wife how happy I am out here, she'd be happy for me, too. But that doesn't make me feel any better when I think about her home alone."

Windermere stared across the table at him, and he felt flushed, embarrassed by his openness and the directness of her gaze. "What?" he said finally. "What are you looking at?"

"You think she thinks there's something going on here?"

"What, between us? There's nothing going on."

"That never seems to stop Mark from thinking it." She paused. "I guess it's natural, maybe. Us being on the road so much."

Stevens shrugged. "People do it." He grinned at her. "Why? Are you falling in love?"

Windermere laughed. "You'd like that, wouldn't you?"

"Big-shot FBI agent falls for small-time state policeman? I admit it would maybe give my ego a boost."

"You're not small-time anymore, Stevens," Windermere told him. "Like it or not, you're one of us now." She straightened. "Now, what the hell are we going to do about this girl?"

Stevens drained his beer, letting the case bring him back down to normal. In truth, he'd been wondering the same thing ever since they'd left the girl in the interrogation room. "You think she's gonna flip? She seems pretty hardheaded."

Windermere shrugged. "Put twenty-five years in front of her and see if she changes her mind."

"Sure."

"What are you thinking?"

"I'm thinking even if she doesn't flip, she's still a good bargaining chip to have," said Stevens. "Those kids aren't just going to abandon one of their own. If they do, they're a lot stronger than anyone I've ever met. Those kids will come back for that girl, somehow. We just have to hold on to her, and they'll turn up eventually."

Windermere nodded. "Pender loves that girl."

"He does."

"They're kids. They still believe in that stuff."

"What," said Stevens. "Love?"

Windermere shrugged. Shot him a half smile. Stevens was trying to think through a reply when Windermere stiffened suddenly. She felt around in her pockets and pulled out her cell phone. "Windermere. Hi, Wendy." She listened for a minute. "No kidding. Ryan Carew. Stevens is going to love it."

She snapped the phone shut with a new grin on her face. "Florida state police got back to Wendy," she said. "Guess who bought a used Dodge Durango in Hollywood, Florida, day before yesterday?"

"Don't tell me," said Stevens. "Ryan Carew."

"You know it. Navy blue. Paid cash. We got plates and everything." Windermere took a triumphant pull of beer. "I bet they were at the airport when security took down McAllister. Just nobody knew where to look."

"We know now," said Stevens. "Wendy put out the word?"

Windermere nodded. "No way those kids get far."

"Right." Stevens caught the waiter's eye and motioned for the check. He stood. "I'll get the paperwork going on McAllister's extradition."

"I'll do the paperwork, Stevens," said Windermere, pushing back from the table. "You go call your wife."

FIFTY-THREE

D'Antonio stared out along Ocean Drive, watching the women parade back and forth while he drank his mojito. Across the table, Johnston looked around nervously. The cop hadn't touched his beer, but D'Antonio wasn't going to let the kid's discomfort ruin the moment. He sat back in his chair and let the sun wash over him, trying to forget those goddamn kids and the problems they caused.

Across the street, Zeke sat in his Cadillac, reading the newspaper and occasionally looking over at D'Antonio or out toward the ocean, where a cruise ship was slowly making its way out into the Atlantic. The paper said it was thirty degrees in Detroit, and for that reason alone, D'Antonio was determined to enjoy Miami.

Earlier in the day, he'd called Patricia Beneteau from the hotel room. Or rather, he'd returned the call; according to Zeke the woman was going batshit crazy trying to get hold of him and he should call her immediately before she sent goons down to kill them all.

"D'Antonio," she'd said, when she picked up the phone. "I assumed you were dead."

"I'm fine," he told her. "Don't worry."

"I'm anything but worried," she said. "Did you find the kids yet?"

He coughed. "Funny story."

"I don't like funny stories, D'Antonio."

"I hooked up with the girl out west before the government stepped in. She flew down here to Florida. I followed. The rest of the gang is down here, too."

"So you found them."

D'Antonio paused. "No. But they've got heat all over them. Shouldn't be hard to catch up."

"So you've accomplished nothing," she said.

He stared at the phone. "I'll have them in a week, tops."

"You've got three days," she said. "If the heat's as strong as you say, those kids don't have much longer than that, anyway. Three days, understand?"

"I understand." D'Antonio ended the call, cursing the moody bitch. Catching those punk kids in three days would be a real fucking task. It wasn't going to happen just by following cops around. He needed something better.

Now, D'Antonio put down the mojito and stared across the table at Johnston. The kid avoided his eyes. "You wanted to talk," said D'Antonio, "so talk."

The cop took a halfhearted sip of his beer. "I got some news."

"News. I hope it's good this time."

"It's good." Johnston looked up at him. "First, the Feds caught the girl. In Jacksonville."

D'Antonio swore. "That's not good news, you idiot. How am I going to get her if she's in federal custody?"

"I got more." The cop leaned forward. "We found out the name of the blonde."

"Who?"

"Girl who joined the entourage after your boys got put down at the Dauphin. Her name's Tiffany Prentice. Lives with her dad outside Philly, goes to school at Princeton. Rich family. Only child."

"How'd you figure this out?"

"Her friend phoned in a missing person complaint," said Johnston. "I guess they skipped school for a little fun in the sun and the girl didn't show up for the private jet home."

"Her friend phoned it in."

"Girl named Haley Whittaker. They came down for a week, stayed at Loews. Were supposed to head back today."

"This friend," said D'Antonio. "She fly home already?"

Johnston shook his head. "They're keeping her around for questioning. Another day or so, they said."

"No shit."

"They got her at some shitbox out by the airport. The Everglades Resort."

"Armed guards?"

"Nah." The cop shook his head. "Probably just a uniform by the door. She's not in any danger or anything."

That's what you think, D'Antonio thought. He stood up, threw a twenty on the table. "Let me know if you hear anything else."

Johnston stared up at him. "What are you going to do?"

"I'll be seeing you," he said. "Say hello to your bookie for me." Then he turned and left the patio, dodging traffic as he jogged across the street to the Cadillac.

Zeke put down the newspaper as he approached. "Everything all right, boss?"

"I need two goons and a clean car," said D'Antonio. He climbed into the passenger seat. "And we're going to need guns."

Zeke glanced at him, started the car. "Not a problem," he said. "Not a problem at all."

FIFTY-FOUR

They pulled into a roadside roach motel on the outskirts of Macon to spend the night and think over Tiffany's proposal.

Pender lay down on the lumpy bed and stared up at the stains on the ceiling. Another crappy motel room, he thought. He was tired of these rooms. He was tired of the rooms and the piles of greasy food and the miles on the odometer, and he was tired of the aliases and the secrecy and always having to cover his six. He was just tired, period. It was time to get out of this racket.

He lay back on the dirty flowered bedspread and closed his eyes, imagining the Maldives and a beach and a hammock and Marie in a bikini. He fantasized about sleeping soundly, about surfing and fishing and not seeing another person for days.

We'll need a boat to buy food from a nearby village, he thought, or maybe a truck. A Jeep. Or we can fish for food. Farm for ourselves. We'll keep our money in some private account and use the last of our fake names, and we'll never be bothered by anyone.

Pender knew it was foolish to daydream like this. It was important to stay focused on the present, to center on the details and avoid making mistakes. Today, though, he let himself indulge, knowing the days ahead would be more challenging than anything they'd faced so far. It was important to keep a goal in mind. It was important to know why the risks you were taking were ultimately worth the price.

After a couple more minutes of fantasy, Pender blinked away the Maldives and forced himself back to the question at hand.

Tiffany had made her pitch somewhere around the Georgia border, though Pender was sure she'd been saving it for days. "You guys need money, right?" she'd said. "A lot of money? My dad is loaded. Why don't you kidnap me?"

Pender had nearly crashed the car, twisting back to search her face for the joke, but she'd only stared at him, serious, until he gave up and turned back to the wheel.

"I have a better idea," Sawyer said. "Why

don't you just get your dad to give us the cash?"

Tiffany shook her head. "My dad doesn't just *give* money. He's a banker. He's gotta know there's a return on his investment. If you guys hold me for ransom, he'll pay without a fight because he'll know he's getting a great return."

"Hell, yes, he is," said Mouse, pulling her down to kiss him. Tiffany giggled like a new bride.

Sawyer sighed in the front seat, keeping his eyes straight ahead. "No offense, but that's the worst idea I ever heard," he said.

Pender found Tiffany in the rearview mirror. "You're sure your dad won't just ship you some money?"

"Not if I just call him straight up and ask," she said. "He's a stingy bastard for such a rich guy."

"I thought he had a private jet," said Mouse.

"The divorce lawyer made him sell it. Anyway, he needed that for work."

"How much could your dad get us?" said Pender.

"I don't know." Tiffany shrugged. "Maybe a million. How does that sound?"

A million dollars. Pender sat awake in the Macon hotel room, listening to trucks growl past outside and trying to work out a strategy.

Every instinct told him not to trust the girl's scheme. So far, Tiffany had given no indication that her father even knew she was alive. Could be he'd just hang up the phone. Worse, he could be one of those people who took a kidnapping personally. Parents could be dangerous and irrational.

They had pulled their most successful scores after days of hard-core preparation and intelligence work. Now they were considering taking a monster gamble on a guy nobody knew, based on the testimony of some superrich girl who'd given up all her toys to be a professional kidnapper. Pender didn't like it at all.

Still, they needed the money. A million bucks would go a long way toward fixing Mouse and springing Marie.

Someone knocked on the door. Pender stood, stretched, and peered through the peephole. Sawyer. Pender opened the door. "What's up?"

Sawyer walked past him and into the room. "You should turn on the news," he said. He picked up the remote and switched on the TV to the local news station. Pender looked up and saw his own face on the screen.

It was a picture of him and Marie, taken in the San Juan Islands north of Seattle the summer before they graduated. If he closed his eyes, Pender could see the picture where he'd stuck it on their fridge in Queen Anne, and he reeled, wanting to be sick.

This is not a surprise, he told himself. You knew the FBI was in your apartment, and you knew they would search the place. This is all part of being a criminal. Suck it up and deal with it.

The news anchor was talking, and Pender turned up the volume as the pictures changed to a shot of Sawyer and another of Ben "Mouse" Stirzaker, both pictures Marie had taken and stored on her laptop.

"While FBI agents have captured one of the alleged kidnappers," the anchor was saying, "three others, including ringleader Arthur Pender, twenty-eight, of Port Angeles, Washington, remain at large. Federal agents say the suspects were last seen in the Jacksonville area but are highly nomadic by nature, and are advising anyone along the I-95, I-10, and I-75 corridors to keep a lookout for these dangerous men. The suspects are believed to be driving a dark blue, late-model Dodge Durango and may be in the company of Tiffany Prentice, twenty, who vanished from a South Beach resort earlier in the week. The suspects are considered armed and dangerous and should be avoided at all costs."

The anchor switched stories, and Pender turned down the volume. He took a deep breath and glanced at Sawyer, who was staring at the floor between his feet. "We gotta ditch that truck," he said.

"Armed and dangerous," said Sawyer. "What a crock."

Pender stared at the TV. "You think we can get a million for her?"

"I don't know," said Sawyer. "How much money do we have right now?"

"Enough for a piece-of-shit car, not much more."

Sawyer scratched his head. "We could do a lot with a million bucks."

"We'd have to move fast. Get out of here *tonight*." Pender tried to think fast. Fuck it, he thought. A million bucks and we're golden.

"We're doing it," he said. "Tell Tiffany to get in touch with her father. A million cash, unmarked bills, forty-eight hours. You know the drill. Then get those guys ready to travel. We leave tonight. Drive as far as we can and swap the Durango in the morning. We can make Philadelphia tomorrow, and with any luck we get the money tomorrow night."

"Done," said Sawyer. He was on his way to the door when a couple of harsh knocks outside made them both go cold. Sawyer glanced back at Pender, who put his finger to his lips. He gestured one minute, and watched as Sawyer took out the Glock he'd stolen from the dead assassin in Miami.

Sawyer stood beside the door, holding the gun pointed to the ceiling, and Pender peered through the peephole. He let out a sigh, gestured to Sawyer to relax, and opened the door. Tiffany walked in, glanced at Sawyer and the Glock and then back at Pender. "You're famous," she said. She was smiling.

"We're all famous," he said. "Bona fide household names."

"What are we going to do?"

"You're going to phone your dad," he told her. "You've just been officially kidnapped."

FIFTY-FIVE

D'Antonio sat in the parking lot of the Everglades Resort, watching jets make their final approach into Miami International. Zeke had hooked him up with his girlfriend's Ford Explorer and a couple of big, dumb bundles of muscle who sat in the backseats, staring out the window and breathing through their mouths. They were quiet, though, and they were armed; both men carried TEC-9 machine pistols in their waistbands. For D'Antonio, Zeke had found a clean .45 caliber Glock and a couple magazines of hollow-point bullets, more than enough firepower to scare a teenaged girl into submission.

The Everglades was a single-story block of drive-up units with a lobby on one end and a dumpster on the other. All of the units faced the road, and behind the motel was a chain-link fence and a railroad siding behind. Out front of the fourth door from the lobby stood a lazy-looking uniform, posted up against the wall with his eyes half closed and his mouth wrapped around a cigarette. A pile of butts lay at his feet. The parking lot was deserted except for the uniform's radio car.

D'Antonio parked behind the cop. He climbed out of the Explorer and gestured for one of the goons, Paolo, to follow. The other guy, Leon, made himself comfortable in the driver's seat as D'Antonio walked toward the officer.

The cop — his badge said Bramley — opened his eyes, giving D'Antonio and Paolo the lazy once-over as they passed him. D'Antonio put on a smile and shoved his hands in his pockets. "Howdy," he said. "I'm Detective Carl and this is Michaels. You heard we were coming?"

Bramley squinted at D'Antonio. "Carl," he said, scratching his head. "What division?"

Paolo was working his way around to flank Bramley again, scoping out the parking lot from the corner of his eye and waiting for D'Antonio's signal.

D'Antonio grinned wider. "CID. Here to talk to the girl."

Bramley glanced at Paolo and then back to D'Antonio. "Nobody tells me shit around

345

here," he said at last. He took out a room key on a plastic key ring. D'Antonio waited until Bramley had unlocked the door and then gave Paolo a nod. The goon brought the butt of his gun down on Bramley's skull, and the man let out a soft grunt before he crumpled to the ground, his body pushing open the door as he fell.

D'Antonio stepped over the cop and into the room, letting his eyes adjust to the dim light. Double bed, old TV, flimsy furniture. Bathroom toward the back and no apparent escape routes. He relaxed a little.

The girl was lying sprawled on her stomach on the bed, propped up on her elbows, watching a cartoon hamster fight a frog on the TV set. She was attractive in a sitcom-starlet kind of way, and she stared at D'Antonio and Paolo with more curiosity than fear.

D'Antonio examined her for a minute, waiting for the cracks to show. "Haley Whittaker?" he said.

She frowned. "Who are you?"

"Your new best friend." D'Antonio gestured back to Paolo, who stepped over Bramley and walked to the bed. The girl let Paolo pick her up in a fireman's carry and take her back toward the door.

D'Antonio caught her eye as Paolo carried her past him. "Where are you taking me?" she asked him, disarmingly calm.

D'Antonio ignored her. He walked deeper into the room and examined the girl's belongings. She had a novel on the nightstand and a laptop computer on the dresser. He took the laptop and, after a moment's thought, the novel as well. The kid was going to get bored.

They were in and out in ten minutes total. Paolo put the girl in the backseat, and D'Antonio sat beside her as Leon drove slow and steady out of the parking lot. The girl still hadn't struggled, still hadn't screamed. She stared straight ahead through the front seats, watching the road while D'Antonio watched her.

After maybe five minutes, she looked up at D'Antonio. "So what is this, like a kidnapping or something?"

D'Antonio smiled at her. "It's something like that."

"You're going to hold me for ransom?"

He shook his head. "Not exactly."

"Kidnapping." She looked him up and down. "That's really cute. You're supposed to be some kind of bad guy?"

She was prettier like this, D'Antonio thought. She was ballsy.

"Is this what you do? You kidnap girls? Is

that how you get your kicks?"

He laughed. She was staring him down, a smirk on her face. "I'm no kidnapper," he told her. "From what I've been told, that's Tiffany's job."

The girl barely blinked. "Where is she?"

"You tell me."

"The hell should I know? She ditched me like days ago."

"We're looking for her," said D'Antonio. "I think you'll see her again soon."

The girl stared at him, her eyes hard. "She's no kidnapper," she said. "We came down from Jersey for a week on the beach, fella. The only one doing any kidnapping is you."

D'Antonio laughed. "Then I guess I'm a kidnapper after all. What does that make you?"

"Fucking unlucky," she said. "How much is my ransom?"

"No ransom," he told her.

She frowned. "Oh, you're just going to rape me and then cut me up into pieces, are you? You're one of those kinds of perverts. I understand."

"I'm no pervert," he said. "We're going to use you as bait."

"Bait," she said. "Like for fishing?"

He smiled. Shook his head, leaned in close

to the girl. "You're going to help us get Tiffany. You understand now?"

She stared at him a second, real close. Then she sat back in her seat and stared out the window again. Frowned deeper. "You want Tiffany," she said. Then she sighed. "They *always* want Tiffany."

FIFTY-SIX

"So listen," the female agent — Windermere — called over her shoulder. "It's probably going to be about fifteen hours to Detroit. You might as well get comfortable."

Marie glanced through the iron bars of the U.S. Marshals Service van at the agent, who sat up front riding shotgun — literally. There was a big Mossberg 12 gauge at the ready between Windermere and the driver, a big black marshal who hadn't said a word as he wrapped Marie in handcuffs and leg irons and locked her into the back of the van.

"Comfortable." Marie looked at the chains around her wrists and ankles, the hard steel bench she sat on, the iron bars on the windows. "You're kidding, right?"

Windermere shrugged. "Sorry," she said. "Tried to get you on JPATS — that's Con Air — but the scheduling wouldn't work. But hey, at least you get some privacy."

Windermere, being the federal agent, had drawn the task of traveling with the prisoner on the nine-hundred-mile drive north from Jacksonville to Detroit. Stevens, meanwhile, got his state policeman's ass on a plane and was flying up to Minneapolis right now to spend an evening with his wife and kids. He'd fly back to Detroit in the morning, and they would meet up with the prosecutor to prepare for the arraignment.

Stevens, the lucky bastard, thought Windermere. The guy had a wife who understood, while she had Mark. Lately, going home had become more like work than work itself, and Windermere dreaded the close of the case for the return it would mean to their life of long silences and sudden, explosive confrontations.

Windermere turned back to face the McAllister girl, who sat staring at her feet in the middle of the van, her eyes open but her body so still it was almost scary. "Let me ask you something," Windermere said. The girl didn't look up. "You and your boyfriend. How did you make it work?"

The girl finally moved — barely. She lifted her head an inch or so in Windermere's direction. "I don't know what you're talking about."

"How did you keep it fresh? You were

together for what, like five years? On the road, too. How did you not get sick of each other?"

Marie looked back down at her feet. "I'm not saying anything without my lawyer present."

"Come on," said Windermere. "I'm not interrogating you. None of this is admissible unless you sign away your rights."

The girl said nothing, did nothing. Windermere watched her for a minute. "All right," she said, shrugging. "Suit yourself." She leaned forward and fiddled with the radio dial until they picked up a jazz station. Somebody was giving it on the saxophone, and Windermere settled in to enjoy the solo.

In the back of the van, Marie stared down at her feet. Maybe that's what happened to Pender, she thought. Maybe he just wasn't interested anymore.

Stevens climbed out of a taxicab and crunched through the fresh snow that lined the walk outside his house in St. Paul. I'll have to shovel this tonight, he thought, surveying the blanket of white that covered the sidewalk and the driveway. He shivered as he paused on the steps, enjoying the sensation of cold on his skin after the suffocating Florida heat. Nancy complained about the weather all winter long, but to Stevens there was nothing like the bitter Minnesota chill to remind a man what it felt like to be alive.

Of course, half the joy of winter was the warmth when you came in from the cold. Stevens pushed open his front door and stood in the landing, peeling off his coat and basking in the bright, welcome familiarity of his home.

"Daddy!" It was J.J., running down the front stairs, nearly toppling over his feet in his hurry to reach the bottom.

"Hey, fella." Stevens wrapped his son up in a bear hug. "How's it going? Where's your mother?"

"Mom's in the living room. Daddy, I made a dinosaur picture at school."

"Wow," said Stevens, setting him down. "You're going to be an artist, hey?"

"No," said J.J. "A dinosaur hunter!"

Stevens kicked off his shoes and walked into the living room, where his wife sat semiconscious in her favorite chair, dozing with a mountain of papers spread out before her. J.J. followed him into the room. "We're getting a dog, Daddy!"

Nancy opened her eyes slowly. She smiled up at her husband, sheepish. "Is this true?"

Stevens asked her.

"Yes, Daddy, a German shepherd!"

"I told them they could have a dog for Christmas," said Nancy. "But only if they're really good."

J.J. nodded. "We're calling him Triceratops!" He ran from the room, and Stevens heard him dashing up the stairs, feet pounding a rhythm into the hardwood. He realized he'd missed the sound.

"Are you upset?" said Nancy. "Do you think it's a good idea?"

"What, the dog?"

"I just thought it would be nice to have a pet," she said. "The kids get scared without you." She smiled. "Sometimes I get scared, too. This big, empty house."

He stared down at her. "Honey, I'm sorry. I've been gone too long."

"No, don't be sorry. You're doing your job."

"I'm done with this job." He lifted her to her feet and wrapped his arms around her. "Another week, tops, I'll be home."

Nancy kissed him. "Home, you say."

"Nothing you can do about it."

"No more running around with Agent Windermere."

"You'll *wish* I was gone."

"One week," she said, snuggling into his

arms. "Then I'm going to lock you away for my personal use, and I'm going to keep you locked up for a very long time."

"I'll hold you to that," he said, and he kissed her back, both of them listening like a couple of teenagers for the telltale creak of the floorboards. He pulled her down onto the easy chair on top of him, kissing her deeply and letting his hands slide under her sweater. He felt her breathing start to quicken, her skin warm on his hands, and then the front door flew open, sending a shock of cold air through the house and filling the landing with the sound of happy teenagers, the laughter and teasing and stomping feet as his daughter and her friends came in from the cold.

Later, lying in bed with Nancy curled up beside him, Stevens stared at the glowing numbers on the alarm clock, listening to his wife's light snoring and wondering how Windermere was doing on the road.

She had been right, what she'd said about cracking the case. It was pleasant to come home every night, it was a wonderful luxury. But working suicides out in the hinterlands couldn't compare to a case like this, to the glamour of kidnapping schemes and interstate prisoner transport, bargaining chips, and, Stevens realized, a partner like Windermere. He knew if things went well they had maybe a week left on the case, and though he ached for the satisfaction of locking up his suspects, Stevens knew that once the case was closed, so, too, was his relationship, professional and otherwise, with Windermere.

You're being selfish, he told himself. *If you're lucky enough to solve this case, you'll come home to a wife who understands you, and a couple of kids who worship the ground you walk on.* You're a cop, he told himself. You solve crimes. Nobody said anything about glamour.

Still, it took hours for Stevens to fall asleep. He thought of nothing but the case, watching the hours tick by toward dawn, and when the morning finally came and his plane took off for Detroit, Stevens was passed out in his window seat, asleep on a plane for the first time.

Fifty-Seven

"You know," said the salesman, studying Pender across the hood of the van. "You look awfully familiar. You from around here?"

Pender nodded. "Got cousins in Mooresville," he said. He gestured to the car and tried not to breathe through his nose. "Someone die in this thing, or what?"

The salesman turned to examine the vehicle, a ten-year-old Chrysler minivan with a bad paint job and a rank odor inside. He shook his head. "Reeked like this when they traded it in. Could have someone take a look if you want."

"That's all right," said Pender. "I'll just crack the windows. You said a thousand?"

"Yeah." The salesman cleared his throat. "You sure I couldn't interest you in something in a little better condition?"

"Got anything around three grand?"

"Got this old F-150," he said, gesturing

across the lot at a red Ford pickup. "Low miles, asking thirty-five hundred. I'll give it to you for three grand flat."

Pender shook his head. "I need something with room. The van's fine. Maybe throw in an air freshener or ten."

A half hour later, Pender drove off the lot, the windows down and air fresheners hung all over the car. The guys are going to love this, he thought, but we're two grand up. They can't complain.

It seemed a shame to ditch the Durango, and Pender was almost tempted to try and sell the thing. But then he caught a glimpse of his face in a newspaper box, and he pulled his hat lower and he knew they had to burn it.

They had gotten away from Macon clean, leaving the hotel around two in the morning, he and Sawyer swapping shifts as they traversed the back roads toward Charlotte while Tiffany tended to Mouse in the back. The kid was degenerating rapidly, Pender realized. He'd been barely conscious when they moved him out of the motel, and he hadn't said a word on the drive so far. We've got to get him looked at and fast, he thought. He'll die if we keep going like this.

Tiffany called her father from a rest stop on I-20, waking the man up and putting on her best scared voice as she repeated what Pender had scripted for her. She danced back to the car smiling and told Pender her dad would come up with the money, just like in the movies. Pender didn't remind her that in the movies, the cops always won in the end.

He tried to play out the next few days in his head. We get the money, he thought. We leave Tiffany with her father. Then we drive south, get Mouse fixed up. Then down to Jacksonville. Fly Carter down and get Marie out of jail. Then we get the hell out of the States and try to retire on half pay. It was a heavy gamble, but there was really no other option short of abandoning Mouse at an emergency room, leaving Marie to rot in prison, and getting out of the country alone.

Pender drove the minivan to the outskirts of town, retracing his tracks until he found Sawyer and others sitting low in the Durango, hidden behind a patch of old shipping containers and jumpy from being out in the open for so long. "Jesus," said Sawyer. "Thought you'd never come."

"What is that, a Voyager?" said Tiffany.

"We can't all drive Bentleys," said Pender. "Let's get Mouse aboard and get going."

They torched the Durango behind the shipping containers and hit the road again, stopping for food somewhere in Virginia and then bombing north toward Pennsylvania. They hit the outskirts of Philadelphia around rush hour, relying on Tiffany's directions to navigate them around the traffic toward Bryn Mawr.

Sawyer kept his nose in a gas station map book, and they made camp in a Super 8 alongside Interstate 76.

"We should get points for all the money we spend in these places," said Sawyer, setting his bag down on the first bed he saw.

"You want to send in the receipts, be my guest," Pender told him.

They muscled Mouse inside, Pender and Sawyer holding him upright and Tiffany running interference in case anyone came looking. They had to drag the kid to his bed, barely conscious, and when they set him down he passed out again. "This is not good," Pender told Sawyer. "We gotta get him help, fast."

Later that night they ate takeout, chewing in silence, everyone preoccupied. It was Mouse, Pender knew. Where normally they'd be keyed up and nervous the night before a job, now they were scared and their minds were nowhere near ready for what they'd have to do tomorrow.

Pender put down his chicken wing. "All

right," he said. "We're all worried about Mouse." He glanced over. The kid was out cold, his thin chest barely moving in time with his weak breathing. Pender shook his head. He glanced at Sawyer, at Tiffany. Sawyer chewed a forkful of fried rice, watching him. Tiffany kept her eyes on Mouse.

"This is our biggest job yet, and we're doing it shorthanded," Pender told them. "I need you guys to be focused. As long as we get the money, Mouse will be fine. So let's make sure we pull this off, okay?"

Sawyer nodded.

"Tiffany?"

"We'll pull it off," she said, "and it's going to be badass."

As far as pep talks went, it was pretty weak, Pender knew. But the whole thing felt wrong. He retreated to his own room and tried to fall asleep but couldn't, lying awake on top of the covers instead and feeling the knot in his stomach grow ever tighter.

FIFTY-EIGHT

D'Antonio knocked on the door once and then pushed it open, balancing the tray against his hip with the other hand. The girl was sitting on her bed, staring at the wall. Her novel sat where he'd left it for her on the nightstand, and she didn't look to have moved much herself.

"Brought you some food," he said. He put the tray on the bed, and the girl stared down at it. She hadn't eaten in a day or so, but she sure didn't look hungry.

"What is it?" she said.

"Meat loaf."

"I'm a vegetarian."

"Not today you're not," he said. "We're fresh out of tofu."

The girl sighed. She looked at D'Antonio. "Okay," she said. "If you're not some pervert, then what the hell are you after with Tiffany?"

D'Antonio walked over to the nightstand,

examined the novel. Trashy chick lit. Typical. "Tiffany's mixed up with some people," he told her. "We're just trying to get her back."

She scoffed. "That's a lie. You're no guardian angel."

"These people did something wrong," he said. "Something bad."

"What did they do?"

He walked to the front of the bed, feeling the girl's eyes on him. "That's not something you need to worry about."

"You might as well tell me."

He looked her over, admiring her long tan legs, the swell of her body in that tight shirt. "Why's that?"

She frowned as if she could read his mind. "I'm obviously not going to tell anyone."

"That's what they all say."

"I saw your face," she said. "The other guys', too. You didn't even bother to blindfold me when you brought me into this house. You're going to kill me."

She said it so calmly, D'Antonio thought he'd misheard. "We're not going to kill you," he said.

She gave him a cold smile. "Bullshit. Soon as you get Tiffany, you're going to cut me up and dump me somewhere. I watch TV."

D'Antonio stared at her. She stared back,

unblinking, her smile scaring the shit out of him. "They killed a man," he said, surprising himself. "They tried to kidnap him and the job went sour. So they killed him."

"And you worked for him."

"I work for his wife," he said. "And for people who work with his wife. She wants revenge. That's where I come in."

"Wow," she said. "A real live gangster."

He examined her face, trying to decide if she was serious. She stared up at him, eyes wide, lips parted. "I bet you get lots of girls," she said.

"Come on."

"You come on." She lay back on the bed, stretched out. Her eyes on his, watching him watch her. "You're so sweet and dangerous. Girls must love you."

He studied her some more. Almost fell for it. Then she sat up and laughed in his face. "So, fucking kill me, then. If that's what you want."

D'Antonio straightened, adjusted his tie. He stood and walked to the door. "I don't want to kill you," he said. "I don't want to fuck you, either."

"You sure?"

He turned back to her. "I want you to bring me your friend. And her friends. That's all."

The girl rolled her eyes. Sank back on the bed as he stepped out of the room. "Always Tiffany, huh?" she called after him. "Christ, be original."

He walked down the hall, breathing a little heavier than normal, trying to wipe the girl from his mind. The girl played tough — hell, she played fearless. Like this kidnapping thing was a game. D'Antonio couldn't remember ever facing down anyone who'd stared back at him so damn nonchalant.

"Boss." Zeke, from the living room. "Your phone."

Zeke handed over his cell phone, and D'Antonio held it to his ear. "Yeah."

"It's Johnston." The cop. "You, uh, didn't have anything to do with that dustup at the Everglades, did you? The girl I was telling you about?"

"Of course not," said D'Antonio. "What do I want with a girl?"

"Yeah, I guess not. The guy they had posted, Bramley or whatever, hasn't been much help. Made the attackers as two weirdos trying to pass themselves off as detectives."

"He give descriptions?"

"Said they were big and white. That's all he got."

"I haven't heard anything," D'Antonio

365

told him. "Any word on the kidnappers?"

"Nothing serious. APBs out for the Durango. About a thousand anonymous tips from here to Macon, Georgia, with nothing to show. Oh, they moved the girl from Jacksonville up to Detroit. Guess they're going to arraign her for your boss's murder."

"He was my boss's husband."

"Yeah, exactly. What'd I say?"

D'Antonio ended the call, and walked into the kitchen, where Zeke and his massive Cuban-American girlfriend were at an impasse over the meat loaf. He grabbed the girl's laptop from the counter and returned to her room.

Haley hadn't moved, hadn't touched the meat loaf. "You're going to turn carnivore or you're going to starve to death," he told her.

"Better than getting shot."

"Not really," he said. "You starve to death, it'll take weeks." He put the laptop on the bed and opened it, booted it up. "Let's see if your friend checks her e-mail."

The girl rolled her eyes. "You looking for a pen pal?"

"Just shut up and type what I tell you," he said.

The laptop hummed to life, and D'Antonio watched as the girl brought up her e-mail provider and typed in her password. He watched over her shoulder as her account loaded up. "You tell her to get her ass back to Miami, or else, understood?"

She typed. " 'Or else.' Original. Anything else?"

"She have any other accounts? What about Myspace?"

"Nobody uses Myspace," she said. "She has a Facebook account, but it's linked to her e-mail."

"All right," said D'Antonio. "What else? She have a cell phone, a pager?"

"She left her cell phone in the room to charge," said the girl. "And nobody has a pager anymore."

"Well, then." D'Antonio put his face close to hers, looming over her, trying to draw an ounce of fear from the girl. "I'll say it again. What else have you got?"

The girl didn't flinch. She thought for a second. "I could call her house. Her dad's place in Pennsylvania. He's never around. Maybe she went home."

"Or maybe he can get a hold of her better than you can. Call her house if you want. But you got two days to make this girl materialize before we start taking body parts."

"Fuck off," she said. He slapped her,

surprising them both. Her head snapped
back, but she didn't make a sound. She
brought her hand to her lip, her eyes wide.
She glared at him. "Give me the goddamn
phone."

FIFTY-NINE

"Daddy?" Tiffany whimpered into the pay phone. "Daddy, it's Tiffany. No, I'm okay. They want to know if you have the money."

Pender listened, watching the pay phone for eavesdroppers. Should have bought burners, he thought. He felt bare naked, standing outside this run-down convenience store in the middle of the day. No burner, no intel. This whole thing is a farce.

"Okay, I'll tell them," Tiffany was saying. "Just leave it at the McDonald's by the SEPTA station. The back dumpster. I love you, Daddy."

She hung up the phone. Flashed Pender a smile, wrapped her arm around his. "He got the money," she said. "What did I tell you?"

"I'll believe it when we're stacking cash," he said, climbing into the minivan.

"You worry too much. We're practically home free."

"Knock on wood."

Tiffany leaned forward into the driver's seat, knocked on Sawyer's head. "Not funny," he said, but he smiled.

"Drop's good for two-thirty?" said Pender.

Tiffany nodded. "Uh-huh."

"Fine." He checked his watch. Ten minutes to two. Forty minutes to showtime.

They swung back to the motel, and Pender and Sawyer dragged Mouse out into the minivan. They laid him across the backseat, and then Sawyer got behind the wheel. "Tiffany," said Pender. "Ride shotgun."

Tiffany glanced back at Mouse. "Why?"

"Just do it," said Sawyer, and Tiffany frowned and got in the front seat.

Pender climbed in back with Mouse, his heart like a drum machine as Sawyer started the van and they pulled out of the motel lot. They were at the McDonald's in what seemed like half a minute, though the clock said it had taken fifteen.

These drives never take long enough, thought Pender. He felt good now, caught up in the nitrous oxide rush, the crazy burst of adrenaline that always came before the job. I'd forgotten how good this feels, he realized.

They drove around the block, scoping out the McDonald's and peering down alleys for half-hidden radio cars and unmarked units lying in wait. They found nothing.

The McDonald's faced out into the street, with a drive-thru track that made a giant U-turn around the property along the inside of the parking lot. The dumpster was in back, across the parking lot and up against a corner of heavy green fencing. Pender soured on the scene as soon as he saw it. If anyone called the cops, they would be easily trapped by a couple of cruisers out on the main road, no matter what exit they chose. "Shit," he said. "Let's hope this guy's as good as his word."

"He'll be here," said Tiffany.

A couple of minutes later, she pointed out the front window. "There's my dad's car," she said, sitting up in her seat and pointing to where a gray Bentley was pulling into the McDonald's lot, as incongruous as a stripper at an inauguration ball. Pender watched the big car disappear into the back of the parking lot. "You told him drop the bag off, then leave, right?"

Tiffany nodded. "I told him everything you told me."

After maybe five minutes, the Bentley appeared on the other side of the building. Pender watched the driver, a very calm-looking middle-aged man, peer out into

371

traffic and then make a right-hand turn. He drove to the end of the block, made another right, and disappeared. "This is it," said Pender.

Sawyer pulled into the parking lot. "Let's get paid."

The bag was sitting exactly where Tiffany had instructed, a glorious green plastic garbage bag playing cool at the base of the dumpster. Pender saw it and felt his heart start to race. Shut up, shut *up*, he told himself. You haven't done anything yet.

Sawyer pulled the van up to the dumpster, and Pender slid open the rear door. He reached out and grabbed the bag, hefting it into the back of the minivan. It felt heavier than normal, bulkier. A million bucks is a lot more paper than we're used to, he reminded himself, and he set the bag on the floor to examine its contents.

Sawyer looked over at Tiffany. "Okay, get out."

"What?"

"Your dad paid the ransom. It's time to go. Beat it."

Sawyer reached across to try and open the passenger door. Tiffany struggled with him. "Sawyer, *quit it*," she said. "This wasn't the plan. We got the damn money. Let's jet."

"We don't have the damn money," said

Pender. He looked up from the bag, now wide open on the floor of the van, its contents a cargo of sweaters and T-shirts and blue jeans: laundry. "We don't have shit."

Tiffany slammed her door closed. "What the hell are you talking about?"

"Maybe that's not the right bag," said Sawyer. "You see another bag around?"

Pender went to the side door, searched the ground around the dumpster. No bags, anywhere. Then his heart went cold. Sirens. Over the crush of traffic and the mumble from the drive-thru, he could hear the wail of sirens, maybe a coincidence and more than likely not. "We got sirens, Sawyer," he said, climbing into the van.

Tiffany was reaching into the garbage bag, examining the clothes inside. She pulled out a vintage Jimi Hendrix T-shirt. "We got the right bag," she said. "This is my shirt."

"This is bullshit," said Sawyer. "Where's the goddamn money?"

"We got sirens, Sawyer," said Pender. "We gotta go, now."

Tiffany glanced up at Pender. "Maybe the money's underneath."

"There's no money," said Pender. "Forget it. We got played. Now drive."

Sawyer stared at Tiffany for a long moment and then stomped on the accelerator and the minivan leapt forward with a roar. Pender slammed the side door shut, and Sawyer steered down the side corridor of the lot, cutting off a Buick coming out of the drive-thru line and pulling out into traffic just as the first police cruiser rounded the corner, lights blazing, siren *loud.*

"Go," Pender told him. Sawyer nodded, found a hole in traffic and aimed for it, the van's engine howling as Sawyer kept his foot on the gas.

They ran a red light and kept driving, Tiffany laughing — *laughing* — in the front seat, hysterical, and Sawyer staying calm, picking his spots and changing lanes, one eye on the rearview mirror and the other plotting his course.

Pender glanced back toward the McDonald's and saw a light show of red and blue out front of the restaurant, two cruisers and an unmarked sedan angled across traffic, blocking the parking lot and nobody even looking in their direction. "Slow down," said Pender. "Make a turn, and, for Christ's sake, slow down."

"Slow down?"

"Blend in. Make for the highway. I don't think they saw us."

Sawyer took his foot off the gas, and

Pender let himself breathe. Even Tiffany was quiet, both hands gripped tight on the armrests. "Holy crap," she said, gasping. "That was *fun.*"

Sawyer and Pender ignored her. "How did they not see us?" Sawyer asked. "Either they're blind or they're running game."

Pender looked down at the laundry bag, the pile of useless clothes. "Somebody's running game," he said. "I just have no idea what it means."

SIXTY

Sawyer got them on the highway and kept the van moving, hovering just above the speed limit and blending into traffic. He caught Pender's eye in the rearview mirror. "Where are we going?"

"Drive," Pender told him. "We'll figure it out on the way."

Sawyer nodded and turned back to the road. Tiffany twisted in her seat. "What are we going to do?" she asked Pender.

"I need to think," he said. He looked up at her. "What does all this laundry mean?"

Tiffany shook her head. "Maybe it's a joke."

"Some joke," said Pender. "This is your life he's playing with."

He picked up the garbage bag and spilled the contents onto the floor of the van. Clothes. Mostly sweaters and a couple pairs of pants. No explanation given. He thought about it a moment, realized, this isn't so bad. "I think we're in pretty good shape here," he said.

Sawyer found him in the rearview. "How do you figure?"

"The guy set a trap. We got out. We got his daughter, and he knows he pissed us off. He's going to be eager to settle. All we have to do is get a hold of him and let him know how mad we are. Double the ransom. He won't screw up again."

"It's good," said Tiffany. "Only this time, don't expect me to leave once you boys have the money."

"Are you kidding?" said Sawyer. "You're the goddamn hostage."

"I'm part of your *team*," she said. "I'm nobody's hostage."

Sawyer glanced in the rearview. "Boss?"

Tiffany twisted back in her seat. "Don't listen to him, Pender. I'm one of the bad guys now."

Pender was barely listening. He'd spotted something in the pile of laundry. Something small and metallic, about the size of an old film canister. He unwrapped it from a faded warm-up jacket and untangled it: an MP3 player, the cheap kind that comes free with your fifth oil change or the purchase of a DVD player. Headphones attached. Pender held it up, showed it to Tiffany. "This look familiar?"

Tiffany shook her head. "I have an iPod."

"You've never seen this before in your life."

"I told you no, didn't I?"

"Anything on it?" said Sawyer.

Pender pressed the on switch. The thing came to life, its little LCD display firing up radioactive green. One track. Pender put the headphones to his ears and pressed Play.

Sounded like a telephone call. A girl's voice. "Hello," she said, her voice calm. "Mr. Prentice, this message is for Tiffany. It's, uh, Haley Whittaker from school, and I'm kind of in trouble. Tiffany's hooked up with these dangerous guys, these, uh, kidnappers. They've pissed a bunch of people off and one of those people is standing right next to me and he wants to know where Tiffany's friends are."

The girl paused for a moment, then came back on. "Um, please don't call the police," she said. "They promised they won't hurt Tiffany if she just gives up her friends. But the guy said he'd hurt me if Tiffany's friends didn't show up in the next two days. So I'm really hoping you'll pass this along and tell Tiffany to check her e-mail soon. Okay. Thank you. I'm sorry for all this. What?"

There was another pause. "Oh. Oh yeah,"

she said. "Um, please, *please* don't call the police. He said he'll kill me if you do. Okay. I'm sorry. Bye." There was the click of the phone hanging up, and then the file ended.

Sawyer was staring at him in the rearview mirror. Pender took off the headphones. "What do we got, boss?"

"Tiffany," said Pender. "Who's Haley Whittaker?"

Tiffany frowned. "She's my friend. She came to South Beach with me. Why?"

Pender stared down at the pile of laundry. Haley Whittaker. Andrew Prentice. The guy wanted the police to catch us, he realized. But he put this message in here just in case we got away clean. Is it legit? Who would have kidnapped this girl?

Donald Beneteau's people, obviously. The same people who shot up the hotel on South Beach. They lost our trail, so they reached out for whatever they could find to get us back. They snatched up Tiffany's friend, and now they're holding her for ransom. And *we're* the goddamn ransom.

He handed over the MP3 player, and Tiffany put the headphones in her ears. Pender watched her in profile as she played the message, her eyes getting wide and her hand moving to her throat. Sawyer turned back to Pender. "Jesus, boss. What's up?"

379

"Beneteau's people snatched her friend to bait us."

"How the hell did they find her?"

"Damned if I know," said Pender. "She was on South Beach, too."

Tiffany put down the headphones. "I need to check my e-mail. Now."

"We'll find a place as soon as possible," said Pender. "We gotta figure some things out first."

"We're going to get her, right?"

Pender didn't answer. "Boss," said Sawyer. "What the hell are we doing?"

Pender shook his head. "I don't know," he said. There was no chance of getting money from Andrew Prentice now that he knew the score. They *had* to get Mouse to a doctor, and they had to save Marie, too. Could they afford to go running after Haley Whittaker just so Beneteau's people could settle the beef? "We need cash," he told Sawyer. "We need it now."

Tiffany sat up. "Haley's got fifty thousand dollars," she said. "From her grandmother. Graduation present. Will that help?"

"Will she pay us?"

"If we save her life," said Tiffany. "Of course she will."

Sawyer glanced at Pender. "We could fix up Mouse with *half* that money."

Tiffany nodded. "Exactly. The minute we get Haley free we'll get Mouse to a doctor. You can use the rest to help Marie."

Sawyer and Pender swapped looks. They needed money, and they needed it yesterday. For fifty grand, Pender would have built a rocket and flown to the moon. "All right," he told Tiffany. "We're in. We gotta get that money, though."

"No problem," said Tiffany. "But I gotta check my e-mail. Now."

Pender nodded, and Sawyer flicked on the turn signal, cutting across three lanes of traffic toward an off-ramp and a stack of neon motel signs in the distance. Fifty grand, Pender thought. I guess we're in business again.

SIXTY-ONE

"You're never going to believe this," Windermere told Stevens, handing him a coffee. "Tiffany Prentice tried to hold herself for ransom."

Stevens rubbed his eyes and took a sip, watching the procession of travelers stream past the baggage carousels at Detroit Metro Airport. "One more time?" he said.

Windermere led him out of the terminal and across to the parking garage, talking quickly as she walked. "Prentice called her dad in Pennsylvania a couple days ago. Said she was a hostage with a million-dollar ransom. Forty-eight hours. No cops."

"A million bucks," said Stevens. "Those kids are getting desperate."

They walked up a flight of stairs and deep into the garage, where Windermere pressed a button on her key chain and a forest-green Crown Victoria chirped in response. "Get this," she said. "Daddy Prentice didn't have any idea his daughter was in Florida, much less that she'd gone missing."

"He thought she was in school."

"You got it. Anyway, he got the money together and he was going to pay it, the whole drop-it-off-at-McDonald's deal, when he gets this phone call."

They reached the Crown Vic and climbed inside. Windermere turned the key, and the car rumbled to life.

"You know how Prentice's friend reported her missing, right?" she said. "Haley Whittaker. She went and got herself kidnapped a few days later. Someone snatched her from a Miami motel room."

"Get out of here," said Stevens. "Our gang?"

"No, sir," said Windermere. She drove the sedan out of the garage. "Somebody else. Somebody who made Whittaker call Daddy Prentice and beg him to make Tiffany give up her friends."

"Beneteau's people. D'Antonio. He's using Whittaker as bait."

"So Prentice hears Whittaker's message and decides he's not going to pay. He drops off a phony bag and calls the cops, but they get there too late to pick up our boys."

"Too late?" said Stevens. "Come on."

"City cops, right? But he also put the message from Whittaker in the bag, so I guess he's hoping Tiffany will give up on her boys and come on home."

They were driving up I-94 now, cruising past the miles of low factories and railroad yards toward the city. "What are we hoping?" said Stevens.

Windermere shrugged. "We're hoping they think Marie's more important. We don't know where D'Antonio is or how he managed to snatch the Whittaker girl. Frankly, nobody's too happy with the idea of these kids getting caught up in a personal vendetta against Beneteau's crew."

"So let's keep pressing McAllister," said Stevens. "Maybe we leak something to the press, something that will get the boys interested again. Do they know she's in Detroit?"

"Not sure," said Windermere. "We can get that on the news. Try to angle the boys up in this direction."

"Sure. In the meantime we can press Beneteau's people for information on D'Antonio. Talk to your people in racketeering. Maybe they've got something on the mob scene in Miami, huh? What about this guy Zeke?"

Windermere changed lanes, pulling out to pass as the highway curved alongside a giant Ford complex. "Still nothing on Zeke," she said. "No known address or aliases. Miami PD is supposed to be on it, but they're corrupt as shit. Probably it comes back blank."

"This guy's a professional, anyway," said Stevens. "He's not risking a kidnapping unless he knows he can beat the rap."

"Maybe," said Windermere. "Maybe we get lucky, though." She glanced across at him. "You owe me for that prisoner move."

"Why's that?" said Stevens. "No fun?"

"The girl said not a word for fifteen hours straight. All the way up from Jacksonville, she just sat there staring at her feet. Every time I asked her something, she told me she wanted her lawyer. It's not like I was interrogating her. I just wanted some company."

"What about the marshal?"

"Clayton?" Windermere laughed. "We talked football for a minute. Then I asked him if he'd read a good book lately, and he clammed up real tight."

"Aw," said Stevens. "You missed me."

"Hell, no. I know you can't read, either."

Stevens laughed, smiling out the window as the bleak Detroit landscape appeared on the horizon.

"Good visit home?" said Windermere.

"Sure," said Stevens. "It was good. Uneventful."

"Tough to leave?"

He shook his head. "I'm happy to be back. This case is gonna fall."

"Give it up," said Windermere. "You missed me, too."

Stevens glanced at her. "Maybe just a little," he said.

Windermere stared at the road ahead, the hint of a smile at her lips. "Get your fix while you still can, Stevens. We're taking this thing down in a week on the outside."

Stevens laughed again and turned back to the window, letting his smile slip away as he focused once more on their labyrinthine case. As Windermere drove, he watched the skyline approach, searching for the big FBI building on Michigan Avenue where Marie McAllister sat alone, the cheese in their better mousetrap, waiting for Pender and Co. to get hungry enough to bite.

SIXTY-TWO

D'Antonio sat in Zeke's living room, choking down a noxious tuna casserole, drinking beer to mask the taste, and watching the news for any sign that the cops were making progress on the Whittaker case.

There was nothing about the girl, but as the news switched to regional and D'Antonio closed out his dinner, he heard something on the TV that made him forget about Zeke's girlfriend's cooking and sit forward in his seat.

"A startling new development in the South Beach shooting that left two men dead at Miami's historic Dauphin Hotel," the anchor was saying. "Federal investigators now name twenty-year-old Tiffany Prentice a suspect following a bizarre kidnapping attempt in suburban Philadelphia."

D'Antonio listened as the anchor outlined the new developments. The kidnapping had been foiled, according to official reports, thanks to the timely arrival of Bryn Mawr law enforcement officials on scene. But the cops hadn't captured the kids, and the girl was still at large.

D'Antonio listened, trying to make sense of the twist. They'd tried to stage a kidnapping. The kids were desperate, and the girl was in on the game. Interesting.

He turned off the television and carried the dirty dishes into the kitchen. Then he grabbed Whittaker's laptop and walked down the hall to the girl's room.

She'd at least poked around at the tuna casserole this time, D'Antonio noticed. The girl had had maybe a forkload or two before she opted out, and now she lay paging through her novel on the bed, her meal cold and forgotten.

D'Antonio closed the door behind and walked into the room. "So you're a carnivore now."

The girl made a face. "That was supposed to be meat?"

"It was tuna."

"I decided you must be trying to poison me, so I didn't eat it." The girl sighed. "I feel so dirty. Can't you bring me a change of clothes?"

"Where would I get a change of clothes?"

"At least a shower. This is cruel and un-usual."

D'Antonio walked to the bed and sat down beside the girl, watching the way her hair splayed out on the comforter, reading over her shoulder as he opened the laptop. "Good book?"

She shrugged. "It's okay."

He peered down at the page. "Who's Alexis?"

The girl frowned at him. Then she glanced down at the book. "I guess she's supposed to be some kind of advertising executive in Manhattan." She shrugged. "I don't really read this kind of stuff. I just borrowed it from Tiffany."

D'Antonio turned back to the laptop and opened the girl's Internet browser.

"Do you read?" she asked. "*Can* you read?"

"Of course I can fucking read," he said.

"So?" She looked up at him. "What do you read?"

He stared at her a second. "I read a lot of those books they sell in airports. Paperback thrillers. Self-help books sometimes. My brother-in-law buys them for me every year for Christmas. I don't know if they do any good."

"They make self-help books for killers?"

"For businessmen," he said. "He doesn't really know what I do." He cleared his throat. "Time to check your e-mail."

The girl stared down at her book for a moment or two. Then she twisted her body so she was facing the computer, her face nearly touching D'Antonio's leg. "You think she wrote back?"

"There was a dustup in Pennsylvania," D'Antonio told her. "Your friend tried to hold herself for ransom."

The girl looked up at him. "What do you mean?"

"She tried to fake her own kidnapping. Something went wrong. I think your little phone call made an impact."

The girl typed in her password, and they waited as the screen loaded up. She twisted on the bed so she was lying on her back, staring up at him, her long hair fanned out and her eyes fixed on his. "I was thinking," she said. "Maybe we could work something out."

Here it comes, D'Antonio thought. "You tried this one already," he said.

"I'm serious this time. You kind of like me. I can tell." She sat up and pressed against his arm, her body close and her lips brushing his ear. "You could have me if you wanted. You could do whatever you liked."

She put her hand on his leg, high. This is fake, D'Antonio told himself. You have a job to do. He shook her off. Pointed to the computer screen. "There. One new message."

She barely glanced at the screen. "I've got fifty thousand dollars," she said, "I could pay you. Like a ransom. I'd give them false information. I could tell them you were, like, a black guy from Jamaica or something. Nobody would have to know."

Christ. The girl was staring at him with such hope in her eyes that he found it hard to look at her. Never again, he thought. Never again with this hostage shit. "I don't want you," he said. "I don't want your money, either."

She stared at him for a long moment. D'Antonio refused to meet her gaze. She turned back to the computer screen. "She wrote back," she said. "A couple hours ago."

"Read it."

She opened the message and read it aloud. Tiffany had heard the phone message. They were in Pennsylvania. They were coming back to get Haley.

The girl looked up at him, waiting for his answer. The kids were in Pennsylvania, he thought. We're safe in Florida, but those kids are at the top of the Most Wanted list.

I don't want them caught before I get my chance with them.

D'Antonio turned back to the girl. "Write her back," he said. "Tell them forget coming to Florida. Go to Cincinnati instead."

"Cincinnati?"

"Yeah," he said, standing. "We're going to take a little road trip."

SIXTY-THREE

"Cincinnati," said Pender. "What the hell is in Cincinnati?"

Tiffany looked up from her computer and shrugged. "I guess it's better than Florida. You guys are wanted as hell down there."

"You're wanted, too," said Sawyer. "Remember?"

They'd turned on the TV as soon as they booked a room, hungry for cheap intel and wondering how the cops were going to spin the kidnapping. Tiffany went pale when her face came on screen, but she kept her composure, and after a couple White Castle hamburgers and a cherry Pepsi she seemed to be enjoying her newfound notoriety. "This is kind of cool," she told Pender. "I'm a legit outlaw now. Like Thelma and Louise."

Now she sat on Mouse's bed with his computer on her lap, reading out Haley's kidnapper's instructions.

"Cincinnati's better for us, anyway," said Pender. "Now that they moved Marie. We get Haley back, and then we swing up to Detroit to get Marie. What time are we supposed to show?"

"Day after tomorrow," said Tiffany. "That's plenty of time."

Day after tomorrow, thought Pender, staring at Mouse. We drive tomorrow. We deal with this Whittaker situation the day after — though how they were going to handle it, he had no idea — and then we get Mouse to a hospital that evening. That's assuming he can make it that far.

Pender stood and walked over to Mouse's bed. His friend looked almost childlike, as though he'd shrunk in the wash. What the hell have we done, Pender thought, listening to his friend's ragged breathing. Nobody was supposed to get hurt. "Mouse," he said, touching his friend's shoulder. "You there, buddy?"

Mouse opened his eyes halfway. He smiled slowly. "Pender."

"Listen," said Pender. "We have to drive to Cincinnati tomorrow. Means you won't see a doctor until the next evening at the earliest. You think you can hold out?"

Mouse nodded. "Of course. Do what you have to do."

"I'm serious, Mouse. No hero shit. We can drop you at an emergency room tonight if you need it."

"Emergency room," Mouse said. "They'll arrest me for sure."

Pender glanced around the room. Sawyer and Tiffany were watching, silent. "Better arrested than dead, right?"

"Bullshit." Mouse struggled to sit up, his face flush and frustrated. "Get me some drugs, and I'm fine for a couple more days."

"You're sure."

"I promise." He turned toward Tiffany. "Pass me that computer, babe?"

Tiffany handed Mouse his laptop, and Pender watched as his friend perched the computer on his sunken chest. "What are you doing?"

"We're getting out of this," said Mouse. "Soon as we spring Marie, we're getting the hell out of this country."

"Fine," said Pender. "But what are you doing?"

Mouse was hammering keys, only half listening. "Getting in touch with my guy," he said. "We'll have two days in Cincy. That's enough time to cook up passports and Social Security numbers. I'll have my guy ship them tomorrow."

"Good idea," said Pender. Mouse is invaluable, he thought. If we lose him, we're royally screwed.

Mouse made eyes at Tiffany. "Now, then, beautiful," he said. "What would you like your new name to be?"

The next day they were up early and out the door, packed into the minivan and on the road ahead of rush-hour traffic. They drove west on I-76, Tiffany dozing in back beside Mouse and Sawyer riding shotgun, fiddling with the radio dial as Pender watched more highway disappear behind them. He kept his eyes out for the state police as he drove, not knowing whether the minivan was compromised or if they'd gotten away clean. It's like driving with a hand grenade, he thought. We blink the wrong way, and it blows up in our faces.

They stopped for fuel and food in Columbus and then continued south toward Cincinnati, the sun starting to set and the shadows getting longer. Sawyer found an alt-rock station and sat back in his seat, drumming along to the beat on his knees. He sniffed the air and turned to Pender. "Be glad to get out of this van," he said. "This thing's got a *stench* to it. I mean, goddamn, Pender. You had to pick the smelliest car on the lot."

Pender smiled. "Security system, bro."

"Ah, that's why we got away back there. Cops were afraid of how bad we smelled."

"You got it."

"Well, shit." Sawyer turned back to watch Ohio, low and flat and farmy, pass outside his window. "I'd maybe rather be arrested than have to spend much longer in this heap."

"No, you wouldn't," said Pender. "You really wouldn't."

They put a few more miles beneath the wheels, Sawyer drumming along to the music and Pender watching eighteen-wheelers pass in the opposite direction. Then Pender spoke up again. "What do you think of this whole scheme?"

"This Beneteau thing." Sawyer stopped drumming. "Haley and all that."

"How's it going to work out?"

"The ransom."

"We've never been on this side of a deal before," said Pender. "I'm just running on instincts."

"If those guys think we're just going to give ourselves up for that girl, they're retarded." Sawyer glanced at Pender. "Right?"

Pender kept his eyes on the road, pulled out into the passing lane. "We're not giving anybody up," he said. "As far as I'm concerned, we're running game on these people."

"They'll bring guns."

"We're walking into a trap," said Pender. "I know it. We're not assassins. We don't even have ammunition. But we need that fifty grand, Sawyer."

Sawyer said nothing for a moment. "Can you think of any other way to do this?" he said finally.

Pender looked over at his friend. "No," he said. "I really can't."

SIXTY-FOUR

First-degree murder. Two counts of kidnapping. Conspiracy to commit murder. Two counts of conspiracy to commit kidnapping. The FBI agent read out the charges with undisguised glee, punctuating the list with a wink at Marie and a parting shot. "Trust me, honey," Agent Windermere said. "There will be more where that came from, just as soon as we peg you down for the rest of the jobs."

Marie barely listened to the woman. Refused to give her the satisfaction of a response. She'd known the charges were coming as the days began to pile up, first in Jacksonville and then, after that excruciating ride, in Detroit. Marie had felt her defiance withering, her resolve nearly vanished, and she sat in her cell now, defeated and miserable, fully aware that Pender wasn't coming for her and that he wasn't sending her a lawyer, either. She would have to face her consequences alone.

Her parents refused to talk to her. She'd tried to call them from the FBI office in Detroit the day after she'd arrived. Her sister picked up on the third or fourth ring, and the sound of her voice had brought Marie momentarily back to life, but her sister was like stone on the other end of the line. "Mom and Dad don't want to talk to you," she said. "Anyway, I don't think they could bear it."

"Marney, please," Marie said. "I need to hear their voices."

"No," said her sister. "You don't understand. You almost killed them, Marie. They're devastated. Dad looks like he's aged ten years since the FBI showed up. All Mom can talk about is the lies you told. Kidnapping, Marie. What the hell were you thinking?"

"I need to talk to them. Please."

"I can't put them through it, Marie. I'm sorry," she said, and she paused. Then: "Please don't call here again."

And then she'd hung up. Marie could still hear the dial tone.

She floated through the bail hearing, barely noticing the judge or the prosecution or her own appointed defender, a well-dressed middle-aged woman who introduced herself as Gloria Wallace, Assistant Federal Public Defender, and who argued strenuously and in vain against the assistant U.S. attorney's request that bail be denied.

Wallace apologized after the hearing and looked like she really meant it, but Marie, still floating above her own head like she was watching herself on television, just allowed herself to be led from the courtroom and back to her desolate cell.

I could not sit here for twenty years, she realized. I would die behind these walls. My body would just give up, and I would die. Or I would find a way to kill myself. I couldn't bear to be alone for the next twenty years of my life — and twenty years, she knew, was just a baseline number. She might never be free again.

Those guys are long gone, she thought to herself. They're on a beach in Thailand sipping fruity drinks and spending all the money you helped them make. They're home free. You've got nobody to live for but yourself.

"Shut up," she said aloud. Her words echoed in the cell and in her eardrums.

But that insidious little voice kept talking, kept pouring poison in her ear. And as Marie lay down to try and sleep on her lumpy cot in that dirty cell, she felt herself starting to give in to the voice, to listen to its promise.

And the next morning, when Assistant Federal Public Defender Wallace showed up at the prison to start preparations for the pretrial hearing, Marie didn't immediately shut her down when she broached the subject of a plea bargain. That little devil's advocate in her head had grown powerful overnight, and even though Marie felt sick even thinking about betraying the boys, she let the voice take the mic and speak for her.

And instead of telling Gloria Wallace, screw off, I'm innocent, Marie floated above her own head again, watched herself lean forward and tell her attorney, "All right, I'm listening. What kind of deal can we get?"

Sixty-Five

"The CSX yards," said Tiffany. "Dusk."

Dusk, thought Pender, trying to think like a mobster. So it was meant to be a firefight. If they'd gone for a populated area, we'd know they were going to play it straight. But they went industrial, deserted, and dark, which means they're not even bothering with pretense. They're going to kill us then and there.

He turned to Sawyer. "What do you think?"

Sawyer shrugged. "I think we've got an Uzi and a handgun and not nearly enough ammunition. We'd be stupid to go in there like that."

"How many men do they bring?"

"We're close enough to Detroit. They could bring a whole army."

"Haley said this is the last time we'll hear from them," said Tiffany. "If we're not where they want us, when they want us, they're going to kill her."

"They're going to kill her, anyway," said Sawyer. "We can't let them kill us, too."

"If Haley dies, you guys don't get paid."

"We're not letting your friend die," said Pender. "Look, we're always going to be in this spot, whether it's now or tomorrow or next week. They want to kill us. We're going to have to beat them."

"We can't just walk in there," said Sawyer. "We don't even know what the place looks like."

Mouse coughed from his corner of the bed. "Street View," he said, trying to sit up. "Search the intersection on the Internet and scope the terrain. Almost as good as field work."

Tiffany punched the intersection into Mouse's computer. "He's right," she said. "Come look. This place is a wasteland."

According to the Internet, the meeting spot was a neighborhood of warehouses, abandoned factories, parking lots, and vacant space. A couple of weed-choked railroad spur lines snaked between the buildings, and in the distance, the CSX classification yards could just barely be seen. "Genius, Mouse," Pender said. "Now how are we going to play this?"

"We could call the police," said Tiffany.

"They gave up their location. We call the police, and they storm the neighborhood."

"What if they don't have the girl on site?" said Sawyer. "Police grab the bad guys, and the girl gets shot up in some motel room somewhere because we didn't pull through."

"No police," said Pender. "Any other ideas?"

He waited. For a minute, nobody said anything. Then Sawyer sighed. "I have an idea," said Sawyer. "Listen up."

They listened as Sawyer outlined his plan, and then they argued it over, picking it apart for flaws and putting it back together. It wasn't nearly perfect, thought Pender, but there was no way to be sure the girl would stay safe unless they got in the mix and dirtied their hands.

Dusk came quicker than any of them would have liked, and they packed up the minivan with the light already waning and their watches barely reading five. Pender drove from the motel into the city, and they watched the sun like a doomsday clock. Nobody spoke, the only sound Mouse's labored breathing from the shotgun seat.

They pulled off the freeway and crossed over the CSX yard toward the meeting spot, but before they reached the intersection Pender pulled a quick right and dashed down a side street. He pulled into a factory lot and put the car in park. He exhaled, slow, and forced his hands to stop shaking. Then he twisted in his seat to face his team. "Everybody ready for this?"

He searched their faces one by one. Tiffany was drawn and taut, beating a rhythm on the floor of the van with her feet. She met his gaze and looked away. Sawyer's eyes were low, his mouth set. He stared back at Pender and nodded when their eyes met. Mouse flashed him a weak grin in the passenger seat.

"Let's go through this one more time," said Pender. "Tiffany, you know how to use that Glock?"

"Point and shoot," she said. "Just like in *Resident Evil.*"

"Perfect. Mouse, you're cool?"

"What have I got to lose?"

"Sawyer?"

"Long as you don't shoot me with that Uzi, boss."

"I'll try my best." Pender looked out the window. The last of the day's light was disappearing below the factory line. He unbuckled his seat belt and picked up the machine gun. "It's time," he said. "Remember, wait for Sawyer's signal before you drive."

"Affirmative," said Mouse. He grinned at Tiffany, who was climbing into the driver's seat. Then he turned back to Pender and seemed to summon what remained of his strength. "If shit goes down, you've got parcels waiting for you at the Amtrak station. You remember how to get a hold of the money once you're on foreign soil?"

"I remember. But you'll be there with us, buddy," said Pender, and he stepped out of the van and met Sawyer coming around from his side. "Ready?"

"I'm ready." Sawyer held out his hand. Pender clasped it, and they shook. Then Pender watched his friend creep into the shadows by the side of the road and disappear along the railroad tracks. He waited until he was sure Sawyer was gone, and then he, too, crept forward, casting one glance back at the relative safety of the van before walking quickly down the road, hugging the building that lined the curb and cradling the Uzi like a baby, the weapon heavy and menacing in his hands.

Sixty-Six

D'Antonio drove the girl to the drop zone in the Explorer while Paolo rode along in the Tahoe with the three fresh goons from Detroit. The girl was fascinated by his gun, kept sneaking looks, as though staring at it would make the thing disappear.

She made her last pitch on the drive over. "You really don't have to kill me," she said. "I'm not going to snitch on you."

She said it lightly, almost flirtatious. Her nonchalance was still shocking. "How could I be sure?" he asked her.

She leaned toward him, smiling. "I know you have a thing for me. How are you going to pull it together long enough to shoot me?"

"I've killed plenty of people before."

"Never anyone like me."

"Yeah," he said. He leaned forward and fiddled with the radio dial. Found a rock station and turned up the volume. "There's a first time for everything."

That shut her up. She sank back in her seat and said nothing more. D'Antonio avoided looking at her for the rest of the drive.

It was true he'd killed people before. More often than not, they didn't deserve to be dead. He did his job well, and he never lost sleep. But D'Antonio liked to kill fast. He'd show up in the shadows when the mark walked in the door at night, put a bullet in his forehead, and walk right out again. He didn't spend time with his victims. Didn't talk to them. He certainly didn't feed and clothe them while he waited for the right time to pull the trigger.

This girl. He could have killed her already. He realized he was putting it off. Something inside him didn't like the idea.

D'Antonio found the intersection on the Explorer's navigation system and backed into the shadows in a parking lot a half a block away. He could see the Tahoe parked on the other side of the intersection and imagined Paolo and the goons spread out in the darkness, their ambush immaculate.

"When the kids come, we're going to show your face just so they know you're alive," he told her. "That way they'll all come out in the open. When we've got all four of them,

I'll let you go."

She turned to face him. "Really?"

He tried to hold her gaze. "Really," he said, thinking, you're getting too damn soft.

She stared into his eyes. "You lie," she said, and her voice was like damnation.

Pender crouched low and ran through the shadows, clutching the Uzi and keeping his eyes open for Beneteau's men. I feel like a Marine, he thought. Urban warfare.

He ran down the side street a couple blocks from the kill zone, expecting to hear gunfire as he made his way forward. But no gunfire came, and he was alone in the darkness. He reached the end of the block and zagged up toward the drop site.

He stopped a block away and stared up toward the spot, searching the distance for any signs of life, any cars in weird places, any assassins with heavy weaponry. But everything seemed normal. Nothing and everything felt out of the ordinary.

He stayed as far off the road as possible, his jeans rubbing against weeds and his sneakers ruffling through the fall's last moldy leaves as he crept up the block. They'd scoped the intersection on the Internet and decided that the vacant lot on this south side would be the likely staging ground for the kidnappers, and as Pender approached he scanned the dark hulks of parked cars for anything fresh and out of place.

The whole street was silent, the only noise the occasional rumble and clank from the switch engines in the CSX yard a few blocks down, and Pender tried to fight the panic in his gut, tried to block the terrifying knowledge that there were multiple men out there in the dark whose only purpose was to kill him.

He crept toward the vacant lot, one eye on the road and the other on the first brief row of cars. There were three vehicles that he could see, all rusted and broken and abandoned, and he crouched down and took cover behind the first, holding the Uzi to his chest and wondering what to do.

He was staring through the spiderweb window of the first rusted hulk when he saw the SUV parked hidden in the back of the lot. It was a late-model Ford, and it looked untouched and new, incongruous in the bleak surroundings.

Had to be them. The truck was too pristine to be sitting in this neighborhood more than a couple of hours. It sat about twenty feet away, angled out, facing north toward the intersection with the passenger windows pointed in Pender's direction.

Twenty feet away. Twenty feet of pure empty space. There was a chain-link fence running the length of the lot and a mostly empty yard behind. No shadow until the other side, where a factory overhang and a row of trees cast camouflage onto the gravel. Twenty feet. A mad dash and a gamble.

He stayed in a low crouch and peered out around the car's rear bumper. The lot was dark, but anyone watching from the road would see him clearly. No getting around it.

Pender forced himself to take a deep breath, and he let it out slow. He took another deep breath and this time closed his eyes and ran. He stayed low but the noise of his feet on the gravel sounded like gunfire already, and he seemed to be running in molasses; it took an hour to close the twenty feet before the shadows but he kept running, kept low, every step a prayer.

He reached the back of the lot and the long, safe darkness and crouched down again behind the Explorer, hunched over and daring to hope that nobody inside had seen him. He sat for a minute, catching his breath, listening hard, but there was nothing but the distant rushing backdrop of the city.

Pender peered around the passenger side

of the Explorer and out into the lot. Nobody anywhere. Maybe we got the wrong intersection, he thought. Maybe we got the wrong time. Maybe there's nobody in this Explorer and we're all running around like idiots. But then he caught a glimpse of something in the passenger-side mirror, a face. A girl's face. She caught his eye for a second, then looked away.

That must be Haley, he thought. Perfect. He slouched back behind the truck and tried to figure out a plan. If he snuck up along the driver's side, he'd be spotted in an instant. He could sneak up the passenger side, but then he put Haley in between the Uzi and the target.

Pender crept back around the passenger side and stared at the girl's face in the mirror, trying to catch her eye again. After a minute or two, she glanced in the mirror, and Pender held up his hand. How many, he mouthed, holding up one finger. The girl nodded, quick and almost imperceptible. Pender nodded. Distract him, he mouthed. She frowned. He held up his free hand and made like a talking mouth. Pender watched as she turned to the driver and started to talk. Then he crept around the other side of the Explorer and slowly made his way up to the front of the vehicle.

■ ■ ■ ■

The girl leaned over toward D'Antonio. "I'm bored," she said. "Where are these guys?"

D'Antonio scanned the intersection. "They should have been here by now."

She put her hand on his leg. "Can't we do something while we wait?"

D'Antonio let himself enjoy her touch for a few seconds. When this is over, he thought, when these kids are nothing but gristle and shell casings, I'm going to go back to Detroit and I'm going to take a long nap. Then I'm going to have Rialto send over a couple girls, and I'm going to forget all about this crazy bitch. He shook his head. "Just wait."

D'Antonio saw the gun before he saw the man. Just outside his window, a submachine Uzi with an extended clip. Hard-core hardware. Then he saw the shooter. It was one of the kids, and for a second he was confused. How did those little punks get their hands on artillery like that, he wondered.

"Don't make a sound," the kid told him, keeping his gun trained on D'Antonio's head. His voice came muffled through the glass, but D'Antonio could sense the kid's nerves, his false courage. "Open the door, slow."

The kid stepped back to give him room, and he let the Uzi drop just enough that D'Antonio saw his chance. Slowly, he reached down with his right hand until his fingers met the steel of his Glock. He wrapped his hand around it, and then he moved quickly, bringing the gun up and spinning to jam the weapon hard against the girl's throat.

"Hey!" The kid jumped forward, shoving the muzzle of the Uzi against D'Antonio's neck. "The fuck do you think you're doing?"

"You shoot, I shoot," D'Antonio replied. "Think about it."

The kid went silent. D'Antonio could hear him breathing hard, trying to keep it together. "All right," D'Antonio said, his voice smooth as butter on toast. "Now drop the weapon before I drop this girl."

"I'm not dropping anything." The kid's voice was shaky. "You even move and I'll put a whole clip in your head."

D'Antonio smiled. "This isn't the movies, kid." With his left hand, he reached up to the steering wheel and punched down on the horn. The noise echoed around the abandoned buildings, loud as a jet airplane in the silence of the night. "I'd say you have maybe a minute until the cavalry arrives," D'Antonio told him. "You want to make a decision, make it fast."

SIXTY-SEVEN

Sawyer crept down the spur line, keeping to the weeds on the side of the right of way and trying to stay in the shadows as he headed toward the intersection. He kept his head on a swivel, trying to imagine where Beneteau's goons were hiding.

This is just like Xbox, he thought. On some Call of Duty shit. He made his way slowly up toward the level crossing and peered out from around the side of a warehouse toward the intersection. The streets were deserted.

Somewhere out there, Pender is running around with an Uzi, he thought. That's a scary idea. He listened close, straining for a cough or the snap of a twig, something to give away the bad guys' locations, but he heard nothing.

Christ, he thought. Where the hell are those guys? He kept listening, hardly daring to breathe, searching the shadows for any signs of life.

Then he saw it. So brief he thought he'd imagined it. A little chuff of condensation, hot breath in cold air. It came from a shadow on the other side of a loading dock, about halfway between the tracks and the intersection. Sawyer stared at the spot, and a couple seconds later he saw the cloud reappear.

Sawyer flattened himself against the wall and slunk forward toward the loading dock, trying to pick the guy out in the darkness. He reached the dock, a five-foot shelf that jutted out toward the road, and he crouched down below it. The man was on the other side, barely ten feet away, and now Sawyer could hear his muffled breathing, the shuffle as he shifted his weight. Bingo, he thought. Now we see whether it's possible to be stupid *and* lucky.

He stayed so low he was almost crawling, inching around the loading dock until the man was maybe two feet away. He peered around the side of the dock. The man was facing away from him and dressed all in black. He was huge. Probably six foot six, a real heavyweight lunkhead. The man cradled a machine pistol in his hands, and he was staring out toward the empty intersection.

Sawyer crept back to the other side of the

loading dock and felt around in the weeds for something big enough to use as a weapon. After a minute or two of searching, he got his hands on a length of four-inch-thick cast-iron piping, and he picked it up, testing it. A little short, but it would do.

He made his way back around the base of the loading dock. This time, something made him hesitate. The man was right there, waiting to be taken down, but something wasn't right. Sawyer waited. He could hear the man breathing, heavy, and then he knew: The thug had turned away from the intersection. He was facing Sawyer now, so close Sawyer could have reached out and tied his laces together.

Shit, Sawyer thought. He stayed crouched, silently begging the guy to turn around. Then he heard the car horn, and he knew he had his chance.

It rang out from across the vacant lot, close enough that it had to mean something. Sawyer heard the thug beside him tense up and turn to face the intersection again. Sawyer stood quickly, holding the pipe like a baseball bat, and he swung for the bleachers, catching the goon square on the jaw, the pipe shattering bone with a sickening crunch and sending the man reeling back toward the warehouse wall, back and down.

Sawyer worked quick, following the guy backward and teeing up with another home-run swing before the thug could grab his gun. This time the man's skull made a sound like a burst pumpkin, and the pipe came back bloody. The guy sunk to the ground and stayed there.

Sawyer stared down at the thug for a second, his heart pounding. Then he reached down and unclipped the gun from around the guy's neck, dropping the pipe by his feet. The gun was warm in his hand, and for a second Sawyer felt sick. Then he caught himself. He straightened up and shook it off and turned back to the street.

Two more thugs, both similarly super-sized, were in the middle of the intersection, walking from opposite corners toward the vacant lot. One guy had a machine gun, looked like an Uzi, and the other a big sawed-off shotgun. Big guys. Big fucking guns.

Sawyer examined his own weapon, a full-sized TEC-9 machine pistol with what looked like a fifty-round clip and a ventilated shroud on the end of the muzzle. The thing was a killing machine, but Sawyer had played enough video games to know you sacrificed quality for quantity when you shot a TEC-9. No sniper shit, he thought. We spray and pray.

The thug with the shotgun was closer, but Sawyer wanted to neutralize the Uzi first. He danced through the shadows up to the corner of the intersection, and then he dashed across the street, making for a Buick on blocks on the other side of the pavement.

He got there and crouched behind the car and watched the thugs, both starting across the lot by now, the guy with the Uzi about forty feet away. Just like the movies, he thought. Exhale slowly, then fire.

Sawyer held the gun in both hands. He took a deep breath, then stood and drew his mark. He let the breath out and pulled the trigger.

The sound was deafening, the gun jumping all over the place with the recoil, and Sawyer let off a burst of maybe ten shots before he got the gun back under control. The thug with the Uzi was down on the ground, but Sawyer couldn't tell if he was hit or just diving for cover, and meanwhile the other thug was making for a line of cars at the edge of the lot.

Sawyer advanced across the street, keeping low and heading for the cover of the building on the edge of the lot. The guy with the Uzi looked back and fired a wild burst, and the Buick's windows smashed to nothing on the other side of the street. Sawyer shot from the hip as he ran, holding tight with both hands and keeping the trigger pulled until the thug was laid out and screaming.

He made the side of the building and leaned back, out of sight, trying to catch his breath. Then he peered back into the vacant lot. The thug with the Uzi was flat on his back, blood pooling around him. Sawyer scoped out the row of junker cars, searching for the second shooter. He spotted him crouched between the first and second rides, the barrel of the shotgun giving him away.

Where the hell is Pender, Sawyer thought. That shotgun will blow me away at close range.

Sawyer peered back around the wall. The shooter had crept forward out of the cover of the parked cars, and now he was making his own dash for the wall. Sawyer stepped out and fired, bracing himself against the wall. The first burst missed, and the shooter fired a blast from his hip and kept running. The shotgun sounded like the end of the world, and Sawyer ducked for cover.

Gotta get him before he gets to the wall, he thought, and he forced himself up and out again, diving into the middle of the lot as the shotgun boomed behind him. The thug was aiming at the corner of the building, and Sawyer caught him with about ten rounds before he could swing the shotgun around. The thug let off one more blast, but it went high and wide, and then he was slumping down, the shotgun falling to the gravel beside him.

Holy shit. Sawyer ran to the cover of the row of abandoned cars and crouched down, staring out over the vacant lot and the carnage. He saw the truck parked way in the back of the lot, nearly hidden by shadows, and he decided that was where the horn had come from. That's where the big boss is camped out, he thought. But where the hell is Pender?

Then he felt the gun at his back. "Stand up, motherfucker."

Sawyer stood, cursing himself as the thug pressed his gun hard into the side of his neck.

"Drop the gun." The voice was vaguely Mediterranean. "Drop it now."

Sawyer felt the adrenaline rush subsiding, and all of a sudden he just felt tired and he knew this was where it was all supposed to end. He let go of the TEC and it clattered to the ground and the guy spun him around, a big ugly grin and a nickel-plated MAC-10.

"You had to get cute, huh?" the guy said, pressing the gun harder against Sawyer's skin. He leered into Sawyer's eyes, drunk on power. Then he shoved Sawyer backward. "Well, come on, then, cutie," he said. "Hope you saved me a dance."

SIXTY-EIGHT

D'Antonio watched as Dmitri hauled the kid to his feet, the muzzle of his machine gun pressed tight to the kid's neck. Jesus, but that little punk had done a lot of damage. Yuri and Dario both done, and where the fuck was Paolo? Either dead or dying somewhere.

They'd watched from the darkness as the kid had come out of the shadows and laid waste to both goons like the angel of death. D'Antonio kept his Glock pressed tight to the girl's ear, holding her close and daring the kid with the Uzi to try something stupid. Now they watched as Dmitri roughed up the punk, whipping him with the butt of his gun, laughing in his face, having a little fun before the kill. "You must be Pender," said D'Antonio. "The man with the plan."

The kid spat. "And who the hell are you?" His voice was still shaky.

"I work for Donald Beneteau's people." He shifted a little. "You ever fired a gun before?"

"I killed your goons in Miami, didn't I? Tell your man to let my friend go."

"Not a chance."

"Let Haley go, at least. She's got no part in this."

"You're in no position to be making demands," said D'Antonio. "If you drop the Uzi, then maybe we talk. Maybe I let Haley go."

The kid pressed the gun tighter. "Not good enough."

Outside, Dmitri had the punk stood up, but barely. The kid was punch-drunk and reeling, his mouth a bloody mess and his left eye half closed. D'Antonio honked the horn, and Dmitri glanced over and nodded, briefly, before kicking the punk backward and leveling the gun at his forehead.

"Fine," said D'Antonio. "Then you all die. Starting with your pal out there."

Sawyer was beat-up and rotten. His head throbbed. He felt his legs giving out when the horn blared and the thug quit beating on him at last. The guy kicked him back, and he nearly collapsed, but just barely held on and stood upright. I'm going out standing, he thought as he stared down the gun. I can say that at least.

The thug had a flair for the dramatic. He gave Sawyer a wink and made kissy lips and then straightened the gun, and Sawyer braced for the kill shot. He closed his eyes. Then he heard the roar of the engine, and he opened his eyes again, quick.

The thug wasn't staring at him, but at the minivan as it sped out from the shadows, its ancient motor straining under Tiffany's heel. The van headed right for Sawyer, and for a moment he could swear he saw Tiffany smiling.

The thug spun away from Sawyer and fired a long angry burst across the front of the van, his shots arcing up and to the left, shattering the windshield. The engine revved higher, Tiffany's eyes all murder and vengeance, and she slammed into the thug doing forty or so, rolled over him twice and came to a stop halfway down the block.

Sawyer ran back to the thug, who lay broken and bleeding on the pavement. He kicked the machine gun away from his hand and stared down at the bastard, the thug's face all grease, glass, and grit, his breathing ragged and bloody. Sawyer stood over him for a minute, watching the man struggling to breathe, and then he picked up the

MAC-10 from the side of the road and put a burst through the thug's chest.

Then, when he was sure the bastard was dead, he stepped over the body and walked onto the lot.

D'Antonio watched the punk step over Dmitri's body, and he tried to keep his composure. He still had the girl, and he still had the trump card.

The kid Pender kept his Uzi pressed tight. "Let her go," he said. "You can't win."

"There's winning and there's winning," said D'Antonio. "You want her to live? You're going to play it my way."

Haley was staring at him. "You don't have to kill me," she said. "It doesn't have to end like this."

"I'll tell you how it ends," he said.

She put her hand on him again. "Put the gun down. It's over."

D'Antonio glanced out the front windshield, the punk getting closer. "You're crazy," he told the girl. "Totally fucking nuts."

The girl was moving closer to him, her breath warm against his cheek. "I am crazy," she said. "I think I might even like you. But you're not going to kill me. You know you can't do it."

He barely blinked, but she caught it and wrenched at the gun. She was quick, but he was stronger and he knew he had a shot. If he pulled the trigger now, he'd blow her head clean off. But he hesitated, just for a second, and she had the gun wrestled clear by the time he did pull the trigger. The shot shattered the passenger window and was gone.

Then the kid Pender was wrestling him out of the car, throwing him to the ground, and the girl had got hold of the gun. And he fell to the gravel, faceup in the shadows, with Pender standing over him, some punk kid with an Uzi and a big pair of balls. D'Antonio wanted to laugh at the absurdity of it all, wanted to laugh at the thought that some fucked-up little girl had played him for his life, but more than wanting to laugh, he knew he wanted to see her face, wanted to understand what she was thinking, what she was feeling as she watched him die.

Instead he got the kid Pender, and when he opened his mouth to call out to the girl, the kid let him have it, a point-blank burst from the Uzi. Then he walked away, leaving D'Antonio to die in the shadows.

Sixty-Nine

Pender met Sawyer at the front of the Explorer, the Uzi still hot in his palm. "You all right?" he said, examining his friend's face. The thug had done a job on him: Sawyer's face was covered in welts, his one eye swollen shut and his mouth a jumble of blood and missing teeth.

"Fine," said Sawyer. He looked past Pender to D'Antonio's body, then into the Explorer where Haley sat curled in the passenger seat. "We cool?"

Pender nodded. "I think we got them all."

Sawyer walked over to Haley's door. He peered in through the broken window. "Hey, listen," he said. "How many of those dangerous cats did they bring?"

Haley blinked and looked up at him like she'd just noticed he was there. "I think five," she said. "Three from Detroit and two from Miami."

"Five plus the boss? Or five in total?"

"Five in total," she said. "Including D'Antonio."

"Who the hell's D'Antonio?"

Haley winced. She pointed out the driver's side. "That one over there."

"We've only got four bodies," said Pender. "Where's the last?"

Sawyer shook his head. "I took care of him."

Pender heard footsteps behind him, and he spun, lifting the Uzi reflexively. Tiffany ducked for cover. "Jesus Christ, don't shoot me," she said, gasping. "You guys gotta come quick. Mouse is hurt."

Pender swapped looks with Sawyer, and then he was running, clearing the vacant lot and huffing it down to where the minivan sat shot-up and haphazard.

Pender got there first. He put the Uzi on the roof of the van and peered into the passenger seat to see Mouse, his shirt torn up, bleeding all over. The kid had taken two or three shots to the chest and shoulder and was breathing blood, half conscious, his eyes lidded and distant. Mouse gave him a weak smile. "We winning?"

Pender turned to Tiffany. "This thing still run? We gotta find a hospital."

"It runs."

"Get in there and put pressure on the

431

wounds," he said. "I'll drive."

Mouse was shaking his head. "No time," he said. "Get out of here."

Pender climbed into the front seat. "We're not leaving you." He heard sirens in the distance as he fumbled with the ignition, willing the engine to turn over.

Mouse reached over and touched Pender's arm. "You remember how to get out of here?" He coughed blood and it spattered on the windshield. "I'm going to die," he said. "You guys should just go." Then his ragged breathing faltered.

Pender stared at his friend, half aware of the sirens getting louder and Tiffany sobbing, his brain slowed to a crawl. Mouse's eyes were half open, and he wasn't moving anymore. He was gone.

Beside them, Sawyer slammed to a stop in the Explorer, Haley in the passenger seat. "What the fuck are you waiting for?"

Pender looked at him across Mouse's body. "Mouse is done, Sawyer."

"Oh, Jesus." For a moment, Sawyer's face slackened. Then he blinked. "Look, we gotta go."

"We're not leaving without him," said Tiffany. "We can't."

"We have to," said Sawyer. "Pender, haul ass."

Pender sat silent for a second, hardly comprehending, and then his brain re-booted. Like someone had pressed the Reset button. He heard the sirens loud. "Tiffany," he said. "We gotta go."

He climbed out of the van and picked Tiffany up off Mouse. She held on to Mouse's body and Pender thought she might drag him along, but then she let him go, crying, and Pender carried her to the Explorer and piled her in back. Then he slid in beside her, and Sawyer gunned the engine as he slammed the door shut. Only when they were at the end of the block and turning did he let himself look back at the wrecked minivan. And then they were speeding away and the minivan was gone.

SEVENTY

They ran up the west side of the CSX yard, Sawyer taking side streets with his foot planted firmly on the accelerator. When they reached the top of the yards, they slowed and crossed over the tracks on a long, double-deck bridge. They came down the other side and turned south into the city, navigating down the east side of the tracks until they came to the train station.

Sawyer parked in a handicapped spot, and they climbed out of the car, leaving Haley in the passenger seat as they hurried into the terminal and found the baggage counter. The clerk served them all in turn, staring at Sawyer's battered face but saying nothing as he handed them identical manila envelopes with their given names on the outside.

They tore open the packages in the concourse, ripping the envelopes into tiny pieces and disposing of them in multiple trash bins before examining the contents.

Mouse had scored them all goodie bags: passports, birth certificates, driver's licenses, and credit cards. Everything they'd need to get out of the country. Pender's package had the same for Marie.

They walked back to the Explorer and found Haley as they'd left her, curled up and vacant in the passenger seat.

She hadn't said a word since they'd asked her about the thugs, and she hadn't even looked at Tiffany. But Pender had other things to worry about, and frankly he wasn't altogether happy about trading this bleary-eyed rich girl for one of his best friends. Shut up with all that, he told himself as Sawyer drove out of the station complex. Shut up and stay focused.

Sawyer glanced back at him. "Where are we going, boss?"

Pender didn't answer for a moment. Then he shrugged. "We drop these two off somewhere. Then we run for Detroit."

Tiffany stared at him. "You're still going after your girlfriend?"

"What else can I do?"

"Get out of here. You have a passport. Be happy you're alive."

"I can't leave her. I won't."

"In the short term," said Sawyer. "Which way are we headed?"

435

Pender glanced at Tiffany, then Haley. "Where do you want to go?" he said. "Airport? Police station? Where?"

"If you guys are going to Detroit, I'm coming with you," said Tiffany.

Pender stared at her. The girl was covered in Mouse's blood, her cheeks still tracked with tears. "We could take you to the airport," he told her. "You could fly anywhere in the world."

"Alone? I don't think so. I don't have enough cash. Now that my dad knows I'm with you, I'm as good as broke."

"I want to go home," said Haley.

Pender leaned forward in his seat, trying to make eye contact with the girl. She avoided his eyes. "That's fine," he said. "We can take you to a hospital if you want. Or a police station."

"I just want to go home."

"You want to go to the airport?"

"I don't know," she said, and then her face screwed up and she was crying. She's here because of us, Pender thought. If we hadn't taken Tiffany, if we hadn't killed those hit men, if we hadn't fled to Florida, if we hadn't killed Donald Beneteau . . .

He didn't have to continue any further to know where the list was headed. Snap out of it. Get the girl home. Get Marie back.

Get out of the United States. "Okay," Pender said. "We're going to drop you at a hospital."

Sawyer frowned in the rearview mirror.

"We can't just put her on a plane, Sawyer. She's in no shape to fly."

"They'll call the police," Sawyer replied. "She knows where we're headed. She'll tell the cops everything."

"We gotta take that chance," said Pender. "We can't take her with us."

Sawyer sighed but kept driving, and when a hospital sign appeared on the road ahead he followed it into the city. He pulled the Explorer into the emergency entrance, and Pender climbed out and walked around to Haley's door. He opened it and leaned in to unbuckle her seat belt. Haley watched and said nothing.

Sawyer was making eyes at him in the driver's seat. Pender caught his gaze, and Sawyer rubbed his fingers together like a greedy bellhop. Pender shrugged and shook his head.

"Why not?" said Sawyer. "We saved her goddamn life."

Pender glanced up at Haley again. She watched him through vacant eyes, her cheeks sunken and hollow. "We've taken enough from her, Sawyer."

Sawyer glared at him, but Pender shook his head. "Fifty grand won't do much for us now, anyway."

He reached his arms around Haley and helped her out of the car. She let him move her without reacting, and Pender was afraid she'd crumple to the ground when he let her go. But she stood unsteadily, and Pender helped her to the sidewalk, where he let her stand on her own. "We're going to let you off here," he said. "Okay?"

Haley stared at him. She nodded slowly.

"I'm sorry," he said. "Believe me, I am." He pushed her gently toward the emergency room doors, and then he walked back to the Explorer and climbed inside. He looked back at Haley as they pulled out of the lot, watched her totter into the hospital like a helpless child, and he felt guilty again and miserable for Mouse. What a rotten world we've created, he thought.

Sawyer gunned the engine and pointed the truck toward the highway. "On to Detroit," he said, glancing over at Pender. "You got a plan, boss?"

Pender thought hard. They had next to nothing besides a truck and a little cash and a lot of automatic weaponry. Carter wanted a hundred grand to spring Marie, and they had no means of paying him. They had no way of getting the money short of robbing a bank.

Robbing a bank. That stopped Pender short for a minute, and he remembered Marie in the apartment in Seattle, pitching her half-cocked criminal plan. We're not bank robbers, thought Pender, but we need a Hail Mary. We're going to have to do something crazy.

"Boss?" Sawyer was staring at him. "You look like you're cooking something up."

"Yeah," said Pender. He stared out at the miserable night. "I just had a really bad idea."

SEVENTY-ONE

"So let me get this straight," said Windermere. "Your client wants full immunity if she gives up the details to the rest of the jobs her little gang pulled off." She stared across the table at Gloria Wallace, who glanced at Marie and then nodded.

"That's right," said Wallace. "Ms. McAllister will give you full access to her team's body of work, including the names of victims, cities, methods, and aliases. Everything you need to build a case against the three ringleaders of the gang."

Windermere laughed. "Come on, Ms. Wallace. You know you're going to have to do better than that."

Wallace stiffened. "My client was bullied and abused into playing a minor role with a group of sociopaths. I'm fully confident that a jury will agree Ms. McAllister is nothing but a victim of Stockholm syndrome taken to the extreme."

"If you were really sure," said Agent Stevens, "you wouldn't be trying to bargain your way out of a trial."

The assistant U.S. attorney, a tall toothpick named Obradovich, leaned forward in his chair, his eyes like black marbles fixed square on Marie. "The agents are right," he told Wallace. "We're going to need something more. And we're not prepared to offer full immunity."

"Five years' probation," said Wallace. "Ms. McAllister will undergo counseling."

Windermere scoffed, and Wallace shot her a glare. Obradovich scratched his head and rubbed his eyes. "What more can you give us?"

"What more does my client have?"

Marie listened to the scene play out, her eyes on the floor. She kept picturing Pender's face, imagining the look of disappointment he'd give her if he found out she was betraying them.

"I want to know where these guys are headed," said Obradovich. "I want to know where they are right now. And if we can't get that from your client, I at least want to know where they plan to go when they finally flee American soil."

Fat chance, thought Marie, and she suddenly felt sick. They wanted her to give up the Maldives. That's what they were asking. They wanted her to sell out Pender's Dream.

"My client can't be expected to know where the kidnappers are at this precise moment," said Wallace. "She's been in prison almost a week. However, if she did have any knowledge as to where the men might decide to run, we would happily agree to provide that information in exchange for a probationary period contingent on counseling and community service at the aid of other battered and abused women."

Windermere snorted again. Wallace ignored her, staring hard at Obradovich. The assistant U.S. attorney leaned back in his chair. "The government would be willing to grant your client five years in a medium-security facility and five years' probation."

"One year, minimum security. Three years' probation."

"Three years, minimum security. Three years' probation. You're not going to get any better than that, Gloria."

"Fine," said Wallace. "That works for me if it works for my client."

Marie looked up. Everyone was staring at her. She swallowed. Tried to speak but couldn't, and she didn't know what she would have said if she could. This was wholesale betrayal they were laying on her now. There was no justification but selfishness.

There was a knock on the door. A junior agent poked his head in the room and searched out Windermere, his eyes wide. "We've got news," he said. "It's big."

Stevens stood, and Windermere joined him. She shot Marie a wink. "Hold that thought." Then the agents vanished, leaving Marie alone with the lawyers, grateful for the stay of execution.

The agent, Hall, led them out into the corridor. Windermere glanced at Stevens when the door closed behind them. "You believe this shit? Full immunity. Give me a break."

Stevens smiled. "We got her, Carla. She looked about ready to crack."

"You're right," said Windermere. "She's good as flipped." She turned to Hall. "This better be good."

Hall was a young kid with cornrows and impeccable white teeth. He flashed them at Windermere. "It's better than good," he said. "It's off the charts."

"So spill."

"Big shoot-out in Cincinnati. Five dead, one wounded. That we know of."

"Cincinnati," said Stevens. "What the

hell's in Cincinnati?"

"Bodies. Three Detroit hoods, first off. Dmitri Georgiev. Yuri Frolov and Dario Pescatori. All tied in with Johnny Rialto."

Windermere glanced at Stevens, who shrugged.

"Rialto's tied in with the Bartholdi family," said Hall, hopping like a first grader with a full bladder. "Sole survivor's a kid named Paolo Vasquez. Miami guy. Tight with the boy Zeke, who's tied in with the Bartholdis. Paolo's a vegetable. Head smashed in with a pipe."

"You said five bodies?" said Stevens. "I count three so far."

"First let me say that everyone else on the scene caught serious lead. Multiple gunshot wounds from semiautomatic weaponry. The place looked like a war zone."

Windermere frowned. "Anyways."

"*Anyways,* found dead in the back of a vacant lot with about eight slugs in his body from a 9 mm machine gun was one Alessandro D'Antonio, also of the Bartholdi family. I think you guys know him."

"They find the girl?" said Stevens. "Whittaker? She the fifth?"

Hall held up one finger. "Hold that thought. She's not the body. They found her in an emergency room in downtown

Cincy, totally unharmed. Yes, she was talking, and yes, I'll fill you in in a second. But first, the final body."

"Spill."

"Ben Stirzaker." Hall's smile grew wider. "Also known as Mouse. Also known as Eugene Moy."

"And about a hundred other aliases," said Stevens. "Holy shit."

"They were in Cincinnati," said Windermere.

"D'Antonio must have met them with the girl and the goons. Tried to ambush them, but once again, those kids got the better of them."

"Just barely. They lost Stirzaker. What the hell happened out there?"

"According to Whittaker, D'Antonio wanted to trade her life for the gang's," said Hall. "Said he'd let her go if they gave themselves up. Somehow the kids got their hands on some guns and blew the roof off the joint."

Windermere and Stevens shared a look. "What else did she say?"

"Oh, here's the kicker," said Hall. "She said the survivors, Sawyer and Pender and the girl? Yeah. They're coming to Detroit."

Seventy-Two

"Christ on a cracker," said Windermere. "They're going to try a jailbreak."

Stevens watched the smile grow wide on his partner's face. She looked like she wanted to hug him. Stevens wasn't sure he shared her enthusiasm.

Pender and his gang were coming to Detroit. And they had guns. These kids were audacious. It could mean a bloodbath.

Windermere spun on her heels and started away from the interrogation room, headed for the elevators. "Let's go, Stevens," she said. "We've got plans to make."

Hall watched her go. "What about the girl?"

"What about the girl?" said Windermere. "What do we need with her now?"

"She'll make damn good bait," said Stevens. "Those kids could have run for the border at any time. They could be home free. But they're coming to Detroit to chase this girl instead." He started after Winder-mere.

Hall took a step to follow. "What about the plea bargain?"

"Let the lawyers worry about it. We're doing fine without her."

Stevens caught up to Windermere at the elevators. She grinned at him. "You think we should tell her?" he asked her.

"About Stirzaker?"

Stevens nodded. "Might shock her into submission."

"Pitch it like we've got to end the violence," said Windermere. "Save them from themselves. Hall!"

Agent Hall appeared from around the corner. "Go tell the girl about Stirzaker," she told him. "Tell her she could save her boyfriend from ending up the same way."

"Will do," said Hall. He turned to go.

"And Hall —" Windermere looked around. Grabbed a wastebasket and handed it to him. "Bring this along. It's liable to get messy in there."

The agents got off the elevator a couple floors up, Windermere still giddy, and made their way over to the makeshift office that was serving as de facto case headquarters for the duration of their stay. It was a tiny third-floor room, one hazy window looking

447

out onto Michigan Avenue, barely enough space for one double-wide communal desk and two ancient computers. They'd plastered every available surface with case information; the place looked like the offices of a couple of sad-sack associate professors at some second-rate university. Home sweet home.

"So, what?" said Stevens when they'd reached their flimsy chairs. "You really think those kids are going to try and storm the jail?"

Windermere laughed. "Let them storm it. I *hope* that's what they do. Then we just mop up the mess, nice and easy."

"You sure?" said Stevens. "From the sounds of it, those kids can make one hell of a mess."

"This is the FBI, Stevens," said Windermere. "We specialize in big messes."

Stevens thought about it. "Yeah, but if it comes down to a shoot-out, chances are they all die. And don't you at least want to meet these guys?"

Windermere had picked up a pencil and was doodling, idly, on a photocopied Wanted poster. She shrugged. "What for?"

"We've been chasing them for weeks," said Stevens. "They've pulled a shit ton of kidnapping jobs, and we might have never

known it if they hadn't killed Donald Beneteau."

"You had them before Beneteau. You had
them with Harper."

"Yeah, maybe. But the trail would have
gone pretty cold if they hadn't shot up that
mobster."

"True," said Windermere. "Okay. But I
still don't care if I meet them."

Stevens peered into an old cup of coffee
and frowned at its contents. "I want to know
them," he said. "I want to see how they
compare in real life to the images in my
head. I want to look at Arthur Pender just
once and try and figure him out. I want to
know *why.*"

Windermere drew a mustache on Arthur
Pender's Wanted photo. "The way this case
has gone, Stevens, I'm going to guess you'll
get your chance to hear the why. Personally,
I'd rather just see these kids locked up."

"You finally getting sick of this?"

"Hell, no," she said. "I'm having fun. I
just think motive's overrated. You get caught
up in stuff like that you start forgetting
about the crimes. You start rationalizing. We
know who did it, and we know how. The
fun's not in the why. The fun's in getting
ahead of these kids, outsmarting them.
Bringing them down and laughing as we

lock them up."

Stevens poured out the remains of his coffee. "Well," he said. "Let's hope we both get what we're looking for."

"We will," she said. "Hall!"

A moment later, Agent Hall showed up in the doorway. "Yeah," he said. "I'm here. What's up?"

"You tell the girl?"

"I told her."

"She puke?"

Hall shook his head. "No puke. She cried. Then she told her lawyer she was done talking."

Windermere waved her hand. "We don't need her. Tell us more about the Cincinnati angle. Give us all you got."

"Okay," said Hall. "I'll give you the easy stuff first. They're driving a late-model Ford Explorer with Florida license plates and a shot-out passenger window. I don't have the tag number."

"Hospital might."

"Hospital don't. The emergency room camera is from like 1988. Picture's too fuzzy. But the truck's dark green, if that helps."

"Can't hurt," said Stevens. "What else?"

"Whittaker said they were coming up to Detroit to get Marie. Didn't say how. But she said they had guns. Machine guns, lots of them."

"So they're coming in hot," said Windermere. "Anything else?"

Hall nodded. "She said they stopped off at Amtrak before they dropped her off. They all came out with manila envelopes. I have no idea what that's about."

"Someone's shipping them something," said Windermere. "Money?"

"Passports," said Stevens. "They're getting ready to leave the country." He turned to Hall. "There should be a fourth envelope at Cincinnati station with Ben Stirzaker's name on it. See if you can get a hold of it and find out where it came from."

"And let us know if this Whittaker girl gives up anything else," said Windermere. "She's probably got plenty of intel on this guy Zeke in Miami, so give racketeering a heads-up as well."

"I'm on it." Hall gave a mock salute and then disappeared. Windermere and Stevens watched him go.

"Kids," said Windermere. "These FBI brats get younger every year."

Stevens glanced at her. "I thought you were supposed to be the youth movement around here."

Windermere punched him on the arm.

"Thanks," she said. "Guess I'm getting old before my time."

She glanced down at Pender's Wanted poster and shuffled it away. "Okay," she said. "We need to put an APB out on that green Ford Explorer. Anything with Florida tags gets stopped. We need to double security around here, and we've got to get Pender's and Sawyer's pictures up on every street corner." She stared across the desk at him. "If those kids aren't in Detroit already, they're just about here. We've got to figure them out, and we've got to be ready for them."

"Roger," Stevens said, and he leaned back in his chair and stared out at the city. This is it, Pender, he thought. What are you going to do?

Seventy-Three

"Hey, Tessa? It's me. It's Matt."

From across the room, Pender watched Sawyer cradle the phone. His friend's laconic baritone was gone, replaced by the gentle tenor the big guy reserved for his sister and his grandmother. Or some semblance of it, anyway; the big guy was still speaking through broken teeth and split lips from the beating he'd taken in Cincinnati, and frustration showed on his face as he struggled to connect with the woman he loved most.

It was funny, Pender thought. Sawyer had never wanted a real girlfriend: he took women to bed with ease, but come morning they were invariably gone and forgotten. The guy loved his sister, was fiercely protective of her, and Pender had sometimes wondered if his friend was only looking for Tessa in the women he seduced and rejected.

"I know," said Sawyer. "Tessa, I'm sorry I lied."

Mouse used to mock Sawyer for the way his voice rose an octave or two on these long-distance phone calls, and Pender usually laughed along with him. Now, though, listening to Sawyer try to keep his voice steady, Pender didn't find it funny anymore.

"No, I'm fine," Sawyer said. "I just didn't want you getting hurt."

Sawyer glanced over at Pender, who raised an eyebrow in commiseration, but Sawyer just frowned and turned away. Pender felt guilty for eavesdropping, and he turned on the television and muted the sound. He lay back on his bed and wondered who he would call when it was time to say good-bye.

He wondered what his parents would say if he tried to call them. Wondered what they'd thought when the FBI showed up at their door. Had they been surprised? Had they cared, even?

Marie was his real family. He'd been so consumed with planning and logistics that he hadn't had time to think about her. Now, with the planning almost done, he yearned for her. He kind of liked missing her, he realized: it made him feel human, made him feel like they were doing the right thing.

Earlier in the evening Tiffany had gone out for food. She'd returned with a bag of cheap tacos and a copy of the *Free Press*, a big smile on her face. "I got us our target," she said, pointing to an article below the fold and a picture of a balding white man in his mid-forties, a movie producer with a young family and a home in a tony Detroit suburb. His name was Jason Cardinal.

"Says here he banked fifteen million last year alone," Sawyer read. "This cat is loaded."

"His wife is twenty-three, and they already have two kids," said Tiffany. "We could write our own check if we snatched his wife."

Pender saw Haley Whittaker's face again and he shook his head. "No women, no children." From the start, he'd tried to rationalize the kidnappings, told himself the victims weren't seriously affected, but one look at Haley's face had shamed him into seeing the truth. One more job, he thought. I'll be damned if we're going to take a woman.

So Jason Cardinal became the final target. And now, holed up in another cheap dive, this one off I-94 just north of Detroit, Pender tried to put a plan together. It would be their most ambitious job yet, their most visible. The fame of the target and the demands they would make would mean exactly the kind of publicity Pender had tried to dodge from the outset.

It was a bad plan, and Pender knew it. It was a desperate plan. But he couldn't figure out anything better, and he'd be damned if he was going to let Marie rot in prison while he walked free.

If everything went right, Pender thought, this would be the last crummy motel room they would ever sleep in. If everything went right, their next beds would be beachside hammocks.

Pender glanced at the television and sat up on the bed. His face was on screen, and then so was Sawyer's. Sawyer was on the beach with a bottle of Corona and a big goofy grin. Pender was with Marie in the San Juans. He still got a chill when he saw that picture. The heading on the TV screen read, "Coming to Detroit."

Well, it wasn't surprising. Haley had talked, like he'd known she would. The girl was shell-shocked and beaten when they left her, and he suspected she felt closer to D'Antonio than she did to anyone else.

Pender turned up the volume just in time to hear the anchor make the case for their green Ford Explorer with Florida plates. So that's a plus, he thought. Sawyer had swapped the Florida tags for Michigan plates courtesy of a beat-up Nissan Altima in a Super Kmart parking lot the day they rolled into town. It would take some time for the police to catch up to the change.

"All right, listen," Sawyer was telling his sister. "I gotta go." Christ, Pender thought. The guy sounds close to tears.

"No, I gotta go," he said. "I'll be fine, Tess. Don't worry." He paused. "Look, I love you, okay? Whatever happens."

Then he hung up the phone. He stared at it for a minute, and then he sighed and straightened his shoulders. He turned to face Pender, his expression unreadable. "Goddamn," he said, his voice back to normal. "That was really fucking hard, man."

Seventy-Four

Jason Cardinal's house was a vast redbrick mansion on a quiet street three blocks from Lake St. Clair. It sat on acres of land: plenty of trees and a football field front lawn, a fitting house for a millionaire movie producer.

Cardinal left for his office at quarter to nine, commuting alone in a bright red vintage Jaguar. Sawyer's eyes goggled when he saw it. "What the hell is he thinking?" he said. "Driving that thing at this time of year. That car's worth a hundred grand, easy."

"So he's careless with money," Tiffany said. "He'll pay the ransom just fine."

"It's not the ransom I'm worried about," Pender replied, pulling the truck into the street behind the Jag.

They followed Cardinal into a modern industrial park and to his office, a nondescript warehouse marked Cardinal Rule Studios. Then they drove to get breakfast and came back and parked across the street

458

outside an electronics plant. They turned on the radio and settled in to wait.

After seven or eight hours of talk radio, cheap tacos, warm Cokes, and glossy magazines, the studio doors opened and Jason Cardinal walked out again. He climbed into the Jaguar, fired up the engine, and reversed out of his parking space. Sawyer tapped Pender on the arm. "See that?"

The Jag was halfway down the block by the time they pulled out, and Pender was half afraid they weren't going to catch up in time. But he stood on the accelerator and pulled alongside Cardinal a couple miles down the road, and then he beat a yellow light a couple blocks farther, leaving the Jaguar staring at red.

Pender drove back to Cardinal's neighborhood. He brought the truck to the curb a half block down from the producer's house, and Sawyer jumped out. He opened the rear door and reached into the back of the truck for the .45.

Pender watched Sawyer tuck the gun into his waistband and walk casually to the end of the block. Then Pender put the truck in gear and pulled into a driveway a few houses down from Cardinal's. He turned to Tiffany. "Grab a gun," he said. "Another pistol if we've got one. Sawyer's going to throw him in the back and you keep your gun trained on him, cool?"

Tiffany nodded. "Cool."

Pender stared out the window at Sawyer, who loitered on the corner doing his nonchalant act. Sawyer checked his watch and then perked up. He glanced back at the Explorer and nodded, and Pender turned the key in the ignition. The truck rumbled to life, and he backed it out of the driveway and into the street, angling it so it blocked any access but would still allow them to get away clean.

A couple seconds later, Pender heard the Jaguar's engine behind him and saw the car pull into the street, as red as a fresh strawberry in the gray winter backdrop, Cardinal's head poking up above the windshield.

The Jag slowed to a stop about ten feet behind the Explorer, and Cardinal peered out at the truck. He glanced in the mirror and looked ready to lean on the horn when Sawyer showed up on the driver's side, waving the Glock in his face.

The producer went pale as Sawyer wrenched open the door. He dragged Cardinal out of the car and hustled him over to the Explorer and into the backseat. Tiffany flashed him her teeth and showed him the pistol. "Hello," she said. "Please don't try anything stupid."

"Who are you?" said Cardinal. "What do you want with me?"

Tiffany gestured with the gun. "Buckle up."

Sawyer ran back to the Jaguar and parked it by the curb. Then he came back to the truck and climbed in the shotgun seat, and Pender hit the gas. Sawyer let Cardinal watch his house disappear and then twisted around to face him. "So listen," he said, holding the Glock aimed steady at the producer's face. "This is a kidnapping, bud. How soon can you get five million dollars?"

Seventy-Five

Windermere stared at the phone on her side of the desk. On his side, Stevens had booted up the ancient desktop and was using every bit of RAM to search the Internet for model train sets for his son. *Christmas and toy trains,* he thought. *Does anyone still do that?*

Suddenly, Windermere sat up in her chair, startling Stevens away from his search. "Hall," she yelled. "Get in here!"

They had been sitting in their crummy office for almost two days, waiting on Arthur Pender to make a move. Security was doubled downstairs, and Detroit PD had a tactical team on standby. There was a helicopter waiting on the roof and plainclothesmen posted at the airport and train station. The green Explorer was all over the news, and there was nothing to do, thought Stevens, but wait.

Agent Hall appeared in the doorway. He flashed Stevens a grin and then turned to

Windermere. "What's up?"

"I'm bored, Hall," she said. "Tell me we're making progress."

Hall shrugged. "We got maybe ten reports of Ford Explorers. Half of them green. None with Florida plates. We got people all over the map phoning in sightings of these kids, especially the blond girl. I bet every blonde in Michigan is pissed as hell at Tiffany Prentice right now."

"That's all?"

"Not quite," said Hall. "Talked to Amtrak in Cincinnati about that Stirzaker thing. Picked up that fourth envelope just like you called it. Passport, credit card, birth certificate, and driver's license. Stirzaker's face, but the name was Adam Goulding."

"What about the shipping address?" said Stevens.

"Shipped from Buffalo. We're tracking down the shipper as we speak."

"Okay," said Windermere. "Keep us posted."

When Hall was gone, Windermere turned to Stevens. "Goddamn it, Stevens. I feel like Christmas Eve over here. Where are those kids?"

"Savor the anticipation," said Stevens, but he was feeling it, too. Antsy and restless.

Hall poked his face back in the room a

minute later. "Hey," he said. He gave Stevens a strange look. "You guys have a phone call. Line Two. Some guy asking for the special agent in charge of the Marie McAllister case."

"No kidding." Stevens looked down at the phone where line two was lit up and blinking. He felt his heart start to pound. "He say what he wants?"

Hall shook his head. "Just wanted to talk to you guys."

Stevens glanced at Windermere. "You want it?"

"You go ahead," she said. "You have the people skills around here."

Stevens inhaled for as long as he could and then slowly let his breath out. He reached for a notepad and gestured for Windermere to listen in on her extension. Then he picked up the phone. "This is Agent Stevens," he said. "Who am I talking to?"

The man's voice was clear and calm. He sounded like he was ordering a pizza. "Hello, Agent Stevens. You're in charge of Marie McAllister?"

Stevens glanced at Windermere. "That's correct. Who is this?"

"This is Arthur Pender. I'd like to make a deal with you."

Windermere was up and scrambling, gesturing at Hall for a tape recorder, reaching for her own legal pad. Stevens cleared his throat. "Okay, Arthur," he said. "Where are you right now? Are you in Detroit?"

"Earlier today my team kidnapped a man named Jason Cardinal from the street outside his home," Pender said. "If our demands are not met within forty-eight hours, we are prepared to kill our hostage."

Jason Cardinal. Jason Cardinal. Stevens searched his brain. He shrugged at Windermere, who scribbled something on her notepad: Movie producer. Big-time.

"Okay," said Stevens, feeling the blood start to pound in his temples. "What exactly are you looking for here, Arthur?"

"Mr. Cardinal's ransom is five million dollars, to be wired to a bank account of my specification. This is what we demand from Mr. Cardinal's family to ensure his safe return. We've already informed his wife of the situation."

"Five million dollars," said Stevens. "Okay. We'll work on that, Arthur."

"I'm not finished, Agent Stevens. From the United States government, we demand the release and safe passage of Marie McAllister to a nonextradition treaty country of our specification. Ms. McAllister will be safe on the ground within forty-eight hours or we will execute Mr. Cardinal."

"Now, hold on," said Stevens. "That's going to take some doing."

"I will communicate with you and you alone," said Pender. "I trust our demands are clear. I'll contact you again in twenty-four hours with further instructions."

Pender hung up the phone. Stevens and Windermere turned immediately to Hall. "Can we trace it?"

"Already done," said Hall. "Pay phone in St. Clair Shores. We have Detroit PD units on the way."

"Jesus Christ," said Windermere. "The balls on that kid."

Stevens let out a long sigh, his heart still pounding. "They're desperate."

"He has to know we're not giving up McAllister."

"If he knew that, he'd be gone already." Stevens stared down at the telephone. "He thinks he has a chance."

SEVENTY-SIX

Jason Cardinal's whole block was a zoo. The producer's long driveway was choked with police cruisers, and the street beyond was equally clogged, filled with civilian machinery and a flotilla of mobile news broadcast trucks. Windermere leaned on the horn as she crept the unmarked car up the street, blaring the siren in vain at the swarms of looky-loos who had taken to the night. "Shit," she said finally, giving up a half block from the epicenter. "I guess we walk from here."

They pulled up to the curb behind a vintage Jaguar convertible. Stevens cast an admiring glance as he got out of the car.

"That's Cardinal's ride," said a uniform nearby, a young St. Clair Shores cop with a buzz cut and excitement in his eyes. "Pretty sweet."

"Who's in charge of this debacle?" said Stevens. "This place is a mess."

"If you're the Feds, then it's you," said the uniform.

"It's us," said Windermere. She glanced at the rookie's name badge. "All right, Stent. Grab some guys and set up a perimeter on each end of the block, would you? Nobody gets in or out unless they're neighbors or witnesses or the kidnappers themselves, clear? And watch out for reporters. Those slimy bastards will tell you anything to get inside."

Stent stood up straighter. "Yes, ma'am."

Windermere watched him go. Then she turned to Stevens, a wry smile on her face. "I bet you were like that once."

Stevens laughed. "Bright-eyed and buzz cut and destined to save the world? Maybe. Weren't you?"

Windermere shook her head. "I went to law school, Stevens. That means I'm a born cynic."

They walked up the driveway and through Cardinal's front door, flashing their badges at the uniform standing guard. "FBI," said Windermere. "This is our case. Where's Mrs. Cardinal?"

The uniform pointed them back into the kitchen, where a group of five or six middle-aged women were huddled around a very young, very blond woman who clutched a baby with one hand and a tissue in the other. A little girl about three years old sat playing with building blocks at her feet.

Windermere addressed the crowd. "People, I'm Agent Windermere with the FBI. Unless you're a witness, you need to clear out while we talk to Mrs. Cardinal, okay?"

The women grumbled but started for the doors. Windermere approached Angel Cardinal. "Why don't we sit down, Mrs. Cardinal?"

The woman nodded. Windermere took her arm and guided her to the kitchen table, and they all three sat, Angel Cardinal silhouetted in a last-gasp sunset that streamed in from the kitchen window.

"All right," said Windermere. "Now, Angel, I want you to understand that there's really no reason to panic just yet. These kids who took your husband, we know them. They don't want to hurt or kill him, okay?"

Cardinal stared at her through swollen eyes. "Okay," she said softly.

"Good. Now, I understand you talked to one of the kidnappers on the phone. Is that right?"

She nodded. "Yeah."

"Okay," said Windermere. "That was Arthur Pender." She nodded to Stevens, who produced a picture of Pender from his pocket. "This is what he looks like. Twenty-eight or so, sandy blond hair. About six feet tall. Have you ever seen him before?"

Cardinal shook her head. Stevens handed her pictures of Matt Sawyer and Tiffany Prentice. Cardinal shook her head again.

"Do you recall seeing a green Ford Explorer on your street today?"

"No," Cardinal said, her voice wavering just below hysterical. "Are those the people who killed that guy in Birmingham?"

"Donald Beneteau," said Stevens. "They are."

"Oh, God." Cardinal started to sob. Stevens snagged a box of tissues from the counter as Windermere tried to console the woman.

"They killed Donald Beneteau because his family tried to play games," she said. "They thought they could solve the problem themselves, and they never called the police. They got stupid, okay? The fact that we're here right now means you're smarter than them."

"So I should pay the ransom?" Cardinal blew her nose. "I should pay them the five million dollars?"

Windermere leaned forward and touched the woman's arm. "We think we can catch these kids without you paying the ransom," she said. "But in the end it's your call."

"We'll back you either way," said Stevens. "But you should know that these kids have made some unusual demands of the government, and even if you pay the ransom, there's no guarantee they'll let your husband go."

Cardinal's eyes went wide. "What do you mean? What kind of demands?"

"Arthur Pender's girlfriend is in federal custody awaiting trial for kidnapping and murder," said Windermere. "He's demanding that we release her."

"Are you going to do it?"

Windermere glanced at Stevens. "We're confident we can get your husband back without compromising our investigation," she said. "We can't let a federal prisoner go."

Cardinal moaned. She let her head sink to the table, and she started sobbing again. "Oh, God. They're going to kill him," she said. "You're going to let them kill my husband."

They put a uniform with Angel Cardinal and let a couple of her friends back in the room for damage control. Then they walked back out the front foyer, and Windermere made a call back to Hall at the Detroit office. A couple seconds later, the kid was on the line. "Hey, ma'am," he said. "How's life at ground zero?"

"This place is a gong show," said Windermere. "And cut the ma'am crap."

"Here, too," said Hall. "This whole office is gone crazy. People running around yelling at each other, pretending they know what they're doing. Everyone's waiting on you guys."

"Yeah? Well, grab a pen. I need to set up a tracing system at Cardinal's place. We're going to camp out here. If Pender calls the office, you redirect him to this line and we'll trace the call from here, okay?"

"Okay."

"Make sure the tactical team is on standby and try to commandeer another helicopter, all right? And get someone to draft a press release. We've got reporters up our asses."

"Done," said Hall. "I'm on it."

Windermere hung up and turned to Stevens. "Let's go face the vultures."

They walked down to the front gate and waded through the traffic jam of neighbors and cops back to Stent's roadblock. The rookie had angle-parked his cruiser at the foot of the block, and beyond his car was a line of news vans with cameramen shooting footage of the street. Stent grinned when they approached. "You like?"

"We like," said Windermere. "Good work."

"Stevens!"

Stevens turned to see a police detective approaching. Stevens made him for Paul Landry, the Birmingham homicide cop who'd handled the Beneteau murder. "Kirk Stevens and Carla Windermere, right? You guys look better dry, I'll tell you."

"Detective Landry." Stevens shook his hand. "Fancy meeting you here."

"Yeah, well." The cop shrugged. "Heard there was a chance your guys were my killers. Figured I'd come down and see for myself."

"Sure," said Stevens. Then he had a thought. "Hey, maybe you can help out."

Landry nodded. "Just say the word."

"These kids like to stay in crummy little no-tell motels, you know, right off the interstate. We're thinking they're looking to make a quick getaway. You think of anywhere that fits the bill?"

Landry rubbed the stubble on his chin. "Let me give it some thought," he said. "If it's all right with you, I'll take a ride, maybe have a look at some places."

"Whatever you can do," said Stevens. "The local boys are going to send some cruisers around, but it wouldn't hurt to have another pair of eyes."

"Perfect," said Landry. He shook Stevens's hand again. "I'll be in touch."

Stevens watched the detective walk back to his cruiser, and then turned to catch up with Windermere, who was already talking to a couple reporters.

"I told you, I can't give you anything on camera," she was saying. "But we need you guys to get the word out about these kidnappers. Post their pictures as much as possible. Push the green Explorer. They're probably hiding in some sleazy motel on this side of the city. Push that. Get it out there. Get people looking around, all right?"

She turned on her heels and started back through the barricade. She punched in Hall's number on her phone and held the phone to her ear. "Hall," she said. "How are those tracer units coming?"

"Headed out the door right now," he said.

"Good," said Windermere. "Listen. Get those guys to bring us down some takeout as well, got it? We're in it for the long haul, and this place is going nuts."

She snapped the phone closed, squared her shoulders, and marched back into the chaos. Stevens watched her clear a path. Then he took a deep breath and followed her in.

SEVENTY-SEVEN

Pender woke up to a siren in his ear. It sounded only briefly, just one quick blast, but it was enough to get him up and out of bed, his heart racing and his hand reaching for the TEC-9 on the table beside him. He felt the gun with his fingers, and then he blinked, still half asleep. You're going to shoot a cop, he thought. Are we at that stage already? He withdrew his hand and checked for the time on the alarm clock. Ten past seven.

Sawyer was already at the window, rubbing his eyes with one hand and holding the Uzi in the other. He glanced back at Pender, one eyebrow raised.

Pender shook his head and held his finger to his lips. On the beds, Cardinal and Tiffany both lay asleep. Cardinal was a snorer; he'd kept Pender awake the whole night. When he wasn't snoring, he was talking in his sleep, tossing and turning and muttering to himself. I guess it's not his fault, Pender thought. He's tied up for ransom in some dingy motel room. The man has a right to be nervous.

Pender walked to the window as Sawyer peered through the crack in the middle of the blackout curtains, searching through the filmy day curtain for the police.

Pender put his hand on Sawyer's arm and the big man stepped back. Pender looked through the curtains and for a moment he was blinded by daylight. Blinking, he pushed back the day curtain and let his eyes adjust.

For a moment he saw nothing, just a row of anonymous parked cars and the burger joint beyond. Then he heard the crunch of tires on the crumbled parking lot pavement, and a second later the front of a police cruiser made his stomach flip over.

He had to fight himself not to jerk the curtains together. Instead he stepped back slowly, keeping the curtains as still as possible. "Shit," he said. "Shit, shit, shit."

Through the crack in the curtains, he watched the cruiser roll by, slow and steady, a Grosse Pointe city cop peering out at the row of motel units and the cars parked in front. "What is it?" Sawyer whispered. "Cops out there?"

"One cruiser," said Pender, feeling like

the cops could hear every word. "They're searching the lot."

"They see you?"

Pender shook his head. "Don't think so."

"What about the truck? Where'd you leave it?"

"I hid it around back," Pender said. "Behind a dumpster and an old tractor trailer. Should be all right." I *hope* it's all right, he thought. Depends how diligent these cops turn out to be.

He watched through the curtain as the cruiser crept away from the window, and then he stepped back and exhaled and sat down on Tiffany's bed, running his hands through his hair. He looked up and saw Sawyer staring at him, and he forced a grin. "Let's hope these are lazy cops."

They waited. Sawyer peered out the window while Pender sat frozen on the bed, his ears perked for any sign they'd been made.

Tiffany sat up on the bed beside him. She rubbed her eyes. "What is it?"

"Shh," Pender told her. "Keep quiet a second."

They waited in silence, the only sound Cardinal's rhythmic snoring. After four or five minutes, the siren sounded again from the other end of the building, and Pender imagined his world was collapsing. But then nothing more came, and after another ten minutes, Pender dared to open the door.

He peered into the parking lot and saw no cops. "I think we're safe," he said. He walked back into the room and pulled on a hooded sweatshirt, and then he ventured out into the parking lot again, the hoodie pulled low over his eyes.

He walked along the side of the motel toward the back, expecting every moment to see the cruiser come rocketing around the corner after him. But nobody came, and he made it to the back of the lot unharmed. The cruiser was gone, and there were no police crawling over the Explorer, either. He walked back to the room, where Sawyer opened the door slowly. "Anything?"

"They're gone," said Pender. "We caught a break."

"Cops?" said Tiffany. "There were cops here?"

"They must have figured we like motels," said Pender. "They're checking every one of them."

"We gotta move," said Tiffany. "We're not safe here."

"Are you kidding?" Pender grinned at her. "We're safer here than ever. They just crossed this place off their list. We're golden."

A couple hours later, when he was sure the police had moved on from their seedy strip of motels, Pender put on a baseball cap and pulled his hoodie back over his face again and set out into the street, finding a convenience store a couple blocks off the freeway and paying for a pair of prepaid burner phones.

He left the store and started walking, hiking through alleys along the side of the freeway until he'd walked at least a couple miles. We're doing this the old-fashioned way, he thought. Foot soldiers and all.

He stopped in back of an abandoned butcher shop to unwrap the first phone. Then he dialed Jason Cardinal's home number and slunk into the shadows to talk. The phone rang once, then again, and then Cardinal's wife picked up. Someone else picked up, too. "H-hello?" said Angel Cardinal.

"This is Arthur Pender," said Pender. "Do you have the money?"

"I have most of the money," she said.

Most of the money, thought Pender. "No stall tactics. Have all the money ready within twelve hours. I'll call back with instructions for the drop." He was about to hang up when another voice spoke.

"Arthur, this is Agent Stevens with the FBI."

"Agent Stevens," said Pender. "I was just about to call your office."

"No need, Arthur. We've moved in with the Cardinals." He was keeping his voice cheerful. Nonthreatening. "Where are you right now?"

"Where is Marie McAllister?"

Stevens sighed. "We're having a bit of trouble with that one, Arthur. Might need a little more time to process her release."

"No more time," said Pender. "You have thirty hours to put her on a plane or we kill Jason Cardinal."

A third voice broke in, a woman's. "Come on, Arthur. Do you really think the government is going to give away a criminal just to make you happy?"

"Who am I speaking to?"

"This is Agent Windermere, FBI."

"Well, Agent Windermere, I don't care how you swing it, but if you don't let her go, you're going to have Cardinal's blood on your hands."

Windermere sighed. "I have to tell you, Arthur, the money is no problem. Angel Cardinal wants to pay the ransom, and we're fine with it. But you're putting us in a bind here. We can't just let your girlfriend walk."

"Listen to me," said Pender. "If Marie McAllister isn't free within thirty hours, Jason Cardinal will be dead. End of story."

Pender ended the call and started walking. He was about to chuck the phone when it started to ring. I should just ignore this, he thought. I've made my demands, and they know what I want. But he raised the phone to his ear again and said nothing.

"Arthur? Agent Windermere here. Look, I know you want your girlfriend back. I respect that. But, listen, you want my advice, take the money."

"Not an option," said Pender. "Goodbye."

"She talked, Arthur." Windermere paused. "I'm not supposed to tell you this stuff, but I kind of feel bad for you. So listen, man. Your girlfriend flipped."

Pender felt his stomach start to crumple. "Bullshit."

"Not bullshit. She told us everything she knew about you guys. Got a slick lawyer and worked out a deal. Full immunity, Arthur, yeah. She gives you up and she walks. Is that what you want? Listen, she sold you out. Take the money and get out of here."

The agent kept talking, but Pender wasn't

481

listening. He pressed the End button, and he threw the phone to the pavement and crushed it, feeling the plastic crack under his feet. He stood in the alley for a minute, his vision blurred and his head spinning. Then he regained control.

The cops had traced the call by now, he realized. He turned and ran, as fast as he could, out of the alley and back toward the motel.

SEVENTY-EIGHT

Windermere hung up the phone and glanced around Cardinal's living room, now transformed into a mobile command center. Banks of computers and sophisticated phone-tapping equipment took up most of the room, and an army of FBI techs and local police officers sat hunched at the consoles. "You guys get all that?"

Agent Hall, sitting by a bank of computers in the corner, stood up. "It's a prepaid cellular phone. We're triangulating the location by GPS right now."

"Can you figure out where it was purchased?" said Stevens.

Hall frowned. "I'll talk to the cell phone company," he said. "Might be tough."

"This is life or death, Hall," Windermere said. "Get it done."

"Will do." Hall picked up a phone and walked out of the room. Windermere glanced at Stevens.

"What do you think?"

"What the hell was that? The girl flipped on you? We never discussed that. What if he walks away?"

"If he walks away, Stevens, we get Cardinal back. If we can't or won't get Marie McAllister out of prison, there's a good chance Pender decides to get violent. Right?"

Stevens stared at her. "I'm here to catch these kids, Carla."

Windermere put her hand on his arm. "So am I, Stevens. I'm just trying to get Pender divorced from the idea that his girlfriend has to be a part of the ransom. Now maybe he brings it back to his team and they decide five million bucks is more important than getting a snitch out of jail."

Officer Stent led Angel Cardinal into the room. She held a tissue to her face and stared around the living room, searching out Stevens with hopeful eyes. "How did we do?"

"I think we did fine," Stevens replied. He walked over to Cardinal and put his hands on her shoulders. "*You* did great."

"But my husband. Will they —"

"Listen to me," said Windermere. "Right now that kid is freaking out, talking to his friends about how his girlfriend's a snitch

484

and the FBI said take the money. By tonight they'll cave and forget about the girl. We'll drop off the money tomorrow, and you'll get your husband back."

"That's if we don't catch them first," said Stevens. "We've got police looking everywhere for those kids. We'll find them. If we're lucky, we'll get Jason back free of charge."

Hall came back into the room, pocketing his cell phone. He shrugged apologetically. "Phone company's a no go. They say two days to get that information to us. At least."

"Damn," said Windermere. "What else have you got?"

Hall sat down at the bank of computers. He scrutinized the monitors for a second. Then he looked up. "Got the location of that phone call."

"Spill."

"Kelly and 9 Mile," he said. "Eastpointe area. That's south of here. Along I-94 headed back to Detroit."

"Where's the phone now?" asked Stevens.

Hall punched a couple of keys. "Looks like it went off grid. Must have turned it off. You wanna check out the locale?"

"Yeah," said Windermere. "Let's have a look."

They parked the Crown Vic on Kelly and

walked up to the intersection. The place was a collection of low-lying local auto mechanics, gas stations, and pawnshops. No motels in sight. Windermere stared up and down 9 Mile. "There's nothing here," she said.

"He knew we'd trace him," said Stevens. "He called from a neutral site."

"You think they drove here? Would he risk it in the Explorer?"

"Maybe they have a second car."

"It's possible." Stevens turned to Hall. "What did they drive to Cincinnati?"

Hall shrugged. "They found Stirzaker's body strapped into a beat-up Dodge Caravan. A real piece of shit."

"Old?"

"As the hills, man."

"What did they drive before, a Durango?"

"Yeah," said Windermere. "Nearly new."

"And every other car they bought was nearly new. Off lease return or whatever. These kids didn't screw around with used cars."

"Except the minivan."

"Yeah," said Stevens. "When they started running low on cash."

Stevens spun around, taking in the intersection. An abandoned butcher's shop halfway down. A couple tire stores and a muffler joint. Heavy traffic on 9 Mile, a steady stream of trucks and a city bus every five or six minutes. "Hard for them to buy a second car when they're running out of money, running out of aliases, and their pictures are on the nightly news," he said.

"You think he walked," said Windermere.

"Well, let's just say hypothetically. We got any motels nearby?"

"Wait a sec." Hall walked back to the Crown Vic. He came back with a handful of printouts and gave them to Stevens. "These are the accommodations listings in the Yellow Pages. Looks like there's a bunch of motels a couple miles down I-94 in both directions."

"But nothing closer. So he'd have to walk a couple miles to get here. Then a couple miles to get back."

"Unless he drove. Maybe they stole a car."

Windermere spoke up. "Anyone check those motels?"

Hall nodded. "Franklin and Georges checked every one of those spots. Couldn't find a thing. No Explorers, no kids."

"Double-check that," said Stevens. "Let's make sure they checked them all."

Hall nodded and pulled out his cell phone. He wandered back to the car to make the call, and when he came back a minute later, he was wearing a half smile. "Apparently some guy named Landry's been trying to get through to you. You know him?"

"Paul Landry," said Stevens. "Homicide cop. He's running point on the Beneteau murder."

"Okay," said Hall. "He's posted up at the Motor City Motel right now. You wanna guess what he's sitting on?"

"Dish."

"Dark green Ford Explorer. He found it hidden in back of the lot. Only thing is it's got Michigan plates. But the passenger window is missing, and he figured you guys would want to take a look."

Windermere frowned. "I thought Franklin and Georges checked out that motel."

"Landry said the truck was well hidden. They probably just missed it."

Windermere shot Stevens a look. Stevens fought down a smile. "So where is this place?"

"South," said Hall. "Two miles off I-94."

Windermere unlocked the Crown Vic. "Get in and buckle up," she told the men. "And you'd better call for backup. We're taking those kids down tonight."

SEVENTY-NINE

"Wait, what are you saying?" said Sawyer. "Marie's a snitch?"

Sawyer sat at the motel room table, staring down at his gun. Tiffany was lying on one bed while Cardinal sat up on the other, watching intently but keeping his mouth shut.

"Five million dollars," said Tiffany. She'd been watching TV, but now her focus was all Pender. "They said we could just walk away with the money."

"Yes," said Pender. He sighed. "And yes."

"What did you tell them?"

"What do you think I told them? I told them shove it."

Tiffany stared at him. "You turned down five million dollars. Just like that."

"I didn't turn down anything," said Pender. "But if it's a choice between Marie and the money, I know which way I'm going."

Tiffany frowned and turned back to the TV as Pender locked the door. "You think it's worth five million dollars just to take back a snitch?"

Pender didn't answer. He'd been running the same question in his head since he'd hung up the phone. The job would go smoother if it was just a straight ransom gig — that much was for certain. Trying to get Marie back was a monster gamble. And if Marie had sold them out, well, it was a hell of a thing to be risking so much for a girl who'd betrayed you.

Sawyer caught his eye. "You think she really did it, boss?"

Pender shook his head. He wasn't sure what he thought. He knew something had changed in Marie when they'd killed Donald Beneteau. Maybe she knew she was finished with this kidnapping thing — with *us* — when she got on the plane to Seattle, he thought. Or maybe she just spooked at the jail time. Anyone would get scared in a situation like that.

In his heart, though, he felt stabbed, sick at the thought she'd betrayed them.

"We should have found her another lawyer in Jacksonville," he told Sawyer. "We should have moved quicker."

"We had no money. Mouse was shot."

"She must have thought we'd left her behind," Pender said. He was pacing the room now. "I mean, how do we know what she told them for certain?"

"What did she really know, anyway? She knew aliases, bank accounts, all the old jobs. Fine. The Feds could have figured all that out."

"She knew where we're planning to retire."

"So we change locales. You don't get to retire in the Maldives. That's all."

"It doesn't matter what she told them," said Tiffany. "Fact is, she betrayed you guys. And you're still willing to risk everything to save her. We could walk away *right now*. Think about it."

"You're rich," said Sawyer. "What the hell do you care?"

"My dad cut me off," said Tiffany. "My credit cards and everything. I have about a hundred bucks to my name."

Pender stared at the floor, charting every stain on the carpet. He could feel Tiffany's and Sawyer's eyes on him, and he knew they were waiting for his decision. He thought about taking the five million dollars, and then he thought, what the hell would I do without Marie? Snitch or no snitch, I'm in love with the girl. I could have all the ransom money in the world and I'd never forgive myself if I walked away. He looked up, first at Sawyer, then Tiffany.

"Well?" Tiffany said.

"It's like this," Pender told them. "I'm staying until Marie's out of jail. You guys can stay or go as you like. You've got passports and credit cards, and there's money waiting on the other end. If you don't want to stick around, you can go. No judgment."

"She's a *snitch,* Pender," said Tiffany. "You're making a huge mistake."

Sawyer slammed his hand down on the table. "She's no fucking snitch," he said. "She's part of the team."

Tiffany stood up. "All right," she said. "I can see how this one's going to end. I'm out."

Sawyer stared. "You're leaving?"

"Let her go, Sawyer," said Pender. "Better she walks out now than when we really need her."

Tiffany walked to the door. She looked back at them. "You guys are going to let this girl bring you down," she said. "I can't be here when it all falls apart."

Then she turned to the door, but before she could reach the handle, a knock on the other side froze the room. Sawyer and Pender stared at each other, and Sawyer reached for the Uzi. "Who is it?" Pender called.

"Arthur Pender," came the voice from the other side. "This is the FBI. Open up. We've got you surrounded."

EIGHTY

Tiffany stood frozen in midstride. Sawyer picked up the Uzi while Pender stared at the door, feeling like he'd just jumped out of a plane without a parachute.

They'd been made. Somehow the FBI had found them, and the entire game had changed. They had moved from a simple kidnapping to a hostage situation, and Pender didn't need to go to the window to imagine the scene outside. There would be police cars and Feds, helicopters, news reporters, SWAT teams, snipers, and hostage negotiators. They were now in the middle of something huge, something disastrous.

Okay, he thought. Don't panic. He turned back to Sawyer. "Help me move this bed," he said. "We gotta barricade that door."

Sawyer stood and helped Pender drag the bed to the door. They fit it tight against the wall, and then Pender stood back to survey the room. So this is it, he thought. Our Little Bighorn. This is where we make our stand.

Another knock on the door. "Arthur, we know you're in there."

Must be Stevens. Pender walked to the window and slipped the heavy curtain apart as gently as he could. He peered out into the parking lot, and after his eyes adjusted to the light, he saw the scene exactly as he'd imagined it, spread out and surreal like some kind of movie.

He saw two Grosse Pointe PD cruisers and two unmarked sedans, the cruisers angle-parked and their occupants kneeling behind open doors, their service revolvers drawn and aimed square at the motel room door. At the door stood two FBI agents, a middle-aged man and a younger woman, both with guns drawn. The man reached up and knocked again. "Arthur," he said. "If you don't open up, we'll have to break down the door."

Pender stepped back from the curtains and drew them tight. "Go ahead," he said, forcing his voice to sound calm. "You come in here with anything less than five million dollars and you'll have yourselves a dead hostage."

There was a pause. Then the woman

spoke. "Arthur," she said. "Listen up. We have you surrounded. There's no way you're getting out of there alive. This game is over, okay? Make it easy on yourself."

"This game is not over," said Pender. "And if you think you can force our hand, you're dead wrong."

He walked to the bedside table and picked up the TEC-9, glancing at Sawyer as he did. Sawyer nodded, and he walked back to the door.

"If you want to give Angel Cardinal her husband back in one piece," Pender continued, his voice barely his own, "I'd suggest you pay closer attention to our demands this time around. Are you listening?"

Pender waited. Finally Agent Stevens spoke. "We're listening, Arthur."

"Good," said Pender. "We want the ransom within twelve hours. We want safe passage to the nearest airport and a jet airplane and pilot package capable of flying us to Asia or northern Africa. You will deliver Marie McAllister to the airport and put her on the plane. When we've verified the delivery of the money and that the plane meets our requirements, we'll release Mr. Cardinal and you can forget about us."

"Arthur." Windermere spoke. "We've been over this. The money's no problem. But we can't get you Marie. I'm sorry."

"This is not a negotiation," said Pender. "Any deviation from our demands will result in Mr. Cardinal's being shot. We're not willing to listen to excuses."

"I've got a jet." Cardinal's voice surprised them all. "I've got a Gulfstream 550 at Coleman Young airport. You can have it and my pilot. The money, too, no problem. Just don't kill me."

"You get that?" said Pender. "Cardinal's going to help you out with the jet. That just leaves Marie and the money. You've got twelve hours."

He walked back from the door and picked up the television remote, cycling through the channels until he found the news, and he sat down on the edge of the bed to watch the coverage, remote in one hand and machine gun in the other, focusing on the screen and trying to calm his racing heart.

EIGHTY-ONE

Agent Stevens watched the first news helicopter arrive and began to trace its urgent pattern above the Motor City Motel, a droning speck against a glorious sunset. Then he brought his eyes back down to earth and surveyed the parking lot and the circus contained therein.

He and Windermere had cleared out the motel as soon as the desk clerk confirmed it was Pender and his gang holed up on the property. Now the displaced guests crowded outside the yellow police barriers, littering the sidewalk with fast-food wrappers and getting in the way of the police moving in and out of the lot.

Grosse Pointe PD had mustered a handful of uniformed cops and cruisers to work crowd control and contain the danger zone around the outside of Pender's unit 23. Officer Stent from St. Clair Shores was posted up somewhere with Angel Cardinal and her

498

children, trying to keep the woman calm. Meanwhile, Detective Landry waited with his partner in his unmarked sedan, both of them riding out the storm with a fresh closure on their minds. Those kids inside had killed Donald Beneteau, and as soon as they were cuffed and booked, Landry would get credit for a high-profile case solved, good for at least a month's worth of goodwill from the duty lieutenant in homicide.

And then there were the tactical officers, the superheroes in body armor and assault rifles, the FBI's Hostage Rescue Team. They'd flown in from Quantico as soon as Stevens and Windermere notified the Detroit office of the situation, and they were commanded by a burly special agent named Wellwood who'd spent the last half hour trying to wrest control of the scene away from Windermere.

"These kids aren't trained for this," Wellwood was saying. He had the motel blueprints spread out in the back of the FBI's tactical van and was examining them as he spoke. "We can get in there with a flashbang grenade and take them out inside of a minute. Problem solved, we all go home."

Stevens shook his head. "As soon as they see you coming, they'll grab that hostage and put a bullet in his head."

Wellwood looked up from the blueprints. "All due respect, Agent Stevens, but my guys are professionals. We'll take them down before they get a shot off."

We're professionals, too, Stevens thought, and I want those kids alive. I don't want to see them shot down. I want to talk them away from the ledge, get them out of that motel room, and walk them into FBI headquarters in cuffs. I've worked this case too damn long to see those kids shot up by a bunch of cowboys with M16s.

Windermere stepped up into the van, flipping her cell phone closed. "Gilbert says we have the ball for now," she said. "If things start to look ugly, Agent Wellwood, you and your guys take over. For now, we try to talk them down peacefully. Clear?"

Wellwood frowned. "You want my negotiators to play the point?"

Windermere shook her head. "We know these guys. They're only talking to us." She turned to Stevens. "So let's do it, big guy. How do we get them out of there?"

Stevens stared back at the motel, listening to the ambient chatter of radio calls and the drone of the helicopters overhead. "Where do we stand on their demands?" he said.

"Angel Cardinal's willing to pay the ransom. She can wire the money anywhere in the world. Confirmation in seconds. That's the easy part."

"The jet?"

"Hall talked to Cardinal's aviation company. They're fueling the plane as we speak. Pilot's being briefed on the situation."

"So it all comes down to Marie."

"Yeah." Windermere turned back to the motel. "I'll get on that plane my damn self before I let that girl anywhere near it. Cardinal can give them his money and he can give them his plane, but those kids aren't getting our girl."

"Agreed." Stevens stared across the parking lot at the row of police cars and the dark motel room beyond. He pictured Arthur Pender holed up behind that door, and he wondered what the kid was thinking. Was he scared? Was he angry? Did he think he was in control?

He turned to Windermere. "Those kids want to see McAllister," he said. "Let's show them McAllister."

EIGHTY-TWO

Marie was asleep when the FBI agent arrived. She'd been dreaming, and she woke up with the sickening feeling that Arthur was in danger. It had been days, maybe weeks, since they'd locked her away. She slept when she was tired, and the rest of the time she stared at the wall of her cell and listened to the other prisoners and tried to imagine she was somewhere else. Sometimes when she woke up there was a plate of bland food sitting in front of her door, and sometimes a blank-faced guard took her outside for an hour of exercise in the barren yard. But mostly she was alone with her thoughts, and she would sleep, or try to sleep, and think of Pender and Sawyer and always of Mouse.

She woke to the sound of a key in the door and looked up to see the FBI agent, Stevens, standing in the hall. "Get up," he said. "We're gonna take a ride."

She thought at first he was taking her to another court hearing, but when he led her out of the holding area, she saw the way the guards looked at her, the way the police openly stared, and she knew this was something different. Something was wrong.

Stevens signed a couple of forms and led her out to the parking lot, where his unmarked sedan waited. He stopped beside the back door. "Hold out your wrists."

She looked at him, saw the handcuffs. "I'm not going to run," she said.

He shook his head, cuffing her wrists in front of her. "Sorry," he said. "I'm going to get in enough shit for this as it is."

He opened the door and ushered her into the car. Marie sat down in the backseat, still half asleep and confused.

The agent got in the driver's seat and pulled out of the parking lot and onto a grimy Detroit street. Marie watched him drive for a minute. Then she leaned forward. "Where are we going?"

Stevens glanced at her in the rearview mirror. His eyes caught hers, and she watched him examine her. He looked back at the road and drove a few blocks. Then he spoke. "You know," he said, "I'm not even an FBI agent."

What the hell does that mean, Marie

thought, but she said nothing.

"I'm an agent with the Minnesota Bureau of Criminal Apprehension, the state police. I don't usually work kidnappings."

Marie watched him in the rearview mirror. He kept his eyes on hers.

"That's mainly because we don't get too many up in that part of the country. I guess you probably knew that, being a professional kidnapper."

He swung a right turn and headed down another long street, his eyes flicking back between Marie and the road. "I have a wife and two kids up in St. Paul," he said. "Haven't seen them in a week. I haven't been home, really home, in about a month. Never figured a state policeman would have to spend so much time on the road."

He made a quick left across traffic, and then they were descending onto a freeway, the car's engine roaring as it picked up speed.

"I miss them," said Stevens. "I miss them like hell. But it's funny. If you told me I could see them tonight but I'd have to give up your case, just let it go, I wouldn't even consider it. There's some part of me that doesn't even want to catch your boyfriend and his pals. There's a part of me that loves working this case so much I'd be happy if it never ended."

He stared forward, watching the freeway rise and fall as the car sped on. Marie sat back in her seat. "Where are you taking me?"

They turned onto an off-ramp and drove back to street level, Stevens's eyes on the road again. He said nothing. Marie stared out the window and sighed. "You gonna tell me or what?"

Stevens didn't answer, but he gestured out the front of the car. In the distance, Marie could see what must be their destination. It was a mass of lights, flashing and blinking and sweeping the ground, a great confusion of people and cars, and rising above it, the faded marquee of the Motor City Motel.

They pulled up to the swarm of onlookers, and a uniformed cop waved them on, lifting a yellow cordon as Stevens drove through. Marie could feel the faces of the crowd all turn toward her, could sense every eye looking in her direction, and she sunk low in her seat to avoid them.

Inside the lot, the confusion was more organized but no less urgent. A collection of police cars lined up like children's toys, uniformed officers running this way and that, and the roar of the helicopters overhead. And everyone's attention focused toward a spotlit motel door, unit 23, surrounded by a half circle of police and their cruisers and nobody moving in or out.

"What is this?" Marie asked, a sick feeling in her stomach. "Why are we here?"

Stevens stopped the car. "Your boyfriend's in there," he said, gesturing to the door. "Arthur and Matt Sawyer and their new girlfriend, Tiffany Prentice. They've got a hostage, a man named Jason Cardinal. He has a wife and two children. They're somewhere around here, too. Terrified, obviously."

"Oh my God," said Marie.

"Your boyfriend is asking for five million dollars' ransom and a private jet to Africa. The family's willing to pay the ransom. The hostage is lending them his jet. But that's not enough for your boyfriend. He wants you, too."

Stevens spun in his seat and stared at her. "He's not getting you, Marie. There's no way in hell. Now, there's a tactical team here itching to just storm in there with machine guns and grenades, but we don't want that. We want everyone out peacefully. But we're running out of time."

Marie stared at the man and then out to the chaos beyond. Pender was in that motel room, and Sawyer was with him.

"We need you to talk to Arthur, Marie," said Stevens. "You could save his life."

Marie felt her insides go numb. The flashing lights seemed to bore into her brain, the voices and engines and radio static all echoing inside her skull until it was too much and she knew she was going to black out. She fought it for as long as she could, a few desperate seconds, and then she gave in, fainting flat in the back of the FBI cruiser.

EIGHTY-THREE

Marie woke inside her nightmare, the FBI agent and a paramedic standing over her outside the unmarked police car, the handcuffs biting into her wrists. "Get up," said Stevens. "We don't have time for games."

It's not a game, she wanted to tell him, but she thought if she opened her mouth she would probably throw up. So she kept quiet as he lifted her to her feet and led her from the car, the whole world watching her in her orange prison clothes, the cuffs, her limp scraggly hair and her bleary eyes.

He hadn't abandoned her, after all. Even after Mouse died. Pender hadn't abandoned her, hadn't flown away to Thailand or the Maldives. He hadn't escaped. He was here, in this mob scene. Pender had done this for her.

Marie looked around, at the police and the reporters and the bystanders in the shadows, and she felt more afraid than she

508

ever had in her life. Why didn't he just go, she wondered. What the hell made him think this was a workable plan?

She realized, cold and guilty, she hadn't wanted to be abandoned. She'd wanted Pender to come back for her and now he had. This was what she'd wanted all along, wasn't it?

Stevens led her through the mob to a big blue FBI van. He helped her up into the back, where a couple of FBI techs sat staring at a mass of computers and electronics equipment. Agent Windermere was sitting in front of a monitor, and she looked up when Marie came in. "Ms. McAllister," she said. "The cause of all the confusion. Agent Stevens has briefed you on the situation?"

"I gave her the general idea," said Stevens.

"We need you to talk Arthur down before he gets hurt, understand?"

Marie wished she could sit down. She nodded.

"Now, listen," said Windermere. "We told Pender you flipped. This whole mess gets a lot cleaner if he forgets about you. You want him to live, you'll play along, because otherwise, babe" — she glanced up at Marie — "he's going nowhere without you."

Stevens wheeled over a chair and patted the seat. Marie let him guide her down, and

Windermere reached for a phone unit. She handed Marie the receiver. "We're patched in to Arthur's room," she said. "I'm going to connect you now."

They ate the last scraps of food as the sun set and the room got dark and gloomy, the only light coming from the television and the spotlights sneaking in around the edges of the curtains. Pender turned on a lamp, and they sat in the shadows, listening to the commotion outside and watching the news coverage.

There were hundreds of cops outside. The news station switched to a live shot from a helicopter, and Pender noticed the Feds had put a sniper team on an adjacent rooftop. He wondered where else the police could be hiding. The motel room was self-contained; there was no exit but the front door. The bathroom was in the back, and there was a heating duct along the rear that looked too small to fit a human being. All the same, Pender knew the cops would be searching for an angle.

He caught Sawyer's eye. "Keep an ear out for noises," he said. "They might not come in through the front door when they come."

Sawyer nodded. "They brought SWAT guys."

"And snipers," said Pender. "We stay clear of the windows."

The phone rang on the bedside table, and Pender jumped. He glanced at Sawyer and saw his friend had his hand on the Uzi. Sawyer raised an eyebrow, and Pender forced a smile. Then he picked up the phone. "This is Arthur Pender."

"Arthur?" Her voice sucked the breath right out of his lungs. Marie. He tried to answer but couldn't, his mouth moving but no sound coming out. "Are you there?"

"Marie," he said finally. "Where are you?"

"I'm okay," she said. "I'm in a van outside the motel. They brought me here."

"I couldn't leave without you," he said. "I missed you so much."

"Arthur, this is crazy. Do you know how many cops are out here? They have guns, baby. They all want to kill you."

"I know," said Pender. "It won't be much longer. Then we'll be free."

"Arthur, please. If you take the money now, you have a good chance of making it out of here. Forget about me."

"Marie —"

"Just listen, Arthur. It's my fault the police caught us. I used the Ashley McAdams credit card in Seattle. Everything's my fault. Don't let them hang you for my mistakes."

"I'm not leaving without you."

Marie paused. When she came back, her voice was stronger. "Arthur, I snitched. I told them everything. I sold you out." Her voice cracked, and he could tell she was crying. "I'm not worth it, Arthur. I'm not worth risking your life for."

"You're worth it," he told her. "Whether you snitched or not. I'm not leaving without you."

"Arthur," she said, her voice pleading. "Think it over. Be professional. *Walk away.*"

He stood there a moment longer, and then he hung up the phone. He had to. Any longer and he might have believed her. Any longer and he might have given up just to see her.

EIGHTY-FOUR

Pender sank back against the bedside table. Be professional, she said. Walk away. He knew she was right. A professional would be on Cardinal's jet right now, sipping champagne and toasting to a life of leisure. A professional would have cut his losses and run when there was still room to run.

They could still be professional. If he took Marie's advice and said to hell with her, they could be on a beach within twenty-four hours, drunk as sailors and rich and free. All it would take was a truckload of balls and a whole lot of selfishness. Maybe that's what it meant to be a professional.

Sawyer caught his eye. "You all right, boss?"

"Yeah," said Pender. "Marie wants us to give up on her. Told me be a professional and walk away."

"Be professional," said Sawyer. "Nice touch."

"She told me we should take the money and get on the plane and forget about her. She told me — she said it was her fault she got caught in the first place. I guess the FBI caught her when she used the wrong credit card in Seattle. She told me this all is on her."

"Bullshit," said Sawyer. "It's my fault we got caught."

"No."

Sawyer looked right through Pender, avoiding his eyes. "I shot Beneteau. Dumbest thing in the world. If I don't kill that guy, we get away clean. Nobody connects us to anything. This is my fault."

Pender looked hard at Sawyer. "It's nobody's fault," he said. "We won as a team, and we lost as a team. We all could have been better."

Sawyer said nothing.

"Marie told me she snitched, Sawyer. I know we should ditch, but I can't."

Sawyer still didn't respond, and the words hung there in the room until Sawyer finally looked up and caught his eye. "I can't do it, either," he said. "We're the guys who're supposed to take the fall for *her*."

Tiffany sighed, loud, from the corner where she lay curled up on the floor. Pender looked over, and she averted her eyes, her face set in a scowl. If she'd left a few minutes earlier, she might have made it, he thought. Instead she's locked in with us in what might be the last days of her life.

"You knew what you were getting into," he told her. "If you wanted something different, you could have gone back to Princeton. I gave you plenty of chances to run."

Tiffany glared at him. "I'm sick of this," she said, standing. "We've got a chance to walk out of here, *alive,* holding real money, and you guys keep talking like there's any other choice. I can't do this anymore."

She walked to the door and started hauling away at the bed. Pender followed her and grabbed her from behind, wrapping his arms around hers. She struggled against him, flailing and cursing. "Let me go," she said. "I'm not going to give up my life just because you guys are too stupid to see what's in front of you."

"You walk out that door and they'll throw you in jail," Pender told her. "We're beyond the point where you can just walk away."

"Maybe for you," she said. "My dad's almost a billionaire. He's got famous lawyers. I'll tell them it was Stockholm syndrome and you guys forced me into it. Let me *go!*"

Tiffany wrenched away from Pender's

arms, wriggling free, and he watched as she struggled to drag the bed back from the door. Sawyer reached to hold her back, but Pender intercepted him. "Let her go," he said. "We're better off without her."

"Hell, no," Sawyer said. "She's not walking out of here and getting off scot-free. No way, boss."

Pender held him back, struggling against his friend as Tiffany dragged the bed back from the door. She turned the knob and had the door halfway open when Sawyer broke free from Pender.

"Get back here," he said, dodging Pender and climbing over the bed after Tiffany. He grabbed her as she crossed the threshold, and they fought for a moment in the police spotlight. Sawyer had his hand on Tiffany's arm, yelling something Pender couldn't make out, and she was trying to get loose of his grip. But Sawyer held tight, and he was dragging her back to the room when Pender heard the shot.

Sawyer staggered back, and Tiffany broke free and disappeared out into the parking lot. Sawyer leaned against the door frame, a red rose starting to blossom on the back of his shirt. Pender grabbed his friend and pulled him inside the room and slammed the door behind him. He took Sawyer to

516

Cardinal's bed and told the hostage *move,* and Cardinal scrambled to his feet as Pender laid Sawyer down.

The big guy was quiet, his eyes wide and his face pale, his hands feeling at the entry wound as the blood poured out of him. Pender locked the front door and pushed the bed back into place, and then he walked back to Sawyer's bed and stood with the TEC-9, listening to his friend strain to breathe and waiting for the SWAT team to break through the door.

EIGHTY-FIVE

Stevens heard the gunshot and then the gasp from the crowd a moment later. He ran around the side of the FBI van just in time to see Tiffany Prentice wrench away from the big guy and make a dash for the line of police cars. Then he saw Windermere pushing angrily through the crowd toward the van, where Wellwood stood yelling something into his headset. Stevens flagged a Grosse Pointe uniform and stood him on guard with Marie McAllister and then pushed his own way to the van.

Windermere collared Wellwood and shoved him, hard, against the side of the van. "What the *fuck* are you doing?"

"My guys had a shot," Wellwood told her. "They had to take it."

"Who the hell told them they could shoot?"

Wellwood just stared at her.

"Great," said Windermere. "Now there's a

pissed-off kid in there with a machine gun, and God knows what he's going to do. You've fucked up our entire situation."

Windermere looked ready to punch the big tactical officer. Stevens stepped forward before she decided to do it. "That was a terrible call," he told Wellwood. "There's a chain of command here and you broke it. But we still have a hostage inside, and as long as he's alive we've still got a situation. So let's calm that kid down, all right?"

"I'm going to get him on the phone," said Windermere. "We gotta get him back on our side."

She disappeared inside the command van just as Detective Landry walked up with Tiffany Prentice beside him, handcuffed and squirming. "Let me go, you bastard," she said. "Those guys made me do it, I swear."

Landry raised an eyebrow in Stevens's direction. "This one claims she was a hostage."

The girl gave Stevens a scared-kitten look through her mess of blond hair. He wanted to laugh in her face. "She's no hostage," he said. "Get Hall to book her and take her downtown."

The girl blinked and her scared look disappeared. "This is bullshit," she said, kicking at Landry. "My dad will have your ass for this. That's a promise."

Stevens watched Landry frog-march the girl to his unmarked, and then he climbed back into the command van where Windermere was waiting, staring at a bank of monitors. She reached for a phone and held out the receiver as Stevens walked in. "Connecting you to Pender's room," she said.

Stevens took the phone and held it to his ear. There was a click and then the electronic ringing as he waited for Pender to decide what to do. The kid was freaking out, Stevens knew. Any mistakes now could blow the whole scenario — assuming it wasn't already blown.

The ringing stopped, and there was silence. Stevens glanced at Windermere, who nodded quickly. "Arthur?" he said. "It's Agent Stevens."

There was no answer. No sound whatsoever. Windermere motioned for him to keep talking.

"Arthur," said Stevens. "We didn't order that shot. Somebody screwed up, and we'll make sure they pay for it, all right? We just want to make sure you're not thinking of doing anything rash right now."

Finally Pender spoke, and his voice was flat calm and deadly. "You've compromised your mission and lost my trust," he said. "You put the life of the hostage needlessly in danger. And you're warning *me* not to do anything rash?"

"I'm sorry," said Stevens. "We know we messed up. But we're still committed to getting you out of there peacefully, all right?"

Pender said nothing.

"Arthur," said Stevens. "We can still do business together. Right?"

Another pause. Then Pender spoke again. "No more games," he said. "You fuck up again, you will regret it."

He hung up the phone. Stevens hung up a second later. He was drenched in sweat, and his heart was pounding. He turned to Windermere. "We still got him."

Windermere exhaled. "Those meathead bastards," she said. "I'll have them working evidence lockers in Anchorage."

Stevens stood, walked to the door of the van. Across the parking lot, the spotlights lit up unit 23's door like an alien tractor beam in an old B movie. "Where does this leave us?" he said. "Does he still walk away without McAllister?"

Windermere shook her head. "He just saw his best friend get shot. No way he leaves without the girl."

"That means he's not leaving," said

Stevens.

"Means the hostage isn't leaving, either."

Stevens rubbed his chin and stared at the motel door. "Not necessarily," he said, turning back to face Windermere. "Call Hall. I have another idea."

EIGHTY-SIX

Pender stared down at Sawyer, watching his friend struggle to breathe, the gunshot wound a gaping hole. The big guy still hadn't screamed, hadn't said a word. He just lay on the bed, staring at the ceiling like he was waiting to die.

Pender watched him. The commotion outside was just background noise now; he felt detached. Like he was watching himself on the television in some shitty action movie.

He'd failed his friends. They'd put their faith in him, and he'd brought them to disaster. Mouse was dead, and Sawyer wasn't far behind. He'd probably die in this motel room himself, and Marie would spend the rest of her life in jail. And it was all of it on his shoulders.

Sawyer reached out and touched his arm, wheezing from the effort. Pender looked down into his eyes, and Sawyer forced a smile. "Now I know how Mouse felt," he said. He rested his head back against the pillow. "Little bastard was tougher than he looked."

Pender said nothing. A professional would have walked, he thought. He watched Sawyer struggle to breathe and wondered how long it would take him to die.

Cardinal sat in a chair in the corner of the room. He'd watched in silence since the FBI had shown up. Now he caught Pender's eye. "It was never about the money, was it?" he said.

Pender looked up at him. The man had relaxed into some kind of acceptance over the last few hours, and now he stared at Pender, unnervingly calm. Pender held his gaze. "What are you talking about?"

"The ransom," said Cardinal. "You never cared about it, did you?"

"You think I kidnapped you for fun?"

"You had your reasons. But money had nothing to do with it."

"You're wrong," said Pender. "I pulled jobs for the last two years saving up to retire. If the police hadn't figured us out, we would still be at work and I would have a couple years, tops, before I could get the hell off this continent and never work again. But we screwed up and they caught on and we ran out of money and needed one last score to make it stick. So here we are."

"No," said Cardinal. "Here you are. If it was all about the money, you would be gone right now. You kidnapped me to get your girlfriend back, plain and simple, but you're not getting her back and you know it. The FBI will let me die before they let her go."

Pender shrugged. "They know what we want. Whether or not they choose to comply is completely up to them."

"Yeah," said Cardinal. "Let's just say I'm not holding my breath."

Pender picked up the TEC-9 and walked over to Cardinal. "Hold your breath or don't," he said. "It makes no difference to me. Whatever happens to me — or you — that girl out there is not going to spend the rest of her life in jail. Understood?"

Cardinal stared at Pender and then at the gun. He swallowed. "Yeah," he said. "Fine. Understood."

EIGHTY-SEVEN

"No," said Stevens. "It was my idea. I can't let you take the risk."

They were standing in the command van, waiting on Agent Hall to come back with body armor. Women's body armor.

"You worry too much," said Windermere. "I'll be fine."

"Forget it. I'm not letting you walk in there like this."

Windermere walked over to him. She put her hands on his face and stared into his eyes. "You're sweet," she said. "And I appreciate it. But you have a family, Stevens."

"You have Mark."

"Forget about Mark. He's probably found someone else already."

Stevens stared at her. "This is ridiculous."

"Don't be silly," said Windermere. "I'll be fine. Besides, I'm leaving you the tough part. I just have to go in there and look helpless. You've gotta keep things moving out here."

"What if you get hurt?"

She winked at him, then turned to Hall, just now returning with a Kevlar vest. "That's what the armor's for."

Hall handed her the gear, and the men watched her fit it over her blouse. When the vest was tight she pulled her coat over the top and posed. "What do you think?"

Hall shook his head. "I can't believe we're doing this."

"Better me than Cardinal, right?" said Windermere. "Come on, guys. This is progress."

"Speaking of progress," said Hall. "The Buffalo office came through with a name on that Amtrak drop. Guy named Rod Stirzaker."

Stevens stared at him, momentarily distracted. "Ben's —"

"Brother, yeah. Caught up to him in a basement with about a hundred grand worth of computers and printing equipment. Squealed like *Deliverance* when they caught him."

"What did he say?"

"Gave up aliases, passport numbers, and credit card details for Pender and Sawyer. Then some clown told him his brother got shot and the kid started crying and clammed up. Wouldn't say another word."

"Well, hot damn," said Windermere. "I guess our boys aren't getting far even if they do get out of this shitstorm." She smoothed her coat down over the vest and glanced at Stevens. "You ever shoot anyone, Stevens?"

Stevens looked at her a moment. Then he nodded. "Just once," he said. "In Duluth. Kid holed himself up in a convenience store with a shotgun."

"You kill him?"

He nodded again. "He was a half second away from shooting the clerk."

Windermere watched him a second. "You're going to have to shoot this guy," she said. "Pender. Even if it means he shoots me."

"I'm not going to put you in danger," he said.

"Stevens." She gave him a look. Then she leaned in and kissed his cheek. "Take the shot. Don't let this bastard go." She straightened and looked over at Hall. "You fellas ready? Let's get the kid on the phone and get moving."

Hall moved over to the phone bank and started punching in numbers.

Stevens stared at Windermere a moment. "I'll get Marie," he said finally. "Might be more useful if she plays the voice of reason."

■ ■ ■ ■

Marie took the phone from Agent Hall's hand and listened as the computer connected her to Arthur's room. The phone rang for a few seconds, and then he picked up. "What?"

"Arthur, it's me."

"Marie," he said. He paused. "Did you hear about Sawyer?"

"I heard," she said. "Arthur, this isn't worth dying for. Both of us alive and in jail is better than one of us dead."

"Not if you're free."

"I'm not going to be free," she said. "Take the money and go."

"I'm not leaving without you," he said. "I'm working on something. Is this what you're calling about?"

"No," said Marie. She looked around the command van. Stevens nodded at her. "They want to trade hostages. Cardinal for an FBI agent, Windermere. They want to take Cardinal out of the picture."

Pender went silent. "Fine," he said finally. "She comes in unarmed."

Marie glanced at Stevens, who nodded again. "Of course."

"You'll check her yourself."

529

"I will."

"All right," he said. "But I have conditions. Put one of the agents on the phone." He paused. "I love you, Marie. No matter how this plays out."

"I know," said Marie. "I love you, too. Be safe."

She passed the phone to Stevens and sank back in her chair, feeling like it was goodbye for good. Beside her, Stevens was talking to Arthur, and Marie picked up his spare headset, fumbling to hold it with her wrists still cuffed. Windermere glared at her, but she ignored the agent and listened in on Arthur's conditions.

"If we're going to do this," he was saying, "you're going to have to earn it. You guys shot up my best friend. Don't expect much of my trust."

"All due respect," said Stevens. "Your best friend is a kidnapper and a murderer. He knew what he was getting into."

"If that's the way you want to play it, I'll send Sawyer out with Cardinal's body. Then you guys can come and get me."

"All right, all right," said Windermere, picking up her headset. "You're both macho men. We believe it. Let's hear your conditions, Arthur."

"Fine," said Pender. "I want Cardinal's

plane to remain fueled and ready. I want Cardinal's five million dollars transferred to a bank account of my choosing immediately. You get me the money, and we trade Cardinal for Windermere. Then we can fight over Marie."

"Okay," said Windermere. "Anything else?"

"I want food. I don't care what it is, but Windermere's going to eat it, too, so don't poison it. When Windermere arrives, she'll be unarmed. Marie will verify or there's no deal. And when Cardinal comes out, he brings Sawyer out with him and your people give him medical treatment. Those are my conditions. Take them or leave them."

Windermere glanced at Stevens. "We can work with that," Stevens told him.

"Good," said Pender. "Get a pen. Here's where I want the money." He listed overseas bank information. Stevens wrote it down and repeated it back.

"Okay," said Pender. "Send Windermere in with a wheelchair for Sawyer."

EIGHTY-EIGHT

Pender hung up the phone. He turned back to Sawyer, who lay breathing weakly on the bed. "We don't have to play it like this," Pender said. "If you think you can hang on, I'll keep you right here beside me. But I don't want you dying in here."

Sawyer stared up at him for a long moment. "Let me go," he said finally. "I'll die if I stay here."

"They'll put you in jail."

Sawyer nodded. "I know."

"I can still get you out of here. You just have to hold on."

Sawyer shook his head. "It was my fault, Pender. I'll take the fall."

"We're a team," Pender told him. "It's everyone's fault."

"Let me just do this." Sawyer reached for Pender's hand. He took Pender's fingers in his weak grip and held them. "For you and Marie. You bailed me out enough times. Let me do this."

Pender stared at his friend for a long moment. Christ, he thought. This is not how it's supposed to go. Then the phone rang. Sawyer gripped his fingers one more time, and Pender straightened and picked up the phone. "Yeah."

"Arthur, it's me. Windermere's clean. No gun. I made sure." She paused. "But she's wearing a vest. I told them you wouldn't like it, but they wouldn't listen."

Pender swore. "I'll deal with it. The money?"

"It's sent. The Imperial Luxembourg bank."

"Okay," said Pender. "Thank you."

"They want to come in now, Arthur. Be careful."

"I'll see you," he said. He hung up the phone and walked over to Cardinal, keeping the gun trained with his left hand and untying the man's wrists with his right. "Good news for you," he told the hostage. "We're getting you out of here."

Cardinal nodded. "Thank you."

"Don't mention it," Pender said. Then he smiled. "When you make this into a movie, I hope you'll give me more muscle definition."

Cardinal smiled back. "Whatever you want."

Pender pushed the man toward the door. "They're going to come with a wheelchair," he said. "You're going to be my shield. We take the wheelchair into the room, put Sawyer in it, and you wheel him back out. Don't look back. Understood?"

Cardinal nodded.

"All right," said Pender. "Let's move this bed."

Pender and Cardinal dragged the bed away from the door and then sat down to wait. A few minutes passed, and then somebody knocked on the door and Pender peered through the peephole to see Windermere on the other side with a wheelchair.

Pender gestured for Cardinal to open the door and took up a position behind him. Cardinal unlocked it and swung it open, and immediately the noise of the night filled the room. The sweeping spotlight landed on the doorway, and Pender squinted out into the parking lot and saw the half ring of police cars and the officers behind, all staring down the barrels of their guns at him. He saw the command van and the crowd in the distance and the news helicopters hovering overhead, and he imagined he could see the snipers on the rooftop opposite, watching him through their scopes. He shivered and took a step backward. Then Cardinal took the wheelchair and they closed the door again.

Pender brought the wheelchair to the side of the bed where Sawyer lay waiting. Sawyer gave him a smile. "So this is good-bye."

Pender reached over and gripped his friend's hand. "You know you don't have to do this," he said.

"Just get out of here safe," Sawyer said. "Understand?"

Pender stared at him a moment longer. Then he forced himself to move. He lifted his friend gingerly into the wheelchair. "Come here," he told Cardinal.

Cardinal wheeled Sawyer to the front door, and Pender peered through the peephole again. Windermere stood on the sidewalk, holding a bag of fast food.

Pender held the gun to the back of Cardinal's head and told him to open the door. Cardinal swung the door open again, and the noise and the light rushed inward.

Windermere waited beside the door. "Give me the bag and step into the room," Pender told her. He gave Cardinal a push with the gun.

Cardinal wheeled Sawyer out into the parking lot, and Windermere took his place.

Pender took the fast-food bag in his left hand and trained the gun on her with his right. He backed her slowly into the room. "Close the door," he said. "Lock it."

She obliged without a word, and Pender opened the food bag, half expecting to see a bomb at the bottom. Instead he saw cheeseburgers and French fries. "I hope you're hungry."

"We didn't poison them," she said. "That food's poison enough already."

"Yeah," said Pender. "Somehow I think I'll die of other causes long before the fast food gets me."

He put the food on the bed, and he frisked Windermere, patting her down and feeling for the telltale lump that would give her away. He stopped, feeling the bulk beneath her coat. "Hear you're wearing a vest."

She stared at him, stone-faced.

"Yeah, that's not going to fly," he said. He trained the gun on her. "Take it off."

Windermere stared at him a moment. Then she sighed and began to unbutton her coat. "You planning on getting me shot?"

Pender shook his head. "Just don't want you getting creative when the game's on the line."

He watched as Windermere peeled off the armor and left it discarded on the bed.

"Don't get comfortable," he told her. Then he picked up the phone. "Get me Agent Stevens."

Pender waited for the cops to connect him, his mind flashing red lights as he worked out a plan. It was a risky idea, and it hinged on Sawyer staying alive and taking the team's weight on his shoulders. But if it worked, it meant both he and Marie would go free. It has to work, Pender told himself. We're running out of options.

The phone picked up. "This is Agent Stevens, Arthur. How's the food?"

"Food's fine. I took the liberty of removing Windermere's body armor, Agent Stevens. So keep that in mind if you're going to try anything fancy."

Stevens paused. "Duly noted."

Pender kept his gun trained on Windermere. "Good. Then it's time for the next phase. I want a van and driver to take me to Cardinal's jet. The driver will be unarmed. I want Cardinal's jet fueled and ready for a transoceanic flight. If you satisfy these conditions, I'll release Agent Windermere once I'm aboard the plane."

There was a pause as Stevens thought it over. "And Marie?"

"The girl?" Pender said. "You can keep her. I've decided I like flying solo." He paused. "You have one hour, Agent Stevens."

EIGHTY-NINE

Stevens stared across at the motel, wondering what the kid was thinking. He'd spent all night fighting to bring the girl along, and now that he'd gotten his ransom he was throwing her away. What had changed when they swapped Cardinal for Windermere?

Stevens turned away from the motel and looked back at Marie McAllister, who sat disconsolate on a chair inside the command van. "What's he doing?" he asked her. "You guys have some kind of secret code or something?"

She looked up at him and shrugged. "No code," she said. "Maybe he just came to his senses."

Stevens stared at her a beat. She's as confused as I am, he thought.

Agent Hall rustled a fourteen-passenger Chevy van from a nearby motel, and he pulled into the parking lot, leaning on the horn and sending cops and civilians scattering. He pulled up beside the command van and climbed out.

"This stuff make any sense to you?" Stevens asked him. "This turnaround of his?"

Hall shrugged. "Maybe he saw a chance to get his friend out and he took it."

"Sawyer. How's he doing?"

"He's in tough shape right now." He glanced at Marie, who looked down at the floor. "Pretty big hole in his chest. They're saying it's a toss-up whether he lives or dies."

Stevens nodded. I'm not convinced this is all about Sawyer, he thought, watching Hall disappear out of the command center. There's something bigger at play here.

"Agent Stevens."

Stevens turned to find Wellwood behind him. The tactical officer regarded Stevens for a long moment. "My guys could be useful if you plan to intercept this kid before he gets on the plane."

"I agree," said Stevens. "Get your men and set up positions around Cardinal's jet. We'll spot him the drive to the airport and hope to suppress him before he gets on-board. But your guys wait for my okay before they shoot, clear?"

"Roger."

Stevens watched Wellwood disappear, feeling the adrenaline start to course. The climax was approaching, and he stood, nervous, wondering how it was all going to play. "Take the shot," Windermere had said. Stevens remembered her lips on his skin and wondered if he could do it.

Hall came back with a Kevlar vest, and Stevens flashed him a thumbs-up. "Give me a minute to call Pender. Then I'll give you the go-ahead."

Hall nodded, and Stevens stepped back inside the command van. He picked up the phone. "Patch me in to Pender's room."

The phone rang, and Pender picked up. "Pender."

"This is Stevens. We're sending a van for you now."

"Okay," said Pender. "We're ready to roll."

Stevens turned to Hall. "Get in that van and drive it to their door. We'll have a police escort for you all the way to the airport. Don't get scared and don't get jumpy. Don't try and be a hero, all right?"

"Yes, sir."

Hall disappeared out of the command van, and Stevens turned to see Marie staring at him. "What about me?" she said.

"We're done with you," he told her. "I'll

have another agent take you back to your cell."

"No," she said. "Please. Take me with you."

"To the airport."

She nodded. "I need to see it. I need to know how it ends."

Stevens rubbed his chin. "Fine. But you stick close to me at all times. You try anything funny, and I'll shoot you where you stand."

He led her out of the command van and down to his unmarked. He sat her in the backseat and then climbed in the front and edged the car through the crowd and through the half ring of cruisers. He pulled up outside unit 19, four doors down from where Hall had the van parked and waiting, and he watched through the front windshield as the door to Pender's unit opened and Windermere walked out with Pender behind, his machine gun pressed to the back of her head and an Uzi in his other hand.

Windermere climbed into the back of the van, and Pender climbed in behind. He kept the gun pointed at Windermere and made her close the door, and then Hall shifted into drive and the van pulled away from the motel.

Stevens let his foot off the brake and followed the van as it made its way around the back side of the motel and pulled in behind a pair of Grosse Pointe cruisers. In the rearview, he saw Wellwood's tactical van and another pair of cruisers follow. The convoy pulled out into the street and started for the airport, the noise and the crowds falling back into the distance.

NINETY

Pender kept the gun trained on Windermere as the van rolled along. With his free hand, he held out the bag of food. "Eat," he said. "Playing hostage must get exhausting."

Windermere opened the bag and took out a cheeseburger in waxed paper. She unwrapped it and took a bite. "So tell me something," she said as she chewed. "Why the sudden change of heart? What's wrong with Marie?"

Pender stared at her. "She ratted me out."

"You think?"

"She said so. You said so. I guess it finally sunk in."

Windermere took another bite. "She was scared for your life. And we'll say anything if we think it will get you to put down your guns."

"So you're saying she didn't snitch."

She shrugged. "Think what you want. But I don't believe that's why you changed your mind."

"It doesn't matter," said Pender. "Either way, I'm getting out of here."

"Maybe," she said. She reached in the bag and took a handful of fries. "You happy now? I can quit with this stuff?"

Pender nodded. She passed him the bag, and he took out another cheeseburger and unwrapped it. It was a tiny lukewarm patty on a stale bun, but it was the first real food he'd eaten in more than eight hours and it tasted better than filet mignon.

The city passed by around them, lit up by the flashing blue and red lights of the police escort. Pender watched through the windows as the driver guided them past low-lying strip malls and little houses, industrial zones and more dingy motels. They slowed as they passed a restaurant, and Pender caught a glimpse of the customers inside, families and young couples and old couples and solitary old men, and he felt a little sad. It would have been nice, he thought, to live a normal life like that. A decent job and a house and a standing dinner date Saturday night. But the driver stepped on the gas again, and he pushed those thoughts from his head. I haven't given up on life just yet, he thought. Not even close.

The airport appeared in the distance, a

vast, flat expanse of blinking lights and shadowed terminals beyond razor-topped chain fencing. The lead police cruisers drove away from the terminals to the far side of the airfield, headed for a hangar and a fuel station and Jason Cardinal's jet, bathed in light and miniature in the distance.

"One more question," said Windermere. "Why'd you do it?"

Pender turned back from the window. "What?"

"I don't really care why you kidnapped all those people. I know the how and the who, and that's fine with me. But my partner, Agent Stevens, he cares about the why. He told me that's all he really wanted, was to look you in the eye and try to understand what made you kids do it."

She stared at Pender, kind of shrugging, a wry smile on her face. The driver watched them in the rearview mirror. Pender stared out the window. "Look around, Agent Windermere," he said. "We didn't really have options."

She followed his gaze. "I'm not sure what you mean."

He gave her a tight smile. "I mean, have you seen the job market these days?"

Windermere laughed, long and loud. "You kids just needed jobs? Damn, Arthur. The

FBI's always hiring."

"We figured we were smart enough to pull this off," said Pender. "Kind of a redistribution of wealth thing, you know what I mean? We wanted to test ourselves, see if we could do it."

"You wanted to test yourselves," said Windermere. "How do you think you did?"

Pender watched the hangar approach, the jet out on the tarmac, sleek and gleaming white and promising freedom. "Ask me tomorrow," he said.

The police cruisers led the convoy onto airport property and out toward the hangar, then fell back as the van drove out to the jet. Pender twisted in his seat to watch the Crown Victoria and the second van fall back as well.

"They brought the SWAT team," he said.

"HRT," said Windermere. "Hostage Rescue Team."

"Whatever. The guys with the big guns."

"They won't do anything unless Stevens gives the order."

"That's good," said Pender. "Stevens kind of likes you."

"You think?"

Pender glanced at her. "You tell me."

"I guess he does," she said. "He'll hold them back."

Pender leaned forward in his seat. "Driver," he said. "Take us right up to the plane. Park in front of the stairs. Passenger side in, so you're facing the HRT guys. You climb out first and go up into the plane. Do what I say and I won't hurt either of you."

He turned to Windermere. "When he's inside the plane, you open your door and go into the plane as well. I'll verify the plane's ready to fly, and I'll let you both go. Understand?"

Windermere nodded. The driver nodded, too. He drove across the tarmac and swung the van around, pulling up alongside the plane's staircase. Pender watched as the driver put the van in park and then climbed over to the passenger seat. He opened the door and stepped out onto the tarmac and climbed the stairs up into the plane.

"Okay," said Pender. "Time to go."

He nudged Windermere, and she obeyed, reaching over to open the rear passenger door and climbing out of the vehicle. Pender followed, the gun held tight to Windermere's neck as she started the climb up into the cabin.

"All right," she said. "Don't do anything crazy now."

"I'm not the one you have to worry about," said Pender. They climbed one step at a time, Pender well aware that his back was exposed to the SWAT team behind him. "If they shoot me, I'll squeeze the trigger and you'll be dead." He told Windermere. "So keep your fingers crossed they don't get cute."

Then the driver appeared in the cabin doorway. "Get back in the plane," Pender told him. "We'll be there in a second."

The driver shook his head, and then Pender saw the gun in his hand, a little cap-gun revolver. The kid stared at Pender, raising the gun to his face. "Let her go."

"Calm down," said Pender. "Don't get stupid. Drop the gun."

"Let her go." The kid was trembling, the gun shaking and his voice unsteady. "Let her go or I shoot."

"Drop the gun," Pender told him. He held Windermere tight and kept the TEC-9 pressed into her skin.

"I swear to God I'll shoot you."

Pender pushed Windermere forward, and she climbed another step. "Then shoot," he said. "But do it quick."

"Do it, Hall," said Windermere. "Take the shot."

The kid blinked. Stared at Windermere. Shaking harder now. Pender took the gun from Windermere's neck and pointed it at him. "If you don't drop that gun, I'll shoot you here and now."

The kid stared Pender down. Pender watched his finger tighten on the trigger. "Goddamn it," he said. "Have it your way." He closed his eyes and let off a burst with the machine gun. Windermere screamed. The kid went down hard.

NINETY-ONE

Stevens watched from across the tarmac as Hall tried to pull his move on Pender. The kid had a gun — Pender had never frisked him — and Stevens watched with mounting horror as the junior agent tried to force the kidnapper's hand. Pender shouted something at Hall, and then time seemed to slow as the kidnapper put a burst through the kid's abdomen. Stevens could hear Windermere's screams from a hundred feet away.

Stevens watched Hall's body crumple as Pender pushed Windermere past and they both disappeared into the plane. Hall was in a heap at the base of the staircase, and the kid wasn't moving.

He stormed over to Wellwood's tactical van. "Who the hell gave Hall that gun?" he said. "How the hell did he get a gun on that plane?"

"Wasn't us," Wellwood told him. "We had nothing to do with it."

"Goddamn it," said Stevens. "No more mistakes. Have your men set up a perimeter around the plane. I want snipers with a clear shot at the cabin doorway."

"Roger. What about the female agent?"

Stevens swallowed, aware that Wellwood was watching him closely. "If you guys have a shot, you take it."

"Understood." Wellwood turned back to his crew, and Stevens watched while the tactical team dispersed. He turned back to the plane as his radio crackled to life.

"Agent Stevens." Pender. He must have grabbed Hall's radio.

Stevens picked up the radio. "Arthur, that was a mistake. We don't know how that gun got on that plane."

"Bullshit, Agent Stevens. You're going to keep making your little mistakes until I'm dead. Well, listen up. I now have two hostages. The pilot and your Agent Windermere. By my count, that makes Windermere extraneous."

Stevens felt his skin start to crawl.

"What I should do, Agent Stevens, is kill Windermere and keep the pilot to myself. But I'm not going to do that yet. Where's Marie?"

"Back at the motel," Stevens said. "I'm sorry."

"Bullshit. You're still playing games. I can see Marie in the back of your car. Get her out of there."

"Whatever you're planning, Pender, it's not going to work."

"Get her out of there or I kill Windermere now, Stevens."

Stevens stared at the plane. "Fine," he said. He walked around the side of the Crown Vic and opened the door. Marie frowned at him and let Stevens help her out of the car.

"Uncuff her," said Pender.

"Arthur —"

"Do it."

Stevens stared at the plane a moment. Then he turned back to Marie. Dug out the key to the handcuffs and freed the girl's wrists. She glared at him, rubbing her raw skin. Stevens turned back to the plane.

"We're going to make a trade," said Pender. "You're going to put down your gun and bring Marie to the cabin door, and we'll swap."

"Not going to happen."

"All right, then, I'll kill her," said Pender.

Stevens swore. "We swap," he said, gritting his teeth.

"Good. Put your gun down."

Stevens made an exaggerated show of

reaching into his holster and removing the FBI-issue Glock. He left it on the seat of the Crown Vic and held both hands high.

"Now bring Marie to the plane."

Stevens put down the radio. He took McAllister by the arm and began to lead her across the tarmac. He could hear Wellwood yelling something in the background, but he tuned the tactical officer out and kept walking.

The Gulfstream's twin jet engines were spooling up as he approached.

Stevens felt naked and vulnerable as he crossed the tarmac, the walk seeming to take hours. The girl was shaking in his arms, whether from fear or excitement, he couldn't tell. Finally they reached the stairway and Hall's bloody body, and Stevens stared down at the kid; his eyes were open wide. It wasn't as easy as it looked, was it, he thought. You can't just *want* to be the hero.

Then he saw the kid's gun, a .38 revolver lying forgotten a foot away from his right hand. Either Pender had missed it or he just hadn't cared. Either way, there it was.

Stevens pushed Marie up onto the stairway and then bent down as though to nudge Hall's body out of the way. With his right hand he swept up the gun and tucked it into his pocket. Then he followed Marie up the stairway, keeping himself behind her so the bulge didn't show.

Marie willed her heart to stop racing as she climbed up the stairs and ducked her head beneath the doorway to enter the Gulfstream. She paused at the entryway and took a breath and then turned and walked into the passenger cabin. It was a luxurious little aircraft: cream-colored leather seats and deep-pile carpeting and three or four flat-screen TVs — and in the rear of the plane stood Pender, holding Windermere in front of him with a machine gun in his hand, the pilot sitting in the seat beside them, staring at Pender's gun.

"Arthur," she said. She wanted to throw up and pass out and die. Pender smiled at her and even his smile looked alien.

"Everything's going to be fine, Marie," he said. He was calmer than she'd ever seen him. "We're free. You don't have to be scared any longer."

She heard Stevens climb into the airplane behind her, and Pender's eyes shifted to him. "Agent Stevens," he said. "Ready to make that trade?"

"I'm ready," Stevens said. "Let's do this and be done with it."

"Don't do it," said Windermere. "We worked too damn hard on this case to give it all up like this."

"Shut up," said Pender. "You'll have other cases. I'll just be the one who got away." He turned back to Stevens. "I'm going to bring Windermere closer, and we'll pass them off, get it? Then you both get the hell off this plane."

"Fine," Stevens said. Marie felt his hand tense on her back as Pender started toward her. "Let's go."

Stevens watched Pender push Windermere forward and held tight to the back of McAllister's shirt, looking for an opening. With his right hand, he reached into his pocket, keeping the girl square in front of him.

Pender and Windermere came closer until Windermere and McAllister were almost touching. Pender kept his eyes on him as they walked, his hand tight on the machine gun. Stevens stared back, watching Pender advance, waiting for the kid to stumble.

Pender took another step and then stopped. He glanced down at McAllister, just barely, and Stevens made his move. He pulled the revolver and stepped back, holding McAllister tight and pointing the gun across the plane at Pender. "Get back," he told the kidnapper. "Get back or I blow you away."

Ninety-Two

Stevens stared across the plane at Pender, pointing the revolver square at the kidnapper's face. "I can't let you do it," he told Pender. "I can't let you go."

Pender stared at him, any trace of a smile now gone. His eyes stayed dead calm, though, and Stevens wondered what the kid was thinking. He sure didn't look scared.

"You kill me, I kill Windermere," Pender said. "Think about it."

Stevens looked at Windermere. She stood ramrod-straight in Pender's grip, the machine gun pressed into the side of her neck. She was staring at Stevens like, ice this kid. Stevens shook his head.

"You kill her, you get rid of your last bargaining chip," he said. "Then you know how this ends."

"You're forgetting the pilot."

"You need the pilot. You kill the pilot and you die on this tarmac."

Pender stared at him. "You've got five seconds to put that gun down. Then I shoot your girlfriend."

"I'm married," Stevens said. "Go ahead."

Pender held his gaze a moment longer. "One," he said.

Stevens shifted his eyes to Windermere's. "Shoot him, Kirk," she said.

"Two," said Pender.

"Last chance to put the gun down, Arthur."

"Three."

"Arthur." Marie's voice was plaintive. "Put the gun down, baby, *please*. I don't want to do this anymore."

"I'm getting you out of here," Pender said. "Four, Agent Stevens."

"Listen to Marie, Arthur. This doesn't have to end this way."

"I guess it does," said Pender. "That's five."

Pender counted, the gun pressed tight against the FBI agent, and he knew he would have to do something by the time he reached five. He drew the count slow, trying to bluff Stevens into folding his hand, feeling a sick sort of emptiness start to well up inside him as he realized that bluffing wasn't going to work this time, that he was going to have to shoot Windermere.

He reached four, and then as if he was standing outside his body, he heard himself tell Stevens five and he felt his finger tense on the trigger and Windermere stiffen beneath him. But he paused, just barely, and glanced over at Marie, saw her face stained with tears, heard her screaming, and he came back inside himself. He stood there in slow motion, unable to move.

And then Windermere wrenched away, her strength surprising him, and the decision was no longer his. He struggled with her and he heard her screaming, but her partner wasn't shooting, and for a second or so he knew he had her, knew he had the agent and Marie and he was getting away clean. And then the first shot sounded, and he felt the slug in his shoulder.

Windermere ran and Pender lifted the machine gun, intending to put a burst through both agents, and then the second and third slugs hit and Pender dropped the machine gun, more from the shock than the actual pain, and then he felt himself dropping to the cabin floor beside it.

He heard Marie screaming, and he saw her face as she bent over him, saw her tears. He suddenly felt the pain and it was worse than anything he'd ever felt in his life, and he could feel his strength waning and he knew he was going to die. He closed his eyes and tried to imagine that he was drifting away from the airplane and the FBI and the bullets, that he was lying on that dream beach somewhere in the Maldives. He could picture it, watching the surf roll in from a hammock strung between two palm trees.

He let himself lie there, imagining how the sun would feel, forgetting everything he knew about a cold Detroit winter. And Marie was there and she was crying and he didn't know why, but he smiled up at her anyway and he tried to touch her face. "I'm sorry," he said, but she didn't stop crying.

Marie pressed her cheek against Pender's and begged him not to go, but he wasn't listening to her and she could tell he was somewhere else already.

He smiled up at her and whispered he was sorry, and she wanted to tell him he didn't need to be sorry, that everything was okay. But he had stopped moving, and his face seemed frozen and distant, and she could tell he was gone.

She knelt over him for as long as she could, feeling the blood seeping out of his body and all over her clothes. Then the FBI agents took her by the arm, first Windermere and then Stevens, and she struggled and shouted and kicked at them until they both reached under her arms and picked her up and took her away, screaming and sobbing.

They took her out of the plane and down across the tarmac, stepping over the body of the young FBI agent. They walked her back to where the cars were parked under the sodium lights of the hangar, and they handcuffed her again and put her back in the unmarked sedan.

Stevens climbed behind the wheel and started the engine and Windermere got in on the passenger side and they drove past the hangar and out of the airport, Marie twisting in her seat and staring back, watching the airplane disappear in the distance until there was nothing more to see.

They took her back through the wintry Detroit streets, and neither of them said a word to her as they drove.

NINETY-THREE

It took several long days after Arthur Pender's death to tie everything off and clean up the last messes, and even then, Stevens knew, there would be more paperwork waiting back in Minnesota.

They wrote reports in triplicate in the confines of their little office, and then, four days after Pender's body was wheeled from the cabin of Jason Cardinal's Gulfstream, they stood pressed close in a Detroit cemetery and watched Agent Hall's coffin as it was lowered into the cold December earth.

It was a miserable affair: a wet, rainy snow falling on the mourners, Hall's family sobbing and Windermere crying, too, burying her face in Stevens's coat and pulling him tight, her eyes clouded with tears.

When the service was over they took a cab from the cemetery to the Metro airport and got on a late-afternoon Delta Airlines flight to the Twin Cities. As the plane took off,

Stevens held Windermere's hand in his own, though this time he wasn't sure whether it was supposed to be for his comfort or hers. He stared out the window and watched the city shrink smaller below, a damp gray maze of freeways and factories. In the distance, he thought he could see Coleman Young Airport and the hangar where Pender had died, and before the city disappeared beneath the clouds, he traced the Interstate's serpentine line to where the Motor City Motel still stood. Then all went white, and he looked away.

"We'll be back," Windermere said from the seat beside him. "The Sawyer kid's preliminary hearing is in a month or so. And God knows what they're going to do with the girls."

The girls, Stevens thought, would probably get off pretty light. Tiffany Prentice, true to her word, had had her father hire the savviest criminal law firm in the country, and Stevens had no doubt that the girl's Stockholm syndrome defense would meet with a sympathetic jury — if the case even got that far. Cases like hers tended to get quietly pled down to fines and community service and then were conveniently forgotten.

McAllister, on the other hand, was relying

on Gloria Wallace, the public defender. And though the woman was paid with taxpayers' money, she wasn't exactly a slouch in the courtroom. Matt Sawyer's initial statements put McAllister nowhere near Donald Beneteau at the time of his murder, and indeed, the big guy was taking everything on his shoulders so as to keep McAllister as far away from the crimes as possible. Sawyer's cooperation meant Wallace had more than enough to keep her client away from any serious jail time, and Assistant U.S. Attorney Obradovich was at this moment finalizing a pretty plum plea deal for the girl, Stevens's and Windermere's objections not counting for a whole hell of a lot.

It was dark when the plane landed in Minneapolis, and a light blanket of snow coated the runways and the city streets beyond. Stevens and Windermere walked together to the baggage terminal and made a friendly bet whose bag would come out first.

Windermere won the contest, and she laughed at Stevens as she hefted her suitcase from the conveyor belt. "I guess I'll see you Monday," she said, turning back to him. "We gotta start unpacking those early cases. See what else Sawyer and McAllister got up to."

"Oh," said Stevens. "I thought you knew.

BCA wants me back onboard. I've wasted enough time doing the FBI's job for them."

Windermere laughed. "Come for the party and leave me to clean up, huh? Isn't that just like a state policeman." They smiled at each other for a few seconds, and Stevens wondered what he was supposed to say next.

He'd been thinking about this moment for a couple of days, but when he looked into Windermere's eyes, he saw she was already pulling away. "So I guess I'll see you around," she said. "It's going to be weird not seeing your mug every morning."

"Sure," said Stevens. "It was kind of fun, wasn't it?"

"It was. Even if you did get all moony on me."

"Moony?" Stevens laughed. "Bull. I nearly shot you."

She let go of her suitcase and wrapped him in a hug. Then she kissed his cheek. "That's how I knew you were into me, dear."

She pulled back too soon. Stevens had to fight himself not to hold on to her longer. "Maybe we'll see each other," he said.

She nodded. "It would be nice to have friends in Minnesota." She picked up her suitcase. "All right, Stevens. I'll see you around."

"Good luck," he said. "With Mark."

She barely looked back. "Thanks. Enjoy your family." Then she was gone, disappearing through the crowd of passengers and out the terminal door. Stevens gave her time to catch a cab, and then he turned back to the baggage conveyor, where his bag was among the last few unclaimed. He picked it up and walked to the exit, gasping in the bitter cold and catching himself searching for Windermere on the empty sidewalk. She was gone. She was gone, and that was that.

He took a cab back into St. Paul, watching the snow falling through the beams of the streetlights and staring through living room windows at the bright half-second tableaus beyond. His own living room was dark when he arrived, the bedroom light on in the second-floor window.

Stevens paid the driver and stepped out into the street, the snow crunching beneath his feet. Someone had shoveled the walk in his absence, and he idly wondered who as he made his way up to the front porch. He fit his key in the lock and opened the door and stepped into the dark hallway, smelling the familiar smell of home.

He stood in the silence of the front hall for a few minutes, wondering why he was hesitating, seeing Arthur Pender and Marie

McAllister in the shadows. Then he put his bag down and walked through the house, descending into the basement and settling down in his favorite chair. He turned the television on to *SportsCenter* and put his feet up on the coffee table and leaned back to watch the basketball highlights.

After a few minutes, he heard a creak on the floorboards above and Nancy Stevens's fuzzy pink pajama bottoms appeared on the stairs. "Are you a burglar?" she called.

"Relax," he told her. "I'm a cop, ma'am."

She came down the stairs, and Stevens watched her come into view, tired and mussed-up and beautiful. "Figured you'd have to be a pretty stupid burglar to want to come around down here," she said. "Nothing in this room dates from later than 1980."

She stood on the landing and watched him, and after a moment he stood and walked over to her. He took her in his arms and kissed her, tasting the mint of her toothpaste and smelling her skin cream. "I'm sorry I've been gone," he said.

"Are you back now?" she asked him.

He nodded. "I'm here. For good this time."

"Good." She stepped back and stared into

his eyes. "Then come on up to bed. We've all missed you."

ACKNOWLEDGMENTS

I've been very fortunate to count among my allies my wonderful agent, Stacia Decker at the Donald Maass Literary Agency, and my editor, Neil Nyren, at Putnam — truly a publishing dream team. Without their insight and enthusiasm, this project would never have come to fruition.

This novel owes much to the efforts of the people who worked behind the scenes on its behalf. Thanks to everyone at Putnam who played a part in the publishing process.

Thanks to my teachers, who played their own part in the publishing process. In particular, thanks to Michael James, Thomas King, and the Creative Writing faculty at the University of British Columbia, especially Steven Galloway, Bryan Wade, Maureen Medved, Peggy Thompson, Meah Martin, and the indomitable Pat Rose.

Many friends and family members offered

encouragement and support. I could fill a book listing their kindnesses; suffice it to say, I am humbled by their generosity, and grateful to them all.

Ariane Thompson-Campbell remains my best friend, my voice of reason, and, above all, my inspiration. I'm a better man to have known her, and a better writer, too.

Thanks, finally and especially, to my family: to my brothers, Terrence and Andrew Laukkanen, and to my parents, Ethan Laukkanen and Ruth Sellers, whose faith in me has never wavered, and whose support has made all the difference.

ABOUT THE AUTHOR

Broke and jobless after graduation, **Owen Laukkanen** answered a Craigslist ad — and for the next three years, he was the tournament reporter for a poker website, traveling from the luxurious casinos of Monaco and Macau to the sketchiest cardrooms of Atlantic City. A resident of Vancouver, he is now at work on a second book featuring Stevens and Windermere.

Mount Laurel Library
100 Walt Whitman Avenue
Mount Laurel, NJ 08054-9539
856-234-7319
www.mtlaurel.lib.nj.us

The employees of Thorndike Press hope you have enjoyed this Large Print book. All our Thorndike, Wheeler, and Kennebec Large Print titles are designed for easy reading, and all our books are made to last. Other Thorndike Press Large Print books are available at your library, through selected bookstores, or directly from us.

For information about titles, please call:
  (800) 223-1244

or visit our Web site at:
  http://gale.cengage.com/thorndike

To share your comments, please write:
  Publisher
  Thorndike Press
  10 Water St., Suite 310
  Waterville, ME 04901